Also by Ann H. Gabhart
and available from Center Point Large Print:

The Believer
The Seeker

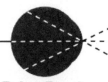

**This Large Print Book carries the
Seal of Approval of N.A.V.H.**

ANGEL
SISTER

**Center Point
Large Print**

ANGEL SISTER

ANN H. GABHART

CENTER POINT PUBLISHING
THORNDIKE, MAINE

This Center Point Large Print edition
is published in the year 2011 by arrangement with
Revell, a division of Baker Publishing Group.

Scripture used in this book, whether quoted or
paraphrased by the characters, is taken from
the King James Version of the Bible.
This book is a work of fiction. Names, characters,
places, and incidents are the product of
the author's imagination or are used fictitiously.
Any resemblance to actual events, locales, or persons,
living or dead, is coincidental.

The text of this Large Print edition is unabridged.
In other aspects, this book may vary
from the original edition.
Printed in the United States of America
on permanent paper.
Set in 16-point Times New Roman type.

ISBN: 978-1-61173-003-6

Library of Congress Cataloging-in-Publication Data

Gabhart, Ann H., 1947–
Angel sister / Ann H. Gabhart.
   p. cm.
ISBN 978-1-61173-003-6 (library binding : alk. paper)
1. Kentucky—History—20th century—Fiction. 2. Domestic fiction.
   3. Large type books. I. Title.
PS3607.A23A85 2011b
813′.6—dc22
                                                            2010046535

To my mother, Olga,
and in memory of her sisters,
Evelyn, Margaret, and Bill,
who shared their memories of growing up
during the Depression years and
made this story possible.

1

Something woke Kate Merritt. Her eyes flew open and her heart began to thump in her ears. She couldn't see a thing. Not even a hint of moonlight was filtering through the lace curtains at the bedroom window. The dark night wrapped around her like a thick blanket as she stared up toward her bedroom ceiling and fervently hoped it was nothing but a bad dream shaking her awake.

Next to Kate, Evie's breath was whisper quiet. Her sister obviously hadn't heard whatever it was that had jerked Kate from sleep. Slowly Kate's eyes began adjusting to the darkness, but she didn't need to see to know how Evie's red hair would be spread around her head like a halo. Or that even in sleep she'd have a death grip on the top sheet so Kate couldn't pull it off her. Kate always woke up every day with her pillow on the floor and her hair sticking out in all directions. The total opposite of Evie, who got up with barely a rumple in her nightgown.

Just a couple of mornings ago, their mother had laughed as she smoothed down Kate's tangled dark brown hair. "Don't you worry about not being as ladylike as Evangeline. Your sister's going on seventeen. When you get older, you'll be more like her."

Kate jerked away from her mother. "Like Evie? I don't have to be, do I? That would be awful. Really awful," she said before she thought. Kate was always doing that. Saying things before she thought.

But she didn't want to be like Evie. Ever. Evie wouldn't climb trees or catch frogs down at the creek. She even claimed to prefer reading inside by the oil lamp instead of playing hide-and-seek after dark. The truth was she was scared of her shadow.

Evie wasn't only worried about things in the dark. Day or night she shrieked if anybody so much as mentioned Fern Lindell. True, Fern—who lived down the road—was off her rocker, but Kate wasn't a bit afraid of her. At least not unless she was carrying around her little axe. Then anybody with any sense knew to stay away from her.

One thing sure, Kate had sense. That was because she was the middle sister, and the middle sister had to learn early on to take care of herself. And not only herself. Half the time she had to take care of Evie too, and all the time Tori who turned ten last month.

In the cot across the room, Tori was breathing soft and peaceful. So Tori hadn't been what woke Kate, but something had. Kate raised her head up off her pillow and listened. The middle sister had to make sure everything was all right.

Kate didn't mind. She might be only fourteen, but she knew things. She kept her eyes and ears open and did what had to be done. Of course sometimes it might be better to be like Evie, who had a way of simply ignoring anything that didn't fit into her idea of how things should be, or Tori, who didn't worry about much except whether she could find enough worms to go fishing. Neither of them was holding her breath waiting to see if the bump in the night might be their father sneaking in after being out drinking.

Victor Merritt learned to drink in France. At least that's what Kate overheard Aunt Hattie telling Mama a few months back. They didn't know she heard them. She was supposed to be at school, but she'd run back home to get the history report she left on the table by the front door. Kate tiptoed across the porch and inched the door open to keep it from creaking. She aimed to grab the paper and be in and out without her mother hearing her. That way she'd only be in hot water at school and not at home too.

They didn't know she was there. Not even Aunt Hattie, who just about always knew everything. After all, she'd delivered nearly every baby who'd been born in Rosey Corner since the turn of the century thirty-six years ago. A lot of folks avoided Aunt Hattie unless a baby was on the way or they needed somebody to do their wash, but not Mama. She said you might not be able to depend on a lot in this world, but you could depend on Aunt Hattie telling you the truth. Like it or not.

That morning last spring when Kate had crept back in the house and heard her mother and Aunt Hattie, it sounded as if Kate's mother wasn't liking a lot of things. She was crying. The sound pierced Kate and pinned her to the floor right inside the door. She hardly dared breathe.

She should have grabbed the paper and gone right back out the door. That was what she should have done, but instead she stood still as a stone and listened. Of course she knew her father drank. Everybody in Rosey Corner knew that. Nothing stayed secret long in their little community. Two churches, one school, two general stores—the one run by Grandfather Merritt had a gasoline pump—and her father's blacksmith shop.

"But why?" Kate's mother said between sobs.

Aunt Hattie didn't sound cross the way she sometimes did when people started crying around her. Instead she sounded like she might be about to cry herself. Kate couldn't remember ever seeing Aunt Hattie cry. Not even when she talked about her son dying in the war over in France.

"Some answers we can't be seein', Nadine. We wasn't over there. But our Victor was. Men right beside him died. He got some whiffs of that poison gas those German devils used. He laid down on the cold hard ground and stared up at the same moon you was starin' up at but without the first idea of whether or not he'd ever be looking at it with you again. He couldn't even be sure he'd see the sun come up."

"No, no, that's not what I meant." Kate's mother swallowed back her tears, and her voice got stronger, more like Kate was used to hearing. "I mean, why now? I grant you he started drinking over there, but when he got home, he didn't drink all that much. Just a nip now and again, but lately he dives into the bottle like he wants to drown in it."

"It ain't got the first thing to do with you, child. He still loves his girls." Now Aunt Hattie's voice was soft and kind, the voice she used when she was talking to some woman about to have a baby.

"The girls perhaps. Me, I'm not so sure anymore." Kate couldn't see her mother, but she knew the look that would be on her face. Her lips would be mashed together like she had just swallowed something that tasted bad.

"You can be sure. I knows our Victor. I's the first person to ever lay eyes on him when he come into the world. And a pitiful sight he was. Barely bigger than my hand. His mama, Miss Juanita, had trouble carryin' her babies. We lost the two before Victor. You remember Miss Juanita. How she was prone to the vapors. She was sure we would lose Victor even after he made the journey out to daylight and pulled in that first breath, but no how was I gonna let that happen. Raised him right alongside my own boy. Bo was four when our Victor was born."

Kate heard a chair creak as if maybe her mother had shifted to get more comfortable. Everybody knew it wasn't any use trying to stop Aunt Hattie when she started talking about her boy. "My Bo was a sturdy little feller. Stronger and smarter than most. Soon's Victor started walking, Bo took it upon hisself to watch out for him. Miss Juanita paid him some for it once he got older." Aunt Hattie paused as if realizing she'd gone a little far afield. "Anyhows that's how I knows Victor hasn't stopped carin' about you, girl, 'cause I know our Victor. He's just strugglin' some now what with the way things is goin' at his shop. Folks is wantin' to drive those motorcars and puttin' their horses out to pasture. It ain't right, but a pile of things that happen ain't right."

Kate expected Aunt Hattie to start talking about Bo dying in France, but she didn't. Instead she stopped talking altogether, and it was so quiet that Kate was sure they'd hear her breathing. She wanted to step backward, out the door, but she had to wait until somebody said something. The only noise was the slow tick of the clock on the mantel and the soft hiss of water heating on the cooking stove. Nothing that would cover up the sound of her sneaking out of the house.

Kate was up to fifty-five ticks when her mother finally spoke again. "I don't believe in drinking alcohol to hide from your problems."

"No way you could with how your own daddy has been preaching against that very thing since the beginnin' of time. Preacher Reece, he don't cut nobody no slack."

"There are better ways of handling troubles than making more troubles by drinking too much." Mama's voice didn't have the first hint of doubt in it.

"I ain't arguing with you, Nadine. I's agreein' all the way."

"Then what am I supposed to do, Aunt Hattie?"

"I ain't got no answers. Alls I can do is listen and maybe talk to one who does have the answers."

"I've been praying."

"Course you have, but maybe we can join our prayers together. It says in the Good Book that where two or more agree on something, the Lord pays attention. Me. You. We's two."

"Pray with me right now, Aunt Hattie. For Victor. And the girls." Her mother hesitated before she went on. "Especially Kate. She's picked up some of the load I can't seem to make myself shoulder."

In the front room, Kate pulled in her breath.

"Don't you be worryin' none about that child. She's got some broad shoulders. Here, grab hold of my hands." Aunt Hattie's voice changed, got a little louder as if she wanted to make sure the Lord could hear her plain. "Our holy Father who watches over us up in heaven. May we always honor ever' living day you give us. We praise you for lettin' us have this very day right now. And for sending us trials and tribulations so that we can learn to lean on you."

She fell silent a moment as if considering those tribulations. Then she started praying again. "Help our Victor. You knows what he needs better than me or even your sweet child, Nadine here. Turn him away from the devil's temptations and bring him home to his family. Not just his feet but his heart too. And strengthen that family and watch over them, each and every one. Increase their joy and decrease their sorrow. Especially our Katherine Reece. Put your hand over top her and keep her from wrong."

Kate didn't wait to hear any more. She felt like Aunt Hattie's eyes were seeing right through the walls and poking into her. Seeing her doing wrong right that moment as she stood there eavesdropping on them. Kate snatched her history paper off the table and tiptoed out of the house. Once off the porch she didn't stop running until she was going up the steps into the school.

The prayer hadn't worked yet. At least not the

part about her father resisting the devil's temptation to go out drinking. Kate worried that the Lord hadn't answered Aunt Hattie's prayer because Kate had been listening when she shouldn't have been. As if somehow that had made the prayer go sideways instead of up toward heaven the way Aunt Hattie had intended.

Now Kate stayed perfectly still to keep the bedsprings from squeaking as she listened intently for whatever had awakened her. The front screen door rattled against the doorframe. That could have been the wind if any wind had been blowing, but then there was a bump as somebody ran into the table beside the door. Kate let out her breath as she sat up on the side of the bed and felt for a match. After she lit the small kerosene lamp, she didn't bother fishing under the bed for her shoes. The night was hot, and her father had made it through the front door.

"Please don't get sick." She mouthed the words silently as she adjusted the wick to keep the flame low. She hated cleaning up after him when he got sick. From the sour smell of alcohol creeping back into the bedroom toward her, she guessed he might have already been sick before he came inside.

She looked back at Evie as she stood up. Evie looked just as Kate had imagined her moments earlier, but she didn't fool Kate. She was awake. Her eyes were shut too tight, and Kate couldn't be positive in the dim light, but she thought she saw a tear on her cheek. "No sense crying now, Evie. Daddy's home," Kate whispered softly.

Evie kept pretending to be asleep, but tears were definitely sliding out of the corners of her eyes. Kate sighed as she turned away from the bed. "Go on back to sleep, Evie. I'll take care of him."

Kate carried her lamp toward the front room where her father was tripping over the rocking chair. She wondered if her mother was lying in her bed pretending to sleep and if she had tears on her cheeks. She wouldn't get up. Not even if Daddy fell flat on his face in the middle of the floor. She couldn't. Not and keep cooking him breakfast when daylight came. Kate knew that. She didn't know how she knew it, but she did.

2

Nadine Merritt heard her husband step up on the porch. She'd been staring into the dark waiting for that sound for hours. One minute she would send up impassioned prayers that he'd make it home safely, and the next she would berate herself for not turning over, going to sleep, and leaving him to his just deserts. Victor was a grown man. He made his own choices. She couldn't make them for him. The trouble was, he wasn't the only one who had to live with the choices he made. They all did. Not just Nadine, but the girls too.

Drinking took money, and heaven only knew, there was little of that in their pockets right now. In anybody's pockets, for that matter. The whole country was deep in depression. President Roosevelt had started some work programs, but plenty of people were still hungry. Some of them had moved past being merely hungry to starving out west where the dust storms had blown away even the chance of growing something to eat. At least here in Rosey Corner, Kentucky, anybody with a patch of ground could grow a few vegetables to keep food on the table. Nadine had just spent the whole day canning beans. Stifling heat from the long hours of boiling the jars lingered in the house.

Of course Father Merritt wouldn't let them go hungry. He ran a tab for them and just about everybody else in Rosey Corner at his store. People thought Preston Merritt was a hard man, and Nadine wouldn't argue that he wasn't, but he didn't hold back beans or cornmeal from anybody. And he didn't hold back anything from Victor's family. At the same time he didn't make it easy when Nadine needed a sack of sugar or flour. His eyes would squint and his mouth would twist sideways as he pulled out his ledger book, licked the tip of his pencil lead, and added the price of whatever she laid on the counter to what they already owed.

Then he'd look up at her through his bushy gray eyebrows and say, "Victor should have never let his uncle Jonas talk him into taking over that blacksmith shop. I told the boy shoeing horses wasn't going to make him any money. People need gasoline now, not horseshoes. That's how come I put in that gas pump out front. A man has to keep up with the times. But Victor never did have much head for making sensible choices, now did he?" Sometimes he said the words out loud and sometimes she just heard him thinking them. And she knew she was one of those choices that he was talking about.

There was another store in Rosey Corner. Smaller, but with most grocery stock a person might need. But there was no way she could go buy anything from Bill Baxter instead of going to Father Merritt's store. So she had stopped going to the store at all. Evangeline and Kate fetched whatever she needed. Nadine had pretty much stopped going anywhere except to church.

She might have stopped that too if her father hadn't been the preacher. She wouldn't have stopped believing in the Lord. She would have just stopped going to sit on the church pew and knowing people were whispering about her and Victor. Worse, sometimes her father preached straight at her. As if she could go back in time and break that first bottle Victor had picked up. Over in France.

At least that's where Aunt Hattie said he'd learned to drink. France. But Nadine wasn't so sure about that. What about Victor's sister? Gertie was all the time swallowing handfuls of aspirin to get through the day. She'd never been in France.

Out in the living room Victor stumbled over the rocking chair and muttered something under his breath. Nadine shut her eyes and whispered the beginning of a prayer. "Dear Lord." Then the boozy smell wafted back to her and her stomach turned over. She put her hand over her nose. Through the door she saw the flicker of an oil lamp and heard Kate talking to Victor.

"It's all right, Daddy. Come on over to the couch and I'll help you take your shoes off." Kate's voice was low, not much more than a whisper, but Nadine heard every word.

"I'm sorry I woke you up, my Kate. I was trying to be extra quiet. I really was." Victor sounded like he might cry.

"I know, Dad."

"I didn't aim to stay out so late, but the boys wanted me to have a little drink with them. I couldn't turn down the boys."

The boys? Who were the boys who were more important than his family? Nadine wanted to scream out at him. But it never did any good to yell at him when he was drunk. He just cried, and then she cried and the girls cried. All but Kate. She hadn't cried over a half-dozen times since she was out of diapers. So it was better to let Kate get him down on the couch. Nadine slid out of bed and crept over to the open window. She needed more air.

"I turn down the boys all the time," Kate was telling Victor.

"What boys?" For a minute Victor sounded almost sober.

"All the ones who want me to marry them, of course." Nadine could hear the smile in Kate's voice.

"You're joshing me, aren't you, Kate? You're way too young to be thinking about marrying. What are you now? Twelve?"

"Fourteen, Daddy. And I know girls who got married at fourteen."

"Big mistake." The couch springs creaked under his weight.

Kate laughed softly. "And not one I'm going to make. Unless I kiss a frog and he turns into a handsome prince."

"You been kissing frogs?" Victor asked her.

"At least one a day if I can catch them. You never know where that handsome prince might turn up. But alas, all I've gotten so far are warts."

Victor laughed. "Oh, my Katherine. You're one for the books. Maybe someday I'll write a story about you. I used to tell my mother stories, you know. She said I was going to grow up and be a famous writer."

"Then why didn't you?"

"She said it. Not me."

"You're always reading. You and Mama both."

"Your sainted mama." The tears were back in Victor's voice now. "Oh, to be the man she deserves. But me, I'm lower than the lowest worm."

Again it was all Nadine could do not to shout out at him that he was the man she deserved and wanted. But not drunk. Never drunk. Nadine leaned closer to the window and pulled in a deep breath. If only she could go back to those early days when they sat together in the evening and read to one another. What had happened?

"Don't you start caterwauling on me," Kate said firmly. Nadine heard her set Victor's shoes down on the floor beside the couch. "Now, not another word. Go to sleep. You have to get up and make horseshoes tomorrow."

"Horses need shoes. Clip clop. Clip clop down the road." The tears were gone again as Victor sang the words of a song he'd made up for Victoria when she was a baby. She had giggled every time he said clip clop and bounced her up and down on his knees. "I like horses, Kate. Do you like horses, Kate?"

"Everybody likes horses," Kate said.

"I wish I had one. I wish you had one. Haven't you always wanted a horse?"

"I don't need a horse. I've got rollerskates. Goodnight, Daddy."

"Rollerskates. Do you think I could make rollerskates?"

"I guess you could try. Now hush and go to sleep. It will be morning soon. And no bad dreams. Not one. Do you hear me?"

"Yes sir, Sergeant Kate. Whatever you say, Sergeant Sir. I will not sing. I will not cry. I will not make any noise at all till the morning sun comes up in the sky." Victor laughed a little. "A poet I am. A poet you will see. Call me Willy and Willy I will be."

"I don't want a daddy named Willy. I like Victor," Kate said.

"Nay, nay. Willy I say. A new day. A new way."

"All right, Daddy. Be Willy if you want, but that's enough poetry. You promised not to make any noise till morning. So keep your promise and go to sleep." Kate picked up the lamp and moved away from the couch. Nadine saw the shadows dancing on the wall above her head.

"Go to sleep. Not a peep. Promises keep."

"Daddy." Kate tried to sound stern, but Nadine could hear a giggle in her voice.

"Accidental poetry, my Kate. A danger to the liter-ate." He stretched out the last word to make it rhyme with Kate.

Kate laughed, and even Nadine staring out her bedroom window into the dark night couldn't keep her lips from curling up. Victor had always been able to make her smile. Even at the worst of times. He'd left her smiling when he climbed aboard the train to be shipped out to France. He'd made her smile after her father had refused to perform their wedding ceremony. He'd kept her smiling through the long months of carrying Evangeline with the memory of her mother dying in childbirth stalking her every moment.

And now, even now with her heart breaking because he chose the bottle over her, he could still make her smile. At least for a fleeting moment. In the living room, Victor was snoring already. Over the snores, Nadine heard Kate's bed creak as she settled back beside Evangeline.

Nadine shut her eyes and whispered softly, "May the Lord rock you in his arms and give you sleep so peaceful." She'd been whispering that same prayer over her girls ever since they were newborn babies. In the words, she heard the echo of her mother's whispered words over her from years before.

What mother didn't want the Lord's protection over her children? To shield them from hurt and bad things. And yet she hid in her bedroom and offered Kate no help. *Forgive me, Kate.*

She tiptoed to her bedroom door to peer over toward the girls' bedroom. She needed to see with her own eyes that Kate had turned out the oil lamp so there would be no danger of it getting knocked over in the night and catching the curtains or bedclothes on fire.

Nadine feared fires. Had seen houses engulfed in flames. Had heard people speak of parents who didn't wake in time to reach their children before the fire blocked their way. So many reasons to fear. Snakes. Storms. Childbirth. Death. The wrath of God. Victor told her it wasn't the Lord's wrath she feared, but instead the wrath of her father. As a child, Nadine had thought they were one and the same.

She wanted to slip over to the other bedroom and stand over her sleeping children. She wanted to tuck the covers up under Victoria's chin, touch Evangeline's beautiful red hair, and lay her hand on Kate's warm cheek. She wanted to stand over Victor and stroke his head and be glad he was home even with the smell of alcohol on him. But instead she turned back into her room.

Nadine didn't bother lying back down. Even if her mind wasn't swirling with memories, she wouldn't be able to sleep through Victor's snoring. She'd been a light sleeper since the age of twelve, when her mother had died bringing Essie into the world. Her father had been unable to even look upon the baby, so Nadine had taken over her care. For two weeks she fought for the life of her tiny little sister, but she lost the battle.

The baby joined her mother in heaven. People said it was for the best.

Now Nadine quietly moved a straight chair over to the window. She sat down and rested her head on the windowsill. Out in the woods beyond the creek, a whippoorwill called. And she remembered falling in love.

3

The first time Nadine really saw Victor, he was reading from *Evangeline* by Henry Wadsworth Longfellow. It was a Wednesday in November, with a cold rain hitting the classroom windows as though the drops might be turning to ice. They had no more than sat down at their desks in English class when Miss Opal jumped up on the small platform she kept in front of the chalkboard and shouted, "Poetry day!"

Miss Opal needed the platform because she was shorter than any of her students, but when it came to poetry, every inch of her petite body seemed to vibrate and expand with enthusiasm.

"Poetry is a gift from the good Lord, and it is my calling to see that your young minds are opened to the joys of that wonderful gift," she was fond of saying. Then she would pop her ruler sharply on her desk as she ordered, "So get cracking."

While some of her classmates groaned at the mention of any poem, Nadine loved poetry. At times she hugged the very volumes of verse tight against her chest in an attempt to absorb the words that so stirred her heart while her favorite line from John Keats's *Endymion* sang through her head. *A thing of beauty is a joy forever.*

That was what Victor's reading of Longfellow's *Evangeline* was that day. A thing of beauty. So beautiful that Miss Opal didn't stop him to allow anyone else a turn. She just settled into his empty desk and let him keep reading about Evangeline searching for her lost love. Nadine couldn't take her eyes off Victor. It was as if she had never before seen him, although that, of course, wasn't even close to the truth. She had seen Victor. Hundreds of times.

They had both been born in Rosey Corner, had lived there all their lives. They learned their 3 Rs together as children in the same schoolhouse. On top of all that, Victor had been waiting on people at his father's grocery since he was tall enough to see over the counter, and Nadine was the preacher's daughter. Everybody knew the Reverend Reece. He'd been telling people at the Rosey Corner Baptist Church how the Lord wanted them to live since before Nadine was born.

Victor and his family didn't attend her father's church. They went to the Rosey Corner Christian Church across the road, but the churches were always having this or that special service together. Nadine had lived her whole life right alongside Victor Merritt.

But until that day, she had never paid him much attention. Never gave any boy much more than a passing glance, even though she was seventeen. She had her fill of boys at home with her older brother, Orrin Jr., and her little brother, James Robert. She spent half her time nagging after them to chop the wood the right length for the cookstove, to wash their bodies, to not ruin their good clothes, to leave snakes or various other wild creatures outside the house, to go to school, on and on. She had no desire to invite another male person into her life.

Not that a few of the boys her age hadn't done all they could to catch her eye. This or that boy was always trying some foolish stunt to get her to notice him, and Jackson Perry followed her around like a puppy dog, telling her how pretty she was. She didn't need him to tell her. She had a mirror. She could see that her features lined up nicely and her eyes were an exceptional shade of blue. When she tied her honey brown hair back with a ribbon at the nape of her neck, it curled softly down her back.

Her father lectured her on the dangers of vanity if he caught her looking in a mirror, but he had little reason to worry. She only used the mirror to be sure her face was clean and her hair was neat.

If she had extra time after she finished her chores, she certainly didn't waste it staring in a mirror. Not with all the wonderful stories out there waiting to be read.

Another danger, her father warned. Novels encouraged impure thoughts. She should concentrate on the truths in the Bible. She had read the Bible. All the way through once, by reading a couple of chapters every day the year she was sixteen, but her heart ran after the romantic stories and poems her teachers let her carry home from school. Books she wrapped in her bloomers and stuck in the back of her underwear drawer, away from her father's eyes.

She hated the darkest months of winter when her chores took all the daylight hours after school. On those winter evenings, she had no choice but to sit beside her father by the fire or the lamp while he studied his sermons. There in his shadow she could only read her textbooks or Sunday school lessons. Her father said they wouldn't be good stewards of the money the Lord had given them if they wasted it on extra oil for a lamp they didn't need to light. Now and again she smuggled the end of a nearly burnt-down candle into her bedroom. The stories she read by those candles—lit after her father was asleep—were the most exciting of all. She felt blessed when she reached the last line of the story before the candle guttered out.

But reading about romance and love didn't mean she had any plans to seek romance for herself. Certainly not with any of the boys who had presented themselves to her as candidates. And definitely not Jackson Perry, who sometimes came to her house to pitch small rocks at the kitchen roof in a vain attempt to get her to come out and talk to him. He didn't have the nerve to walk up on her front porch and knock on the door. None of the boys did. Not and face the possible ire of the Reverend Reece.

There were times when Nadine thought she might marry the first boy with nerve enough to knock on her front door. Sort of the way fairy-tale princesses married the suitor who accomplished some incredibly courageous feat. As long as it wasn't Jackson Perry. Nothing could make her look upon Jackson Perry with favor. Something she wished she had told him straight out when he first started following her around. But she hadn't, and one thing had led to another until the church people decided they were a couple just because where they saw Nadine they saw Jackson.

One of the church's busybodies had even brought the courtship that was a figment of Jackson's and the church ladies' imaginations to her father's attention last August, after a revival service. All the way across the field back to their house, her father had preached at her until she almost wished she were in love with Jackson Perry so she could elope with him.

Her father had a strong voice, given to him by the Lord when he surrendered to preach at the age of eighteen, and as they walked through the night, Nadine imagined every ear in Rosey Corner tuning in to his words. "I trust you and Jackson Perry have not done anything to bring shame upon your family and your Lord."

Nadine was glad for the velvety darkness of the summer night as she answered, "I have absolutely no interest in Jackson Perry, Father."

"That's not what Mrs. Miller tells me."

"And who should know the truth of this better? Mrs. Miller or me?"

"Don't be impertinent," her father said sternly. "Mrs. Miller is a fine woman and a good worker in the church."

"Yes sir," Nadine said as she steeled herself to listen silently to whatever he had to say about her and Jackson Perry. She had never been able to win any kind of dispute with her father. He owned the truth, pure and simple.

"I'm not saying Jackson isn't a fine young man. He is. He's grown up in the church. I baptized him when he was twelve, and as far as I know he's never fallen away from his beliefs. He works hard helping his father on their farm. The oldest of ten children. Respectful to his mother."

Nadine began to worry as the praises went on

that her father was going to get in line with all the church ladies and decide Jackson was the perfect match for her. She spoke up. "I'm not ready to entertain suitors. Any suitors."

"What are you now? Sixteen?" He slowed his walk and turned his head to stare at her.

"I turned seventeen in June," Nadine said quietly. "But I have another year of school."

"There are those who think girls have little need for higher learning." He started walking faster again, and Nadine hurried to keep up.

"Thank goodness you don't think that way," Nadine said, praying if she said it quickly enough it would be true. She could not imagine life without school and books. It would just be one endless day of chores after another. That's how she thought life would be with Jackson Perry, who had quit school after the sixth grade and had not picked up a book other than the Bible since. Or so he claimed. Somewhat proudly.

Her father didn't say anything for so long that Nadine's heart started pounding inside her chest. She was sure he was going to say getting her to the high school in Edgeville five miles away would prove to be too much hassle. The last year she'd ridden with Louis Prentice, who took a whole buggy full of girls in to school with him every morning. The other girls paid him a dollar a month, but Louis, who went to their church, didn't charge Nadine. Louis had graduated last spring and was heading to Lexington to study law at Transylvania College. Nadine had found another ride. One of the girls' fathers was going to let her drive a buggy to school, but that girl didn't go to their church and she might expect to be paid. Nadine's father didn't part with dollars very easily even when he had them in his pocket.

They reached their yard and her father lifted the latch that held the gate, still silent and deep in thought. Nadine normally wouldn't have worried one whit about that. Her father often sank into deep silences as he pondered this or that truth from the Bible, but she feared he wasn't pondering Bible truths now. She feared he was pondering her last year of school. With the silence pounding like a pulse against her ears, she said, "It is all right if I ride with Becky to school next month?"

"What's that?" Her father turned toward her as if surprised she was still walking beside him.

"School," Nadine repeated. "I'm supposed to ride with Becky next month."

"Yes, yes. That was all arranged weeks ago." His voice sounded impatient. He looked up and around as though surprised to find himself in his own yard. "Where are your brothers?"

"James Robert is on the steps. I told him he could run ahead. Orrin Jr. was planning to walk Arabelle home before he came in."

"Yes, yes, of course. Did your brother tell you

he has asked Arabelle's father for her hand in marriage?"

"He said he was going to." Nadine looked over at her father, but could not see his face in the dark. His voice did not sound as if he thought it good news.

"They want me to marry them next month. Orrin Jr. says he sees no need to wait since her father has agreed to let them live in a small house on his farm. The boy will probably make me a grandfather before summer comes again."

Her father sighed as he pushed open their door and lit the lamp they always left on the table by the door. After he adjusted the wick and replaced the chimney, he turned to stare at Nadine in the soft light of the lamp. After a moment he said, "'And God said unto them, Be fruitful, and multiply. And it was so.'"

"Arabelle does love children," Nadine said.

"I wasn't thinking of Arabelle." Her father's eyes narrowed on her. "Or Orrin Jr., but you."

"Don't look so concerned, Father. I'm not going anywhere except to school. I'll be here to fix your supper and take care of James Robert."

"But for how long? You do lust after your romantic stories."

Nadine dropped her eyes down to the floor as she said, "Everyone needs a bit of entertainment, Father. Some joy in one's life." She peeked back up at his face to see if she'd said too much.

"I get my joy from the Word of the Lord." His eyebrows almost met over his dark brown eyes. "'I will delight myself in thy commandments, which I have loved.' That's where we find the proper joy."

"Yes, Father." Nadine set her Bible down on the table and carefully lifted the lamp chimney to light a candle as she tried to waylay his lecture on the evils of modern literature. "Would you like some tea and perhaps a piece of the apple pie Mrs. Grant made for us?"

"I would." James Robert made a beeline for the kitchen. At thirteen James Robert was already six inches taller than Nadine and always ready to eat.

Over the following months, Nadine had often caught her father studying her with a frown settling between his eyes, but he did not mention Jackson Perry to her again. For that she was grateful, even as she took more care to hide her books from his eyes. She could not stop reading, but she didn't want to have to defy his orders.

Then Miss Opal had poetry day, and the dreary November day melted away as Nadine saw Victor with more than her eyes as he made the words of *Evangeline* come alive. Nadine knew the story. Had read it herself from beginning to end more than once. Had cried over the love lost through no fault of Evangeline. Tears swelled up in her eyes as Victor read the end of the poem. Love found and lost again.

Miss Opal was dabbing her eyes with her handkerchief, but Nadine hardly noticed. Nor did Victor, as he looked up from reading the last line. Whether it was by accident or intent, his eyes settled on Nadine. She didn't know if he was seeing her for the first time or not, but she did know he was seeing her. All noise in the room faded away, and the air around her held the intense clarity of a moment in time that ever after changes one's life. She looked back at him and knew Victor Merritt was the man she was going to marry.

4

The sound of Nadine stirring up the fire in the cookstove woke Victor Merritt, but he didn't open his eyes. Too much light was already pushing against his eyelids and making the hammers pound inside his head. He dreaded opening his head up completely to the morning sun. Nadine set the coffeepot and skillet down on the kitchen stove. The clang of metal on metal was like a gong right against his ears.

He needed coffee desperately, but the sizzling sound of bacon frying made his stomach lurch even before the smell reached his nose. If only he could crawl under the smell of the bacon to get the coffee. Then his head might not blow apart.

Of course what he really needed was a drink.

And not coffee or water. Alcohol. The evil potion that was pounding hammers against his brain and driving him down the path to destruction. Or so his father-in-law told him, at least once a week. Victor couldn't argue the truth of it, but he didn't know how to stop it.

The drink had hold of him. He could no more free himself from that hold than a spring rabbit could free itself from the jaws of a dog that dug it out of its grassy nest. Preacher Reece told him to give it over to the Lord. To lay it at the Lord's feet. But Victor hadn't been able to find that spot to lay it down. He'd think he had. He'd vow to stop drinking in the morning light, and then the day would grow old and the devil would sneak back in his thoughts.

Just one little drink won't hurt. A little taste to knock out that aching in your shoulder. You can't make horseshoes without swinging your hammer, and you know nothing else can stop the pain in that old war wound. Nobody will know. Not if you only take one little nip. One little taste so you can keep working.

Lately he hadn't been able to take just one little nip. Not if there was more than one nip left in the bottle. Nadine didn't understand. Couldn't understand. He was glad she didn't understand. Glad she didn't have to fight the demons. Glad her sleep wasn't haunted by faces of men dying in the mud in France.

Everybody thought the memories of the terrible things that had happened in the war should be faded away by now. All that had been years ago. They'd won the war, beat down the Germans, and come home. Life went on. The living had to go with it, and for a while he had. He and Nadine had been blessed with babies and had watched them grow into beautiful girls. Life was good, and the war memories stayed locked in a back corner of his mind.

He hadn't intended to ever let them out again, but for some reason the bad memories had started slithering out into his dreams. Then the dreams stayed with him even after he woke up in the morning, until any time he shut his eyes he could see the men on the battlefield calling out for help while their blood turned the ground red around them. He watched them die. His friends. Bo.

He'd never seen Bo in France. He'd looked for him, asked others if they'd seen him, but they never crossed paths in the war. He didn't know Bo had died there in the trenches until he got home. Yet often it was Bo who cried out to him in his dreams. Bo who reached for him. Bo who needed his help. Bo who was dying while Victor was living.

Bo was his best friend when they were young. He couldn't remember a time when Bo wasn't there watching out for him. Making sure the dangers lying in wait along the path of life didn't win over Victor the way they'd won over his brother, Preston Jr.

Victor's father said a man wasn't your friend if he was paid to watch over you. He said that man was a servant, not a friend. It was true that Victor's mother paid Aunt Hattie and Bo. Victor had always known that. It wasn't a secret. More a matter of pride with Victor's mother. And a necessity. Juanita Gale Merritt never enjoyed good health after her marriage. She said the Kentucky air weakened her, until by the time Victor came along she spent most of her time sitting in her chair by the window doing needlepoint. Aunt Hattie ran the house.

Juanita's family, the Gales, were well-to-do landowners in Virginia and, according to Aunt Hattie, not at all pleased when Juanita was swept off her feet and carried away to the uncivilized west by Preston Merritt. The family had insisted Aunt Hattie go along with Juanita. Aunt Hattie could have refused to go. She wasn't the Gales' slave even if her mother and father had been.

Slavery had ended when Lee surrendered to Grant the year before Aunt Hattie was born. She was a free woman who could go and do as she pleased, but going west to Kentucky seemed a fine way to sever the ties with those who refused to forget the time when people of her color could be bought and sold. Plus she'd grown up with Juanita Gale and had watched over her for years, much as her son, Bo, grew up with Victor and watched over him. Money changed hands, but that didn't keep affection from being exchanged in hearts.

Aunt Hattie was more a member of the family than a servant. At least to Victor. And Bo was more brother to him than Preston Jr. Of course Preston Jr. had died when Victor was ten, and Bo had watched over Victor until Bo was eighteen and Victor was fourteen. Then Bo had joined a Negro league baseball team and traveled all over the country to play ball before the war. Victor had gone with Aunt Hattie to see him play once when Bo's team came to Louisville. He was good. Hit two homers. But then Bo had always been good at everything he did.

It was Victor who could never hit a ball much past second base. It was Victor who tripped over his own feet whenever he tried to run a race. It was Victor who had to have a sheet of paper and a pencil to figure up the right change to give customers at the store. It was Victor who had lived when Preston Jr., a true Merritt who could make any father proud, had died. It was Victor who had lived when Bo, the better, stronger man, had died in the mud in France. Victor who lived while hundreds of better men had died.

And he didn't know why. Sometimes he wondered if it was the good Lord's way of laughing at them all. The Lord pulling a joke on them, letting a puny man like Victor live and taking the others on to heaven. Or maybe the Lord just didn't want Victor.

Nadine got upset whenever he said anything like that out loud. She'd glare at him and tell him in no uncertain words how wrong he was. She could not imagine a God who laughed, and Victor did not want to imagine a God who didn't. It wasn't often he saw her father in Nadine, but when she told Victor how he was approaching blasphemy talking about the Lord laughing at him, she had Preacher Reece's fire in her eyes. It wasn't a fire he liked seeing there.

He wasn't going to like seeing the disappointment in her eyes whenever he finally pulled himself off the couch and made his way into the kitchen, either. That's what he was. Perhaps had always been. A disappointment. To his father. To his country. To his wife. To his children. To his Lord. A failure at everything he'd tried. The only thing he was good at was making the boys laugh when he was drinking with them. He supposed that was better than making the Lord laugh at his puny plans.

He used to be able to make Nadine laugh, but he didn't think there would be much chance of that this morning. Not from the sound of pans being banged around in the kitchen. He pulled in a slow breath and held it. He still hadn't opened his eyes, but someone was coming across the floor. Quiet little hesitant steps. Not Nadine. Not Kate. Certainly not Evangeline. His oldest daughter wouldn't even look toward him when he'd been drinking.

He eased one eye open a slit. Just as he thought. Victoria Gale. His baby. Already ten years old, but still and always his baby. She looked like his mother. Fair of skin with almost black hair. A few freckles spotted her nose and upper cheeks, and her eyes were the green of a cold winter pond.

None of the girls looked a thing alike. Evangeline took after Nadine's side of the family with red hair like Nadine's mother and beautiful blue eyes like Nadine. And Kate, well, Kate was Kate. Her hair was an ordinary brown, and her eyes sometimes didn't seem to know what color they wanted to be, the way they changed from green to blue to gray according to her mood. But there was nothing ordinary about Kate. She practically exploded with life, had run after it with both hands ever since she was a little thing. It brought her hard knocks and falls sometimes, but that hadn't ever stopped her.

"Daddy?" Victoria's voice wasn't much more than a whisper. "Are you awake, Daddy?"

The hint of fear in her voice pierced Victor. What had he become that his baby was afraid to stand beside him? He pushed open his second eye. "I'm awake, puddin'." His voice came out raspy, but he managed to put a smile in the sound of it. "Are you awake?"

She looked relieved to see that he really was her daddy and not some stinky hobo who had wandered in off the road. "Of course I'm awake," she said with a giggle. "I'm walking around."

"You could be sleepwalking. Wandering around in dreamland looking for a way out. Any two-headed horses in there?" Victor sat up. He managed not to groan, but only barely. He was the one wandering around in a vast wasteland without a way to get back.

"No, Daddy." Victoria rewarded Victor with another giggle. "I've never seen a two-headed horse."

"Oh, but every girl should see a two-headed horse at least once in her life. They are curious beasts." He leaned back against the couch and breathed in and out slowly. He wanted to close his eyes and pull the couch cushions up over his head, but his baby was watching him.

"Are you sick, Daddy?" Victoria's smile changed to a worried frown.

"I'm not feeling too pert, but no, puddin', I'm not sick." He started to reach out to touch her face, but when he noticed how his hands were shaking, he tucked them down between his legs instead. "Just feeling a little woozy. Not awake enough yet."

"You want a cup of coffee?"

"You bring me some coffee, I'll give you a ride to the moon just as soon as I finish building my rocket ship."

"Oh, Daddy." Her smile was back. "Nobody could go to the moon."

"Are you sure about that? They do it all the time in the books I read. Fly up there and land their rockets and go searching for little green men."

Victoria wrinkled her nose. "Who would want to find green men?"

Victor smiled. "Well, maybe you can go to Venus and find purple girls. But first get me that coffee."

When she brought him the steaming cup of coffee, Victor took it with both hands to keep from sloshing it out as he brought it up to his lips. Another few sips and he might be back among the living. "Thank you, puddin'. You and your mama are lifesavers."

"Mama said to ask if you wanted eggs this morning."

Victor's stomach rolled at the mention of food. "Not today. Biscuits and honey will be enough for me. Just give me a minute or two to drink my coffee and get cleaned up. The rest of you don't wait on me. Go on and eat."

After Victoria skipped back into the kitchen, Victor took another drink of his coffee and leaned back against the couch. The hammers weren't pounding quite so hard. He might try standing up. He needed to be moving. Sanderson was supposed to bring in his horse this morning to get new shoes. Victor couldn't afford not to be there. Even if he was the only blacksmith in Rosey Corner, Edgeville wasn't that far away. Owen Prentice was still doing some horseshoeing there, although last time Victor saw Owen, he was wondering how much longer he was going to be able to hold on to his business with the way automobiles were taking over the roads.

Progress, everybody said, and no man could stop that. His father said no man should want to stop progress. That a man with any gumption would jump on board with the progress and ride it like the opportunity it was. Look at the money he was pulling in off that gas pump he had the forward thinking to put in front of his store.

Victor took another drink of his coffee and massaged his forehead. Thinking about his father made the hammers hit harder.

"Need some help, Dad?" Kate asked from the kitchen doorway.

Victor looked over at her. "Don't worry about me, Kate. You go ahead and eat your breakfast. I'll be along in a minute."

She hesitated a few seconds, as if she wasn't sure she should believe him, then turned back to the kitchen. Victor reached down to get his shoes that were lined up neatly by the couch. Kate's doing, he thought as he pulled them on. She must have helped him get bedded down on the couch the night before, even if he had no memory of it. He thought the shame of that should keep him from ever taking another drink, but so far it hadn't.

He stood up, balanced on his feet for a moment before he tried moving. He went out the front door and around the house to the back porch where they kept the washpans and water in the summertime. It was closer to go through the kitchen, but he wasn't ready to face the kitchen yet.

He stopped at the well and drew out a bucket of water to pour over his head. That drowned out enough of the hammers that he could go onto the porch and wash up. But it woke up thoughts of his father again. Every day his father went out to the pump on the well behind his house and performed his morning bathing rituals. Winter or summer. No matter the weather. Victor had seen him clear a spot in the snow to stand to bathe. A man didn't let a little cold water stop him from keeping his body clean.

When Victor had asked him why he didn't carry the water in the house and heat it on the stove, his father had made a sound of disgust before he said, "That's for women. Women and boys."

The water that Victor washed up in on the porch wasn't heated, but the morning sun was already warm and the cool water felt good. He pulled on the clean shirt somebody—probably

Kate—had laid on the chair for him and peered into the small square mirror on the wall over the wash pan to comb down his hair. The mirror was wavy and flecked in places, but it still showed Victor too true an image of how he looked. Eyes bloodshot. Nose red. Mouth weak. He turned his eyes away from the sight of himself.

He tried to wash the bad taste and the smell of the alcohol out of his mouth. Not that it mattered all that much. Nadine wouldn't be offering him any good-morning kisses. When he finally went into the kitchen and said good morning, she didn't even look up at him.

"Morning," she answered, as if admitting the truth of it being morning but unable to lie and say it was good.

He sat down at his place at the table where two biscuits awaited him on his plate. He wanted to reach across the table and touch her hair. Beg her forgiveness for being such a failure. Thank her for not hating him too much to sit there across the table from him. He wanted to tell her how beautiful she was and how she was the best thing that had ever happened to him. He wanted to tell her how much more he loved her now than he had when they married seventeen years ago. He wanted to kiss her. To feel her smooth cheek under his lips.

He broke a piece off his biscuit and stuffed it in his mouth. And he remembered the first time he kissed her.

5

Victor was going on fourteen when he first realized he was in love with Nadine Reece. Not that he let anybody know he was smitten. Not even Nadine.

In his years working at his father's store, Victor had learned the hard way that just because you felt something, that didn't mean you had to tell other people. People had a way of twisting things around, finding something in the most commonplace remarks to jab at a person and make fun. Of course, saying he was in love with Nadine Reece would hardly be a commonplace remark.

He had plenty of reasons to keep his mouth shut on any romantic topics. First off, nobody would believe he knew what love was at his age. Second, Nadine was even younger than he was. Third, Nadine had never given him the slightest indication that he was anything more than a fixture behind the counter at the store or just another boy to ignore at school. Last of all, Bo told him straight out the first time he noticed Victor eyeing Nadine that only an idiot would fall for a preacher's daughter. Especially Preacher Reece's daughter.

"I'm not falling for anybody," Victor had

protested. "I'm just looking. You told me it was a natural thing for boys to think girls are pretty. And she's pretty." Victor and Bo had been walking down the road to Graham Lindell's house to practice hitting a baseball. Graham was about the same age as Bo and almost as crazy about baseball as Bo was.

"I ain't disagreeing with that. You got a good eye. The girl's a looker. Nobody gonna argue that." Bo glanced over at Victor with a knowing grin as he pitched the baseball back and forth between his hands. Then his grin disappeared. "But that Preacher Reece, he ain't no easy man."

"It's not him I'm thinking is pretty." Victor hoped to make Bo laugh and forget about Nadine or Nadine's father.

Bo did laugh. That had always been one of the best things about Bo. The way he thought things were funny. Nobody else at Victor's house thought much was funny. Victor couldn't remember the last time he'd heard his mother or father laugh. Maybe not since Preston Jr. had died. That had been more than three years ago, but there wasn't much sign that the sorrow was going to lift off the house anytime soon. Preston Jr. was too big a loss. He had been strong, good-looking, intelligent, and ambitious.

Victor's father used to brag about what Preston Jr. would do for Rosey Corner when he was governor. He didn't merely think it was possible for Press to be elected governor. He thought it was a certainty. Then just like that, Press was gone, and all his father had left to pin his hopes on were Victor and his sister, Gertie. Not much chance of anything important coming from either of them, he'd tell people who came into the store. They both took after their mother's side of the family. Weak blood. Weren't a thing like Preston Jr., who was a Merritt through and through. That boy had been destined for greatness.

Sometimes the people listening to Victor's father talk would sneak a look over at Victor. He'd feel their eyes on him, but he would keep doing whatever he was doing as if he hadn't heard a word. He didn't look up and say he was sorry for living when Preston Jr. hadn't. He couldn't say that. Not without lying. He might feel guilty about it, but he wasn't sorry he was still breathing.

It wasn't his fault Press drowned. At least that was what Graham, who was there, and Bo, who wasn't, had told him. Victor didn't really know. His memories of that whole afternoon had been sucked into a murky quagmire in his mind. Some scrap of memory would surface on occasion and then sink right back into the murk again. He did remember lying on the riverbank trying to throw up and breathe at the same time. And he remembered the terrible silence after Graham quit diving into the water and screaming for Press.

Bad things happened, and often as not, a person couldn't do a thing to stop them. That was what Aunt Hattie told Victor, what Bo told Victor, what the preacher who preached Press's funeral told him. Some days he even believed them. But whether it was a day he believed them or not, he kept breathing, kept on living, going to school, working in the store, trying to cheer up his mother.

And he kept laughing. Press had liked to laugh. Even after his face got fuzzy in Victor's memory, his brother's laugh stayed clear as a bell. So it didn't seem right to stop laughing himself, or to let everybody else stop.

Victor set a goal of getting a smile out of his mother at least once a day. He read her Mark Twain's books. He told her silly stories about a family of crows who lived in Crow Town back in the cedar thicket behind the house. He described what some of the Rosey Corner women wore into the store. His mother nearly always found that interesting and often amusing. Victor didn't know why. She herself rarely bothered getting dressed after Preston Jr. died. Spent most of her days in dark purple dressing gowns while she sat in her sewing rocker beside the window, doing elaborate needlework.

Aunt Hattie took care of her. She carried her meals in to her and sometimes spooned the food into her mouth. Victor would hear Aunt Hattie cajoling his mother to eat while he and Gertie sat at the silent dinner table with their father. No conversation was expected or wanted there. Sometimes Victor and Gertie wolfed down their potatoes and beans and stuffed Aunt Hattie's biscuits and ham in their pockets so they could escape to the backyard to eat. There they could talk and laugh.

Gertie was four years older than Victor and a little strange by her own admission. "But then isn't everybody just a little strange?" she'd ask and cock her head to the side. "Especially if their last name happens to be Merritt."

She was short, barely came up to Victor's shoulder. Claimed she was put out on the steps when she was a baby in hopes that somebody might take her, but when no one did, her mother and father had to keep her. She said those days out on the stoop must have stunted her growth and that's why she was so short.

By the time Victor was thirteen and found himself hopelessly in love with Nadine Reece, Gertie was actively looking for a suitor in order to escape her father's house. "He doesn't have to be handsome," she told Victor. "He doesn't have to have money, although I certainly wouldn't turn down a man with means. He doesn't have to be a talker. All he has to say is 'will you' and 'I do.'"

Victor was glad that man hadn't shown up so far. It was bad enough that Bo would be leaving the beginning of June to play baseball for the Blackbirds in the Negro League. Bo was going to play shortstop and hit homers. Lots of them.

Now, as they went up the lane to Graham's house, Bo punched Victor's shoulder and said, "Boy, you is wading out in deep water where you don't needs to be going. You'd best back away. It don't matter how pretty that preacher's daughter is."

"I haven't even put my toes in that water you're talking about, but just in case I do decide to wade in, maybe you ought to stick around to keep me out of trouble." Victor looked over at Bo. He was at least six inches taller than Victor and had shoulders twice as broad. Victor felt scrawny beside him.

"Now don't you start that again. You knows I gotta go. There ain't no place for a colored boy like me here in Rosey Corner and nothin' to do except haul and tote for somebody else."

"That's all I do. Haul and tote for my father."

"Yeah, but what you's haulin' and totin' is all gonna be yours someday."

"Someday a hundred years from now if Father doesn't find a better candidate." Victor kicked a rock out of the path leading up to Graham's house.

"You the only candidate for that, boy. You the onliest one with the Merritt name to pass on to the next generation. You and that pretty preacher's daughter." Bo grinned over at him.

Victor's face turned red. Even in his daydreams he hadn't gotten far enough along to imagine being married to Nadine.

"Oh ho." Bo laughed. "I done got you thinkin' about some interesting stuff now, ain't I? Maybe I'd best be tellin' you all about the birds and bees before I fly the coop."

"I know about the birds and bees."

"You probably does if you can learn about it with your head in a book. Maybe you put your head in the Bible enough, you'll impress that preacher." Bo threw the ball up again.

Victor bumped hard against Bo and grabbed the ball out of the air. "I already told you I'm not trying to impress the preacher. Or anybody else right now. Even if I was, I doubt if I could do anything that would impress her."

Bo looked down at his empty hands and over at the ball Victor was holding. "Don't be sellin' yo'self short, Vic. You just stole the ball from Bo 'Sure Hands' Johnson. Could be you'll be surprisin' some other folks in a few years."

It had taken Victor years to get Nadine to notice him. Oh, she knew who he was. She knew his name and that he was the youngest child of Preston and Juanita Merritt. Everybody in Rosey Corner knew that sort of thing about everybody else. On top of that, she was pleasant enough when she came in the store and would smile vaguely toward him whenever he managed to step into her path at school, but she hadn't really seen him. Not until a November day in their last year at high school and Miss Opal had him read from *Evangeline.* Then he'd looked up from the book at her and her eyes had been on him, seeing him the way she never had before. Perhaps seeing him in a way no one ever had before.

His feelings for her, shut up tight inside him for so long, burst free, and for a minute he thought his skin might split down the front of his chest and let his heart show. He wanted to run down the aisle to her desk and fall on his knees and ask her to marry him then and there.

Of course he didn't. Instead he closed the book and handed it back to Miss Opal, who was up on her step stool trilling on about how nothing could conquer true love as he walked back to his desk as if nothing unusual had happened.

6

As the days passed, Victor wondered if he had imagined those sparks in the schoolroom. Perhaps he had just been carried away by the words of the poem, because after that, Nadine started avoiding him. She stopped coming to the store. Sent her little brother to pick up whatever they needed.

Victor filled the orders and kept the lists written

in her hand. He traced out her letters spelling sugar or flour with his own finger and wished he could rearrange the letters to make them say *I love you*. At school she kept her eyes away from him. It was as if she were afraid to have feelings for him. And he knew no way to change that.

He didn't even have Bo to talk to about it man to man since he was still off hitting homeruns for the Blackbirds. He thought about asking Aunt Hattie, but she might tell his mother. His mother might mention it to his father and then the chaff would fly. That wasn't what he wanted. What he wanted was somebody to tell him how to get Nadine to look him in the eye again. He thought about Graham Lindell, but Graham was away at school learning to be a doctor like his father. That left Gertie. The only person currently residing in Rosey Corner he could trust to keep whatever he told her a secret.

Gertie had found her man to say "will you" and "I do" and had been married to Wyatt Calhoun for almost five years. The union had produced no children, but Gertie didn't seem too worried about that. She assured Victor and anybody else nosey enough to ask that if the Lord wanted her and Wyatt to have babies, he'd send them some. The Bible was full of stories about this or that woman having a baby after everybody else had given up on them. And it wasn't like she was as old as Elizabeth or Sarah in those Bible stories.

Not by a long shot. It still might happen even if her father did shake his head when he looked at her and mutter about weak Gale blood.

When Victor finally got up the nerve to talk to Gertie, she listened to his sad story without showing the first bit of surprise that he was in love with Nadine Reece.

"I'm your sister," Gertie explained. "I probably know more about you than you know about yourself. I like Nadine. She can't help being Preacher Reece's daughter any more than we can help being Preston Merritt's children. We just are." She looked thoughtful for a moment before she went on. "Father won't be happy, but then when was Father ever happy?"

She didn't expect an answer, and Victor didn't give her one. He wasn't worried about his father's happiness, only his own. "But she won't talk to me. She won't even look at me. And now she's stopped coming into the store. She sends her brother when they need something."

"Oh, that means it's serious. Very serious." Gertie raised her eyebrows and smiled. "You do realize that Father and Preacher Reece are not on the best of terms. Or more likely that never occurred to you."

"Nadine's the one I'm trying to get to notice me. Not Father or Preacher Reece."

"Men." Gertie sighed and rolled her eyes. "You're so thick-headed."

"I won't argue that. That's why I'm asking you to help me. Please."

"All right. Now pay attention." Gertie spoke slowly as if explaining something to a backward child. "Preacher Reece is why Nadine's got you out in the cold. She knows her daddy isn't likely to approve of your match or, for that matter, any match for her. And poor Nadine has been living most of her life doing her best to keep from upsetting her daddy." Gertie smiled again. "But there's some things I don't think our sweet Nadine knows."

"What things?"

"Oh, just that the preacher has been paying visits to Carla Murphy down the road. Folks are saying he must be comforting her after the death of her mother a couple of months ago, but I'm thinking the comfort might be going both ways. Carla has always fancied being a preacher's wife. You remember how in her younger days she used to show up at our church regular as clockwork to make eyes at any preacher we called who wasn't already married? None of them ever made eyes back. Poor old Carla never was much of a looker even back then. And that laugh of hers. Sounds like a sick crow." Gertie made a face and shivered a little.

"The woman can't help how she laughs," Victor said, but he couldn't keep from smiling. Carla Murphy did have a laugh that could make a person wince.

"I didn't say she could, but the fact is, when Carla shows up anywhere, people right away forget any funny story they might have been thinking about telling. And who can blame them? She could curdle milk." Gertie put her hands over her ears before she smiled wickedly and went on. "But that won't be a problem with Preacher Reece. I don't think that man has ever told a funny story. In the pulpit or out."

"Not even before he lost his wife and baby?"

"Not that I ever heard of. He says the gospel is too serious for laughing, but don't you think the Lord intended us to laugh?" She didn't give Victor a chance to answer her. "I mean, he put laughter inside us. He surely never intended for us to keep swallowing it down and choking on it and getting all dour and full of gloom, now did he?"

"I'm no expert on the good Lord's intentions. But do you really think Preacher Reece has gone courting?" Victor could hardly believe that.

"Stranger things have happened. And it could be that the Reverend has opened his eyes and looked at Nadine and seen that he won't be able to keep her home forever to wash his shirts and cook his breakfast. Poor girl has spent enough years in servitude to that man already."

"You must have your mean shoes on today. That's not a very nice way to talk about a preacher." Victor frowned at Gertie.

"He's not my preacher. And fact is, nobody that I know of made him king of Rosey Corner. Being a preacher doesn't mean you can tell everybody what to do any more than holding somebody's grocery tab does." Gertie leaned back in her chair and crossed her arms over her chest. "This is going to serve the both of them right."

"Not if she won't even look at me."

"We'll make her look at you. I'm thinking it's time the two churches got together for one of those box suppers to raise money for the Orphans' Home. All you've got to do is outbid everybody else for Nadine's box supper."

"What if she doesn't bring one?"

"She'll have to. It's for the orphans."

So three weeks later, on the last day of 1916, Victor offered two dollars straight off for Nadine's box supper, and how he felt about Nadine Reece was no longer a secret. Nobody in Rosey Corner had ever paid that much for the pleasure of sharing any girl's box supper.

They retired to a corner pew in the back of the Christian Church. With hands that trembled a bit, Nadine spread a white kerchief between them. Her cheeks flushed pink as she lifted the food out of her basket. She kept her eyes away from his face as she offered him a rather flat biscuit with ham. "I fear I'm not a great cook. Not like your Aunt Hattie. People say her biscuits are so light they almost float up off the plate."

"Biscuits are biscuits," he said as he reached for the biscuit. He let his hand touch hers a bit longer than necessary. He spoke softly to keep any of the other couples around them from hearing. "It's the company I was bidding for. Do you like other poems besides *Evangeline*?"

Her eyes came up to his then, and sparks exploded between them the same as in the classroom. He pulled a tiny volume of poetry out of his pocket and held it out to her. "A late Christmas gift," he said.

This time she let her hand linger on his as she took the book. The food sat forgotten between them. She started to open the book but then seemed to remember she was in a church where surely it was a sin to read any book other than the Bible. Instead she slid it into a pocket in the folds of her skirt as she said, "I do love poetry of all kinds. Thank you."

Victor didn't remember eating the food, but he supposed they did because it disappeared. Then he asked if he could walk her home, and she nodded shyly. The night was clear and cold and their breath was frosty on the air as they walked across the frozen ground to her house. But in the soft moonlight it was easier to talk, and both of them seemed reluctant to reach her yard gate and have the evening end.

Inevitably the gate was there in front of them. In the glow of a lamp in the front window of her house, they could see her father reading his Bible. He hadn't come to the social held at the Christian Church. While he could hardly condemn the gathering since it was to benefit the orphans, he didn't have to give it the blessing of his presence. Gertie had counted on that when she arranged the event.

Nadine glanced toward the house and then lifted the latch on the gate. The hinges creaked as the gate swung open. "Perhaps we should say good night here."

"I'll walk you to the door," Victor told her.

She stared up at him a moment before she said, "I believe you would." Then whether by intent or not, she stepped nearer to him until he could feel the warmth of her breath near his face.

He had never kissed a girl. A few girls had given him the opportunity, but it had never seemed the right thing to do since he had already given his heart to Nadine. But he had read about many kisses in the poems and stories he read. So he put his fingers beneath her chin and lifted her face up toward his. She did not try to pull away. He could see the shine of her eyes in the moonlight as he dropped his head down to softly cover her lips with his.

Her hand came up to touch his cheek, and even after he lifted his lips from hers, they stood there with their breath intermingling for a moment while the earth shifted beneath their feet. None of the poetry he had read had done kissing justice.

Somehow he managed to walk her on to her door even though his legs felt as wobbly as two willow limbs. And then he raced back across the field straight to Gertie's house. She was just coming home from the church, and as she came into her yard, he caught her up in a giant hug and swung her around while he let out a war whoop.

She laughed and said, "Two dollars well spent, I see."

7

At the breakfast table, Kate broke a little piece off her biscuit and played with it a minute before she put it in her mouth. She was never hungry at breakfast time and especially not on mornings like this when her mother and father seemed to be separated from one another by a wall only they could see.

Beside Kate, Tori poured a big puddle of ketchup on her fried egg. Kate averted her eyes and tried not to think about how much it looked like the blood that pooled under the chickens after her mother tied their feet to the clothesline and cut off their heads. Mama said if they wanted fried chicken, they couldn't afford to be squeamish. It was a fact of life that somebody had to cut the chicken's head off, pluck the feathers, and clean the innards out of it. Kate didn't think she was squeamish. She helped pluck and clean frying chickens all the time. Still, watching Tori dip her egg into that pile of ketchup did make Kate's stomach flip over. So maybe she was squeamish.

But that was the only way Tori would eat her eggs, and Tori needed to eat her eggs. She was too skinny, and the doctor said that was why she caught everything that went around. Kate had always been healthy as a horse, so it didn't matter whether she ate breakfast or not. She chewed her piece of biscuit ten times before she swallowed it.

On the other side of Kate, Evie was cutting up her bacon to eat it with a fork. She was the only person Kate had ever seen eat bacon with a fork. Evie said that ladies never picked up any piece of meat with their fingers. Not even chicken legs. She'd read a book that said so.

Sometimes Kate thought eating breakfast was going to drive her crazy. She took a sip of water as Tori chattered on about digging worms to go fishing. Kate didn't want to go fishing. She'd rather pick beans.

But they'd done that yesterday. The beans wouldn't need picking again until the next day and maybe not then if some rain didn't come. It had been dry. They'd been carrying water from the well to water some of the tomato plants, but they couldn't water the whole row of beans. Out west it was so dry they were having dust storms. Kate had read about it in the newspaper last week. It sounded awful. The air thick with dirt. Dirt in your eyes and ears and nose. Dirt flying around when it ought to be on the ground letting people plant stuff in it.

At church Grandfather Reece had been praying for rain even as he warned them about the signs of the time. Kate hated sitting on the pew at Rosey Corner Baptist Church listening to Grandfather Reece shout about how the dust storms and all the wars and rumors of wars from over in Europe were signs right out of the Bible. Punishment for a society gone astray. And all they deserved after the states had repealed Prohibition.

Every week it was the same, and every week Kate wanted to put her hands over her ears and block out his sermon. She didn't want to think about the end of the world, even if that did mean going to heaven. She just couldn't get as excited about that idea as Grandfather Reece. He'd raise his hands in the air and get a look of rapture on his face as he talked about the Lord coming back to take them home. He was ready to go and all the rest of them needed to be ready too.

Kate wasn't all that ready. Oh, she'd walked down the aisle and been baptized. She believed in the Lord, but at the same time Kate liked it here on earth even if it was dusty and dry. She had a lot of living still to do. So she was always glad when her mother let her go to church with Aunt Gertie. The preacher at Rosey Corner Christian Church was young. He and his wife had two little kids, and he didn't preach about the end of time. At least not every Sunday. He sounded as if he might like to delay going on up to heaven a little longer the same as Kate.

Aunt Gertie told Kate not to fret too much about the end of time. "The Bible says straight out that nobody knows when the Lord is going to come back. And that includes your Granddaddy Reece," she said one day when they were walking home from church. "This or that preacher has been studying the signs and calling for the end of time ever since I can remember, but the plain truth of it is they don't know. And that's the best way, else the good Lord wouldn't have decided on it. His way's always best. Even your Granddaddy Reece can't argue the truth of that."

Kate didn't know about that. She wasn't about to try to argue anything with Grandfather Reece or Grandfather Merritt. Not only would it be disrespectful to disagree with her elders, it would be useless. Her father said tying a piece of cold iron in a bowknot would be easier than changing the mind of either one of her grandfathers. They knew what was true whether it was or not.

She looked over at her father, who was advising

Tori that the best worms might be found in the soft ground just outside the barn. Kate shuddered a little. Worms were the last thing she wanted to think about at the breakfast table. She gave up on eating her biscuit and bacon and pushed her plate away from her.

"Don't waste food, Kate," her mother said as she picked up her teacup and took a sip. She had already finished off her bowl of oats before Kate's father got to the table. Oats. Another stomach turner for Kate. Gooey gray glop.

"I'll save it and eat it later," Kate said. "I'm not hungry this morning."

"You're not hungry any morning," Evie said as she attempted to fork another piece of bacon. It broke and scooted away from her fork. Undeterred, she slid her fork under the bacon and carefully lifted it. The bacon piece fell off before she got it to her mouth.

"For heaven's sakes, just pick it up and eat it, Evie," Kate said.

Evie sent her a mean look. "You eat the way you want to and I'll eat the way I want to."

"Girls," their mother said. "Don't start. Not today."

Kate stared down at the table in front of her and muttered, "Sorry." After a moment she looked up and asked, "Do you have chores for me this morning?"

"I thought you might go with your father. See if

his shop needs sweeping out or anything." Her mother kept her eyes on her teacup.

"But somebody has to go fishing with me," Tori said. Then she brightened. "Or I could go by myself."

"Not yet, Victoria," their mother said. "Maybe next summer."

"But I'm already ten," Tori started.

"Don't look at me, Mama." Evie finally got the piece of bacon to her mouth on her fork and chewed a moment before going on. "Besides, you promised to help me sew the collar on my new dress today. I want to wear it Friday night when I go out with George." Her face took on her "dreaming about George" look.

Kate thought any old dress would do for George, who was a goof. A goof with a car, which was nice when he let Kate ride along to Edgeville with them to take in a movie, so she bit her lip and didn't say anything. Kate loved going to movies, and sometimes George even paid for her ticket as long as she promised not to sit anywhere near him and Evie. Of course George called her Evangeline. Nobody shortened Evie's name except Kate. After all, Evangeline had been named after the romantic and tragic heroine of a poem. A poem that both Mama and Daddy loved.

Kate wished she knew a few lines of it by heart so she could say them now and try to get her parents to smile at each other. Instead neither of them showed even a whisper of a smile. Mama stared down at her tea while Daddy's words bored a hole through the wall between them.

"I don't need a guard, Nadine. Kate can go with Victoria." He finished off his coffee and stood up.

Mama kept her eyes on her cup. Her fingers were white where she was squeezing the handle so hard. "I didn't say you did, Victor. I merely thought you might need some help this morning."

"There's no doubt of that," he agreed pleasantly enough, but there was an edge to his voice. Still it was hard to tell if he was angry with himself or Mama or someone who wasn't even in the kitchen.

Kate didn't think it was her, so she dared to speak up. "Mama needs some sugar and baking soda, so I'll walk along with you to the store."

"I want to go too," Tori said.

"You have to get those worms before it gets too hot," Kate said quickly. "They'll go too deep once the sun starts baking the ground."

When Tori started to fuss, their mother spoke up. "Kate's right, Victoria. You can't go fishing without bait."

Kate loved having time alone with her father. Sometimes she could get him to tell the best stories. But today as they started up the road toward his blacksmith shop in the middle of Rosey Corner, he wasn't in a storytelling mood.

He pulled his hat brim down low and frowned like the sun was hurting his eyes.

To fill the silence between them, Kate started chattering. "Mama's making raspberry jam. That's why she needs sugar. And she said she might have enough raspberries for a pie."

"The raspberries are ripe?" Daddy sounded surprised. "Well, I guess it is the middle of June. Where has the year gone?"

"A lot of it's still left." Kate spun around and walked backward for a moment in front of her father. "I love summer. Don't you love summer?"

"A smitty gets hot in the summer," he said, but his frown was gone.

"I guess so." Kate said as she turned to walk beside her father again. "And I suppose this summer's not so great for a lot of people."

"I wasn't aiming to make you sorry you like summer, Kate. You're young. You're supposed to like summer. No school. Time to go fishing."

"I hate fishing." Kate made a face.

"I know, but you're a good big sister. Tell Victoria to bait your hooks too. She doesn't mind worms."

"I don't mind worms. I just don't like squishing them on hooks." Kate shuddered. "And then you have to sit there quiet as stone and wait for some fish that's too little to make a raccoon happy. Then you have to work the hook out of that little bitty fish's mouth and throw the poor thing back

69

in to grow bigger, but it remembers about the hook and you never catch it again no matter how big it gets. On top of that, it already smells like a fish, which I suppose makes sense since it is a fish and your hands end up stinking like fish. Worst of all, if you do happen to catch something big enough, you have to clean the thing and try to keep from swallowing a bone when you eat it. Now tell me what's fun about any of that?"

Daddy actually smiled, which is what Kate was trying to make happen. That and to keep him from looking over toward the little square house they were passing where a person could buy a drink. It was closed in the mornings, but Kate had seen men go up to the door at all times of the day and somebody always opened up. Grandfather Reece called it a den of iniquity. Kate had looked up "iniquity" in the dictionary and found verses that talked about it in the Bible, but she still wasn't sure what went on in the little house. Except she knew it wasn't good, even if her father was singing when he came home after being there.

"You're a good daughter too, Kate," Daddy said. "I didn't cause you trouble last night, did I?" He reached over and touched her hand as they stopped in front of Grandfather Merritt's store. Gas fumes floated out to them from the gas pump where a man was filling up his car's tank.

"No, Daddy. You never cause me trouble."

"Oh, if only that were true." His smile was gone again. "But you can tell your mother not to worry today. Tell her I'll look forward to that raspberry pie tonight."

"Great, Dad," she said before she tiptoed up to kiss his cheek. The stubble on his unshaven cheek poked her lips. She stood in front of the store and watched him walk on up the road to his shop. It would take him awhile to get his forge hot enough to shape a horseshoe, so it was just as well no one was outside waiting. And in her heart, a little prayer circled. *Please let that be true about Daddy coming home to supper. Please.*

8

Tori found worms. When Kate got back with the sugar and baking soda, Tori was waiting on the back porch with a couple of cane poles. She dug around in the can of dirt she was holding and pulled out a plump pink worm to show Kate.

"He's a wiggler." Tori looked very pleased as she held up the worm. "We'll catch a big one with him."

"Then I guess we'll be eating fish for supper. I'll tell Mama to have the skillet ready when we get back." Kate tousled Tori's hair with her free hand. "Give me a minute to get a jug for us. It's already hot. We'll need water."

Kate carried the groceries on into the kitchen, where her mother was washing and picking through a pan of raspberries. When Kate told her Daddy promised to be home for raspberry pie at suppertime, Mama managed a little smile as she said, "Then I guess I'd better bake one. Here, take a berry bucket in case you find some vines around the pond. That way you won't have to fish the whole time." She handed Kate the small metal pail she'd just emptied into her pan. "And don't worry if you don't get back by noon. Evangeline can carry your father's lunch to him."

"By noon it'll be sweltering. It's already too hot for the fish to bite." Kate lifted her hair up to give the back of her neck some air.

"You hope." Mama really smiled now as she laid her hand on Kate's cheek. She looked her straight in the eyes and said, "Thank you."

"Sure, Mama. You know I'll run to the store any time you need something." Kate knew that wasn't what her mother was thanking her for, but there was no way the two of them could talk about what had happened last night.

"I know you will." Her mother dropped her hand away from Kate's cheek. "I guess you're going to Graham's pond."

"Yeah, it's closest and Tori says the fish bite better there."

"If you see him, tell Graham hello for me, and if you run across Fern, you leave her alone."

"I always leave Fern alone," Kate said.

"Make sure Victoria does too. That child is too curious sometimes. I don't think she's ever met a stranger."

"There aren't any strangers in Rosey Corner to meet."

"What about all the people passing through on the road out front? Gypsies. Hoboes. Men down on their luck. Sometimes it seems like half the country has taken to the roads to try to find work or something to eat." Mama frowned and shook her head a little. "Thank goodness we still have food on the table."

"And enough to share." Kate had carried food out to a man who'd knocked on the door asking for something to eat just two days before. "But Graham's pond is back in the woods way off the road. Nobody but Rosey Corner folks know about it. No strangers."

"True enough, but plenty of us Rosey Corner folk have some strange quirks. Fern Lindell for one, and while I don't think Fern would hurt anybody, I wouldn't want to test the truth of that with Victoria. So you see that she behaves."

Kate and Tori cut across the fields to Lindell Woods. By the time they climbed the second fence, sweat was running down both their faces. It felt good to move under the shade of the trees. Graham said this part of the woods was old growth that had never been cleared away for farming. Kate loved looking up at the huge oaks and elms and poplar trees. Sometimes she just stopped right in the middle of the trees and started singing "Praise God from whom all blessings flow" to thank the Lord for letting her live so close to something so beautiful, but today Tori was in a hurry to get to the fish.

They left the big trees behind and entered a part of the woods that had once been cleared for farming. Here cedars had sprung up so thick that Kate and Tori had to walk bent over to get through the trees. They went straight for the pond and didn't go by Graham's cedar pole cabin to ask if they could fish. He'd already told Tori she could fish there anytime she wanted.

Graham was one of those Rosey Corner people with strange quirks Kate's mother had been talking about. One of the strangest was the cedar pole one-room cabin where he lived winter and summer, when a big two-story frame house full of furniture stood empty out closer to the road. Graham's parents had lived there before they died in the influenza epidemic. His father was a doctor, but there wasn't any way to doctor people who had the influenza. The person either died or didn't, Graham said. And a lot of the people in Rosey Corner had died. His father was one of the first to succumb because he was out day and night helping people and he brought the sickness home.

Graham didn't catch it. He didn't know why. He just didn't. He'd worn the garlic necklace some hoped would ward off the sickness, but then so had Fern and his mother. His mother died a week after Graham buried his father. Fern burned with the fever for days after that, and Graham thought she would die too. Then the fever left her, but Graham said it carried some vital part of her away with it. Graham always looked sad when he said Fern's name.

Fern didn't live in the big house either. At least not the way a normal person lived in a house— sleeping in one of the beds, washing sheets, and cooking meals in the kitchen. She just drifted in and out of the house, eating whatever Graham left on the cabinet for her and sleeping on the floor one night, and the next, bedding down out in the woods in a shelter she made by chopping down cedars and piling them up for walls.

Some people said Graham didn't live in the house because he was afraid of Fern, but Kate thought it was more that he'd turned the house into a shrine of sorts to his parents. He liked taking Kate and Tori over to the house to show them his mother's hats. There were shelves of them. Graham would always talk about how beautiful and fashionable his mother had been as he brushed the dust off the hats for the girls to try on.

Kate asked him once why he didn't give the

hats away. Everybody else Kate knew packed up the clothes of any family member who died and sent the box off to the orphans' or the old folks' home. But Graham had looked genuinely shocked at the idea of giving away his mother's hats. "I couldn't do that. She might need them," he said.

At the time, Kate had been too afraid to ask him what he meant by that. She already got the heebie-jeebies sometimes when she was in the parlor where Lillie Lindell's portrait hung. She was sure the woman's eyes were staring at her no matter where she moved in the room. Kate didn't like putting on the dead woman's hats either, but sometimes she did it to keep from hurting Graham's feelings. She never let the hats sit on her head more than a couple of seconds, as if they might still be carrying some trace of the influenza that had carried their owner away from the living world.

This morning, when Kate and Tori finally pushed through the cedar thickets and trees and came out on the pond bank, the water looked cool and inviting. Kate wasn't a bit surprised to see Graham and his long-eared hound, Poe, sitting on the east bank of the pond in the shade. As she and Tori walked around the pond toward him, frogs hopped out across the green moss clinging to the edges of the bank and plopped into the water.

Graham wasn't fishing, but his pole was on the bank beside him. "Done drowned all my worms," he told them. "We got here before sunrise and caught me and Poe a mess for dinner, so the rest of them out there are yours, Victoria, if you can get them to bite." Graham looked up at the sky. "The sun's already getting high in the sky."

"I know." Tori made a face as she dug a worm out of her can of dirt and scooted it on her hook. "Kate had to go to the store." She held the can out toward Kate.

Kate waved it away and set her cane pole down. "You can catch whatever's left, Tori. I'll go hunt for raspberries." She held up her berry bucket. "Mama's making jam."

"Yum," Graham said as he stood up. "I'll tell you where some good ones are if you promise to bring me a jar. Of course there might be snakes." Poe raised his head up off his paws and gave his owner a sad-eyed look to see if they really were leaving such a good resting place.

"I'm not afraid of snakes."

"I wasn't either till one bit me some time back. My leg swelled up big as a fence post. Probably would've died if I hadn't known some cures. Still goes dead on me from time to time if I don't drink my adder's-tongue potion." Graham stomped his right foot.

Kate never knew whether to believe Graham or not. He had studied medicine. Had planned to be a doctor like his father before the influenza epidemic interrupted his plans. He did come up with special potions from roots. Not to give to other people, but sometimes when somebody in Rosey Corner had a sick animal, they'd come after Graham.

Folks said he should hang out a shingle as an animal doctor, but he didn't. He wouldn't even take any money for helping the animals. That way the farmers couldn't get mad at him if the potions killed their livestock instead of helping them, he said. He did sometimes take a jar of beans or slab of bacon. He had to keep food on the table for Fern and Poe.

Graham wasn't destitute even though some people thought he was because of the way he lived. Kate's father said Graham always had cash money to plop down when he bought something at the store. That was more than a lot of the people in Rosey Corner could do right now. The Barclays—Graham's mother's family—had money. His grandfather was a state senator, an influential man in Frankfort before he died of grief after Graham's mother passed on. At least that was what Graham claimed killed him. Kate's mother said it was a heart attack, that she remembered reading in the newspapers about how Senator Barclay had dropped dead right in the middle of a session of the legislature.

Kate had no idea how old Graham was. Age didn't seem to matter all that much to him, as if he'd always been old and didn't worry about it.

The skin on his face was stretched so tight over his cheekbones that it showed tiny red blood vessels tracing a pattern across his cheeks. His shirts hung loose off his shoulders the way they might on a scarecrow in somebody's garden, and Kate had never seen him when his ankles and some leg weren't showing below his pants. That was because he wore his daddy's old clothes, and his daddy had been shorter than him.

Every other week or so he shaved whenever he decided he should show up at one of the churches, and he just whacked off his hair with his pocketknife when it got down in his eyes.

"I gave up on having a wife a long time ago," Kate had overheard him tell her mother once. "No woman I ever met would take on a sister-in-law like Fern. But I pledged to my mother on her deathbed that I'd see to Fern as long as she needed seeing to. I guess Mother must have had a premonition that Fern was going to be damaged by the fever. She laid down sick one woman and got up a whole different one. But that didn't change her being my sister."

Now Graham touched Poe on the head and told him he could stay with Tori. The old dog sank happily back down on the pond bank and dropped his head on his paws as he blew a burst of contented air out of the sides of his mouth. "We were out late last night chasing coons," Graham explained.

"Did you catch any?" Kate asked as she followed him around the pond toward some vines growing at the edge of the woods.

"Naw, not the way you're talking. Me and Poe, we like to get them up a tree, but then we just exchange pleasantries and all of us go on home. It's the chase we're after, not the raccoon."

"You can sell raccoon skins," Kate said.

"I couldn't do that. Me and Poe, we're way too familiar with our coons to want to skin them." Graham stopped and pointed toward the raspberry vines. "Looks like the birds haven't gotten all the ripe ones yet. Or me. I ate some for my breakfast this morning before we started fishing."

"Now that sounds like a good breakfast." Kate stepped into the vines to reach for some of the bigger berries.

"Careful. You'll get all scratched up. Not to mention those snakes."

"Raspberries are worth it." Kate pulled off a berry and put it in her mouth. "Nothing better."

Graham waded into the vines beside her and picked a handful of berries to drop into her bucket. They picked awhile without saying anything. In a tree nearby, a mockingbird was running through his repertoire, and behind them Tori's hook splashed in the water. Above their heads a red-tailed hawk floated across the opening over the pond and let out a shrill whistle.

"Life is good," Graham said as he stared up at the hawk.

"But not for everybody," Kate said.

"Well, no, I guess not everybody can be fishing or picking raspberries on a pond bank, but that doesn't mean we can't be happy we are." Graham dropped another handful of berries into Kate's bucket.

Kate didn't say anything for a minute as she stepped deeper into the berry bushes, carefully mashing down some of the vines with her foot. Then she said, "You and Daddy, did you used to go fishing together when you were kids?"

"Your daddy is some years younger than me, but he was always hanging around Aunt Hattie's boy. Bo was about my age. And we both liked hitting a baseball. Your daddy ran after the balls for us. That Bo, he could smack that ball clear to yonder no matter how I pitched it." Graham looked up and off across the pond as if he could see the baseball flying still.

"Was Daddy happy then?" Kate asked.

"Nobody can be happy all the time," Graham said softly before he shook himself a little, as if to get rid of some sad memory. "But he was happy enough when we were playing ball. Course everything was different then before the Great War and the influenza."

"How?" Kate asked.

"Oh, I don't know. I guess because we were

young and full of the future. Bo, he was going to be a great baseball player, and he was on his way before he went in the army and got killed over there. Me, I was going to cure people. That's why I didn't go to the War. I was still in school. If it had lasted longer and the influenza hadn't come along, I was thinking I'd go overseas as a doctor. Help the wounded soldiers."

"What about Daddy? What did he want to be?" Kate held her bucket over toward Graham for him to drop in his berries.

Graham didn't start picking again for a moment as he thought about his answer. "He was younger, like I said. He hadn't come up with what he planned to do. All he knew for sure before the War came along and yanked him away from Rosey Corner was that he loved your mama. I've never seen nobody so much in love when he was just a young sprout. Bo and me thought he'd die of lovesickness before he ever got your mama to notice him." Graham laughed a little. Then his smile disappeared. "I was in love something like that once upon a time."

"You were?" Kate was surprised. "What happened?"

"I had to come home from school to take care of my folks and Fern when they got sick. I guess the girl gave up on me coming back, and she up and married somebody else."

"I'm sorry."

"Well, it was probably for the best. No woman would want to live the way I do now, and you know, I sort of enjoy it. Freedom's a fine thing." He had a handful of berries again, but when Kate held the bucket over toward him, he grinned at her and popped the whole handful in his mouth.

Kate laughed. And behind them Tori yelled that she'd caught a fish.

9

It was hot in the blacksmith shop. A man couldn't bend iron without heating it to the right stage for the work. That meant fire in the forge year-round. Sweat soaked Victor's shirt and rolled down his face as he shaped the horseshoe on his anvil with his ball-peen hammer. Horses' hooves came in all sizes and shapes, and making shoes to protect their feet and legs was an art. Some of it could be learned, according to his uncle Jonas, but the best blacksmiths were born with a natural instinct and feel for the iron.

Victor didn't think he was born a blacksmith. He'd never thought about shaping iron for a living before the war, even though he liked hanging around his uncle's blacksmith shop when his father didn't need him at the store. His great uncle, actually. His father's uncle by marriage.

Uncle Jonas was a big man, broad as an axe handle across the shoulders, and as good-hearted as he was strong. He could swing the heaviest hammer with one hand with ease. Victor never imagined being able to do what Uncle Jonas could do, but Uncle Jonas let him start shaping the iron as soon as he was big enough to swing a hammer. Victor liked bending the iron to his will. Still, he never planned to use what Uncle Jonas taught him. Not until after everything changed in 1917.

The year he turned nineteen started out fine enough. He was looking forward to graduation, and life seemed full of endless possibilities. His mother talked incessantly about sending him to school back in Virginia. She wanted to turn him into a man of letters. A writer or a teacher perhaps. She had dreams for him the same as his father had had for Preston Jr. His father had no such dreams for Victor. He expected him to finish out his senior year and then start working in the store. A man couldn't expect to spend his whole life buried in books.

Preston Jr. had been enrolled in Centre College over in Danville, but that was different. Preston Jr. had been going places, and he needed not only the book learning but also the contacts with the right people who would someday help him get elected governor. Nobody was going to elect Victor to anything, which suited Victor just fine.

He didn't want to run for office, not even for mayor of Rosey Corner if there had been such a position.

That's what people sometimes said his father was. Unofficially. Unelected. But Preston Merritt knew what the community needed. Hadn't he lived there all his life? Didn't he see virtually every person in Rosey Corner most every week? Some of them every day. So he knew what was going on. The only other man some people set forward as leader of the community was Preacher Reece.

Victor's father laughed at that idea. Preacher Reece might know spiritual matters. If somebody wanted to know about getting to heaven, then by all means that person should knock on the preacher's door. But if that same person wanted to get something done, say, on the road through Rosey Corner, then he'd better show up at Merritt's Dry Goods Store and talk to Preston Merritt.

Victor put in his time at the store on Saturdays and after school, but he didn't plan on spending the rest of his life working there. He might not know what he wanted to do with his life, but he was sure it was something finer than measuring out flour and keeping count of the pickles in the pickle barrel. That was thinking his mother encouraged.

The day after he turned nineteen early in

February, Victor heard his parents arguing about it. He'd never heard his mother cross his father before. In fact they rarely spoke to one another beyond an occasional polite inquiry after the other's health. But his mother stood up to his father for Victor's future. She had her inheritance and she would use it how she wished, and that was to see that Victor was properly educated.

She had her heart set on his going to the College of William and Mary in Virginia where all the men in her family had been educated. Victor planned to get her to compromise on a college in Lexington. That way he could come home to help his father in the store on Saturdays and, more importantly, to see Nadine.

It was funny when he thought back on that time now how blind they'd all been. In Europe countries were bombarding one another and men were dying, but none of it seemed to have much to do with America. And nothing at all to do with Rosey Corner. They read the accounts of the war in the newspapers. Every man who came into the store that January railed against the German submarines attacking neutral ships. They thought something should be done when Germany sank the US liner *Housatonic* in February that year, and most of them backed President Wilson's call for Congress to pass a bill allowing the merchant ships to arm for protection.

But it was the rare man in America who was

ready to pack his knapsack and head across the ocean to help fight the war. Even when the newspapers reported the German Foreign Minister Zimmerman's telegram to Mexico proposing an alliance against the United States, most of the men in Rosey Corner still thought the war would stay overseas and never touch any of them.

Victor read the war news in the papers and heard the talk at the store, but he didn't worry about it. He was young and in love, and thoughts of Nadine filled his head. He jumped out of bed every morning with a smile on his face. It didn't matter what his father said to him. It didn't matter what her father said to her. At least not to Victor. Nadine wasn't quite as sure about that.

"Give me a few more weeks to let him get used to the idea," she told Victor when he asked if he could come to her house to call upon her.

"He's never going to get used to the idea. He doesn't like me. He's never going to like me." Victor didn't see any use dancing around the truth.

Nadine frowned at Victor. They had stolen a few minutes to talk outside the school before classes started. "What a thing to say! Of course he will like you once he gets to know you better. Right now he thinks you're like your father."

"If that's true, he's the only person who ever thought that," Victor said. He moved in front of her to block the cold wind off her face.

She had her hands tucked inside the sleeves of the black wool coat one of the church members must have passed down to her. It was too short and showed a wide band of her dark blue skirt sticking out below it. She had let the hood of the coat fall off her head and the wind was blowing strands of her long honey-brown hair across her face. Her nose was red and her beautiful blue eyes were tearing up either from the chill wind or the stubbornness of their fathers.

Victor's hand shook a little as he smoothed back one of her curls. She was so lovely that it was all he could do not to reach out and fold her in his arms and kiss her. But Miss Penman, the head of the school, frowned on romantic embraces between students, so he restrained himself. "If only I could write a poem that would do your beauty justice."

"Beauty is only skin-deep," she whispered.

"Not in your case. You are beautiful inside and outside, through and through, and I love you completely. Desperately. With every inch of my heart and soul, and I always will to my dying day." He wasn't sure behind the school building was exactly the best place to first profess his love to her, but he didn't wish his words back.

Her eyes widened and she sounded breathless as she said, "I don't know what to say."

He smiled down at her. "I could suggest a few words. Three notable ones if they are there in your heart." He lightly touched the wool of her coat over her heart.

She looked truly distressed that she couldn't say the words of love he so wanted to hear. "It's just that I can't imagine what my father will say. Or do."

"Why worry about what your father will say? Why not worry about what you want to say?"

She dropped her eyes away from his. "The bell is going to ring in a few minutes. We should go inside."

Victor put his hands on her shoulders to keep her from turning away from him. He hesitated and then pushed out his next words. "I hear your father has been visiting Carla Murphy."

Her eyes shot back to his with a flash of anger in them. "What do you mean by that? My father visits people in Rosey Corner all the time. They ask his spiritual counsel. He is a preacher. It's his calling to help people."

Victor held his hands up and stepped back. "Right. Sorry. I didn't mean anything by it. Just repeating something somebody told me."

"Well, you shouldn't listen to gossip. Maybe you should read in the Bible what James says about the dangers of an unbridled tongue." She whirled away from him and stormed toward the front of the school.

He waited a few minutes before he followed her. Perhaps he had been wrong to speak of Carla

Murphy and the rumors going around Rosey Corner. Obviously Nadine wasn't ready to surrender her spot in her father's life to another woman. Obviously she wasn't ready to step into the spot Victor had wide open in his own life for her.

He hesitated on the steps into the school and thought about not going inside. He wanted to go down to the stable, get his horse, and ride away from here. To Frankfort or Lexington. Anywhere away from Rosey Corner. Anywhere away from the anger in Nadine's eyes.

How could she be so angry with him when he'd just told her how much he loved her?

He went on into the school just as the bell rang. He wouldn't let her think he was a coward who spoke of his love and then ran away when she didn't speak of her own love in return. He had loved her for many years with not so much as a glance his way from her. He wouldn't give up so easily. He'd fight Preacher Reece for her if he had to, but first he'd reread the book of James in the Bible so next time he'd be readier to bridle his tongue and only say the right things to her.

Something he wasn't sure he'd ever learned to do, Victor thought now as he brought his hammer down and hit the horseshoe on his anvil. He missed the intended spot by a fraction of an inch. That's what he got for letting his mind wander away from his work.

He picked up the horseshoe with his tongs and laid it back in the coals. He was glad Haskell Jenkins had left the heat of the shop to wait outside in the shade for Victor to have the shoe ready for his horse. He wouldn't have wanted Haskell to see him make such a boneheaded strike.

He rubbed the sweat out of his eyes with his shirtsleeve. His shoulder ached. He rotated it to loosen it up, but that just made the ache go deeper. He stared over at the shelves where a bottle was hidden in behind a pile of rags. It was less than half full, but that would be plenty to dull the pain.

He shut his eyes and pulled in a long breath. He held the air in his lungs as new beads of sweat popped up on his forehead, but he didn't let his feet move toward the shelves. He wouldn't pick up the bottle today no matter how much his shoulder hurt. He'd hurt worse. Lots of times. And he'd told Kate to tell Nadine he'd be at the supper table that night. Nadine wouldn't believe it was true, but she'd bake the raspberry pie anyway. She was a far better woman than he deserved.

He loved Nadine as desperately as ever. Much more even than that day he'd first admitted his love, but he kept failing her and falling short of being the man she should have. What had happened to him that made him keep doing the things he knew he shouldn't do and kept him from doing the things he should?

Maybe her father was right. Maybe he did have a demon inside him. A demon that only the bottle could quiet. Or maybe his father was right that some men were born with moral courage while others had to search for it wherever they could find it. Be that inside the pages of a book, with a gun, or in a bottle.

Victor shut his mind to the call of the bottle and lifted the horseshoe out of the coals. It was yellow hot, and this time when he hit it with his hammer, the iron shaped just as he intended.

10

That night Kate's father kept his word and came home to eat a piece of raspberry pie warm from the oven. There wasn't even the hint of alcohol on his breath, and the tired lines on his face vanished when Kate's mother stepped over behind him at the table to massage his sore shoulders.

After supper Kate's mother and father settled down in the next room with their books while Evie and Kate cleaned up the kitchen. Tori got to go on out and play since she'd caught the fish for their supper. Kate started to point out that she deserved the same consideration for getting briar scratches and chancing snakebites when she climbed into the middle of the raspberry vines to pick the berries for the pie, but she didn't want to hear how Evie would moan and cry if she got stuck doing the dishes alone. So Kate just gathered the dishes off the table without a word. Outside the neighborhood kids were yelling as they played kick-the-can. A good group must have gathered out in the Merritts' front yard the way they did almost every evening.

Kate looked at the pile of dishes and sighed. "Everybody will be gone home before we get all these dishes done."

"You're too old to play kick-the-can and hide-and-seek anyway." Evie gave her a look. "When are you going to start acting your age?"

"Never, I hope. Hide-and-seek in the dark is fun. Unless you run into the clothesline. That's not much fun." Kate put her hand on her neck and made a choking noise before she picked up the dishpan and held it out toward Evie. The enamel had chipped off in places, leaving thin black spots, but so far it hadn't sprung a leak. "It's your turn to wash."

"No, it isn't." Evie backed up a few steps as if she thought the pan might bite her.

"I washed last night. It's my turn to dry." Kate kept the pan held out toward Evie.

"Well, maybe so, but please will you wash again?" Evie held up her hands and waggled her fingers. "I filed and buffed my fingernails this afternoon, and dishwater will ruin them."

"Yeah, yeah, and your big date with Gorgeous George is coming up." Kate set the pan down on the cabinet and got the teakettle off the stove. She put the cake of lye soap in the pan and poured the water in on top of it to make the most suds. She hated not having sudsy water when she washed dishes.

"You'll melt all the soap," Evie told her.

"You don't like the way I do it, you can wash them yourself." Kate set the teakettle back on the stove with a thump.

"Stop that fussing, girls," Mama called from the next room.

"Yes, ma'am," Kate answered.

"Now see what you've done," Evie said under her breath. "Upset Mama. And when everything was going so nice tonight."

Kate started to smack Evie in the face with the dishrag. She could almost see the soap bubbles landing in Evie's red hair and her eyes popping wide open, but Kate dropped the rag into the hot water instead. She didn't want to disturb the peace of the evening. Evie was right about that much. Besides, just thinking about it was almost as good as doing it.

For a second she felt guilty as she remembered one of Grandfather Reece's sermons about sin and how if a person thought about doing something wrong in his heart it was the same as doing it. But he was talking about big things like murder and adultery. Not a smack with a dishrag. The Lord would surely understand how a sister could drive a person batty enough to think about doing something a little bit wrong sometimes.

Kate washed the glasses and set them in the drain pan for Evie to dry. In the living room Mama laughed. Maybe at something in her book or something Daddy said. Kate didn't know which. She couldn't hear what her parents were saying over the clank of the dishes in the dishpan, but it was still a good sound. She smiled in spite of the pile of dishes and the games going on outside without her. She even tried to make peace with Evie. "You and George going to a movie Friday night?"

"Probably," Evie said as she twirled the dishtowel up inside one of the glasses. The towel squeaked against the glass. "But don't be trying to get George to invite you to ride along. This is my date. You want to have a date, you get your own boyfriend."

"You can have George. I don't want him or any other boy." Kate made a face.

"Aren't you ever going to grow up, Kate? You're fourteen. Plenty old enough to get sweet on a boy." Evie picked up one of the plates and dried it off. "Maybe sometime we could have a double date. Me and George and you and . . . let's see." She thought a minute. "How about Harry Winters?"

"Harry Winters! I wouldn't walk across the porch to see him. He uses his fingers instead of a handkerchief to blow his nose." Kate shuddered.

"That's disgusting." Evie frowned at her.

"Really disgusting." Kate washed a bowl and then held it up toward the light coming in the window behind them to see if it was clean.

"I mean you telling me that. Ladies don't talk about those sorts of things." Evie picked up another dish to dry. "So maybe not Harry. Who do you think is good-looking? Besides George, that is."

Kate bit her lip to keep from saying the only thing good-looking about George was his car. That would just make Evie squawk and then there would go the peace of the evening down the creek. So instead she shrugged a little and said, "Oh, I don't know."

She ran through the boys in the neighborhood in her head, but she couldn't imagine wanting to *date* any of them. They were all right for playing baseball or catching frogs in the creek or seeing how many gooseberries they could eat without getting the sour shivers, but certainly not for sitting close and holding hands the way Evie and George were always doing. Kate had even caught the two of them kissing. That was really worrisome, thinking about George maybe ending up her brother-in-law. A worry her mother obviously shared, because she was always reminding Evie there was more than one fish in the sea.

Kate was thinking about trying to change the subject to how many fish might actually be in the sea—it had to be in the millions—and how there were probably lots of fish nobody had ever seen, but Evie spoke first. "There's got to be at least one boy who makes your heart go thumpity-thump."

"Well, maybe if we were seeing who could run the fastest."

"That's not what I'm talking about and you know it." Evie sounded disgusted.

"I know." Kate scrubbed the fork she was holding until it shone before she went on. "But . gee whiz, Evie, I've known these boys forever. And most of them have no idea how to carry on an intelligent conversation. I'll bet they've never even thought about how many fish are in the sea. They just want to talk about the latest prank they pulled or about where the best hunting spots are or their dogs. Actually I like talking about their dogs." She laid a handful of washed utensils in the drain pan. "I wish Bullet hadn't gotten run over. But even when they do talk about their dogs, none of them are half as much fun to talk to as Graham."

"I don't know what you see in that crazy old man." Evie shook her head at Kate as she picked out all the forks to dry and put in the drawer before she did the spoons.

"He's not crazy. A little odd maybe, but definitely not crazy."

"You couldn't prove that by me." Evie waved her towel back and forth while she waited for Kate to finish washing the mashed potatoes pan. "What in the world do you talk about with him? Besides how many hats his mother had."

"Oh, I don't know. Anything and everything. Birds, old Poe, freedom. Fish in the sea." Kate handed Evie the pan and picked up the skillet. They were almost through, and the noise level outside was as strong as ever. Nobody had gone home yet. "The past. He tells me things about when Daddy was our age."

"He's got to be lots older than Daddy," Evie said.

"I guess so. But that doesn't mean he doesn't know things about Daddy when he was growing up. We know things about the little kids around here." Finally Kate had the skillet clean. She fished around in the bottom of the dishpan for any utensils she might have missed.

Evie wiped off the skillet and set it down on the cabinet beside the stove. "He doesn't look like he'd know much of anything about anything."

"Funny. I think he looks like he knows about a lot of things. Things I don't even know to ask about, but that maybe I will someday."

"You're not normal, Kate."

"That's a mean thing to say. And after I washed the dishes for you when it was your turn." Kate wrung out the dishrag and carried the pan to the back door to sling the dishwater out in the yard. When she came back in the kitchen to put the pan under the cabinet again, she said, "Besides, maybe I'm the normal one and you're the one who's not normal."

"I don't think so." Evie carefully hung her dishtowel on the rack on the side of the cabinet and then gave Kate a pitying look.

Kate balled up the dishrag in her hand. She could probably hit Evie right in the nose with it if she tried. She shut her eyes and counted to five and made herself shake the rag out and lay it on the cabinet to dry. "Who's got red hair? That's not the normal color. Most people have brown hair like me."

"Hair color doesn't make you normal or weird. Besides, my hair is pretty. Everybody says so."

"Okay. But who cries like a baby when they don't get their way even if they are sixteen?" Kate said. "Who needs somebody to go with them to the outhouse after dark?"

"Now who's being mean?" Evie's cheeks flushed red and her lips trembled.

"Not mean. Truthful. I guess that's one of my weirder characteristics. Not trying to hide from the truth."

"Oh, go on outside and play with your little friends," Evie said with a wave of her hand. "Just be careful and don't let Fern or the gypsies get you."

Kate made a face at Evie. "The gypsies like redheaded girls, and they don't care whether it's dark or daylight. They grab whatever they want whenever they want it."

The color drained out of Evie's face. "They don't really, do they?"

"No, not really," Kate relented. "They just steal apples off your trees or clothes off your clothesline."

"Fern does that."

"True, but Graham always brings whatever it is back or trades you something better for it."

"It's still wrong to steal. That's one of the Ten Commandments."

"But remember she's not normal. Like me." Kate stuck her tongue out at Evie.

"You'd better not steal anything."

"What is the matter with you two? Stop it right now." Mama was standing in the doorway with her hands on her hips.

"Sorry," Kate said quickly and slipped out the back door before her mother could make her go to bed early. She wasn't worried about Evie getting in trouble. Evie never got in trouble. It must have something to do with being the oldest and so ladylike with that pretty red hair like their

Grandmother Reece had had, the one who had died when Kate's mother was twelve.

The next morning after breakfast Mama gave her a talking to about how sisters were supposed to try to get along, and how it wasn't nice to say things that got other people scared and how wouldn't it be good if they could have just one night when nobody was upset with anybody else.

"Yes, ma'am." Kate ducked her head, stared at the table, and tried not to think about Evie gloating in the next room because Kate was in trouble.

"Your sister should be your best friend," Mama said. "I always wanted a sister. Brothers are all right, but a sister, she can understand things about you without you ever saying a word. It's like your heart divided and made another person."

"Twin sisters maybe." Kate looked up at her mother. "Evie and me aren't twins."

"You don't have to be twins to love one another and help one another. Remember, sisters are a gift and a blessing."

"Yes, ma'am, I do love my sisters, but nobody can get along with everybody else every minute of every day, can they?"

"I suppose not. At least not without the help of the good Lord." Mama smiled and reached across the table to pat Kate's cheek before she stood up.

Kate hid her sigh of relief that the sister lecture was over. She got up too and went over to look at the jars of raspberry jam lined up on the windowsill. The light purple jam seemed to absorb the sunlight hitting the jars and then bounce it out into the kitchen. There were only five jars. Even the biggest wild raspberries weren't much bigger than the tip of Kate's little finger, so it took a lot of picking to have enough for jam. "You want me to take Graham his jar of jam this morning? I promised him one for showing me where the best raspberries were and helping me pick."

"You can later, but first take one up to Father. He'll be at the church praying over his sermon this morning."

Kate picked up one of the jars and let her mother kiss her cheek before she went out the back door and cut through the field behind the house toward the church. She hoped her grandfather would be too deep in the Scriptures to want to pray over her this morning. She didn't really mind the prayers. Everybody needed prayers, but sometimes he went on and on until her knees got numb.

Kate climbed the fence in behind the church and looked over toward the back door. It was closed. That was a sure sign Grandfather Reece wasn't at the church yet. She'd go around to the front door and sit on the steps to wait for him.

The steps would be in the shade this time of the morning.

When she came around the corner of the church building, a little girl was already sitting on the steps. She looked up at Kate and said, "Are you an angel?"

11

M e? An angel? Far from it. Just ask anybody," Kate said with a laugh as she squatted down in front of the steps.

The little girl pulled her faded red dress down over her knees as though she wanted to hide as much of her small body as she could from Kate. Little bare feet crusted with dirt stuck out below her dress. The child pushed her dark curly hair back from her face and dropped her chin down on her knees to wait for whatever Kate was going to say next. Tear streaks ran down her cheeks, but she wasn't crying now.

Kate had never seen the child before. "Are you lost, sweetie?"

"No." The child mashed her mouth together, and tears filled her dark chocolate-brown eyes and overflowed to slide down her cheeks. She didn't bother wiping them away as she stared up at Kate with a mixture of fear and hope. "You have to be an angel. Please."

"Why do I have to be an angel?" Kate moved over to sit down beside the child. She started to put her arm around her, but then stopped. She didn't want to frighten the little girl.

"Because my mommy said that if I sat here and didn't cry, an angel would come take care of me and love me and bring me something to eat. I tried really hard. Just like I promised Mommy." The little girl looked down at her feet. After a few seconds she went on in a tiny, sad voice. "But I couldn't keep all the tears in. They just came out."

"Where is your mommy?" Kate asked softly.

"She left. With Daddy. She had to." The little girl pulled her dress down farther over her knees until the hem touched the top of her feet. She curled her toes under as if to hide them too.

"Why did she have to?"

"Because of the baby in her tummy. Daddy, he's gonna find work and then they're coming back for me. But Daddy said this looked like a good place. He said it had gardens and apple trees and two churches. Most places only have one. They kept Kenton because he's sick. Nobody wants a sick boy. I told them I might be sick too, but they said the angel wouldn't care. That she'd make me feel better. They're coming back for me. Mommy promised."

The little girl looked up at Kate as if she needed Kate to say it was true, so Kate did. "Then they will as soon as they can."

The little girl let out a long breath and scooted closer to Kate. "Can I touch you or will my hand go right through you? You know, like a ghost. I've never seen an angel before."

"You can touch me. I'm not a real angel. Those you might not be able to touch." Kate put her arm around the child and drew her close to her side. Her shoulders felt very bony under her dress. "My name's Kate. What's your name?"

"Lorena Birdsong. Mommy told me to say my name every morning when I get up and every night when I go to bed, and that wherever she is she'll be saying it too. My name. Lorena Birdsong." The little girl looked up at Kate. Her lips trembled a little, and she blinked her eyes very fast before she went on. "Names are very important, you know. Mommy told me never to forget that."

"Your mommy is right." Kate squeezed her shoulders a little.

The girl shifted a little to the side and pulled a piece of paper out from under her leg. "She wrote it down for me so that when I start school, I'll spell it right." She ran her finger over the writing on the paper before she held it out for Kate to see. "That and the day I was born."

"Lorena Birdsong. June 1, 1931," Kate read. "That's a very pretty name."

"Thank you." Lorena lovingly folded the paper and held it over her heart for a moment before stuffing it under her leg again.

"Do people call you Lori for short?" Kate said.

"Nobody but my brother, Kenton. He does sometime." She looked very sad again. "I didn't get to tell him goodbye. He's been coughing so bad that he was really tired and he went to sleep. Mommy tried to wake him up, but he was too sleepy. She said she'd tell him for me. He's six."

"And you're five."

"This many." Lorena held up one hand with her fingers spread apart. "I had a birthday."

"I know. It was on your piece of paper."

"We were in the car. We don't have a house."

Kate thought of the people she'd seen going through Rosey Corner in the last few months. Mostly men alone on foot, but some families in cars. Her father said the men were trying to find work, but there wasn't any work to find in Rosey Corner. So they passed on through. He said they were going to the cities where at least they'd be able to find a soup kitchen.

Any time one of the men knocked on their door, Kate's mother would fix a plate of food for Kate or Tori to carry out to him in the front yard. The men always looked so hungry even after they brought the empty plate back up to the door.

"Are you hungry?" Kate asked Lorena.

Lorena licked her lips and nodded her head. "And thirsty. Do angels carry food in their wings?" She tried to peer around behind Kate.

"I'm not an angel, sweetie. No wings for sure."

Kate looked at the jar of jam she was holding and wished for a spoon. Still, the jam would taste better with a biscuit and some milk. "But I know where we can get something for you to eat. Come on."

Kate picked Lorena up. She was all skin and bones and didn't weigh as much as a sack of flour.

"I can walk," Lorena said.

"I know, but you're tired and not very heavy." Kate looked up and across the fields. She could see Grandfather Reece in the distance walking toward the church. She slipped around the side of the church quickly before he noticed them there on the steps. She put the jar of jam right inside the back door. Then she almost ran to the fence and set Lorena down on the other side before she climbed over herself.

She didn't want her grandfather to see them. He'd want to pray over Lorena and ask a hundred questions. Lorena didn't need questions. She needed food and a bath and somebody to keep hugging her.

Kate picked Lorena back up. This time the little girl didn't protest. Instead she giggled and said, "I like being carried." Lorena laid her head down on Kate's shoulder. "You smell like an angel."

"Oh really? And what does an angel smell like?"

"You," Lorena murmured. The little girl's body relaxed against Kate as if she were falling asleep.

Kate didn't say anything as she hurried across the field to her house. She was too busy trying to think of what she would say to her mother. She'd brought home strays before. A cat that still lived in the barn and had kittens regular as clockwork, poor Bullet who'd gotten run over, a frog and a lizard, but never a stray little girl. And never a stray she so wanted to keep.

Kate might not really be an angel, but she could be a big sister. Somehow she'd have to convince her mother that they needed another sister. Four wasn't that much more than three. A little thing like Lorena surely wouldn't cause much trouble. And how could anybody turn away a little girl who needed a big sister?

Kate stopped on the back porch to pour some water in the wash pan and wash Lorena's face.

"Is this your house?" Lorena asked. She didn't try to duck away from the washrag.

"It is. I'm going to take you in to meet my mother."

"Is she an angel too?"

"She's a lot closer to one than I am. That's for sure." Kate laughed as she dried off Lorena's face and then kissed her nose.

Lorena put her arms around Kate's neck. "Can this be my house too? Just till Mommy comes back."

"I don't know. I hope so." Kate started to comb Lorena's hair, but the little girl jerked away.

"Ouch! That hurt." Lorena wrapped her arms over her head to keep her hair away from the comb.

"I'm sorry, but you've got rats' nests in there."

"I'm afraid of rats." Lorena's bottom lip trembled and she held her arms tighter against her head. "They eat your toes if you don't keep wiggling them. Kenton told me."

"Your toes are safe here." Kate put down the comb. "We'll comb that hair later. I'll get you a mirror you can look into and you can help comb, okay?"

Lorena slowly dropped her arms away from her hair. "Do you promise? About the toes?"

"I promise." Kate squatted in front of the little girl and looked her right in the eyes. "No rats in this house. Your toes are safe." She smiled before she reached down and tickled Lorena's toes.

Lorena giggled and backed up. Then her eyes got very round again as she stared at Kate. "Please promise I can stay here."

Kate hesitated. She wanted more than anything to promise, but she couldn't be sure what her mother and father would say. Finally she hugged Lorena and said, "I want to promise that, but I can't. I can promise that somebody will take care of you."

"I don't want to go to an orphans' home. Kenton says those places have lots of rats."

"No orphans' homes." Kate wouldn't let them

send her to an orphans' home. She didn't know how, but she wouldn't. "Come on. Let's go show you to Mama and get you something to eat. Do you like bacon and biscuits and raspberry jam?"

"You have all that food?"

"And honey too."

"I knew you were an angel," Lorena murmured against Kate's neck.

12

On Sunday afternoon, they gathered at the Rosey Corner Baptist Church to decide what to do with the child. Most everybody seemed to think that since the little girl had been left on the Baptist Church steps, that gave the church not only the right but also the duty to determine what became of her. A bad feeling had been growing inside Nadine ever since her father started talking about having a meeting to decide the child's fate. She had no confidence a decision by committee would be best for Lorena. Or for Kate.

Nadine looked over at Kate, who was sitting on the other side of Lorena. The two of them had the child safely sandwiched between them on the front pew, but how much longer was Nadine going to keep that true? She wanted to. From the moment she had seen Kate guiding the child through the back door into the kitchen, she had wanted to. There had been something so wounded and lost about the child, and yet at the same time the little girl had looked up at Kate and then at Nadine with total trust as Kate began talking about this new little sister she had found.

Kate's eyes had beseeched Nadine over the top of the little girl's head as she pushed out her words so fast they were almost tripping over her tongue. "This is Lorena, Mama. I found her on the church steps. She's really sweet, and she needs somebody to take care of her. Do you think maybe the Lord planned on you sending me over there to the church this morning with the raspberry jam for Grandfather Reece?" She rushed on before Nadine could answer. "You know, so I'd find her. He plans out ways to take care of us, doesn't he? I mean, he loves all his children and he tells us to take care of our brothers and sisters, right? And according to the way the Bible talks about brothers and sisters, Lorena is our little sister."

Nadine had looked at the little girl and back at Kate's pleading eyes and wanted to say yes, yes, yes. The Lord was good, and he did love them and expect them to care for one another. She wanted it to happen just the way Kate wanted, but things didn't always happen because Nadine wanted them to. Else Essie wouldn't be dancing only in her memory. Instead her baby sister would be grown, with children who called Nadine aunt. Victor wouldn't need alcohol to get him through the week, and people would still have more need for horseshoes than rubber tires. Aunt Hattie's boy, Bo, would be hitting homeruns somewhere instead of being in a grave in France, and Nadine's father would smile at her and rejoice in the beauty of his granddaughters. So many things she might like to make happen for the better.

Troubles came at some time or other to everybody who drew breath. The Bible was plain about that. A time to laugh and a time to weep. This was surely a time for weeping in America. People without enough food to eat. People so desperate that they would leave a beloved child on the steps of a church in hopes strangers would feed and care for her. Praise the Lord she and Victor were able to feed their girls. In that she was blessed.

They could feed this girl too. Kate was right. One more small mouth to feed and one more body to clothe wouldn't be that much trouble.

Nadine hadn't promised that day or in the days since. It never did to make promises she wasn't sure she could keep. Even to herself. She'd broken too many of those promises already. Aunt Hattie told Nadine she was too hard on herself. That the only one who was ever able to keep every promise he made was the good Lord, and some of those promises cost him agony.

But it was surely better not to promise the moon when a person had no way of pulling it down out of the sky. So instead Nadine had said, "We'll take care of her today."

"But what about tomorrow?" Kate wanted to know.

"We'll worry about tomorrow when it comes," she said before holding her arms out toward the child.

The little girl must have seen the welcome in those arms, because she didn't hesitate as she moved across the floor and let Nadine embrace her. She was so thin that Nadine's heart hurt for her.

The child relaxed against Nadine and let out a long contented sigh. "Mommy was right."

"About what, sweetheart?"

"About the angel coming to help me. But she didn't know about the angel mommy," the child said.

"What angel mommy?"

"You."

Kate explained about the angels while Lorena ate biscuits and bacon and applesauce.

When the child couldn't stuff in another bite she touched a biscuit on her plate. "I wish I cou' give this to Kenton."

"Kenton?" Nadine asked.

"Her brother," Kate said. "Lorena said he ' sick."

Lorena looked sad. "But he likes biscuits. It might make him feel better."

"Do you think he's still in Rosey Corner? That your mother and father might still be here?" Nadine asked. "We could take them some food."

Lorena shook her head as big tears gathered in her eyes. "Mommy got in the car and shut the door. She leaned way out the window and looked at me all the way down the road, but Daddy didn't stop. He kept going till I couldn't see them no more."

"I see," Nadine said. And she did see. Too much. "She was looking back at you because she loves you so much."

"I wish she hadn't gone," Lorena said in a very small voice.

They heated water and let Lorena bathe in the round metal tub out on the back porch. She liked that. She splashed in the water and played with soap bubbles and didn't complain when she had to stand still while Nadine checked her hair for lice and her little body for any sores that might need treating. All she found were a few mosquito bites Lorena had scratched raw. But Nadine had to blink back tears at the sight of the child's little ribs outlined so starkly beneath her skin.

When Victoria came home from playing with Sally Jane across the road, the child was napping on her bed while Nadine and Kate searched

through Victoria's old clothes for a dress that wouldn't completely swallow Lorena. Victoria wasn't the least bit bothered by the prospect of her place as baby in the family being usurped. Instead she put her favorite rag doll beside Lorena and sat down on the floor by the bed to wait for the child to open her eyes.

By the time Victor had come home late that afternoon, Lorena was the same as adopted into their family. That was three days ago. Three days of the little girl sitting at their table eating their food and running around their yard and sleeping in the girls' bedroom. Finding a place in their hearts as they held back tomorrow.

Now tomorrow had come, and Nadine's dismay was almost overpowering as her father stepped behind the pulpit to call the meeting to order. It wasn't simply the look on his face and the way he kept sliding his eyes over Nadine without really looking at her. He knew what she wanted. She had cornered him that morning before worship services in his usual place in the back of the church reading the Scripture and told him straight out that she and Victor were willing and able to give Lorena a home until her parents came back for her.

Her father had breathed a heavy sigh and placed his finger on the Bible page to hold his place before he looked up at Nadine. "You know her parents will never come back for her, Nadine.

They tossed her aside as easily as we might get rid of a stray cat."

"They were desperate. They didn't have any way to feed her," Nadine argued.

Up in the front of the church, the men's and women's Sunday school classes were being taught on opposite sides of the pulpit. Because of the heat, the children's classes were being held outside under the shade tree.

Her father raised his eyebrows and peered at her over his reading glasses. "They had a way to get gasoline. Don't you think food should have come before gasoline for their automobile?"

He didn't expect her to answer him, but she did. "We can't know their reasons or motives."

"That is true, but we can know and examine our own motives. The Lord surely placed this child here for a reason, and we must do what is best for the child without consideration of our own selfish desires. Now leave me so that I may receive the holy message the Lord would have me deliver to my people today." He looked back down at his Bible in dismissal.

Nadine stared at the thinning gray hair on top of his head and dared to speak again. "Doesn't the Lord promise to give us the desires of our heart?"

He pulled in a breath and let it out slowly as if having to work to control his temper. When he did finally speak, his words sounded calm enough, but his eyes showed anger with her refusal to bend to his will. "Psalm 37:4. Nadine, you know it is sinful to pick and choose this or that portion of Scripture to justify one's faulty thinking. The first of that verse says to delight thyself also in the Lord. You must first do that, and then you will be standing in the will of the Lord and not be desiring in your heart things that are not of the Lord."

She refused to back down even in the face of the storm gathering in his eyes. "How could wanting to care for a homeless child not be of the Lord?"

"Enough." His voice boomed out so loudly that the people in the Sunday school classes looked around at them. He stuck his fingers and thumb up under his glasses and rubbed his eyes to compose himself before he went on. "It will be decided what the Lord's will is for the child at the meeting this afternoon. But it would be well for you to remember, Nadine, that the Lord has already blessed you with three daughters."

So it was with much trepidation that she brought Lorena back to the church that afternoon. Nadine's heart sank as she saw the people gathering in the church. Her father and his wife, Carla. Carla's sister, Ella Baxter, and her husband, Joseph. Each time Ella looked over at Lorena, Nadine wanted to scoot a bit closer to the child.

She had never liked Ella. The woman was too much like Carla even though she was closer to Nadine's age. Neither of the two sisters had children, but they were always quick with advice on how children should be raised. Especially Nadine's children. They both liked Evangeline, but Kate was a constant topic of harping complaint. She should be more ladylike. She should listen to her elders. She was too quick with a disrespectful remark. She was too restless in church. She spent entirely too much time talking to that bohemian Graham Lindell. If Nadine took up for Kate and praised her free spirit, then Carla would insist Nadine's father pray over Kate in an attempt to tame that spirit.

Nadine had always countered her father's prayers with fervent prayers of her own. Prayers that her father would see Kate's loving heart and joyful attitude instead of worrying about her occasional lapse of obedience and ladylike manners. Those prayers had yet to be answered, but more importantly her father's prayers had done nothing to change Kate, except perhaps to prove to her that she could sit absolutely still for ten or more minutes without suffering permanent injury.

Kate was sitting perfectly still now. She had her eyes half closed and Nadine could see the prayers rising out of her. Prayers Nadine feared would not be answered as they wished. If only they could have somehow hidden Lorena from the eyes of the other people in Rosey Corner. But nothing stayed hidden in Rosey Corner for long, and by the end of the first day, everyone in the community knew a child had been dropped on the Rosey Corner Baptist Church's steps like an unwanted puppy.

Her father began speaking. "Brothers and Sisters, we are gathered here together this day in order to make a godly decision in regard to the little sister who was left at our church with the hoped-for assurance that the good people in this very church would act with compassion. I thank all of you for the Christian concern and love that brought you back this afternoon. Let us ask the Lord's guidance and his blessings upon our actions." Nadine's father clutched the sides of the pulpit and bowed his head to pray. His voice boomed out so loud as he addressed the Lord that Lorena was startled. She stared up at him with large eyes.

Kate leaned over and kissed the child's head, and Nadine squeezed her hand. She thought about just picking the little girl up and carrying her out of the church. It was not going to turn out well. She'd known that as soon as she'd seen her father's face that morning. It was a feeling that had gotten surer when Father Merritt had shown up and stalked down the aisle to sit ramrod straight on the opposite side of the church from them, looking neither right nor left or making any pretense of bowing his head for the prayer.

Preston Merritt had not stepped foot in this church building for years. For that matter Victor, who sat beside Nadine, had rarely come inside any church since he'd come back from the war, but when Gertie or Aunt Hattie did shame him into attending, he went to the Christian Church on the other side of the road. That was the Merritts' church. Preston Merritt had been on every pulpit committee that church had formed for the last thirty years. And of course, Nadine's father had stood in this church's pulpit even longer.

Now the two men—her father and Victor's—had come together under the same roof with what Nadine feared was a rare unity of purpose. She stared up at her father as he kept praying. He was beginning to show his age. He had always been a stocky man, but lately he had gained some extra weight that made him get out of breath with any sort of exertion. Even while he was preaching, he sometimes had to stop and hold on to the pulpit while he gathered his wind. The skin on his neck lapped over his shirt collar. Today he had surrendered to the heat enough to leave off his suit jacket, but his tie was pulled tight up against his stiff collar, the same as always. His gray hair was carefully combed to hide the balding spot on top of his head and held in place with a liberal application of pomade. But his voice sounded strong and sure as he addressed the Lord.

She let her eyes wander past Victor over to Father Merritt. He was staring straight ahead, his face stony and his eyes wide open like Nadine's as her father's prayer went on and on. He was older than her father, but didn't look it. Victor said stones didn't age, that they stayed hard forever. Father Merritt's body did show a few signs of age—the loss of his hair and the deep frown wrinkles between his eyes. Still, he often claimed to be as strong at sixty-nine as he had been at thirty, and nobody in Rosey Corner challenged the truth of that whether or not they believed it.

He must have felt her eyes on him because he turned to look at her. She ducked her head, but not before she saw pity mixed with contempt in his eyes. It was a look she'd seen before.

13

On Wednesday, April 6, 1917, President Woodrow Wilson signed the declaration of war and, with the strokes of his pen, altered the lives of Nadine and her classmates. The boys at school the next day seemed to have become older overnight as they talked of going to war. Miss Penman called an assembly in the gymnasium to read to the students the president's words asking Congress to declare war on Germany.

" 'The world must be made safe for democracy.' " The newspaper fluttered in Miss Penman's hands, and she stepped behind the podium for support and kept reading. " 'It is a fearful thing to lead this great peaceful people into war, the most terrible of all wars. But the right is more precious than the peace, and we shall fight for the things that we have always carried nearest our hearts. To such a task we can dedicate our lives and our fortunes, everything that we are and everything that we have, with the pride of those who know that the day has come when America is privileged to spend her blood and her might for the principles that gave her birth. God helping her, she can do no other.' "

The students sitting on the wooden stands next to the gymnasium floor were completely silent as she read. No girl adjusted her skirt. No boy scooted his feet against the floor. Even though Nadine had already read the president's words in the paper her father had brought home, she listened just as raptly as the other students. She felt as though she were standing on the edge of a precipice, and any movement might send her plummeting down into a dark void.

Miss Penman laid down the newspaper and stared out at the students in front of her. She mashed her lips together and seemed to be having difficulty speaking. That somehow was even more frightening than the words propelling them into war that she'd read out of the paper. Miss Penman was always in control and always ready with her cane to be sure her students maintained proper control of themselves while at her school.

Control was what a person should strive for at all times, and now their whole world was spinning out of control because of a three-letter word. *War*. Miss Penman tried to slow the spinning. "Young men, many of you may be called upon to serve in this hour of our country's need, and when that time comes, I am confident you will respond with courage. However, that time has not yet come." Miss Penman stared out at them and hit her cane against the floor to emphasize her words. "You must not rush headlong into this battle without proper thought. You who are seniors have only weeks before you will receive your diplomas. Stay the course here, finish your education so that you will be better equipped to serve our great country when you are asked to answer the call."

Miss Penman stepped out from behind the podium and studied the students a moment before she picked up her cane and pointed it at them. "When that time comes and you step up to the line in service to your country, you will strike a blow for freedom."

As though she had punched a hole in the bubble

that had enclosed them and kept them frozen, the entire student body stood up and cheered. Ramon Adams rushed down off the stands and grabbed the American flag that sat beside the podium and waved it in the air. The cheers grew more raucous, and Miss Penman didn't even bang her cane on the floor to settle them down.

Some of the boys talked of enlisting at once in spite of Miss Penman's words, but not Victor. He could have without lying about his age, as some of the younger boys were ready to do in order to serve in this war that would surely end all wars. Victor had turned nineteen in February, but he told Nadine that June would not be too late to join the fight.

In fact June loomed before them and made it seem as if every breath needed to be rushed. There was no longer time to think about their future. There was no longer time to daydream of love. There was no longer time to wait for their fathers to accept them as adults capable of deciding their own futures. If they wanted to have a sure time together, it had to be now.

On the last Sunday of April, Nadine slipped away from the house to meet Victor in the woods behind the church while her father napped. She had never done anything so bold before, and she couldn't imagine what her father might do if he awoke and found her missing. She looked over her shoulder as she hurried across the pasture field toward the woods. No one was watching her, not even James Robert. He'd gone fishing with a friend. But it didn't matter that her father wasn't actually on the porch to catch her sneaking off. Her sure knowledge of his disapproval trailed after her and nipped at her conscience. Even so, she did not stop. She kept moving toward the trees, toward Victor.

He was waiting for her. He took her hand and led her back into the woods. Sunshine streaked down between the budding tree branches to touch them with warmth while over their heads birds sang frantically to their mates. When Nadine leaned back against an oak tree to catch her breath, Victor stepped up close to her and put his hands on her shoulders. Her heart started pounding even harder as she lifted her face toward his in hopes of a kiss.

But he did not drop his mouth down to kiss her. Instead his eyes burned into hers as he said, "I love you, Nadine Reece. I want you to be my wife."

The words knocked the breath out of her again. She hadn't expected a proposal. He had told her he loved her several times, but she had yet to say the words back even though they were swelling in her heart. The thought of actually saying them aloud petrified her. She didn't know why. She had never thought she lacked courage.

After all, hadn't she watched her mother die

and fought death for the life of her little sister? The fact that she had failed did not negate her courage. Didn't she live every day with her father without totally surrendering her own will and dreams? But now in the face of Victor's proposal she quaked with fear. No longer would she be able to drift along enjoying Victor's devotion and hoping that in time her father would accept them as a couple. No longer would she be able to ignore the truth that she might have to confront her father and demand he see her as an adult with the right and ability to shape her own life. He would strike her down. He would squash the idea of her love under his feet. She feared giving him that chance.

She moistened her lips as Victor put one of his hands under her chin to keep her from looking away. "I can't—"

He put his finger over her lips to stop her words. "Yes, you can. I see your heart in your eyes. I know you love me. Else you would not have dared to come out here to meet me." He moved his finger to trace her lips. "Still, I do so desire to hear the words come from your beautiful mouth."

She caught his hand in hers and kissed the tips of his fingers. A wanton move, but it gave her the courage to say, "I do love you, Victor."

His face exploded with joy and he laughed out loud as he grabbed her in a bear hug that lifted her off the ground. When he sat her back down on her feet, he pulled her close and kissed her as he never had before. No chaste kiss of only lips touching lips. This kiss demanded and received a response from her down to her toes. She pushed him away before she melted completely in his embrace and lost all sight of proper behavior.

He leaned back from her, but did not release her from his arms. She had never seen him looking so happy. Up until that moment, shadows of worry always lurked in his eyes even when he was smiling, but now all those shadows had vanished. "And do you say yes?" he asked. "Will you marry me?"

The word yes was on her lips, but she held it back. "You have to give me time."

"What if there is no time to give? We have to take the time we have now and not reach for time on another day." Some of the shadows edged back into his eyes. "You have to say yes. You have to marry me. I can't go to fight over there if you don't marry me first."

"But you haven't even enlisted yet." She wasn't able to voice the yes he so wanted to hear. She had told him she loved him. Why couldn't that be enough for this one day? Why couldn't he give her time to gather more courage? To somehow block her father's sure disapproval from her mind. Another boy perhaps, but not the son of Preston Merritt.

Her father had told her as much after the box supper and the church people had reported to him that Victor had purchased her box of food. "The Merritts think they can buy anything they want. Anything," he had said. "Never forget, Nadine, the love of money is the root of all evil. I will pray that you are protected and guided away from that evil."

Nadine blinked her eyes and pushed away thoughts of her father as she stared up at Victor. He—this man—was her future. The man she loved. Nothing her father could ever say would change that. She concentrated on what Victor was saying.

"Three more weeks. Not even a month. Do you realize how quickly three weeks will pass?" Victor tightened his arms around her.

"You wouldn't have to volunteer. You could wait until you were called up."

The shadows came out of his eyes and darkened his face. "No. My father already thinks I'm a coward. I will not give him more reason to believe that to be true. I have to sign up. I have to step up as an American."

She didn't argue with him. She felt the same. No matter how frightened she was of the idea of war, no matter how terrible the stories of the French and English dead in the trenches in Europe, there was really no choice. Their country was at war. Sacrifices would have to be made, both by the men who went and the women they left behind who loved them.

"You are not a coward." She reached out and laid her hand on his cheek. "You are the bravest man I know. You dared to love me."

He put his hand over hers as he stared into her eyes. "How could anyone not love a girl as lovely as you? A girl whose beauty goes all the way through her body and soul. I would wait for you through all eternity, but please don't make me face going into that eternity without having you for my wife."

"I will marry you." The words were easier to say than Nadine had thought, and speaking them seemed to free something in her spirit that had been bound too tightly for too long. The sun's rays coming down through the trees had a brighter sparkle, and the birds seemed to be singing just for her and Victor. Sinful though it might be, she wanted to dance, while at the same time she felt as if every bone in her body had melted like butter in a dish set in the sun.

"When?" Victor asked in a husky voice.

"Whenever you want." She surrendered her will completely to his and in doing so was surprised to realize that his will matched her own.

"The day after graduation," he said.

She felt a great relief with the decision. Whatever storm their decision brought, they would face it together. They didn't talk about that storm then. By unspoken accord they gave themselves this stolen hour of complete and total happiness. They didn't speak of their fathers or of the war. They spoke only of each other and the beautiful children they would have and how the poetry of their love would never die.

But they couldn't dwell in the magical sunlight dappling the woods forever.

They told her father first. He stormed and raged at them. Said they were too young, too different, too blind, too foolish, and on and on. He quoted Scripture, none of which Nadine thought related to her wanting to marry Victor, and he prayed over them. They endured it all without argument and without any change in their resolve. He finally ordered Victor out of the house.

Nadine went with Victor with no assurance of ever being allowed to cross the threshold back into her house again. James Robert ran after her to beg her not to leave. At thirteen he was already half a foot taller than her, with all the sweetness of his mother and little of the sternness of his father. She had been his only mother for five years, so she hugged him and promised to return. And in truth where else could she go? Her father would surely not bar the door on her even after she married Victor.

They went straight from her house to his parents. Victor's mother wept at the news, but she smiled through her tears and reached for Nadine's hand. Victor's father did not utter a word. He simply looked at them the way he might look at an upside-down turtle flailing its legs in the sun before he left the animal to its miserable end.

Now all these years later, the same look was in his eyes as he stared across the aisle of the church directly at Nadine. She wanted to jump up and tell him they hadn't come to a miserable end. That she loved Victor as much now as she had then and that he was a better husband and father than Preston Merritt had ever hoped to be. But of course she didn't. She could not stand up to the look in his eyes. Nor could Victor. It went back farther than her. And it wounded Victor even more than her father's words wounded her.

All she could do was pray that he would stay as silent on this day as he had on the day they had announced their plans to marry. Even as she whispered the words in her mind, she knew the prayer would not be answered as she wanted. He had not come to the Rosey Corner Baptist Church to remain silent.

14

Kate held Lorena's hand and breathed in and out slowly as her grandfather called for them to pray. She wouldn't panic. Not yet. They couldn't take Lorena away from her. That couldn't be what this meeting was about, even if the church people did keep peering over at Lorena sandwiched between Kate and her mother as though she were some kind of freak at the county fair.

Kate wanted to tell them it wasn't polite to stare, but she bit her lip and kept quiet. An uneasy feeling was growing inside her that nobody was going to listen to anything she said or pay the least bit of attention to what she wanted or even what little Lorena wanted. But surely they would listen to Mama. She was sitting on the other side of Lorena, ready to be Lorena's angel mother. If only she hadn't looked so worried as she helped Kate get Lorena dressed to come.

Kate kept her head bent as Grandfather Reece prayed on and on, but she opened her eyes a slit and peeked through her eyelashes over at Lorena, who was staring first one way, then another with big brown eyes. She was a little doll in the new yellow dress Mama had made for her. Kate had tied a matching yellow ribbon in Lorena's dark hair that fell in curls down around her shoulders.

Kate softly touched the curls, and Lorena looked around at her and smiled. She didn't look worried. She wasn't sure what was going on, but she kept looking at Kate with eyes full of trust. She knew Kate would take care of whatever it was. After all, Kate was her angel.

Now Kate wished she could turn into an angel. Just for a few minutes. Just long enough to convince Grandfather Reece that indeed the Lord had intended for her to find Lorena on the church steps. That the Lord had picked the Merritts, and Kate Merritt in particular, to take care of Lorena. Hadn't she always taken care of Tori and, half the time, Evie too?

They could be four sisters instead of three. Tori was excited about the idea, and even Evie didn't seem to mind. She hadn't made the first complaint when Kate let Lorena climb in bed with them when she had a bad dream the night before. She'd just scooted over to make room.

That's the way it was. They had all made room for Lorena in their hearts. She already belonged, and Kate didn't see why they had to have a big meeting at the church about it. Lorena being left on the church steps didn't have a thing to do with who got to decide where she lived. The Lord had already decided that. He had picked Kate as some sort of earth angel-in-training to watch over

Lorena, and Kate was ready to do her best to earn her wings.

Or maybe it was actually Lorena who was the angel. Perhaps the Lord had sent Lorena as a special gift to them so they could keep focused on what was most important in life. Mama was singing hymns in the kitchen while she cooked. Daddy hadn't forgotten to come home for supper all week. Everybody was happier. And Kate was happiest of all as she and Tori took Lorena to meet Aunt Gertie and then to see Graham.

When her grandfather finally said amen, Kate raised her head and peeked over her shoulder to see if Aunt Gertie or Graham had sneaked in while Grandfather Reece was praying, but she didn't see them. She'd hoped they would be there. To be on her side just in case.

But Graham probably hadn't even known about the meeting since he hadn't come to church that morning, and Aunt Gertie, well, Aunt Gertie acted half afraid of Grandfather Reece sometimes. Besides, Uncle Wyatt expected her to stay home and keep him company on Sunday afternoons since he worked every other day of the week. After Sunday dinner, the two of them sat out on their front porch, weather permitting, and anybody wanting to see them had to go there.

Kate didn't know why she was worried about needing help anyway. Not when the Lord had chosen her to take care of Lorena. But then as Grandfather Reece started talking and her other grandfather kept staring over at her father and mother, Kate's stomach turned over, and all that kept her from throwing up was the knot in her throat.

"A couple in our church have generously offered to give this waif a good home." Grandfather Reece paused and almost smiled as he looked out at the people in the church. He didn't look at Kate's parents. Instead his eyes settled on the Baxters.

On the other side of Lorena, Mama sat stock-still as she stared up at Grandfather Reece. Kate's heart began beating too fast, and the knot grew in her throat until she could barely swallow. Why was he looking at the Baxters instead of her parents?

He went on. "Ella and Joseph Baxter are fine people, grounded in their faith, good workers in the church. They will make excellent parents."

Kate looked at her mother and waited for her to say something. She had to tell Grandfather Reece how wrong he was. Her mother's cheeks were bright red as she clutched her hands so tightly in her lap that her knuckles were white. If her mother had been looking at Kate the way she was staring at Grandfather Reece, Kate would have been ready to crawl under the pew. But Grandfather Reece ignored Kate's mother and kept talking about how wonderful Ella and Joseph Baxter were.

Kate didn't care how wonderful his grandfather thought they were. They may have been the ones he had picked out to take care of Lorena, but they weren't who the Lord had picked out. And if nobody else was going to stand up and tell Grandfather Reece that, Kate would.

She jumped to her feet. Her mother grabbed her arm to stop her, but Kate shook off her hand. She'd always been told that if the Lord was guiding a person to do something, that person should do it no matter what anybody else said. And the Lord was without a doubt telling her to take care of Lorena.

"That's not right," she said. "We're Lorena's family now."

Lorena slid off the pew and wrapped her arms tightly around Kate's leg. "Angel," she whispered. She buried her face in Kate's skirt.

Kate didn't think anybody heard Lorena's whisper over the general stir in the church. An audible wave of shock was vibrating off the church walls because she was standing there defying her grandfather. A mere infant in the faith next to him. He was staring at her with thunder in his face, but Kate didn't care. She stared back without blinking. She was right. He was wrong. She knew it. He knew it, and the Lord knew it.

And as soon as she caught her breath again, she was going to tell him as much.

He shifted his eyes from Kate to her mother. "Nadine, can you not control the daughters you have?"

Kate's mother stood up as though all her bones were hurting and stepped in front of Kate with her back to Grandfather Reece. Kate expected her to be mad that she had dared speak up, but instead Mama's eyes were full of caring as she put her hand on Kate's shoulder. "Kate, take Lorena outside. And Victoria. This is not for you to decide." Her voice was soft and kind. She dropped her other hand to touch Lorena's head.

"But the Lord has already decided for us," Kate said. Lorena's face was pressed so hard against her leg, Kate was afraid the little girl's nose would be bruised, but she didn't try to ease her back. Instead Kate stared at her mother and waited for her to demand the people in the church see the truth of what she said.

"The child is right." A strong voice rang out from the back of the church.

Kate jerked her head around to see Aunt Hattie rising up out of the back pew. Kate hadn't even known she was there. Aunt Hattie pointed toward Grandfather Reece as she went on. "The good Lord don't like us messin' in stuff he's already decided. That's shaky ground to be steppin' out on even if you do feel called of the Lord."

"The good Lord hasn't decided anything," Grandfather Reece thundered. "He certainly hasn't revealed his truth to this child. Or to you."

"Is you saying a child can't hear the truth of the Lord?" Aunt Hattie not only didn't back down in the face of his wrath, she actually stepped out into the aisle to confront him face-to-face. Like David going to fight Goliath. "What about little Samuel in the Bible? Has you put that story out of your mind, Reverend? Seems the good Lord did some whisperin' in that little boy's ears."

"I don't need you to be telling me the Bible, woman!" Grandfather Reece shouted and brought his hand down so hard on the pulpit that Kate wouldn't have been surprised to see the wood splinter and fall apart. "You have no right to even be here." His face was turning an odd shade of purple.

"How come you to say that? 'Cause you don't want my black feet defilin' your holy floor?" Aunt Hattie shook a finger at him. "Let me tell you, it ain't your floor. The church belongs to the Lord, and he spreads open his arms and welcomes all to step in. And this little child here don't belong to you either. Or to you, Ella Baxter." Aunt Hattie turned to point at the woman sitting on the second pew opposite Kate and her family.

"Well, I never," Ella Baxter said as she grabbed a fan from the hymnbook rack and began furiously waving it in front of her beet red face. She was breathing hard and looked about to faint. Her husband pulled out his handkerchief to dab her forehead while Carla jumped up from the front row, where she always sat whenever Grandfather Reece was in the pulpit, to hurry back to see to her sister as well.

Kate had hope for a moment before Grandfather Merritt stood up from his pew and stepped out in the aisle to block Aunt Hattie's path to the pulpit.

"That's more than enough, Hattie," he said without raising his voice.

She seemed to visibly shrink in the glare of his hard eyes as the righteous power drained out of her. Even so she held her ground and didn't completely give up the fight. "You knows it's the truth, Mr. Preston. You knows it. They's doin' that child wrong. They's doin' your Kate wrong. You don't want no part of that on your conscience."

"There are times to speak and times to stay silent. Times when a person gets what he wants and more times when he doesn't," he said. "That's a lesson we all have to learn. A lesson you learned long ago."

"Some lessons is hard to keep fresh in a body's mind." Aunt Hattie ducked her head. Then she seemed to gather herself and looked over at Kate. "Come on, child. Let's me and you and the little ones go find a spot outside in the shade."

"Do as she says," Kate's mother said.

"Yes, ma'am."

Kate picked up Lorena, who burrowed her face into Kate's shoulder. Tori grabbed Kate's arm and clung almost as tightly as Lorena. Before she turned to go outside, Kate looked past her mother, still standing in front of her, toward the pulpit. Grandfather Reece's face looked funny, twisted somehow as he yanked at his collar. His mouth was moving but no sound was coming out. A bit of saliva dribbled down his chin.

Kate's eyes widened as she called out, "Grandfather Reece!"

Everybody else had been looking at Kate or Ella Baxter or Grandfather Merritt and Aunt Hattie. Nobody had noticed Grandfather Reece struggling to talk.

"Father!" Kate's mother cried as she rushed toward him. When he began to sway on his feet, she wrapped her arms around him, but she wouldn't have kept him from falling if Kate's father hadn't grabbed him too. They carefully lowered him down to the floor where she knelt beside him and began frantically undoing his tie.

Carla rose to her feet and screamed before she fell back onto the pew with a heavy thump. Her eyes rolled back in her head, and Ella Baxter began fanning her and patting her cheeks. The woman paused in her ministrations to her sister long enough to glare over at Aunt Hattie and spit out her words. "You caused this."

Aunt Hattie didn't pay her the first bit of attention as she pushed past Grandfather Merritt to join Kate's mother kneeling beside Grandfather Reece. She got down close to his face and spoke in a calm, even tone like she had everything under control and all she had to do was make Grandfather Reece believe it.

"You think on breathing, Reverend. Push that air in and out. In and out. Slow and steady." Aunt Hattie put her hand on Grandfather Reece's chest and watched it rise and fall a moment before she peered up at Kate's father. "You better get somebody to go fetch the doctor, Victor."

There wasn't a doctor in Rosey Corner. Aunt Hattie was the closest they had, but when somebody was sick enough, the doctor came out from Edgeville. Kate's father told Evie to run tell Uncle Wyatt to go for the doctor in his automobile. Tori was sent after water. Nobody asked Kate to help. Her father just pointed at the door and told her to go outside and wait.

This time she didn't argue. She hugged Lorena closer to her and carried her out of the church. She wanted to climb over the fence and take Lorena off through the woods to some spot where no one would ever find them, but of course, she couldn't do that. Even if she found Graham and he helped her. They'd still find her, and then

141

they'd say that her trying to hide just proved they were right. The Lord wouldn't pick somebody to take care of Lorena who would run away. So instead she went over and sat on the stone wall next to the graveyard.

Up the road she heard Uncle Wyatt start up his car and head to town. A few minutes later Evie and Aunt Gertie hurried into the churchyard and up the church steps. Neither of them noticed Kate and Lorena there in the shade.

A bee buzzed past Kate's head, and out on the road a car passed by. It was very hot, but Kate kept her arms around Lorena, and the little girl didn't try to wiggle free. The hushed murmur of voices drifted out from the open windows of the church, but Kate couldn't make out any words. She looked toward the gravestones.

Would the men of the church be digging a new grave there next week for her grandfather? And if they did, would it be her fault for standing up and claiming more knowledge of the Lord than Grandfather Reece? Just thinking about it made Kate quiver inside. How could she have done such a thing?

Lorena raised her sweaty head up off Kate's chest and looked at her. "Was he dying?" she whispered.

"I don't know," Kate said.

"He scared me."

Kate tightened her arms around Lorena. "I

know. It's scary when somebody gets sick like that."

"Before that. Before he looked so funny and laid down. He scared me." She ducked her head down against Kate again.

"It's all right, sweetie," Kate said as she stroked Lorena's hair.

"Do you promise?"

She wanted to promise, but she wasn't really an angel who could make things turn out right the way Lorena hoped she could. Still the Lord did answer prayers. Kate had to believe he would answer this one. "We can pray about it," she said.

"Mommy prayed." Lorena's words were muffled against Kate's chest.

"What did she pray?" Kate asked.

"For rain and that Daddy would find work. And for Kenton and me to have something to eat. She prayed a lot." Lorena leaned back and looked at Kate. "Daddy got mad when he heard her praying."

"Why's that?"

"Because we were still hungry. He said the Lord didn't care about her prayers."

"The Lord always cares." Kate smoothed Lorena's hair back from her face.

"That's what Mommy told me. She waited till Daddy wasn't listening and then she told me so he wouldn't get mad. She said that was why I could know an angel would come take care of me

143

when they had to leave me here. That she would pray extra hard. So hard the Lord would have to hear her." Lorena put her hand on Kate's cheek. "And he did."

"He hears all our prayers," Kate whispered.

"But we have to say them first, don't we?"

"We do."

"Will you say them for me?"

"What do you want me to say? To pray?"

"Pray for us," Lorena said. "And for Mommy and Daddy and Kenton. And for him."

"Him?"

"That man. He scared me, but I don't want him to die." Lorena let her head fall back down on Kate's shoulder.

"Neither do I. I'll pray." Kate laid her cheek against Lorena's head and stroked the little girl's back as she softly spoke the prayer words. "Dear Father in heaven. Watch over us and Lorena's mother and father and brother. Protect them and give them food to eat. And please, please help Grandfather Reece be all right. Amen."

15

They carried the preacher across the field back to his house on a stretcher that Victor's father kept at the store just for emergencies like this. The man couldn't walk. His left side was paralyzed. A stroke, according to Aunt Hattie. She didn't go across the field with them. Said there wasn't anything to be done except to try to keep him as comfortable as possible while they waited for the doctor. And pray.

One of the deacons at the church had stood up and offered up a prayer for their pastor while they lifted him over onto the stretcher. Reverend Reece stared up at Victor out of the eye that wasn't drooping and tried to say something. The words seemed to get all snarled up in his mouth and came out as little better than gibberish. When even Nadine couldn't understand him, the man's face flushed red again and he began flailing at them with his good arm.

"Best try prayin' some calm down on him," Aunt Hattie said as she scooted back out of range. "Else things is gonna go from bad to worse for him."

Nadine pushed his arm down and stroked the sweat off his forehead with her handkerchief. "Shh, Father. You can tell us later. Now you have to stop trying to talk and let us carry you home where we can take care of you."

Carla had to nearly be carried to the house as well. Her sister and brother-in-law got on either side of her and held her up while they helped her walk across the pasture field behind her husband on the stretcher. With each step, the keening wail rising from Carla got a little louder until halfway to the house, Victor's father looked over his shoulder at her and said, "For the love of all that's holy, woman, pull yourself together. The man has not quit breathing as yet, but I know not how much more of that sound he can bear."

Carla stopped walking and clamped her mouth shut for a moment as she glared at Victor's father before she let out an even louder wail. For a minute, Victor thought his father might drop his end of the stretcher and be done with it, but he clenched his jaw and kept moving forward. Victor was calling up some of the same sort of resolve.

Just the sight of the stretcher had summoned up unwelcome memories from the war when Victor saw far too many of his fellow soldiers carried away on similar stretchers. Of course they were the luckier ones. Others lay out in no-man's-land with no hope of being carried anywhere as the war between the trenches went on. Then again perhaps the ones who had passed beyond the misery of war to a better place were luckiest of all. At least they no longer had to crouch in the trenches in fear that if they raised their head a fraction of an inch too high a German sharpshooter would end their misery.

Victor blinked his eyes and tried to push the war memories out of his thoughts. He needed to concentrate on helping Nadine and her father now and not think about the war. He didn't know why the war kept haunting his thoughts lately. It had all happened years ago. It had nothing to do with his life now. Nobody was dying in the mud now. He wasn't running between the trees of a French forest straight toward the German guns, daring a bullet or a piece of shrapnel to slam into his head or chest. He was in Rosey Corner where he wanted to be.

He was one of the really lucky ones who had somehow lived through the cold and the mud and the artillery fire and made it home to his beautiful wife. They had a good family. They might not have a lot of money, but they had a roof over their heads and food on their table. There was need for a blacksmith's skills yet a little longer, and if those motor vehicles did push horses off the road, perhaps he could find a way to adapt and learn to pound out and shape some other need besides horseshoes. Garden hoes perhaps, or iron gates. Something useful.

He couldn't expect to get any money out of the whimsical horse heads he liked to shape out of scrap iron on occasion. Those were just poetry for his soul, something to break the monotony of each day burning into the next. A man needed poetry. A man needed confirmation of his worthiness in this world. Something he'd certainly never received from the man he was carrying on the stretcher across the field or from the man holding up the back end of the stretcher.

Something lately he couldn't even drum up inside himself.

Nadine's father groaned as they carried him up the porch steps. He wasn't a light man, and both Victor and his father were sweating profusely. Victor had tried to get his father to allow one of the other men in the church to help carry the preacher to his house, but Preston Merritt was too proud to admit another man might be stronger than he was, even if age was beginning to chip away at that strength. His father was breathing hard as they maneuvered the stretcher through the front door Nadine held open for them, then on toward the bedroom.

Carla was not a tidy housekeeper, and dirty clothes covered the rumpled bed and spilled out onto the floor. As they moved into the room, a cloud of gnats rose up from a forgotten plate of brown apple peelings on the table beside the bed. Body odor mixed with the smell of talcum powder and liniment. It was not a pleasant combination. When Carla didn't follow them into the bedroom and instead dropped down on the couch in the sitting room, Nadine shut the bedroom door to keep out the church people who had followed the stretcher across the field and into the house.

In the next room, Carla kept up her moaning, but with the door shut between them, the noise was bearable. Nadine pitched the dirty clothes off the bed and smoothed the covers as best she could. "Clean sheets would be better, but heaven only knows where to find them in this mess," she muttered, more to herself than to the two men waiting to put her father down.

They shifted the man from the stretcher to the bed. He was no longer fighting against them, as if he had realized something of what had happened to him. His mouth was still moving, but now Victor thought it might be in silent prayer. At least the Lord would understand his words even if the sounds were as mixed up in his head as they had been coming out of his mouth at the church.

"Thank you for your help," Nadine told Victor's father before she began unlacing her father's shoes. "And I know my father would thank you too if he were able."

Victor wasn't so sure of that as Reverend Reece glared up at Preston Merritt with his good eye. It was just as well he couldn't speak his thoughts. The two men had never gotten along. Even before Victor and Nadine married. It went back farther than that. Farther than Victor could remember.

"No man would do less," Victor's father said as he leaned down to roll up the canvas stretcher. He kept his eyes away from the man on the bed. "Let me know if there's anything else I can do."

"That's kind of you," Nadine said politely. "But Victor and I can manage now."

"Right," Victor's father said.

Victor didn't know how a person could put so much scorn into one little word. His father didn't think they could manage—he had never thought they could manage. Victor curled his hands into fists and thought about slamming him in the face. But what would that prove except that his father was right? He couldn't manage his temper. He couldn't manage his drinking. He couldn't manage his life.

Nadine dropped her father's shoe to the floor and came over to stand beside Victor. Behind her, Reverend Reece tried to say something, but she didn't look back at him. She just stood silent beside Victor, as unmoving as one of those trees standing by the water that the psalmist talked about in the Bible.

He had once thought he could do anything as long as she stood like that beside him. He could face down his father. He could face down her father. He could go across the sea and fight the Germans. As long as Nadine loved him, he could stand his ground and be the man she thought he was. That was before the whiskey sirens started enticing him toward the rocky shores that promised to wreck his life.

He tried to shut his ears to their song and hear Nadine's song instead, but the truth was, he wanted a drink. He hadn't had a drink for four days, but he needed one now. He was weak. He had always been weak. Not strong like his father. Not strong like Preston Jr. Not strong like Nadine. If he let his feet do what they wanted, they would walk right out of this house and go to that place in Rosey Corner where any time of the day or night a man could get a bottle. It just cost more on Sunday. Both in money and self-respect.

As if his father could read his thoughts, he shook his head before he reached for the doorknob to leave the room. Then he turned back for a moment. "The preacher was right. You won't be able to keep her. Not the way you've been living."

At first Victor wasn't sure who he was talking about as he heard an echo from long ago. *You won't be able to keep her.* That was what his father had said to Victor about Nadine almost twenty years ago. The words had traveled overseas with him, lived in the trenches with him, and still tore through his heart at times. He did not deserve a woman as wonderful as Nadine. He had never deserved a woman like Nadine. But yet she was still standing beside him, unflinching in the face of his father's scorn.

But of course it was the child his father spoke of today. Victor frowned at him and asked, "What difference does it make to you? She's just a little girl in need of a home."

"I'll not have you trying to turn some gypsy child into a Merritt." He opened the bedroom door and stalked through the house to the porch with a curt nod of his head to acknowledge the people clustered in the front room around Carla. He'd go home to sit alone on his porch or in his parlor with a glass of water while he waited for the daylight to come on Monday morning so he could go back to the store and count his bolts of cloth or the cans on the shelves or figure the worth of the gallons of gasoline in his pump.

Victor shut the door and turned to Nadine.

"What are we going to do about Kate?" she asked.

"Nothing's been decided yet."

"We can't fight your father." She kept her voice low. "Or mine."

"We're not going to think about it now. Right now we're going to take care of your father. We'll worry about tomorrow when it gets here." Victor put his hand on Nadine's shoulder.

"That's what I told Kate the first day she brought Lorena home. But tomorrow always comes. Always." She looked close to tears. But then her father was making a gurgling noise, and she turned from one worry to another as she hurried back to his side.

She pushed a pillow under his head and wiped the sweat off his face with an edge of the sheet. "The doctor will be here soon, Father."

The man on the bed groaned and flailed his arm against the bed as if he knew the doctor would be of no help. He was trapped in a body that no longer did what he wanted it to do.

Nadine looked up at Victor. "Tell Kate I need her to help me clean up in here."

"What about the child?"

"She'll be all right with Evangeline and Victoria. They can play with her."

"I wasn't thinking about Lorena. I was thinking about Kate."

"Why does everything have to be so hard?" Nadine sighed and her shoulders drooped. Then she pulled herself together and said with more assurance in her voice, "No one will come to take Lorena away today. Tomorrow may come, but it's not here yet."

16

"One day at a time," Nadine repeated under her breath after Victor left. That was how the Bible said a person should live. After all, life was uncertain at the best of times, and no one knew how many days he or she was going to be given. How many times had she heard her father preach about the man who had all his storerooms filled and thought his future was guaranteed, only to find out death held no regard for man's plans? The only place to lay up treasures was in heaven.

Still, no matter where a person put his treasure,

that person never started out the day expecting it to be his or her last, unless perhaps he was marching into battle or she was laboring to bring a child into the world. Certainly her father had not expected to look death in the eye when he'd risen out of bed that morning to go preach to his people. Now he was back in the same bed unable to even ask for a drink of water. What would the man do without his voice? What would the church do without his voice? He had been their leader since before Nadine could remember.

But she couldn't worry about the church now. Not with so much else to worry about. Not with her father grunting again and struggling to sit up.

She put her hands on his shoulders and gently but firmly pressed him back down on the pillows. "You can't get up. If you try, you'll fall and what good will that do you? You might end up with something broken."

He reached over to grab his useless hand. He shook it at her, then dropped it to point at his mouth. She had no problem interpreting his meaning. He was already broken. She mashed her mouth together to keep from showing the pity she felt for him before she spoke in a matter-of-fact voice. "You can't change what has happened. You won't make it better by fighting against the truth of that."

He looked near explosion as he balled up his good hand into a fist. She didn't flinch away from him. He had never hit her. He had always used words to punish her. A frown and a few well-chosen words from him could still turn her into a guilty child afraid to speak. Just as she'd been afraid to confront him in the church.

No such qualms had stopped Kate. If Nadine's father lived through this stroke, Nadine would hear about that. If he remembered. Perhaps the stroke would wipe away that memory. Unfortunately Father Merritt's memory would stay crystal clear. And he too had sided against them.

Kate tapped on the bedroom door before she opened it and slipped inside. Her eyes barely touched on her grandfather on the bed before she whipped them away. "Daddy said you needed me." Her face was pale and pinched looking.

"I do. I'm sorry, but you know Evangeline would be useless at helping me clean up this kind of mess." Nadine spoke in a low voice with her back to the bed.

Kate looked around. "Yeah. Evie would be gagging and holding her nose for sure." She wrinkled her own nose. "So what do we need? Soap? Water?"

"A bucket of hot water and some cold water in a glass for Father." When Kate started to turn away to get the water, Nadine stopped her with a hand on her arm and whispered, "Is Lorena all right?"

"Tori's playing paper dolls with her," Kate said, and then her face twisted as she tried to keep back tears. "They can't give her to Mrs. Baxter, Mama. They can't." Pure despair washed across her face. "Can they?"

Nadine had no answer for her. Instead she folded her arms around Kate and held her tightly for a moment as she smoothed down her hair. "Shh, sweetheart. Nothing's going to happen today." She pulled back away from her. "Nothing that hasn't already happened."

"Mrs. Baxter asked me where Lorena was." Kate looked worried. "Like I should have brought her to her."

"No, no. Nothing's been decided. Besides, Mrs. Baxter has her hands full with Carla right now. Is Carla still carrying on?"

"I don't know. I came in the back door through the kitchen. I didn't want to walk through all the deacons on the front porch. Thought they might be praying, but it sounded like they were just talking about needing rain. Out in the kitchen Mrs. Baxter was talking to Mrs. Taylor and Mrs. Spaulding about doing dishes or something. None of them were praying either." Kate frowned a little. "Shouldn't they be praying?"

"I'm sure they're praying in their hearts just as we are." Nadine peeked over her shoulder at her father, who was breathing easier and seemed calmer. She sighed. "I suppose I should go see if Carla wants to come sit with Father. After all, she is his wife."

At Nadine's suggestion that Carla come into the bedroom to sit with her husband, Carla threw up her hands and went limp in a near faint. "Oh, Nadine, I couldn't. I simply can't bear to see him that way. Your father so strong and now stricken down and twisted by that awful woman's evil words. It's more than I can bear."

"No one's to blame. Strokes just happen." Nadine didn't know why she wasted her breath. Nothing she could say would keep them from blaming Aunt Hattie for angering her father to the point of collapse.

Carla sat up straighter and glared at Nadine. "You heard her. Standing up and defying him in his own church. The shame of it. She's the one who should have been stricken down."

Nadine opened her mouth to defend Aunt Hattie again, but then she could almost hear Aunt Hattie whispering in her ear. *Let it go, child. Better me than our Kate.* What Carla said made little difference anyway. Nadine clamped her mouth shut and pulled in a slow breath. "Father is going to need a lot of care," she said.

Carla let out another moan and covered her face with her hands again. Ella Baxter pushed in front of Nadine. She murmured a few comforting words to Carla before she frowned over her shoulder at Nadine. "Leave her alone. Can't you see how distraught she is?"

Nadine stared past Ella at Carla. The woman was disgusting and useless. Nadine had never liked her, even before the day she came home from school and found her settled into her father's bedroom. Mrs. Orrin Reece. Nadine had never forgiven her father. Not because he had married the woman, although that was bad enough, but because he had not bothered to tell Nadine. Instead, Carla met her at the front door with the news and an infuriating smirk as she stood there, blocking Nadine's way into her own house.

Nadine had heard rumors about her father and Carla that year as she finished out high school. Victor himself warned her of the possibility of a romance between them, but she didn't believe him. She hadn't wanted to believe him. Not her father and Carla Murphy.

Carla had been a devout member of the Rosey Corner Baptist Church since before Nadine was born. In attendance every time the doors were open. Unmarried, she claimed, because her widowed mother who suffered from a nervous condition depended on her, the eldest daughter, to help her at home. Then her mother had passed on, and Carla had needed her pastor to comfort her through her grief. Comfort that had grown and entrapped him.

"How could you?" Nadine had demanded of

him that day when she found him in the backyard stepping off the garden spot for James Robert to dig up.

He paused and turned to her as if he didn't know what she was talking about. "How could I what?"

"Marry that woman. Without so much as a word to me. To us." Nadine threw out her arm to include James Robert, who was leaning on his shovel and digging a hole in the ground with his eyes. "Is that all the consideration you can show us?"

Her father's eyes narrowed on her. "Control your emotions, Nadine Glynn, before your lack of restraint carries you into sin. I have married Carla Murphy. She is now your stepmother and you will treat her with respect."

"Carla Murphy will never be any kind of mother to me." Nadine spat out the words.

He matched her fire with coldness. "That is your choice. We all make choices. Some good and some bad. I will pray for your choices."

Suddenly everything was crystal clear to Nadine. "You're talking about me and Victor, aren't you? That's what all this is about, isn't it? A way to punish me."

"Wrong choices always bring their own punishment."

He had certainly found out the truth of that, Nadine thought now as she went back into the bedroom. Nadine had married Victor the day after graduation and followed him to Louisville where he hired on to help build Camp Zachary Taylor before he enlisted. When he was shipped to France, Nadine had come back to Rosey Corner, but she'd never gone home again. Instead Gertie and Wyatt had opened their home and their hearts to her. James Robert had left the day after Nadine married to go live with Orrin Jr., who had bought a farm in Indiana. Nadine's father was left alone with his choice. It had not been a particularly happy one.

Kate followed Nadine back into the bedroom with the water. Nadine raised her father's head and tipped the glass up as though giving a small child a drink. He tried to swallow it, but most of the water dribbled out of his mouth onto his shirt.

"Hand me that handkerchief off the dresser," Nadine told Kate.

After Kate brought the handkerchief to Nadine, she stood beside the bed and stared up at the ceiling, then down at the floor before she closed her eyes for a moment as if to gather courage. When she opened them again, she finally looked straight at her grandfather's face. "I'm sorry, Grandfather," she said quietly. A tear edged out of the corner of her eye. "I am so sorry."

Nadine tensed, ready to grab her father's arm if he swung it at Kate. She had no idea what her father might do, but then to her great surprise, an

160

answering tear formed in his good eye, and he reached for Kate's hand. He grasped it as if he had caught hold of a lifeline and tried to speak, but none of the sounds added up to words. Kate brushed away her tears with her free hand and listened intently. "You want me to get you something?"

He nodded his head, a look of relief in his eyes that someone had tried to understand. He made more noises as he frowned with a growing look of frustration at their inability to understand him.

"I bet I know," Kate said with a smile. She gently freed her hand from his and picked up the Bible off the table by the side of the bed. She let it fall open in her hands and read, " 'I will lift up mine eyes unto the hills, from whence cometh my help.' " She looked from the Bible to her grandfather. "That's one of your favorites, isn't it, Grandfather? The Lord must have guided my eyes to it for you." She closed the Bible and laid it on the bed beside him.

He pushed a burst of air out of his lungs as he wrapped his hand around the Bible, and one corner of his mouth turned up in a twisted smile, but a smile nevertheless. Nadine could almost see the calm washing over him. He opened his mouth and an actual word came out. "Amen."

By the time the doctor arrived, she and Kate had cleared out the dirty clothes and dishes containing bits of food long forgotten. Nadine had put a bowl of vinegar and water in the window to deodorize the air. The small room trapped the afternoon heat, so she had helped her father out of his suit pants and shirt and sponged his chest and legs with cold water.

It had been years since she'd seen him without his clothes, and he looked diminished lying there in only his underwear. Hours ago he had been in control of his world, ready to impose his will on those around him, and now he was an invalid unable to even empty his bladder without assistance. She had tried to help him as matter-of-factly as possible, but it wasn't something a father wanted his daughter to help him do.

Dr. Blackburn pinched her father's arms and legs and poked the bottom of his left foot with a needle. No response. He prepared a draught of medicine and showed Nadine how to hold her father's head so that all the medicine wouldn't slide out the wrong side of his mouth and down on the bedcovers.

At the doctor's suggestion, Nadine propped pillows behind her father so that he was in more of a sitting position. "That will help him breathe easier," Dr. Blackburn said as he put his instruments back into his black bag.

It did more than that. It also seemed to restore a modicum of her father's dignity as he reached down with his good hand and pulled a sheet across his legs and lower body. He still could not speak, but it was obvious he had no trouble understanding the words spoken to him.

Dr. Blackburn pulled up a chair close to the bed and sat down. "You've been with me in enough sickrooms to know that this is not a good thing, Brother Orrin." The doctor, who was almost as old as Nadine's father, had kind eyes and a caring bedside manner. He always looked a bit rumpled, as though he didn't have time to worry with his personal needs when so many people needed his care.

Nadine's father laid his right hand on the Bible still beside him on the bed and inclined his head a bit.

"However, there are many cases where people do recover some of their faculties, and there is no reason to believe that you won't be one of them. After a time of rest and with the prayers of your people, I would not be surprised to see you regain some use of your arm and leg."

Nadine's father pointed toward his mouth and made an attempt to speak. Still no words they could understand.

The doctor shook his head a bit and looked sad. "It's very trying for you, I know. Not being able to communicate with your voice. You may even feel you are saying the right words in your head, but they aren't coming out of your mouth right. Time and rest may help that too. Lean on the Lord, Brother, and look to him for your strength."

Dr. Blackburn's eyes didn't waver as he stared straight at the man on the bed. "I won't lie to you. The days ahead are going to be very difficult, but you are a man strong in the spirit. I believe you will get better. You must believe that too. Miracles do happen, but in the Lord's own time. Not our time."

On the way out, the doctor stopped to treat Carla for her nervous attack. As Nadine watched him listening to her heart, soothing her with his words and stirring up powders that were probably nothing more than sugar in a glass of water, she thought it would take more of a miracle to get Carla off the couch than Nadine's father out of the bed. But then as the doctor said, miracles did happen.

17

The summer of 1917 was a time of miracles for Nadine. All across the country people were gearing up for war. Uncle Sam popped up on recruitment posters everywhere. Even in Merritt's Dry Goods Store in Rosey Corner. Men between the ages of twenty-one and thirty were required to register for the draft, but younger men were lining up to go fight for democracy too. Factories were being converted into munitions factories. Farmers were plowing new fields. Victory gardens were sprouting in every backyard.

In spite of the dire reports coming in from Europe, enthusiasm and excitement blew hot across the country, fanning the patriotic fires. The American soldiers were going across the sea to save the Allied forces. Lafayette had come across the Atlantic to help America win her independence and now it was time to repay the favor. The song "Over There" echoed in the air.

Nobody wanted to think about the millions of French and English casualties. It would be different when the Americans got there. But first they had to be trained. State militias were mobilized and sent over to France early in the summer, but most of the new recruits needed training in the business of war, so the army began feverishly building training camps to turn men and boys fresh off the farm or out of the factories and schools into soldiers. One of those training camps was outside Louisville.

It was also a summer of love for Nadine and Victor. That too seemed a miracle. They married on the last day of May in Edgeville. Gertie and Wyatt stood up with them. Neither father bothered to note the day in any way.

Nadine had wanted to stand with Victor in the church that was like a second home for her and seek the blessing of the Lord on her marriage. She had also hoped for the blessing of her father.

She and her father had been through so much together. Her mother's death. Lean years at the church. Times of sickness. Nadine had dug potatoes out of the ground, picked beans, and killed chickens to put on their table. She caught rainwater to wash their clothes and heated irons on the stove to iron the wrinkles out of her father's shirts. She brushed and laid out his black suit for him every Sunday. She mothered James Robert. She had carried the load of caring for the household on her young shoulders and done everything she could to seek the love and approval of her father. And even though she always seemed to fall short, she had never stopped trying.

So she swallowed her pride and cornered her father at the church early one Wednesday before prayer meeting to ask him to perform her marriage ceremony. She rehearsed her words all day until they seemed polished and sure. She even spoke them aloud on the way across the pasture field to the church where there was no one to hear but Mr. Archer's cows.

And the Lord. She asked the Lord's help not only in changing her father's heart but her own as well. To give her understanding and not resentment. To help her accept Carla Murphy's presence in her father's life. To help her put away the pride that led to sin. To remember to honor her father as the Bible instructed.

Her heart pounded as she made her practiced speech. "Father, I apologize for my angry words about Miss Carla. I should have bridled my tongue and respected your decisions regarding your own life." She stopped to pull in a shaky breath as a frown began growing between his eyes. She hurried on before he could speak. "I would also hope you might respect the decisions I make. I love Victor Merritt and he loves me."

"A Merritt never loved anything but money," her father growled as the storm grew in his eyes.

She held up a hand and was relieved to see it was not trembling as she said, "Wait. Please let me finish. I am old enough to marry, and now that I am almost out of school and you are married yourself and with the war, I don't want to wait. It would mean so much to me if you would perform the ceremony for me and Victor."

"So you've come crawling to me for my approval?" He took his reading glasses off and carefully folded them before he laid them on his Bible.

She clamped down on her resentment at his words. She had come across the field prepared to beg. If that was what he wanted, then she was willing to indulge him. "Yes."

He looked at her for a long moment before he picked up his reading glasses again and rubbed them off on his shirt. With great care, he positioned them back on his nose and picked up his Bible. Finally he answered her. "You won't get it. Not for marrying a Merritt." He began reading his Bible again.

Nadine stared at his bent head. She knew she had been dismissed and that he expected her to accept his word as final and slink away. All her life she'd done what he said. He was not only her father; he was a man of God. But she had confronted him about Carla and not been stricken down by him or by the Lord. She stood in front of him and let the minutes tick away until he finally looked up at her again.

"Why?" she asked.

He pretended to not know what she meant. "Why what?"

"Why do you hate the Merritts?"

His frown furrows got deeper. "A Christian man cannot hate. 'He that loveth not knoweth not God for God is love.' First John 4:8. So I do not hate. That is a despicable word."

"Then what do you have against Victor?"

"I am only looking out for you, Nadine. Trying to keep you from making a mistake. While I certainly do not hate the Merritts, I do know them. I've lived with them here in this community all my life. Preston Merritt cares nothing for spiritual things, only how much money he can accumulate."

"Victor and his father go to church. Every Sunday."

"It takes more than sitting in a church pew to make a man right with God." Her father pointed his finger at her. "Surely you've heard enough of my sermons to know that. The good Lord wants men to be committed to building up the kingdom of God instead of stepping on whoever is in the way to build up their own kingdoms."

"Victor isn't like that. He's kind and gentle and loving."

"The apple doesn't fall far from the tree," her father said.

"Is it because they have money and we don't?" Nadine sought a reason.

"I care nothing for monetary things. You know that. I trust the Lord to take care of our needs." Her father peered at her over his reading glasses. "Now be off with you. I am deep in the Scripture, and there is nothing you can do to change my mind about saying the words to marry you to a Merritt. I will not do it."

"You are a hard man, Reverend Reece." She stared at him as she ripped free from her need for his approval. The wound hurt, but it would heal. "But neither will I change my mind. I am going to marry Victor whether you say the words or not."

He stared back at her, unrelenting. "Then so be it. I will pray that you will not regret your decision, but not all prayers are answered."

"My prayer has been." Nadine would not let him beat her down.

Her father smiled in a pitying way. "Victor Merritt is no answer to prayer."

"Perhaps not your prayer, but mine, yes."

The wedding ceremony in Edgeville a week later was short. She and Victor stood side by side in a Reverend Barton's parlor as he pronounced the words and proclaimed them man and wife. She and Victor joined hands and lives and didn't go back to Rosey Corner. Wyatt took them to the train station where they bought a ticket for Louisville.

On the platform before they boarded their train, Gertie promised to take care of Victor's mother as best she could. Victor hugged her and promised to write. Nadine stood outside their family circle and felt very alone. She had told James Robert goodbye the night before out in the garden as they knelt among the rows, pulling weeds out of the beans and onions. Beans and onions that neither of them would be there to eat.

Nadine had pushed the dirt up around the roots of one of the bean plants and then fingered the leaves. "These beans are from the same seeds that Mother planted. She loved growing things." Nadine stared at the plant and felt near tears. "I still miss her so much. Do you?" She looked over at James Robert, who had stopped pulling weeds and instead was crumpling dirt clods and letting the dirt sift through his fingers.

"Every day. Was she as beautiful as I remember?" He looked up from the dirt at Nadine.

"Yes. You have her red hair."

"I remember her eyes were blue like yours," James Robert said.

"Do you remember how she used to sing hymns in the kitchen while she cooked?" She looked off across the yard toward the trees as she heard the echo of those songs in her head. "Sometimes she sang the same verse over and over again."

"Yeah, I liked hearing her sing. After she died, I used to cry whenever we sang 'Higher Ground' at church." He looked near tears even now at the thought.

"I know." Nadine reached over and touched his arm. "That was her favorite."

"Yeah. But you know what I remember best about her?" James Robert looked over at Nadine with a hint of a smile.

"What?"

"The way she laughed. How she could make us all laugh." He looked away from Nadine down at the ground again. He picked up a small round rock that looked almost like a clod of dirt and studied it for a long moment before he threw it out of the garden. "Everything changed when she died. Everything."

"She didn't want it to," Nadine said softly. "She wanted us to keep being happy. Do you remember how she had us all come in by her bed the night she died? She made you and me and Orrin Jr. all put our hands on top of hers on her heart and promise that we would take care of one another and never forget how much she loved us." Nadine reached over and took his hand. It was rough and strong and so much bigger than it had been that night so long ago.

He looked from her hand to her face. "I'm fourteen, Nadine. I'm not a little boy anymore. You don't have to take care of me now."

"I know." She tightened her hold on his hand. She didn't want to let go. She was afraid she might never see him again. "You're like our mother, you know. Sweet-tempered. Kind. Loving."

"I don't laugh as much."

"None of us have laughed enough."

He put his other hand on top of hers. "I'm glad you're marrying Victor. I like him."

"I'm going to miss you so much, James Robert," Nadine said as tears began to gather in her eyes.

"We're not dying," he said, a little embarrassed by her tears.

"No, not dying," she agreed. "Do you remember the baby? Essie?"

"Essie?" He frowned. "You mean Mary?"

"Mary was her burying name. Essie was her living name before she died." Mary Reece was what her tombstone read. Their father hadn't named the baby until her burial. But that wasn't her name. Nadine had named her Essie for her mother, Estelle, and she'd never seen any reason to change it just because of some letters chiseled in stone.

"I hated her. I know she was just a little baby, but I hated her, and then after she died, I felt like maybe I'd caused it by hating her." He looked worried as he asked, "I didn't, did I?"

"No, of course not. She was just too little. She needed more than I, more than all of us, could give her after Mother died. And you didn't really hate her. You would have loved her if she had kept breathing." Nadine blinked away her tears as she managed a shaky smile. "She would have been six this year. Sometimes I see her playing out in the yard. I mean not really. Just in my head."

"Do you want me to stay here? Not go to Indiana?" he asked.

"No, no. You'll like it with Orrin Jr. and Arabelle. You'll have fun being Uncle James Robert to their two little ones."

"I'm thinking of telling people my name is J.R. when I get up there. What do you think?" His cheeks turned a little red. "Sometimes people want to call me Jimmy Bob when I tell them my name is James Robert. I'm not a Jimmy Bob."

"No, definitely not." Nadine tried out the new name. "J.R. J.R. Reece. Sounds important. I like it." Her smile was steadier as she pulled his hand up with hers until she held it over her heart. "No matter what happens to us, never forget how much I love you, J.R. You're my brother."

There on the train platform in Edgeville watching Gertie and Victor hug and say their goodbyes, Nadine again felt the ache of tears building up in her eyes, but she didn't let them spill out. As James Robert had said, nobody had died. They were growing, stepping toward their destinies.

So she hadn't cried then. She hadn't cried until the train went through Rosey Corner and there was James Robert standing out in the field by the track, waving at every passenger car that passed to be sure not to miss her. She leaned out the window to wave back, and her tears could no longer be denied. Victor hadn't been upset. He simply held her and whispered promises of love in her ear.

18

The Louisville train station was bustling when they arrived. Soldiers stood on the platform telling their loved ones goodbye. Piles of crates waited for somebody to haul them away. Horses placidly flicked away flies with their tails as they stood hitched to carriages waiting to carry people away from the station. Men in suits hurried about, their steps sure and certain, while other men looked as if they'd just arrived from the country and were as lost as Nadine. She'd never been farther from Rosey Corner than Edgeville.

Victor had. He'd often come with his father to Louisville to buy stock for the store. So he wasn't overwhelmed by the crowds, and Nadine was glad to put her hand in his and let him lead the way. He slung his canvas bag over his shoulder, picked up her valise, and promised the boardinghouse Graham Lindell had told them about wasn't far. Graham had stayed there the year before when he was in Louisville with his grandfather for some kind of political event.

The boardinghouse lady, Mrs. McElroy, was a large round woman who laughed as she took their money and pointed them to the attic room. "You'll have a bit of privacy up there, and you're young so the stairs won't be a hindrance to you." She leaned a bit closer to them and winked. "Plus the man in the room below you is deaf as a post, so you can bounce around on the bed all you want. Being newlyweds and all."

Every inch of Nadine's skin burned red at the woman's words. Of course she'd wondered about her wedding night, but only in a vague, dreamy way. What little she knew about love came from poems and stories. The actual act of lovemaking was not something a proper young preacher's daughter was supposed to think too much about, but now as she looked at the amused glint in Mrs. McElroy's eyes, she felt unprepared and too young. She wanted to get back on the train and go back to Rosey Corner to ask Gertie for advice.

Mrs. McElroy laughed louder and smacked Victor's shoulder with the flat of her hand. "Your little woman's face is about to catch fire. You two are sure you're married now, aren't you?"

Victor smiled back at the landlady, not minding her bawdiness a bit. "Yes, ma'am. Had the knot tied proper and all this very afternoon by a Reverend Barton." He put his arm around Nadine's shoulders and pulled her close against his side.

Mrs. McElroy's face changed, became wistful. "I remember being a bride. Seems a lifetime ago when I think about it. Ah, my Quinn McElroy was a fine figure of a man. He's been gone these many years now. May the good Lord bless his soul." She reached over and laid her hand on Nadine's cheek and looked straight into her eyes. "Don't you worry about a thing, dovey. When you've got love, everything happens like magic, and it ain't a bit hard to see the two of you got love."

The landlady's words proved true. Their wedding night turned out to be a magical time of love. Victor was as innocent in the art of lovemaking as Nadine, but that didn't matter. The two of them shared poetry of the soul and body. Nadine remembered how the Bible said a man should cleave unto his wife and they would be one flesh. That's how she felt lying beside Victor, skin touching skin, breath intermingling. No longer would it be Nadine alone or Victor alone. It would be Nadine and Victor together through whatever the days and years ahead held for them.

Victor had no problem getting a job. The army was hiring all comers to get Camp Zachary Taylor built as fast as possible. The work was hard, the hours long, but though he came home sunburned and dirty, Victor got stronger every day and more at home in his skin away from Rosey Corner.

He hadn't enlisted. He planned to do that in August. That gave them two months. Two beautiful months. Two enchanted months. Two miraculous months. Nadine refused to think about August, about Victor being sent overseas to fight. The news of the war wasn't good. German U-boats were sinking ships every day. The French army was near collapse. The German artillery was pounding the Allied soldiers. The Russian czar and his family were being held under guard in their palace as the government in that country was overthrown. Sometimes when Nadine read the newspapers, it seemed as if the whole world was falling apart.

August was mere weeks away, and Victor was

determined to step up to the recruiting table and answer Uncle Sam's call. Yet in spite of this and the dire news of the war, Nadine rose up every morning with a song in her heart. A song Victor knew every word to.

"You're living in the moment, dovey," Mrs. McElroy told her. "A fine way to live, it is. Fact is, I might go so far as to say it's the only way. Not that I've always made a practice of it, but that don't make it any less so. Even the good Lord told us that in the Bible. Live today. Pray today. Let the Lord take care of tomorrow, seeing as how he knows more about it than we do anyhow."

Mrs. McElroy had taken Nadine under her ample wing. The first two days after Victor started work, Nadine stayed cooped up in the attic room. She read the books she'd brought in the bottom of her case all the way through twice and devoured the newspaper Victor had bought for her. She'd written James Robert, Gertie, Victor's mother, and considered writing her father but decided against it. It would do no good. She could almost see him stuffing it, unopened, in the drawer of the table by the door.

By noon on the third day, the small attic room felt like an oven. Even the air coming in the narrow window that Nadine propped open felt as if it were blowing off a fire. She wandered downstairs, where Mrs. McElroy pronounced her a girl in need of something to do, shoved a broom into her hands, and pointed her toward the porch. Nadine took the broom gratefully. She had little experience with idleness and no comfort with the idea, since her father always preached that idle hands were an invitation to the devil.

Maudie McElroy cut their rent in exchange for Nadine's work, but she treated Nadine more like a favored daughter than hired help. She never asked her to stir the sheets in the boiling pot of water out behind the boardinghouse, but she did let her gather dry sheets off the clotheslines.

"A little sunshine will do you good, dovey," she said. "You're altogether too pale. You wouldn't be in the family way already, now would you?"

Nadine blushed. "That's not something you can know after only a week, is it?"

Mrs. McElroy laughed as if Nadine had told the best joke ever. "Not all girls have a ring on their finger before they do some kissing and cuddling. While kissing and cuddling don't exactly make babies, it can lead to that what does."

"Oh." Nadine's eyes opened wide as she realized what Mrs. McElroy meant. Mrs. McElroy was what the kinder ladies at church had always called earthy. Still, in spite of the way she could make Nadine blush, Nadine enjoyed the woman-to-woman way Mrs. McElroy talked to her.

That was something she'd never had. No one

back in Rosey Corner would dare say the sort of things Maudie McElroy said to Nadine. Not to the preacher's daughter. But here in Louisville, Nadine wasn't the preacher's daughter. She was Nadine Merritt, Victor Merritt's bride, and she refused to think about how fast the days were passing to August.

She kept telling herself perhaps the war would be over before Victor enlisted, or if not by then, before he was trained and ready to be shipped overseas. She said a prayer every morning and every night that there would be peace. That the Central Powers would surrender. That the Allies would prevail now that America was throwing all her resources behind them and General Pershing was on his way across the ocean with the first American troops.

But the battles went on. More ships were sunk. More men died. More artillery shells exploded. Neither side seemed to make any gains as they hunkered down in the trenches that snaked across miles of the French countryside.

Yet even as men were dying across the ocean in this war, she and Victor were blissfully dancing to their song of love. She and Maudie were laughing in the kitchen as they peeled potatoes for the night meal. Old Mr. Benson, the hard-of-hearing boarder, kept on complaining about the summer heat as he sat on the porch and whiled away the hours fanning himself and swatting flies. The neighborhood kids still rolled hoops down the street in front of the boardinghouse. And the days passed even as Nadine tried to cling to them and make them linger.

On the Fourth of July Victor had the day off. The city celebrated the day with a parade and a street fair. Early that morning Maudie helped Nadine pack a picnic lunch.

"Grab all the fun you can, dovey," she told Nadine. "Because nothing lasts forever."

"Love does," Nadine countered.

"You could be right. I still carry the love for my Quinn in my heart, but his time here with me didn't last near long enough. Ah, the two of us should have gone on more picnics, but the good man was working and I had the little ones."

"You have children?" Nadine had never heard Maudie mention children.

"Five boys. One died as a wee child. The others are off seeking their fortunes in the West. The youngest promises to send for me as soon as he strikes it rich, but I won't be holding my breath waiting for that to happen." Maudie wrapped a ham sandwich in newspaper and put it in the basket. "Ah, but it would be nice to have some grandbabes climbing around on my lap." She looked up at Nadine. "I'm sure your mother feels the same way."

"My mother died in childbirth when I was just a girl," Nadine said as she stuck a couple of apples down beside the sandwiches. She kept her eyes on the basket and felt the familiar stab of sadness. "The baby died too. A little girl."

"Ah, some hurts never fade. The same with my little Leslie. Four years old he was. A pot of boiling wash water spilled on him. I would have laid down and died on the spot if it would have kept him breathing." Maudie put her rough hand on Nadine's shoulder. "But we can't change the things that happen. We just have to keep going. And your sweet mother is surely smiling down on you because you're so happy. She wouldn't want to put a shadow on the day, and neither do I. You two children go and have fun."

It was a beautiful day. The sun was bright and hot, but a nice breeze kept the flags rippling and the red, white, and blue banners flapping. Everywhere they walked they could hear a band playing "Over There." Nadine and Victor found a spot in the shade near the courthouse to eat their lunch. Later, after the parade, they strolled hand in hand through the park. As evening was falling and they turned back toward the boardinghouse, Nadine couldn't keep her mind from counting the days to August.

"You don't have to enlist in August," she said. "You don't have to sign up for the draft until you're twenty-one. The war might be over by then."

He didn't say anything or even look at her. Just kept walking along, but she felt him pulling away from her even though he still held her hand. Where a moment before the absence of words between them had been comfortable and right, now it felt tense and wrong.

She tightened her grasp on his hand and said, "I'm scared for you to go."

He stopped and pulled her to the side of the walk. He stared down into her eyes. "I know. I'm scared to go, but I have to."

"Why?"

"Because it's the right thing to do. The only thing I can do. Can you understand that?" He peered down into her eyes.

"But we're so happy here."

"You wouldn't stay happy married to a coward who didn't step up and answer the call of his country to fight for freedom. I have to go."

She stared up into his face, oblivious to the people passing them on the sidewalk. Finally she said, "I know. I love you, Victor Merritt." It was the first time she had ever told him she loved him without his saying the words first.

A smile broke out on his face, and he wrapped his arms around her and kissed her right there beside the sidewalk.

A woman passing by them said, "Young people! No sense of decorum."

A man's voice answered her. "Oh, let them be, Wilma. They're in love. It's a good day to be in love."

On August 1, Victor signed up for the army. He reported to Camp Zachary Taylor two weeks later. Nadine stayed at Maudie's until he climbed aboard the train a month later to go east to ship out to France. Then they were one of the couples trying to cling to each moment before the war ripped them apart.

"The war can't last long now." He stood very close to her, their legs touching in the midst of the swirling confusion of the train station.

She was trying very hard not to let the tears welling up behind her eyes come out where he could see them. "Why is that?" she asked.

"Those German Boches will take one look at this new doughboy and lay down their guns in surrender. It'll be Victor the Victorious."

She smiled just as he'd intended. "You will be careful."

"As much as any soldier can be. But better I'll have your love as a shield to protect me." He stared into her eyes as if he could see to the depths of her soul. "Every night I will look up at the stars and tell the brightest one in the sky how much I love you. All you have to do is look up at the same star and you will hear those words in your heart." He touched her chest above her heart.

"The echo you hear in return will be my words coming back to you." In spite of her best efforts, a few tears were spilling out.

He kissed the tears off her cheeks. "Be brave, my beautiful Nadine, for nothing can keep me from returning to you. You are my love, my joy, my life." He placed his hand on her belly. "And if we have made a baby, my hope. Now give me a smile to carry away with me."

"How can I smile when you're leaving?"

"I think bravely might be the best way."

"I'm not that brave."

"Oh my Nadine, how wrong you are. A braver heart I have never known, and I will carry that heart with me, but I must also have your smile."

The train whistle blew and panic swelled inside Nadine. How could he expect her to smile now? She clutched his sleeves and turned up her lips as best she could.

"Sadly won't do," he said. "You want me to stand on my hands and wiggle my toes in the air?" He started to pull away from her.

She grabbed him and laughed. "Don't you dare." It was a trick he often did in the morning to pull a sleepy smile from her. The train whistle blew again. "You don't have time to take off your shoes, and with your shoes on, I couldn't see whether your toes were wiggling or not. Besides I'd much rather have a kiss."

"Then a kiss it will be, my beautiful bride."

As their lips met, she wanted to crawl inside his skin and go with him. But she could not. He pulled free and touched her cheek one last time before he ran for the train door just as the conductor was pulling up the steps. She ran alongside the train to the end of the platform and then watched the train until it disappeared up the track. The tears flowed unchecked down her cheeks as she walked back to the boardinghouse.

She thought about staying in Louisville. Maudie said she could stay in the attic room, but then three days after Victor left, Nadine got her one and only letter from her father. *Come home. Louisville is a wicked town.* That was all he wrote, but Nadine read more into the words because she wanted to.

She wouldn't go home. She couldn't live in the same house with Carla, but she would go back to Rosey Corner. A person needed family even when that family wasn't always easy to love.

19

As the days passed and her mother didn't come home, worry hung in dark clouds over Kate. Not just about Grandfather Reece, but about Lorena as well. Every time there was a knock on the front door, Kate's heart jumped up in her throat and she froze wherever she was until she found out it wasn't Ella Baxter come to take Lorena away.

Kate simply could not fathom why anybody

could think Ella Baxter would make a better mother than Kate's own mother. Anybody with any sense knew that wasn't true. Why, if a little kid got close to Mrs. Baxter with sticky hands at a church dinner, she nearly went into hysterics. Then there was that time last summer when Paul Whitton threw a caterpillar at some girl out in the churchyard and hit Mrs. Baxter instead. The woman had screamed like a banshee, grabbed Mr. Arthur's cane, and started whacking Paul. Almost broke his arm before Grandfather Reece got the cane away from her. Paul wasn't but ten, but Mrs. Baxter spoke up at the next business meeting and wanted to vote him and his whole family out of the church. All over a worm.

The woman didn't like dirt. She didn't like bugs, and she didn't like kids. Kate couldn't imagine what had made her decide she wanted Lorena. If they were going to pick a mother simply because a woman hadn't been blessed with a child of her own, Aunt Gertie would make a better mother than Ella. Ten times over. While Aunt Gertie might be a little set in her ways and prone to headaches, at least she liked kids. But the intention of the people of Rosey Corner had been plain enough at the church on Sunday. Grandfather Reece's stroke had delayed that, but Kate wasn't sure it had changed anything.

In fact the stroke made it that much harder to change. Kate had stood up ready to fight for

Lorena in the church, and Aunt Hattie had stood up to fight beside her, and look what had happened. Everybody said it was Aunt Hattie's fault that Grandfather Reece had a stroke, but Kate had been the first to speak up against him. She knew who was really to blame.

Daddy said neither one of them was to blame. That sometimes strokes just happened, but everybody knew they happened faster when people got upset. Else why would people keep telling each other not to have a stroke when something was going wrong? And things had been going wrong.

Sometimes the unworthy thought sneaked into Kate's head that Grandfather Reece had the stroke because he was going against the Lord's own plan for Lorena. The Lord had picked Kate to find Lorena on the church steps, not her grandfather. And then Kate would practically melt with shame for even considering the thought that the Lord might look upon her with more favor than he did on Grandfather Reece after all the faithful years her grandfather had served the Lord. If anybody knew what the Lord wanted, it would be Grandfather Reece and not Kate.

By some kind of miracle, her grandfather hadn't condemned her for causing his stroke. Instead he had taken her hand and smiled at her when she had told him how sorry she was. At least he'd smiled as best he could. He wasn't happy. Nobody could be happy lying there so helpless with no way to know if he'd ever get better.

The doctor didn't even know that. He said Grandfather Reece's condition might improve, but then he pulled Mama aside to warn that a second stroke could be even worse and that they needed to keep Grandfather Reece from getting upset again.

Kate didn't know how the doctor expected them to ever do that. Grandfather Reece got upset each time he opened his mouth and the words didn't come out right. He couldn't get out of the bed and walk. He couldn't even take a drink without half the water spilling out the wrong side of his mouth onto the bedcovers.

Rosey Corner Baptist Church was praying for him. So was the Christian Church. They held a special joint prayer service the Sunday night after he had the stroke, but Grandfather Reece didn't sit up and start talking so people could understand. The deacons told Kate's mother not to lose faith. The miracle would surely come in the Lord's own time. That's what Grandfather Reece had always told them when they prayed for something that didn't come right away, whether it was for rain or healing.

The Lord's own time. Meanwhile they didn't have any choice but to keep doing the best they could to take care of him. Miss Carla wasn't any help. She was still having sinking spells and telling anybody who would listen that she wasn't well enough to stand up under the strain of caring for her husband. Every day Kate's mother looked as if she was having a harder time standing up under the strain herself.

On Wednesday when Kate went over to see if there was anything her mother needed from home, she grabbed Kate with a look that verged on frantic and jerked her into the sickroom. "You can sit with your grandfather for a little while," she said.

Kate wanted to pull away and run home. She didn't like being in the sickroom. It had a funny smell. Not a dirty smell. It was clean. She and her mother had seen to that the first day, but there wasn't any way to keep out the sick smell. That smell just seemed to ooze out of the pores of somebody as sick as Grandfather Reece.

But Kate couldn't say no to her mother. Her mother needed help and who else was there to give it? Certainly not Evie, who turned pale at even the thought of having to visit Grandfather Reece, or Tori, who was way too young. No, it had to be Kate, the middle sister, the one who always did whatever had to be done. The responsible one.

So Kate took a deep breath of air that she hoped would be enough to last as she moved a few steps farther into the room. The man on the bed scared her. To be truthful, her grandfather had always scared her. Even when he was patting her on the head as a little girl, she'd kept expecting him to yank her up by the collar and let her have it for something she'd done.

Kate heard her mother go out the front door. Miss Carla was snoring on the couch. No church people were visiting. Nobody there but Kate to take care of her grandfather.

She tiptoed over to the chair by the bed. He was asleep or seemed to be. That was good. She could sit there beside him and be very quiet. Better even than that, she could close her eyes and pray. Sometimes she jumped up in the morning and forgot about praying. She didn't intend to. She just did. And now wasn't a good time to be forgetting about praying. Not with so much she needed help with.

Of course it wasn't right to only pray when she needed something. She was supposed to pray about everything. Good things, bad things, in-between things, ordinary things. The Bible said the Lord wanted to hear from his people. And she was one of his people. She'd been baptized down at the river when she was younger than Tori, and not just because her grandfather and mother told her she should be. She'd felt the Lord telling her in her own heart.

Grandfather Reece had baptized her and Evie, who had run down the aisle that same day after

Kate stepped out. He'd called her Sister Katherine Reece Merritt, thanked the Lord for her soul, and dipped her down under the water. It was the closest she had ever felt to Grandfather Reece.

Now as she sat beside her grandfather's bed, she bowed her head and shut her eyes, but she couldn't seem to settle her thoughts down enough to pray. Her legs were all jerky and itchy. She wanted to move, to run outside and down the road to check on Lorena. *Lorena. Lorena. Lorena. Dear Lord up in heaven, help me take care of Lorena. Let me keep being her sister. I'll try to be extra good and do the things I should and not do the things I shouldn't.*

"Amen," her grandfather said.

She opened her eyes and peeked over at her grandfather to see if he had noticed her praying and was trying to help her out, or if he wanted a drink of water or something. It was hard to tell since "amen" was the only word he said that anybody could understand and he said it for everything.

He was staring at her out of his good eye, and she almost expected him to rise up out of the bed and start preaching at her the way he'd done plenty of times in the past when somebody had told him some wrong she'd done. She'd almost be glad to get preached at that way again, because that would mean he was back to his old self. But instead he just lay there and kept staring at her. Not a stern stare or a reproachful stare. But more as if he wanted her to do something for him.

"Can I get you something?" she said softly after a few minutes.

"Amen," he said.

"You want me to pray?" she asked. "I'm not too good at praying out loud, but I can do the Lord's Prayer if you want me to."

He waved his right hand as if to shoo off that idea and pointed to the nightstand.

"The Bible. You want me to read the Bible to you again? I can do that." She reached over and picked up her grandfather's Bible. "I could read it all the way through for you, but that would take too long. You'd be back preaching before I got out of Exodus. How about if I just open it up and start reading wherever?"

Her grandfather said amen again. She didn't know whether that meant yes or no, but his eyelids drooped down over both his eyes, and he seemed to be listening when she opened up to the Gospel of John and started reading. She remembered him preaching sermons on some of the verses she read, and when she told him that, he opened his eyes and looked at her and said, "Amen." This time it sounded as if the very word he intended came out of his mouth.

By the time her mother came back in the room to let Kate go home, Kate had read through five chapters of John. Before she left, Kate leaned over to kiss her grandfather goodbye, something she hadn't done since she was a little girl like Lorena and her mother told Kate to kiss him goodbye. She hadn't wanted to then, but now it just seemed right. She owed him that much, and some of the worry seemed to evaporate with her lips touching his forehead.

But it came back when her mother asked how things were at home. Kate sort of skipped over the truth. She couldn't tell her how she and Evie kept fighting over who had to do what or that Tori kept saying she wasn't hungry and not eating like she should or that Daddy hadn't come home for supper two nights in a row. So she mumbled something about needing to pick the beans before she kissed her mother goodbye and hurried out the door. It was easy to see her mother was already worried enough without Kate adding to it.

The only person not covered up with worry was Lorena. She was trusting Kate to take care of her. Every morning she got out of bed and stretched up as tall as she could there in the middle of their bedroom and said, "My name is Lorena Birdsong." Every night she did the same thing before she went to bed. Some days she spoke her name in little more than a whisper. Other times she practically shouted it out. The whisper made Kate want to cry and the shouts made her laugh.

Some mornings, Kate would pick Lorena up and dance her through the house to the kitchen, singing her name. "Lorena. Lorena. Lorena Birdsong. My sweet Lorena Birdsong."

That made Lorena giggle, and for a minute Kate could forget all the things she had to worry about. Grandfather Reece might be getting better, and Daddy did finally come home even if it was late. It wasn't that much of a problem to keep the household going while Mama was gone. Getting the fire to burn right in the cookstove wasn't easy—sometimes it just wanted to smoke up the kitchen—but she kept waving the smoke out the back door with a dishtowel and poking at the fire until the stove finally got hot enough to perk coffee and fry eggs for Tori and Lorena.

And Evie was trying to do her part even if she was sort of bossy about it. The first morning she got up and tried to make biscuits just like their mother's, but while Mama's biscuits were light and fluffy, Evie's were hard as rocks. She cried when their father tried to bite into one before he said some things just weren't possible and that he always did like light bread with his honey.

On Thursday Tori and Lorena helped Kate pick the green beans. When they ended up with over a bushel of beans, Kate didn't know what to do. She knew about as much about canning beans as Evie did about making biscuits. She knew about breaking them up and washing them and packing them in quart jars. She'd helped with that plenty of times. Then Mama put them down in big pots of water and cooked and cooked them, but Evie said if they didn't do it right, they'd end up with ptomaine poisoning when they tried to eat the beans come winter.

"But we can't just let them sit here and ruin," Kate said.

Evie eyed the beans a minute before she said, "When's Mama coming home?"

"I don't know. Why don't you go ask her? You ought to go see Grandfather Reece anyway."

"I can't, Kate. I don't do sickrooms very well. I get all trembly and feel like I'm going to faint." Evie grabbed hold of one of the posts on the back porch as if she thought the faint was coming on already.

"You wouldn't faint," Kate said.

"You can't know that. Lots of people faint for all kinds of reasons. Just because you think you can bite nails in two doesn't mean that everybody can." Evie gave her a mean look.

"Who's bitin' nails in two out here?" Aunt Hattie said as she came around the house and found them on the back porch staring at the beans.

"Oh, Aunt Hattie," Kate said with a big smile. "You must be an answer to prayer."

"Why's that, child?"

196

"All these beans." Kate waved her hand at the green beans.

"You's been prayin' over beans?" Aunt Hattie raised her gray eyebrows at Kate.

"Well, no, but I should have been. Mama's still over with Grandfather Reece and Evie says if we don't do them right we could get ptomaine poisoning, but we can't just let them go to ruin. You can help us can them, can't you? Please, please, please." Kate grabbed Aunt Hattie's hand and pulled her up on the porch.

"I was a-thinkin' you might need some help about nows." Aunt Hattie laughed and looked around. Her smile faded into a frown. "Where's the young one?"

"She's inside looking at books with Victoria," Evie said.

A look of relief flashed across Aunt Hattie's face as she shut her eyes for a second almost like she was praying. When she opened her eyes, she said, "Gets them on out here. The storybooks ain't going nowhere. Them young'uns can break beans same as we can." She grabbed the old straight chair they kept on the porch and sat down before she filled her apron with beans and began breaking off the ends. "And bring on out some pans for the beans. We ain't got all day. Canning beans ain't no short job."

Later with the beans in the jars boiling in the kettles and the kitchen so hot Kate could barely breathe, she shoved more wood into the cookstove the way Aunt Hattie told her. She wiped the sweat off her face with her skirt tail and said, "No wonder people put cookstoves outside to can on." She and Aunt Hattie were alone in the kitchen.

"It ain't no bad idea in the kind of summer we's having now," Aunt Hattie agreed. "We'll make us some tea and sit out on the back porch when we're sure we've got the jars boilin' proper. You got any ice?"

"The iceman came yesterday, but we've got it so hot in here, it's probably all melted in the icebox."

"Don't be worryin' over ever'thing, child." Aunt Hattie put her hands on Kate's shoulders and looked straight into her face.

"But I have to, Aunt Hattie." Kate was almost glad for the sweat on her face. If a few tears sneaked out, Aunt Hattie wouldn't notice.

"No, you don't. You can't do one thing about the ice meltin'." Aunt Hattie's brown eyes bored into Kate, and they both knew she was talking about more than ice. When Kate didn't say anything for a moment, Aunt Hattie tightened her hands on her shoulders and said, "I knows about your mama. She's done workin' herself to a frazzle over there with your granddaddy whilst that ol' Carla sits on her hands. I'd a done gone over there and helped her, but I don't figure I'd better show my face around that place right now. But what I don't know is about your daddy. He been comin' home like he oughta?"

Kate dropped her eyes away from Aunt Hattie's to stare down at the floor. She didn't want to answer her. "I don't know," she mumbled.

"You look back up here at me, child." Aunt Hattie waited till Kate raised her eyes back up to her face before she went on. "Ain't no need in you tiptoeing around the truth with me. There ain't nobody on this green earth I ever loved more than I love your daddy except my own boy, Bo. But lovin' somebody don't mean you think they don't never do nothing wrong. Ain't a one of us that ain't done some wrongs."

Kate's throat felt tight, but she made herself say, "He didn't come home last night till almost daybreak."

Aunt Hattie mashed her mouth together and shook her head. She pushed a breath out her nose before she said, "That ain't no way for him to be acting right now."

"No, ma'am, but he can't help it, Aunt Hattie. He just can't help it."

"Ain't no truth in that, child. Ever'body can help it. With the good Lord's help."

Kate stared down at the floor again. She didn't know what to say to that.

After a moment, Aunt Hattie went on. "Your mama, she needs to come on home. You tell her I said for her to let the church people help. Some of them are wantin' to. They think a heap and all of your grandpappy at that church. There ain't no shame in askin' for help. And she's needin' to be home."

"All right," Kate said. "I'll tell her."

Aunt Hattie gave Kate's shoulders one last squeeze before she said, "I'm praying for you, Katherine Reece Merritt. Whatever happens you's gonna be able to handle it just like you is handlin' the heat in this kitchen to fix these here beans. It ain't easy, but you is doin' it."

20

When Victor saw Aunt Hattie coming toward his blacksmith shop, he wanted to run out the back door and hide. She wouldn't be coming for any good reason. Not with the way he could see the frown creasing her face from all the way across the yard. He almost went over and lifted up the saddle blanket on his shelf to take a nip from his bottle. But he knew better. If she saw him, she'd break it for sure.

He wished she'd been there to break the first bottle he'd tipped up to his mouth way back when he was in France. He hadn't messed with the women over there the way some of the other men had. But drinking hadn't seemed so wrong.

He hadn't thought about it burrowing down inside him and coming home with him. At the time he hadn't been all that sure he'd live long enough to come home.

War was worse than anything he had ever imagined. Even before they got to the fighting, the whole thing was one misery after another. He'd thought he couldn't get any more miserable when he boarded the train and left Nadine behind. But then they loaded them on those old ships, stuck them down below, and wouldn't let them up on the deck more than an hour or two here and there on their way to France. Victor was sick the whole way along with most of the other men. In rough water there weren't enough buckets to go around, and sometimes the floor was slimy with vomit. A man couldn't get away from the smell of it.

Things didn't get a lot better in France. Not with the way they stuffed them in trains to go to their training grounds. Then the cooties were waiting at the training camps. It was almost a relief to get to the trenches. At least until it rained and they were walking in mud all day long. And kept raining so that the mud got deeper in the trenches and swallowed up the planks they laid down to walk on and sometimes pulled a man's boots right off his feet. There were stories of men sucked down into the muck never to be seen again.

Victor didn't know if the stories were true, but he did think it possible. The mud was everywhere. In their hair under their helmets, flavoring their food, between their toes in their boots, layering their canteens, permeating their very souls. They couldn't get away from the mud. They slept in it, fought in it, lived in it. Died in it.

Sometimes after a hard downpour a new body part appeared out of the mud. Victor told himself it didn't matter. Whoever he was, the man was dead, gone from his body to meet his Maker. What was left was just bone, sinew, and skin. And if Victor was ordered over the top and got hit by enemy fire to end up one of those bodies sunk down in the mud, what difference would it make if the soldiers lucky enough to still be breathing used his hand sticking out of the side of the trench to hold something up out of the mud. That's how they were using Oscar's. Nobody really knew the dead man's name or even his nationality, but it only seemed right to name him, to make him part of their company when his hand emerged from the side of the trench.

That's how war was. A man had to survive as best he could. He couldn't worry about what he'd left back home. He couldn't worry about how long he was going to live. A man just had to follow orders and give all he had to win the war and save democracy.

War wasn't a thing like Victor had expected or

maybe anything like anybody back in the States had expected. Back there, they'd taught them to march. Wasn't much use for marching in the trenches. It was just hunkering down and hoping a sharpshooter didn't spot your helmet if you forgot and lifted your head a few inches too high. Or that your gas mask would work when the Germans launched their mustard gas barrages. Or that you wouldn't get the order to go over the top.

Up out of the trenches, the German artillery had made rubble of the buildings and splintered the trees. Barbed wire barriers laced the no-man's-zone between them and the Boches. Not a good place to be. Of course sometimes a man imagined it might be better to get the order to charge out into battle. At least then he'd be moving and not just sitting in the mud waiting for the enemy's artillery to find its mark.

Victor couldn't see how they could ever expect to win the war by simply taking up existence in the trenches with the rats and body lice and mud. Squads sneaked out at night to spy out the enemy's position and try to take German prisoners, and the engineer companies kept adding more barbed wire to the barriers meant to deter the enemy from making their way undetected through no-man's-land to their frontline trenches. On both sides above the trenches, men peered out of baskets suspended below balloons tethered to the ground to catch a view of any unusual activity along the enemy lines, and occasionally a plane would buzz over. Some of the soldiers took potshots at the planes when they saw the German colors, but they never brought one down.

If it hadn't been for Nadine's letters making their slow way across the ocean to him, Victor wasn't sure he could have survived the trenches even with no German fire. There were three rows of trenches—the forward front line where the soldiers had to be on guard at all times, the second row where the doughboys were ready to go forward to relieve the front line, and the back trench where a man could relax for a few days without worrying about getting his helmet too high out of the trench. The mud and the rats and the cooties didn't go away, but here at least a man might get a letter from home.

Victor could even now shut his eyes and see some of the lines from those letters written in Nadine's hand although the letters themselves were lost to the mud. *The lilacs are blooming. I took a deep breath of their sweet scent and blew it into this letter for you. I say your name every night as I look up at the brightest star in the sky and it sings like poetry in my heart. I carry you in my prayers all day long.* He especially treasured each and every *I love you*. Simple words, but words he needed to read over and over.

Anytime they had a mail call and Victor's name

wasn't called, his spirits sank so low that he sometimes wasn't sure anything he remembered about the summer was true. Maybe it had all been only a dream and Nadine had never given her love to him. Maybe he was going to wake up and there would be the truth like the mud sticking to him. But then the next mail call he'd have a letter. A letter that said she loved him. That she would always love him. No matter what happened. That she could hardly wait until he came home. That she would be there waiting for him.

Not all the letters were good. Some brought bad news. The one where she told him she'd lost the baby before she got far enough along to show under her full skirts. That had been a sad day in the mud. Gertie's letter a couple of months later, telling him their mother had contracted influenza and died. It hadn't seemed right for bad things to be happening back home when so much was bad all around him. He'd somehow expected home things to be protected in the circle of his memory, to stay the same until he got back to Rosey Corner.

They hadn't written to him about Bo. Aunt Hattie had decided there'd be plenty of time for Victor to be sorrowful about that later on after he got home. The only reason they'd told him about his mother was that he'd know something was wrong when he didn't get any more letters from her.

But Bo had died over there. Killed in action, fighting alongside the French. The American generals wouldn't let the black soldiers go into combat with the white soldiers, but the French didn't worry about color. They needed men to take the place of their fallen comrades. So they embraced the black troops who came ready to fight the German enemy and to die beside them in battle. Like Bo.

Aunt Hattie was afraid Victor might lose heart if he knew Bo had been killed. That he might think if Bo couldn't make it through the war, then there wouldn't be any way he could. Aunt Hattie might have been right. But in a war it wasn't always the best man who came through alive. Sometimes it was the luckiest. The man who was ducking behind a tree when the enemy bullet came his way or the man in the back trenches when the artillery fire came. And hadn't Bo always told Victor how lucky he was? Lucky to have a mother and father with means. Lucky to have him, Bo, watching after him and keeping him out of trouble. Lucky to be able to go to school. Lucky to be fast on his feet. Lucky in love.

That was the last thing Bo ever told him. Bo had come through Louisville before being shipped out after going home to see Aunt Hattie. He came by the boardinghouse, where Maudie McElroy let him sleep on the back porch before he caught his train east.

As they sat out on the back steps, Bo shook his head at Victor and Nadine. "I'm a-lookin' at the two of you and I still can't hardly believe it. You got the preacher's daughter to say yes." He gave Victor's shoulder a playful punch and laughed.

Nadine's face colored up, but she didn't quit smiling. A person couldn't keep from liking Bo no matter what he said.

Victor squeezed Nadine's hand. "I did."

"Will wonders never cease?" Bo laughed again. "I don't know whether you know it or not, Miss Nadine, but this boy here fell for you practically as soon as he was out of knickers. Lovesickest pup I ever saw. And now look at him. One lucky dawg. Luck like as how he's got, it don't never run out, so don't you worry your pretty head about him, young Miz Merritt, if this war drags on and he has to follow me on over there. He'll be comin' back across that ocean. That's for sure and certain."

Victor had thought then that he had to join up. To prove his courage to his father. But nothing had ever proved that or was likely to. Not going to the war. Not coming home. His father wouldn't even think it took courage for Victor to stand up and go to the door of his shop to meet Aunt Hattie. But it did. It took a great deal of courage, because Victor knew what she'd come to say.

"Aunt Hattie." He kept his voice light and

cheerful like she was just another customer come to get some piece of iron bent. "And what can I do for you today?"

"You knows what you can do for me, Victor Gale Merritt." She stepped right up to him and poked her finger in his chest. She'd never been a big woman. Victor had been taller than her by the time he was ten. And now age had stolen a few inches and every ounce of extra fat until she was nothing but skin and bones and pure power. Every wrinkle on her face was frowning as she peered up at him through her steel gray eyebrows. "You can be goin' on home at suppertime and not be letting the alcohol turn your feet off the right way."

He didn't have any defense. Sometimes it was better to just be quiet and take the beating he deserved. He looked down at the ground and felt beaten already. "You're right, Aunt Hattie."

"I knows I'm right. You has got to take care of your girls. What's the matter with you that you'd go off to that wicked place when your girls are needin' you?"

"I don't know," Victor mumbled.

"That ain't no answer. You look back up here at me and come on out with the truth." She waited until Victor raised his eyes back to her face. The skin was still furrowed between her eyes, but now it was a concerned frown. "What's the matter with you, Victor?"

He didn't know how to answer her. What truth could he tell her? He wasn't sure he even knew the truth. The dreams. The ache in his shoulder. The noise of the cars passing on the road out front. Nadine running home to take care of her father. The child Lorena he wasn't going to be able to protect. Kate's eyes when that happened. The emptiness in his soul.

The look on Aunt Hattie's face softened, and she put her rough hand on his cheek. "She ain't left you, Victor. She's standin' right beside you same as she has through all your years together."

"But I'm not good enough for her, Aunt Hattie. I haven't ever been good enough."

She pulled her hand back and gave his cheek a little smack. "Don't you let my ears ever hear you say that again, Victor Gale Merritt. You as good as any man I ever knew."

"You might be the only person who ever thought that."

"How about your Nadine? Didn't she marry you and wait through the war for you and carry your babies? You can't be shuttin' your heart to love like that."

"I'm not doing that," he said quickly. Then he stared at Aunt Hattie. "Am I?"

When she just kept looking at him without saying anything, he went on. "I'd die for Nadine."

"I knows you would, child, but sometimes it's

harder to live for somebody, and that's what you's got to do right now."

Her voice was full of caring, but that didn't keep her words from pounding into him like hammers striking soft metal. Trembles pushed through him. "You told me that once before. A long time ago. When Press Jr. died."

"It ain't always easy to be the one still living." There was understanding in her eyes.

"I've been having dreams, Aunt Hattie. They won't let me be. Even in the daytime all the dead haunt me."

She put her hands on his shoulders and pulled him down close to her face. "You ain't got the first reason to feel guilty about still breathing air when others ain't. It wasn't none of your fault that my Bo died over there in France or that young Press Jr. didn't get out of that river."

"But maybe it should have been me instead of them."

"That ain't for us to decide. Things happen and people die. The good Lord helps the rest of us go on living." Aunt Hattie studied Victor's face. "He'll help you too, with whatever's tormenting you."

"Did he help you when Bo died?"

"I couldn't a made it if he hadn't. That was a bad time." Aunt Hattie dropped her hands from Victor's shoulders and sat down in the chair by the forge.

Victor pulled his stool over to sit beside her and wait till she was ready to start talking again.

She stared off at the wall for a few minutes before she said, "It weren't just Bo, though that was a blow that like to kilt me. But your sweet mama going at almost the same time was nigh on more than I could bear. So many folks dyin' over there and over here. But the Lord, he tol' me he'd let me know when my time was up. That until then, he'd help me keep livin', keep catchin' babies when they got born, keep watchin' over Nadine till you come home. You know how Mr. Preston and Preacher Reece didn't give that girl the first bit of help, and Gertie, well, Gertie, that child does good to keep herself helped."

"I thank you for Nadine." Victor reached over and touched Aunt Hattie's hand on her lap. "And for me."

"No need for thanks. Your Nadine did more for me than I could ever do for her. She understood that I'd lost one son and that I wouldn't be able to bear losin' the other." Her eyes came back to Victor's face as she took hold of his hand and squeezed it. "While you might not be my natural born child, you ever' bit a child of my heart. And I'm proud of the man you turned out to be."

He dropped his eyes away from hers. "I'm not."

"You the onliest one what can change that. And you is the one who has to be there for your girls."

"I don't know if I can. Not the way they need."

"They just need you," Aunt Hattie said softly. "That's all they's ever needed."

"I can't keep back the bad things."

"Nobody can ever keep back all the bad things. It ain't possible for the likes of us. We just has to ride through those bad times together. You need to give Nadine some understanding and not be deserting her when she's needin' you."

"Deserting her? I'm not doing that, am I?"

"That's somethin' you have to answer." Aunt Hattie gave his hand a little shake. "But that ain't all your trouble. You know they's gonna come after that little child."

"I know. Kate won't understand that."

Aunt Hattie let out a long sigh. "That's God's own truth. Our Kate done thinks she been anointed by the Lord to take care of that little one and I ain't doubtin' she has, but there's some that thinks they's more powerful than the Lord. Leastways here in Rosey Corner."

"What am I going to do, Aunt Hattie? I can't fight my father."

"We in the same boat on that one, Victor. Mr. Preston's done wrong about all this. It ain't right givin' that baby to Ella Baxter, but that's what's gonna happen and there ain't nothin' under God's heaven we can do about it." Aunt Hattie squeezed Victor's hand again. "Exceptin' to help Kate through it, and you can't do that from the inside of a bottle."

"Don't you think I want to quit?" Victor cried. "Don't you think I'd have already quit if it was as easy as just wanting to?"

"I done tol' you, child. You can't do it alone. You's got to let the Lord help you."

Everybody kept telling him that, as though it was the easiest thing in the world. As if he could just hold the bottle and his addiction up in the air and the Lord would reach down and grab it all away from him. They hadn't, none of them, carried the bottle around and tasted its temptations. But it wouldn't do any good to tell Aunt Hattie that. So instead he said, "And what about Lorena?"

"We's just gonna have to pray we's wrong about that Ella." Aunt Hattie didn't look too sure that prayer was going to be answered. "Besides, we ain't goin' nowheres. We'll be right here in Rosey Corner if that little baby needs something. And the good Lord watches over his little babies."

She stood up and so did Victor. "Pray for me, Aunt Hattie."

She reached up and touched his cheek again. "I already do, child. Ever' day. And you just remember that in the good Lord's mighty eyes, we's all nothin' but little babies."

21

The next Sunday morning after their preacher was felled by the stroke, the Rosey Corner Baptist Church met for Sunday school as usual and then walked across the road to have services with the Christian Church.

Nadine didn't go to church. Carla went in spite of crying and going on all morning about how she wouldn't be able to bear being at church without Nadine's father there with her, but when Ella knocked on the door, she was out it in two minutes. Once she was off the porch, Nadine stood in the middle of the sitting room and wrapped the silence around her as she thanked the Lord for the respite from the woman's constant moaning or harping. It was like waiting on two invalids—one by stroke and one by orneriness.

Nadine told herself she should ask for forgiveness for her lack of charitable thought when it came to Carla, but then again she'd never read the first word in the Bible that said a person wasn't supposed to face facts. The first fact was Carla was about to drive Nadine over the edge of sanity. The second fact was that Carla wasn't going to lift a finger to do anything as long as Nadine was there to do it for her.

Praise the Lord, Nadine's father had started showing some improvement. While he still struggled to speak, he was saying more words that she could understand. Plus he'd gotten back some of the use of his leg and arm so that with help he could get out of bed and sit in a chair. Even before Kate told Nadine what Aunt Hattie said about letting the church people help, Nadine had decided it was time to go home.

Nobody had come right out and told her Victor was drinking again, but enough of her father's visitors had looked uncomfortable when they tried to make small talk that she'd known. Plus he hadn't come by since Tuesday. He should have come by to see her even if he didn't care about her father. What in the world had ever happened to the young man brave enough to walk up on her porch and ask to court her? But of course, it wasn't her father he was scared to face now. It was her. He knew she'd be furious at him when she saw the drinking signs in his eyes.

She *was* furious with him. He couldn't even stay away from the drink long enough to be there for their girls while she took care of her father. He surely realized she had to take care of her father. He'd have done the same if it had been his father, though heaven only knew neither father had ever gone one step out of the way to help them. Still, they were family and a person had to take care of family. The Lord help her, she'd even have to take care of Carla if it ever came to that. Nadine shut her eyes and said a fervent prayer for Carla's health. Either that or more patience. Lots more patience.

A small voice inside her head said maybe she needed some of that patience for Victor. Things weren't easy for him either. Those dreams from the war had come back to torment his sleep. She'd been patient when he'd first come home from France. She'd seen how the war had bruised his soul and understood he needed time and love. Love she was more than willing to give him. It was so good to have him home. To be able to stop worrying that he'd never come back to her.

Sometimes she had heard that echo in his letters from France. His fear that he'd never make it home. But it was Bo who hadn't made it. Bo who had died in the trenches with the French. Bo who was buried in a cemetery over there. Bo who had always looked so strong and sure of himself even though he was a Negro in a white world. He got a French medal for bravery. They had sent it to Aunt Hattie. People told her she should hang it on the wall, but she took it out in her backyard and buried it as though they'd sent her Bo's body back in that little box.

She and Nadine searched through the woods for the right rock to use as a marker, and then Graham Lindell helped them carry it home. Nadine and Graham both cried when they laid that stone on the ground over the spot where the medal was buried, but Aunt Hattie hadn't shed a tear.

Victor hadn't cried when Nadine told him about Bo either. He was too battle weary. All he'd seen had pushed him way beyond tears. He wouldn't tell her about it. Not the part that haunted his dreams. He told her how the French countryside looked. He talked about the people he met. How he never got to Paris, but some of the other soldiers in his company had. He even talked a little about how cold it was sitting in the mud and waiting, but he didn't talk about the things that made him wake up in the middle of the night sweating and flailing his arms. He said he didn't want to think about it, much less talk about it, but it had kept coming out in his dreams.

So she had whispered words of love in his ear, and he clung to her and loved her in return. Slowly he fought back the terrors of the war, and they stepped forward into their future. He took a drink now and again to dull the ache in his shoulder where he still carried some German shrapnel, but he was home every night rubbing her feet and reading poetry to her and singing silly songs to Evangeline even before she was born.

They had been able to laugh then in spite of his war wounds and her fear of giving birth for the first time. He and Aunt Hattie had carried her through that fearful time as memories of her mother dying in childbirth accompanied each new pain. Now three beautiful girls later, she was just as much in love with him as she had been then, and she had no doubt of his love for her.

Yet something had happened. He was having the nightmares again, and instead of leaning on her, he was going to the bottle for comfort. She didn't understand it. Nothing had changed except that they were older. Shouldn't that make it easier for him to lean on her? Had her anger made her back away from him so he couldn't lean on her?

She didn't deny that the distance that had come between them was partly her fault, but nothing she did seemed to quell the anger when she saw him turning to the bottle. She couldn't pray it away. She couldn't ignore it away. She couldn't yell it away. It was there, a hard knot inside her chest. And now at this time of crisis he had let the bottle call him again.

Didn't he know they had no hope, no hope at all, of hanging onto Lorena if he was staying out all night drinking? It was a funny thing but Nadine's arms seemed to miss holding Lorena more than her own girls. Of course Kate and Evangeline were too old to even consider needing holding, and Victoria was on the way to thinking she was grown up too. Lorena needed her. Nadine hadn't realized how much she'd missed having a little child in her lap until Kate found Lorena. Not that Lorena was exactly a baby. She was five years old, but she needed loving. She needed holding and Nadine needed to hold her.

It had seemed so simple when Kate brought Lorena home. Before her father and Father Merritt got involved. Why did everything have to get so complicated?

With a sigh, Nadine went to help her father get dressed. When she went in the bedroom, he was already sitting on the side of the bed. "Well, Father, you're making progress. Maybe you can go sit on the porch today. You're sure to have a pile of visitors coming by this afternoon."

"Friday," he said.

She hesitated a moment before she said, "No, it's Sunday." It would do little good to avoid saying it was the Lord's Day. Somebody would be sure to mention it was Sunday before the day was over. Carla herself would be home full of what they did at church in a little over an hour.

He reached over and touched the Bible they left on his bed now. He didn't try to read it by himself, but every once in a while he'd open it up and point to something for Nadine to read aloud to him. Once or twice it had even seemed to be a passage he might have intended to point out at the time. "Carmel," he said and then looked irritated.

Nadine picked up the shirt she'd ironed the

night before and helped him shove his stroke-affected arm into the sleeve. "Carla has gone to church." For a second Nadine imagined the same whisper of relief blowing across his face that she'd felt when she'd seen Carla out the door.

As she worked his trousers on his legs, she kept up a steady stream of chatter, about how much they were surely missing him at church. By the time she got his socks and shoes on, her hair was sticking to her forehead and rivulets of sweat rolled down between her breasts. She sat back on her heels in front of him to catch her breath and try to cool off by fanning herself with her apron.

He surprised her by reaching out and touching her cheek. "Amen."

"I'm on my knees and I need prayer. We both do," she said.

He held his hand up in the air and shut his eyes. His lips moved but no sound came out, but somehow she knew he was praying for her and not for himself. The stroke had changed him. He was cross and irritated by his inability to do what he wanted to do, but at the same time he didn't fight against her help. He didn't stare displeasure at her or frown condemnation down on Kate. Instead he had reached out to Kate with gentleness and forgiveness. Two things Nadine had not often seen in her father. Nadine wondered if he knew why Kate had asked for forgiveness. Did he even remember anything about Lorena and what had led to his stroke?

When he opened his eyes, she said, "Amen. And thank you, Father, for praying for me. I know the Lord will help us both."

She waited until he was situated in the big rocking chair in the next room before she pulled a chair up in front of him and said, "We need to talk before Carla gets back."

He shook his head a little before he said, "Need rain."

"Yes, we do, but listen, Father, I have to go home." He shook his head with more vigor, but she kept talking. "You're getting better. Dr. Blackburn said so when he was here Friday. So it's time for me to go home. My girls need me. Victor needs me."

She stopped and pulled in a breath, waiting for the frown that always came when she said Victor's name. But this time her father didn't frown. He just looked sad and maybe even a little scared as he stared down at his hands in his lap.

She reached over and touched his arm. "I'm not deserting you. I'll be back every day." When he looked up at her, she added, "Carla will be here and Elbert Hastings and Bob Smith are going to take turns sitting with you at night for a few days. They're like brothers to you. Good brothers."

"Amen." The word sounded sad.

She felt guilty, but she couldn't tell him she

would change her mind. She couldn't change her mind. She had to go home. She was needed there too. Perhaps even more than here. When she started to stand up to go straighten the bedroom, he reached out and grasped her arm. "Read." He let go of her arm and picked up his Bible. It fell open in the middle and he turned a few of the whisper-thin pages before he pointed at one of them.

"Isaiah 40," she said as she took the Bible from him and sat back down. She had no problem picking out the verses he wanted her to read. They'd been marked by him some time in the past for a sermon perhaps. " 'Hast thou not known? Hast thou not heard, that the everlasting God, the Lord, the Creator of the ends of the earth, fainteth not, neither is weary? There is no searching of his understanding.' "

She stopped, but he motioned her to go on. " 'He giveth power to the faint; and to them that have no might he increaseth strength. Even the youths shall faint and be weary, and the young men shall utterly fall; but they that wait upon the Lord shall renew their strength; they shall mount up with wings as eagles; they shall run, and not be weary; and they shall walk, and not faint.' " She laid the Bible still open to Isaiah back in his lap. "Oh, to be an eagle soaring with the Lord's power."

"With . . . ," her father started but couldn't find

"Then why did he?" Lorena looked at Kate.

"I don't know. Let's go ask Daddy."

Kate's father laughed when Lorena asked him about the lightning bugs. "That's the easiest question I've had all year," he said. "The good Lord made them that way so they can find the special one they love."

"But how can they find the one they're looking for? All their lights look alike." Lorena stared out at the lightning bugs twinkling in the twilight.

"To you perhaps, but not to all those lightning bugs. They're probably looking back at you and saying we all look alike, and wondering how we ever find the right love for us with no little lights to guide us." He smiled at Lorena.

Lorena giggled and looked at Kate. "Your daddy's silly."

"But he has the answers," Kate said.

"That answer." Kate's father sounded a little sad as he looked away from Kate and Lorena out toward the sky. "Not all the answers."

"Nobody ever has all the answers," Kate's mother said softly.

Kate spoke up fast right behind her. She wanted her father to keep smiling and laughing tonight. "I'll bet you can tell Lorena how people find the right love without having flashing lights."

He kept looking up at the stars, but the smile was back on his face. "That I can. It's up there in the stars." He pointed toward the sky. "When

the word he wanted. He clasped his hands together and pulled them up in front of his chest and slowly straightened the fingers of the stroke-crippled hand until he could hold his hands together in a position of prayer.

"With prayer," she said for him. "I think we just had church, Father. Thank you. The Lord must have given you that sermon just for me."

He smiled with half his face. Dr. Blackburn had warned her that the muscles in the face were often the last to make any recovery after a stroke. Then he lifted his hands, even the crippled one without help, and floated them in front of him. "God makes right," he said.

"He'll make you all right again," Nadine said.

"Right here." He put his fist over his heart.

"Amen," Nadine said. She went to the bedroom and stripped the sheets off the bed. When she dropped them on the floor, she wanted to drop down on top of them. She was so tired. She had only slept a few hours here and there all week. But she pushed aside her exhaustion and pulled out the clean sheets and spread them on the bed. She had to keep moving. Keep trying to do what had to be done. Keep hoping the Lord would give power to the faint and strengthen the weak. Keep praying that she could look past her anger and somehow find a way to be strong enough to help Victor. To be there for her girls. To protect Lorena.

22

When her mother came home late Sunday afternoon, Kate couldn't stop smiling. Maybe everything was going to work out after all. Grandfather Reece was better, sitting up in his chair and sometimes even saying the words he intended. Her father was there with them. No work on Sunday and no drinking either, unless Kate's nose was tricking her. Her mother must not have smelled any alcohol on him either as she stepped into his embrace and let him hug her for a long moment. That had made Kate feel best of all.

Evening services at Rosey Corner Baptist Church had been canceled, so they stayed home. They ate peanut butter and jam sandwiches out on the front porch to escape the heat inside the house and washed them down with sweet iced tea. Daddy said they might as well enjoy the ice instead of just letting it melt away in the icebox. Besides, the iceman would bring more on Tuesday. For dessert Kate and Evie had stirred up some caramel icing to spread between graham crackers. Lorena ate so many that Mama said she was sure to be sick.

When the neighborhood kids started showing up after supper, Tori ran out to play hide-and-

seek with them, but Kate stayed with Lorena, who thought hide-and-seek was scary after the sun went down. Kate told her the fading daylight just helped them stay hidden, but Lorena said she didn't want to hide. Ever. Instead they ran after lightning bugs rising up out of the grass and caught them on the wing. They didn't put them in a jar, because Lorena worried that the bugs wouldn't have enough air even if they did poke holes in the lids.

"Why do they light up like that?" Lorena asked as she watched one of the lightning bugs crawl across Kate's hand.

"Because that's how the Lord made them." Kate gently pushed the bug over onto Lorena's hand.

Lorena held her hand very still while the lightning bug crawled across her fingers. "B[ut] why did he make them that way? He didn't ma[ke] the bugs like that back home. None of them [lit] up."

Kate was surprised. "You didn't have ligh[tning] bugs at night?"

"Uh-uh. Mommy woke me up to see the[m] after we crossed over the big river. I thoug[ht they] were fairy lights." The bug opened its w[ings and] lifted off Lorena's hand. She watched it [rise in] the air. "Do you think God made them [so that] we would believe in fairies?"

"I don't think so, sweetie."

each new baby is born, the Lord has one of his angels write that baby's name on a star. Two per star. Then when the right time comes, the boy and girl gaze up at the stars, see their names there, and the rest is history."

"Is it really that easy? That sure?" Kate asked as she gazed up at the stars too. It might be nice to see her name there and know who her one true love was going to be.

Mama laughed a little. "Not at all. Sometimes it takes a poem." She reached across the space between her and Daddy to hold his hand.

"Oh yeah," Kate said. "Like *Evangeline*."

"Evie?" Lorena looked up at the stars and then out toward the road where Evie and George were leaning against his car talking. "Is her name up there on a star with George's?"

"Whoa. Let's slow down. I don't think Evangeline has looked at the right star as yet," Mama said as she held her free hand out to Lorena. "You look tired, sweetheart. Come, sit in my lap and Daddy Victor will tell you a story."

Lorena hesitated. "I can't. I might go to sleep."

"That's all right. I can carry you to bed," Mama said.

Lorena stepped back away from the porch. "I can't go to sleep. Not yet."

Kate touched the little girl's shoulder. "You can go ahead and say it. Right here on the porch. We'll say it with you if you want."

Mama looked puzzled. "Say what?"

"Her name," Kate explained. "Lorena's mama told her to say it every night and every morning so she wouldn't forget."

"Mommy's saying it too. She said if I listened real hard I'd be able to hear her in my heart." Lorena put her hand over her heart and looked at them fiercely as though she didn't think they would believe her. "And I can too." Her fierce look faded until she just looked sad. "Sometimes."

Mama blinked her eyes fast as she reached over to touch Lorena's cheek. "Of course you can. And even when it doesn't sound out real loud, you can be sure your mother's love is still whispering in your heart. Softly like angel wings."

"But you're right about keeping your part of the bargain," Daddy said as he leaned toward Lorena. "So let's hear you say it."

Lorena stepped out to the edge of the porch and raised her arms over her head as she looked up at the stars. "My name is Lorena Birdsong." Her voice was strong and true.

On the porch, Kate and her parents echoed Lorena's name. "Lorena Birdsong."

Out in the yard, Tori shouted out Lorena's name too when she heard them say it, even though it gave away her hiding place to Pete Wiley, who was it. Over by George's car, Evie looked up and called the little girl's name too.

"I hear her." Lorena wrapped her arms around her middle to give herself a hug before she crawled up into Mama's lap and smiled over at Daddy. "Now you can tell me a story."

Kate leaned back against one of the porch posts as her father told a story about two lightning bugs searching for one another. The neighborhood kids began leaving for home, and Tori came up to the porch to lay her head in Kate's lap and listen to the story too. The soft murmur of Evie's and George's voices floated across the yard.

Kate wondered if this was what people meant when they said that God was in his heaven and all was right with the world. She felt so peaceful, so happy. Grandfather Reece was getting better. He wasn't mad at her. Lorena was safe in Mama's lap. Kate's parents were holding hands, and the story Daddy was telling made a smile bubble up inside Kate.

Lorena fell asleep, but Kate's father kept on with his story. Even after he finally had the lightning bugs to their happily-ever-after ending, they sat on the porch and talked about whatever came to mind as the moon came up and cast night shadows across the yard. None of them wanted such a perfect day to end.

But in spite of prayers to hold off tomorrow, Monday came. It started off better than the Monday before, when Kate had smoked up the kitchen trying to get the fire going in the cookstove. So she felt like Christmas in June was still happening when she smelled coffee perking, bacon frying, and biscuits baking when she went into the kitchen.

"You want me to do something?" she asked.

Mama looked over her shoulder at Kate from where she was turning the bacon. "Oh, Kate. You're up early. You should have slept in like the other girls."

"I like being up early." Kate gave her mother a good morning hug. "Especially when it's hot like today's going to be." Kate grabbed a piece of the newspaper off the table to fan herself. "It's hot as blue blazes in here already. How do you stand it cooking in here all summer? Sometimes last week I had to go out on the porch to get my breath. I think we should just eat apples and peanut butter till it gets cooler."

"That's an idea." Mama laughed and wiped the sweat off her face with her apron. "But the good Lord gave us wood and a stove to use it in and good things to cook on it, so I guess I can stand the heat. Besides, I'm used to it. I had to start doing all the cooking when I was twelve."

"Yeah, when your mother died. That had to be awful." Kate took the metal fork from her mother and turned the bacon.

Mama peeked in the oven at the biscuits and then stirred the oatmeal. "Well, the cooking wasn't all that bad, but losing my mother was. I still miss her."

"I missed you last week," Kate said without looking up.

"I wasn't that far away, and you were over there almost every day," Mama said as she lifted some plates out of the cabinet.

"I know, but it wasn't the same. It was scary here without you." Kate flattened one of the pieces of bacon against the pan and watched the grease sizzle out of it.

Her mother set the plates down, took hold of Kate's shoulders, and turned her around to face her. "Look at me, Katherine Reece. What do you mean scary?"

"I didn't know how to do things," Kate said.

"But you did it. Everybody got fed. The beans even got canned." Her mother's hands tightened on her shoulders. "That's what you need to remember."

"But everything was so hard." Kate hated the whiny sound in her voice. She cleared her throat a little. "I didn't think everything would be so hard."

"With no one to help you," Mama said softly.

"Well, Evie and Tori helped. I didn't do it all. And Aunt Hattie helped with the beans or we would have never gotten them done."

"What about your father?" Mama's eyes seemed to burn into her. "He was here to help you, wasn't he?"

"He was at the shop most of the time." Kate slid her eyes away from her mother's face. She couldn't see what it would help to get Mama upset about Daddy staying out all night drinking, even if that was the scariest thing. She wanted to keep having Christmas in June and not open up a box of trouble. "I didn't think he'd know that much about cooking."

Kate's mother pulled her close against her and stroked her hair. "Your father knows about a lot of things. We just need to trust him."

"I do, Mama." Kate's voice sounded muffled against her mother's chest. "I love Daddy."

"I do too, sweetheart. I do too." Her mother stepped back and patted Kate's cheek. "But I guess we shouldn't let breakfast burn up." She turned to take the biscuits out of the oven.

Kate forked the bacon strips and laid them out on a piece of brown paper sack to drain out some of the grease. She wished she could drain out her worries as easily, but the worries were like a thorn deep in her mind that kept poking her. She looked over at her mother. "But what happens when somebody trusts us and we let them down?"

Mama looked up from stirring the oatmeal. "You're talking about Lorena, aren't you?"

"And me."

"You aren't going to let Lorena down."

"But Evie says she was at the store and Ella

232

Baxter was there talking about when she got her new little girl."

Mama looked as if some of those worry thorns were poking her too as she reached over to touch Kate's arm. "We're going to have to trust the Lord to help us on this one, Kate."

"But . . . ," Kate started.

Kate's mother scooted the oatmeal and the skillet with the bacon grease back to the cooler part of the stove and pulled Kate over to sit down at the table with her. She looked at her intently for a moment before she said, "Real trust pushes out the buts. When your father was in the army over in France, sometimes it would be weeks, even months between letters. I'd read things in the paper about this or that battle and almost go crazy with worry. I imagined the most awful things. And then I lost our baby."

"I didn't know you had another baby," Kate said.

"Well, I was only a few months along. Nobody knew I was in the family way except Gertie and Aunt Hattie. He hadn't even quickened in my womb, but I felt the loss as if I'd already borne him and held him in my arms. Somehow losing that sweet promise of life made me doubly afraid your father would never come home and I'd be alone forever." She reached up and put her hand on Kate's cheek. "That I'd never have the chance to hold you beautiful girls."

"You couldn't have known about us then."

"That's where you're wrong. You've always been in my heart." A smile touched her lips and then slid away. "But after I lost that first baby, my arms ached with emptiness and I sank into despair. Aunt Hattie helped me through that dark time. She'd just lost her Bo, but she didn't let that keep her from helping me. She said we can't always understand everything that happens. That sometimes we can't understand anything that happens. And at times like that we have to just hand it all over to the Lord. She taught me a verse out of Proverbs. Proverbs 3:5. 'Trust in the Lord with all thine heart; and lean not unto thine own understanding.'"

"But I don't want it to happen. Lorena belongs with us."

"She does. We just have to keep praying that the Lord will help the others see that too." Her mother squeezed her hands. "Now you run tell your sisters breakfast is ready. I hear your daddy on the back porch."

When Kate went back to the bedroom, Tori and Lorena were up getting dressed while Evie had the sheet pulled up over her face trying to pretend it wasn't morning. Lorena ran to hug Kate's legs. "Tori says we can go fishing this morning in Mr. Graham's pond. She's going to show me how to put a worm on a hook."

"As long as I don't have to show you." Kate

234

made a face as she picked up the little girl and kissed her.

"You'd better watch out that Fern doesn't get you," Evie said from under her sheet.

"Who's Fern?" Lorena asked.

Evie threw back the sheet and sat up. She held out her hands like claws toward Lorena. "Mr. Graham's crazy sister. She'll grab you and make you stay in a house made of cedar trees, just like the witch kept Hansel and Gretel in the gingerbread house."

"Evie!" Kate frowned at her over Lorena's head. She gave Lorena another hug and put her down. "Don't listen to old grumpy grouch. She must be getting up on the wrong side of the bed. On the other hand, there's probably not a right side for her."

Evie shrugged and yawned as she stretched. "Just trying to warn you."

"We don't have to worry about Fern," Kate said. "That's not what we have to worry about."

"What do we have to worry about?" Tori asked as she leaned against Kate for a good morning hug.

"Finding worms if you want to go fishing. Watching you eat your egg with all that ketchup. Yuck! Not enough rain to make the blackberries worth picking. Stepping in chicken doo-doo. Getting tickled by your big sister," Kate dug her finger's into Tori's side and then grabbed Lorena and tickled her too.

Both girls shrieked and ran for the kitchen. Kate gave Evie another mean look. "What's wrong with you?"

"Not a thing," Evie said as she pulled off her gown and started getting dressed. "It's poor old Fern that's got something wrong with her, and one of these days you may be sorry you didn't listen to me."

Kate rolled her eyes at Evie and shook her head before she followed Tori and Lorena to the kitchen. If only Fern was all she had to worry about. It was Ella Baxter she didn't want to see.

23

After Victor left for the blacksmith shop and the breakfast dishes were washed, Victoria and Lorena dragged Kate out to dig for worms. Evangeline grabbed her book and went to settle in her favorite spot by the window in the front room. Nadine stood in the middle of the kitchen and breathed in the silence after the clamor of the day's beginning, but Kate was right. It was hot even though she hadn't fed the fire since she cooked Victoria's egg. Funny how the heat gathered in the summer and sat down on top of a person, while in the winter when you wanted to feel the heat of the fire, it seemed to scoot out of every crack available and leave you shivering while you cooked.

Nadine poured herself another cup of tea and carried it out on the back porch. She had to go back over to her father's house. She had promised, but more than that, she plain didn't trust Carla to properly care for him.

Trust in the Lord and lean not unto thine own understanding. Kate wasn't the only one who needed to surrender to that trust right now or the only one to struggle with trusting the Lord enough to turn her worries over to him. Nadine wished she'd brought her Bible out with her. Not that she needed it for that verse. She whispered the words over to herself again.

Trust. That had been so hard to do with Victor overseas. With the newspapers full of stories of battles and death. Artillery shells and sorrow. Of course she hadn't been the only person in Rosey Corner waiting for news from a loved one, nor had Aunt Hattie been the only one to get the dreaded telegram.

Nadine sat down in the old straight-back chair in the shade of the vines growing up strings on the end of the porch. The climbing vine was one of the few things that didn't seem to be affected by the hot, dry weather. While the bean vines out in the garden were wilting down in the harsh heat of the sun for lack of water, this vine kept putting out more green curling tendrils. Of course that could be because of the wash pans of dirty water she emptied on its roots several times a day.

She reached up and carefully touched the vine. The leaves were rough and irritating to the skin. But it gave shade and a bit of privacy. Gertie had given her a start of the vine when they bought the house after Victor got home from the war. The vine grew up all around Gertie's back porch, and Nadine had spent hours in the solitude of that leafy room writing Victor letters and praying for his safe return.

It had been strange living with Gertie and Wyatt. For the first time in her life, Nadine hadn't had enough to do. She helped with the cooking and cleaning, but Gertie wasn't an overzealous housekeeper, so there were hours every day with absolutely nothing to do. Nothing except worry herself to distraction. Especially after she lost the baby.

Often as the hours of the day crept by, she thought about boarding a train and going back to Louisville to see if Maudie McElroy might have her attic room for rent and chores for Nadine to do. Those months at the boardinghouse seemed like the only happy time in her life since her mother died. But she stayed in Rosey Corner. It was what everybody expected her to do. Sit and wait. Wait and pray.

She wrote to Victor even when weeks passed without a letter from him. She read every book on Wyatt's bookshelves. Victor's mother tried to teach her needlepoint, but Nadine pricked her fingers so often that the "Home Sweet Home" she finally completed was dotted with bloodstains. She still had it stuck away in a drawer somewhere. She went to church and listened to her father's sermons and felt like an unwelcome stranger, sitting in the familiar pews with her father's eyes boring into her.

She had no home. No purpose. Her prayers couldn't even keep her baby safe in her womb. How in the world could she expect them to keep Victor safe halfway around the world?

The weeks became months. The months passed into another year. Winter gave way to spring, and still the war went on. No one had thought the fight would go on so long once the Americans got over there, but the Germans were dug in along their lines. The Allies were dug in along their lines, and there they sat. In the mud, Victor wrote. He was ready to do his duty, to fight for freedom, but at the same time he was miserable, sleeping in the trenches, fighting the body lice that lived in his uniforms, doing his best to keep his feet dry so he wouldn't have trench foot. He didn't write about the soldiers he saw die, but every time Nadine read a battle account in the newspapers, she could see Victor on the front lines, falling for his country.

She lost weight. She lost interest in reading

anything except the news accounts of the war. She missed James Robert. She missed her father, who was the same as lost to her with Carla standing between them. She missed the baby she should have been nursing by now. She missed Victor. She missed the Nadine she'd always been. The Nadine who could handle things. The Nadine who did what had to be done. But now there was nothing to be done. Nothing but wait.

Gertie told her she had to quit letting her imagination work overtime. That she could just as easily imagine good things like the war ending and Victor coming home. Aunt Hattie carried food to her and sat with her until she ate it. Her father sought her out on Gertie's back porch and preached at her. But Nadine stayed in her valley of shadows.

It was a relief, even a blessing, the day Victor's father showed up at Gertie's early in June to order Nadine to be at the store at eight sharp the next morning to wait on customers while he unloaded some new stock. He stared at her with his hard eyes and said, "It's time you started earning your keep."

"Father!" Gertie gasped and half rose up out of her chair on the back porch where she and Nadine had been shelling peas. "Nadine is eating our groceries. Not yours."

"I wasn't talking to you. I was talking to Nadine." Father Merritt turned cold eyes on

Gertie. "God only knows you've never earned your keep. Can't even supply poor Wyatt with an heir."

Gertie sank back down in her chair. She picked up a pea pod that had been caught in her skirt and stared at it a moment before she shelled out the peas and dropped them in the pan beside her chair. She kept her eyes on the peas in the pan as she said softly, "I'm not past childbearing age. The Lord might yet bless me with a child."

"Not likely," Father Merritt said.

Nadine looked between them and thought she should say something to take up for Gertie, who had been so good to her. But she didn't know what to say, the same as she'd often not known what to say to her own father in the face of his unkind spirit.

But Gertie came up with her own retort. Color burned in her cheeks as she looked up at her father. "You could be right. Perhaps it's the Lord's punishment on you. A judgment. If Victor doesn't make it home, then you'll be the one without any heirs."

Nadine's heart turned to stone and sank inside her at Gertie's words. She was speaking out loud Nadine's darkest fear. It was all Nadine could do to keep from clapping her hands over her ears and running off the porch.

"He'll come home," Father Merritt said.

"You can't know that." Gertie's face was beet

red now as she defied her father. "You aren't God. You can't control what happens over there the way you think you can here in Rosey Corner."

"He's a Merritt. He'll come home." There wasn't even the shadow of doubt in Father Merritt's voice. "When the war ends, he'll be back."

"Press Jr. was a Merritt."

For a second Nadine thought Father Merritt might strike Gertie, but he just mashed his mouth together and turned back to Nadine. "Tomorrow morning at eight. Sharp," he said before he stomped off the porch and went around the house without another word.

Gertie told Nadine she didn't have to go, but Nadine wanted to go. She needed something to occupy the hours. She needed something to think about besides the battles going on in France. She wanted to be where she could hear Father Merritt telling people Victor would be coming home, because when he said it, Nadine could believe it.

She worked every day the store was open. She and Father Merritt sometimes went hours without speaking a word directly to one another, but that suited Nadine just fine. There was plenty of talk. People were in and out all through the day, sharing their problems, their worries, their caring. And slowly she began walking out of the shadows.

The store wasn't like the church where she'd

worshiped with most of the people in Rosey Corner at one time or another, but the same feel of community was there. The people liked one another. They cared what happened to the people who lived next door. They cared about Nadine. Always before, she'd thought people were nice to her because she was the preacher's daughter, but there in the store they looked her in the eye and smiled at her and asked after Victor. And they cared. Not because she was anybody's daughter or wife, but because she was one of them.

Gertie begged her to quit at the store when the first people in Rosey Corner came down with the influenza late in 1918. In France, the American doughboys had charged out of the Allied trenches and stormed the German positions in September, pushing the enemy back, but while there finally seemed to be reason to hope the Germans were going to be defeated, influenza was killing people all over the world. Even in Rosey Corner.

School was dismissed until further notice, and church services were canceled. People stayed home behind closed doors to shut out the disease, but it spread relentlessly. Victor's mother came down with it early on. From the first cough, nobody had any hope that she'd recover. In spite of Aunt Hattie's sitting with her every minute and spooning medicine down her throat, she died a week later.

Victor's father closed the store for the burial,

but once the grave was closed he went back to the store. He said people had to have a way to buy what they needed. Not that the store had very many customers. Few people ventured out to the store either because they were too sick or they feared coming into contact with those who were. No household was spared. Not even the doctor or his family, as Dr. Lindell and his wife were early victims, and Fern nearly died. Graham was the only one in his family to escape.

Nadine didn't get sick. Not even a slight case. For a little while, she thought Father Merritt was coming down with it, but he fought it off. He said it was the cold water baths he took every morning that warded off the influenza. At times Nadine thought she and Father Merritt and Graham Lindell were the only people in Rosey Corner who weren't coughing and down with the ague. Even Aunt Hattie came down with it in spite of the garlic amulet she wore around her neck.

Graham and Father Merritt carried groceries to the houses where every family member was sick. Graham cared for their animals and helped bury those who died. Nadine wore paths between Gertie's house and her father's house and Aunt Hattie's as she cared for the sick. From her sickbed, Aunt Hattie told Nadine how to brew a concoction of herbs and roots to strengthen the sick. Whether that was what did it or whether it was their prayers or a combination of the two,

Aunt Hattie, Gertie and Wyatt, and Nadine's father and Carla began showing improvement every day until by the first of the year the worst of the epidemic was over in Rosey Corner.

The war was also over. Armistice was signed on November 11, 1918. The war had ended a few weeks earlier than that for Victor when fragments of an exploding shell imbedded in his shoulder. Nadine didn't receive his letter telling her about his wound until weeks after the Armistice, and then she didn't know whether to shout with joy or cry because he was hurt. The joy won out. A breath of relief swept through her that he was only wounded and not one of the thousands who would never come back across the sea from France. Like Bo.

When she told Father Merritt about the letter, for just a second she imagined she saw a reflection of her joy in his face, but if so, he would never admit to it. "That means he'll be in one of those field hospitals over there," he said with the usual growl in his voice as he peered at her. "Better not stop praying yet, Nadine. The hospitals over there are full of the influenza the same as here."

Nadine didn't duck away from his eyes the way she sometimes did. Instead she looked straight at him as she said, "You don't have to worry about that. I'll never stop praying for Victor, but he won't catch it. He'll be home. And soon." And this time Father Merritt looked to be the one who needed to believe her.

Now Nadine took a last sip of her tea and threw the dregs left in the cup on the roots of the vine. As she stood up to go to her father's house and be a dutiful daughter, she wondered if she had stopped praying for Victor. At least the right kind of prayers. Had she let other worries, other duties, push in front of her first duty to her husband? Were her prayers only for herself?

She prayed he wouldn't drink. She prayed she would be able to bear up under the shame of having a husband who spent money they couldn't afford on alcohol. She prayed the girls would be protected from that shame. But she should have been praying for Victor. That the Lord would remove whatever was tormenting him. Victor didn't want to be pulled away from them. She could see that in his misery on the mornings after he allowed himself to go down the alcohol trail. But still he went, and some part of her couldn't forgive that. Perhaps that should be her prayer. That she could be more forgiving.

As she stepped down off the back porch to head down the road to her father's house, she saw Kate, Victoria, and Lorena digging for worms in the hard dry ground out by the barn. She called to them that she was leaving, and they ran across the barnyard to give her hugs. She held Lorena an extra minute, and the child leaned into her hug, absorbing every bit of it. Inside her heart Nadine was praying, *Dear Lord, spare us hard testing.*

It was a prayer she kept praying as she left them and went around the house to walk up the road. But it wasn't a prayer she had any assurance would be answered. The Bible assured her the Lord never tested anyone beyond that person's ability to bear whatever happened. As long as the person was trusting the Lord and leaning not on her own understanding. That was what she needed to pray. To have the kind of trust she could only receive from the Lord. Yet in spite of her prayer, she felt burdened down with so many reasons to worry. Lorena. Kate. Her father. Victor.

Nadine stopped in the shade of a tree where the lane to her father's house intersected with the main road through Rosey Corner. Up ahead she could see the stores. Not far past that was the blacksmith shop. She wanted to walk on up there, to see Victor, to rest her head in that sweet hollow on his shoulder for just a moment. To let him lift some of her burdens off her shoulders onto his. But he already had too many burdens to carry of his own. Burdens he'd been carrying for years without asking her to help him bear them.

Her shoulders drooped as she began pushing one foot in front of the other again as she turned down the lane to her father's house. She was tired. Bone weary. Spirit starved.

Spirit starved! Whose fault is that? In her mind she could see her father in the pulpit preaching at her while he held up his Bible and shook it. *Hide the words of this book in your heart and feast on its wisdom.*

When she was a child, her father had insisted she memorize a new Bible verse every week, and now a bit of one of those verses rose to the top of her mind. *Cast thy burden upon the Lord, and he shall sustain thee.* No sooner had the verse whispered through her mind than she heard the sound of Victor's hammer striking metal, carrying through the air to her. It was a good sound. Her step was a bit lighter as she headed on down the lane to her father's house.

24

At Graham's pond, Lorena wasn't the first bit squeamish about squishing one of the wiggly worms onto the fishhook the way Tori showed her. It was Kate who made a face and shivered.

"Kate don't like worming hooks," Tori explained to Lorena. "But it's something you gotta do if you want to catch fish." She wiped her hands on the grass, and Lorena did the same.

"Am I ready to catch a fish now?" Lorena asked.

"Almost. Soon as you throw your line out in the water." Tori flipped her line expertly out onto the pond surface and watched her hook sink. "Be careful not to catch your hook on a tree limb."

"Or your ears," Kate added. "Maybe you'd better let me or Tori toss your line in the first few times."

"No, I can do it." Lorena clutched the cane pole and raised it above her head to throw the hook out in the water. It landed a few inches from the bank.

"No fish worth catching there," Tori told her. "Better try again."

Kate moved out of hook range and sat down in the shade. She had hoped Graham would be there at the pond, but he'd think it was too hot to fish. Even Tori said there wasn't much chance of catching anything, but Lorena had been so determined to give it a try. Just as she was determined now to throw her own hook out into the water. On the fifth try, she landed it far enough away from the bank that Tori said she might get a bite. Tori settled into her silent fishing mode, and Lorena settled down beside her, copying her every move.

Kate leaned back against a tree and wondered how long before Lorena got bored with it all. Soon, she hoped, because she was definitely bored with it already. Going fishing with Tori in the springtime wasn't so bad. There weren't so many bugs and the sun didn't try to burn off the top of a person's head. But now here in late June it was hot. Even in the shade. Mosquitoes buzzed around Kate's ears, and she could almost feel the chiggers crawling up into her underwear. She should have dabbed coal oil around their ankles before they left. They'd be scratching chigger bites for days.

Lorena's line bobbed in the water, and she let out an excited shriek as she yanked on her pole. She lost half her worm and didn't hook the fish, but that didn't dampen her enthusiasm. She scooted what was left of the worm down to the end of the hook and happily threw it back into the water. A few chigger bites might not be such a bad trade for Lorena having so much fun.

Kate smiled and waved away a fly that wanted to settle on her nose. Maybe Graham would hear them and come out to see what all the racket was about. Then at least she'd have somebody to talk to. But it wasn't Graham who came to investigate first.

She didn't see anybody right away. Instead she had the creepy feeling somebody was watching her, watching them. Kate remembered all her mother's warnings about tramps wandering through Rosey Corner, and her heart began beating a little faster. It wouldn't be Graham. He and Poe always came crashing through the woods with plenty of noise to let her know they were coming. Kate held her breath and listened harder as she straightened up away from the tree and slowly turned her head to look behind her. Fern was there in the shadows of the trees, watching her. Kate couldn't keep from jumping.

"Scared you, did I?" Fern said in her voice that always sounded rough, like a rusty hinge on a door that wasn't opened very often. She didn't look directly at Kate, but instead kept her eyes on Tori and Lorena.

"You startled me." Kate scrambled to her feet.

"Not scared?" Fern didn't wait for Kate to answer as she stepped out of the shadows. She was carrying her hatchet. "Might be you should be."

"Graham told us we could go fishing here whenever we wanted." Kate pushed a smile out on her face as she edged a few steps away from Fern. She wondered how fast she could grab Lorena and run for home. She didn't have to worry about Tori. With her long skinny legs, Tori could outrun Kate any day of the week.

"It's my pond too." Fern turned her eyes on Kate.

Graham had told Kate that Fern was beautiful as a young woman. Fair skinned with delicate features, light blue eyes, dark curly hair, and a smile that lit up her face. Kate knew it was true because she'd seen her portrait hanging on the wall in the Lindells' house. But it was hard to believe the woman standing before her now was the same young woman who had worn the airy white gown and smiled at the artist while he'd captured her beauty in brushstrokes on the canvas.

Now the skin on Fern's face was weathered and mottled with broken red veins on her high cheekbones, and her mostly steel gray hair looked to be trying to take flight to escape from her scalp. The blue of her eyes had faded like old work jeans and had an unfocused, almost feral look. She wore a pair of overalls with big holes in the knees that she'd probably stolen off somebody's clothesline years ago. Under the overalls was a dirty white slip. She didn't carry any extra weight, but she'd long ago lost her delicate look. She spent her days cutting cedars now to make her cedar houses instead of sipping tea and doing needlework.

Kate licked her lips and backed a couple of steps closer to Tori and Lorena, who were so intent on their fishing that they hadn't noticed Fern yet. "If you don't want us to fish, we'll leave."

Fern showed no sign she heard Kate as she stared past her toward the pond. "I don't like water. People die in water."

"You mean if they can't swim and drown?" Kate said.

"Swim or not. All the same." Fern turned back

to Kate. Her eyes narrowed on Kate's face as she said, "You look like him."

"Who?" Kate asked, curious in spite of herself.

"Him." Fern said it as if Kate should know whomever she meant. Then she looked past Kate back at Tori and Lorena. "That little one. Haven't seen her before. Where'd she come from?"

"Her name's Lorena. We're taking care of her right now."

"She's like me." Fern kept staring past Kate toward Lorena.

Kate looked over her shoulder at Tori and Lorena. They'd seen Fern now and had abandoned their fishing to stare at her. Tori was clutching her fishing pole with one hand and Lorena's hand with the other. She was up on her toes ready to run, but Lorena just looked curious as she started toward them. Tori held her back.

Kate reminded herself that she wasn't afraid of Fern as she turned back to look at the woman. She kept her eyes away from the little axe. "Who? Lorena?"

"That one." Fern pointed with her hatchet. Her arm was covered with scratches in various stages of healing.

Lorena pulled loose from Tori and ran up beside Kate. Kate pushed the little girl behind her and stepped in front of Fern. Again she reminded herself she wasn't afraid of Fern, but the hatchet made her a little nervous. She was starting to say they were leaving when Lorena peeked out from behind her to ask, "What are you doing with that?"

Fern looked at it and then dropped her arm back to her side. "Cutting cedars," she said. "I make palaces out of them."

"Palaces in the woods?" Lorena asked.

"Best place for them. Nobody bothers you out here."

"Oh," Lorena said as if that made perfect sense to her. She edged out from behind Kate to stand in front of Fern. Kate kept her hands on Lorena's shoulders, ready to pull her back out of danger. "My name's Lorena Birdsong. What's yours?"

"Fern Maia Lindell. I never married."

Kate had never heard Fern talk so much. Usually a growled "hello" or "get away" was all she said. So even though Kate thought it might be wise to pick up Lorena and run, at the same time she wanted to hear what else Fern might say.

"Why not?" Lorena asked.

"He died." Fern stared at Lorena as if she'd forgotten Kate or Tori were even there. "He called me Maia. Nobody else ever called me Maia. He said it was a princess name."

"My mommy told me I had a princess name," Lorena said.

"Like me. Your name. Your hair." Fern reached toward Lorena with the hand that wasn't holding the hatchet. Her fingers were bent like claws.

Kate started to pull Lorena back, but Lorena looked up at Kate and said, "She just wants to touch my hair."

Kate held her breath as Fern stroked Lorena's hair. She was relieved when the woman pulled her hand back.

"Pretty hair. He said I had pretty hair." She touched her own hair and something that might have been a smile flickered across her face.

Kate couldn't remember ever seeing Fern smile.

"Was he sick? Is that why he died?" Kate asked.

Fern's eyes sparked with anger as she glared over at Kate. "You're nosy. Brother thinks you're nice, but you're too nosy."

"You don't have to answer," Kate said quickly.

"I can answer, but what difference is it now how he died?" Fern's voice sounded sad. "He died. Brother let him die. He didn't understand."

"Who didn't understand? Graham or him?" The question bubbled out of Kate before she could stop it

"Nosy." Fern raised her hatchet and spun it around over top her head. "Maybe I ought to cut off your nose."

Behind Kate, Tori screamed, "Run, Kate!"

Kate didn't look around at Tori. She wrapped her arms around Lorena and stood her ground. She tried to keep her voice from trembling but didn't quite succeed as she said, "I'm sorry, Fern. I'll stop asking questions."

From the woods behind Fern came the sound of Poe baying, and then the dog and Graham crashed through the bushes out of the trees.

"Fern!" Graham's voice was sterner than Kate had ever heard it. "What do you think you're doing? You know I've told you not to bother Kate and Victoria when they're fishing here."

Fern looked at him and lowered her hatchet. She pointed at Lorena. "That one's like me." Then she pointed toward Kate. "That one's like him. The one you let die."

"Now, Fern, you know I didn't want anybody to die. Especially not him." Graham's voice was calm and gentle now. "You go on and chop on your cedar bushes and don't be stirring up trouble. You hear?"

"I hear." Fern glared at Graham and then at Kate one last time before she turned back to the woods.

She disappeared into the trees without rattling the first bush. Somehow that was spookier than her swinging the hatchet over her head. Poe nudged his wet nose up against Kate's hand to get her to rub him. When she didn't pay any attention, the dog gave up on her and began licking Lorena's face. Lorena giggled and hugged the old dog's neck. Graham asked Tori if she was catching anything, and she told him not yet as she pitched her hook back in the pond, and things almost felt normal again. Almost.

"Tori's teaching Lorena how to fish," Kate said. She hesitated before she added, "I didn't aim to upset Fern."

"She wouldn't have really hurt you. She just sometimes likes to put on a show." Graham frowned and shook his head a little as he looked over his shoulder toward the spot where Fern had gone back into the woods. "I don't know what got into her today. She normally doesn't pay the first bit of attention to you and Victoria fishing here."

"She liked my hair." Lorena pulled a lock of her dark curly hair out away from her scalp. "She said it was like hers."

"Is that a fact? Well, maybe that explains it. Fern did have pretty curly hair when she was growing up. My mother was always making over her and dressing her up like a little princess." Graham smiled at Lorena. "That was all a long time ago."

"Do you think she wanted to be a princess?" Lorena asked.

"Could be," Graham said. "Maybe she thinks she is a princess. Who knows with Fern? She's always out there piling up cedars to make her cedar palaces. Leastways that's what she calls them. Appear to be nothing but piles of brush to me, but it keeps her occupied and mostly out of trouble. She didn't scare you too bad, did she?" Graham looked from Lorena to Kate and back to Lorena.

"Tori was scared, and I was a little bit. But not Kate. Angel sisters don't get scared of anything." Lorena grabbed Kate around the middle and gave her a hug. "Kate's not even afraid of rats biting her toes while she sleeps."

"I told you. No rats at our house." Kate pushed a smile out on her face as she breathed in and out slowly. She felt weak all over, like she'd run to Edgeville and back. She really wasn't afraid of Fern. Not exactly. But hatchets start flying and a person would be stupid not to be at least a little worried. "And I'm not an angel, remember?"

"You're my angel like Mr. Graham is her angel." Lorena turned loose of Kate and looked at Graham. "Did you really let somebody die like she said?"

It was the question Kate had wanted to ask, but she would have never spoken it aloud. Lorena had no such qualms.

"No, I didn't. You can't pay any attention to what Fern says. Back when she got so sick with the influenza, the fever did things to her head. She can't remember things right. The way they really happened."

"She remembered being a princess," Lorena said.

Tori let out a yell. "I've got a bite, Lorena. Hurry up, and you can pull it in."

Kate and Graham watched Lorena run to grab the cane pole from Tori and run backward up the bank to pull the fish in. It was too little to keep, but Lorena didn't care as she jumped up and down and clapped her hands. Tori carefully unhooked the fish and gave it to Lorena to put back in the water.

"Nothing like catching that first fish." Graham smiled before he looked back at Kate. His smile slid away. "Are you all right, Kate?"

"I'm fine," Kate said. It wasn't much of a lie.

"She won't bother you again. I promise."

Kate looked at him. She wasn't sure she should ask, but she did anyhow. "Who was the him she was talking about? She said I looked like him."

Graham mashed his mouth together and for a second Kate didn't think he was going to answer her, but then he said, "That would be your daddy's brother. Press Jr. Fern was in love with him."

"Do I really look like him?"

Graham studied her face a minute before he answered. "The family resemblance is there. Around the eyes and mouth, but that's not a bad thing. Press Jr. was a good-looking boy. Good at everything he did. Your granddaddy thought he was going to be governor when he got old enough. But he never got old enough."

"What happened to him?"

"He drowned."

"Here?" Kate almost shivered as she looked back at the pond.

"No. At the river. A long time ago. 1908. He was nineteen. It was a bad thing, Kate. I don't like to talk about it."

"Was Fern there?"

"She was, but she doesn't remember it right. I don't know that any of us remember it right. Fact is, I don't want to remember it at all." Graham's voice sounded firm. "Enough bad things happen every day to worry over. No need pulling up bad ones from the past that a person can't do one thing about now except feel sorrowful."

"No, I guess not." Kate clamped down on the questions that were circling in her head. Graham didn't want to talk about it. That was plain to see even before he stepped away from her without another word and went over to watch Lorena push a new worm onto her hook.

He was right. She did have enough to worry about already, what with being the middle sister, the responsible one. The one who had to make sure everybody was taken care of and happy. Still, it seemed like her father's brother's—her uncle's—drowning would be something she would know about. Even if it had happened years before she was born.

25

The week passed. On Thursday Grandfather Reece stood up on his own and walked out to the porch with two canes. A slow, shuffling walk, but he made it. He got command of a few more words, and although his right eye drooped and saliva dribbled out of his twisted mouth, the side that did work often as not smiled when somebody sat down beside him on the porch.

Kate's mother said it must be all the prayers his people kept offering up for him. Her father said it was nothing short of a veritable miracle. Either that or his smiling and frowning muscles had gotten messed up the same way his talking had.

But Kate didn't think so. Whenever she sat down beside him, Grandfather Reece would open up his Bible with his good hand and point out verses for her to read aloud. He liked Psalm 91. He could find the middle of his Bible with his thumb and more times than not it fell open to that chapter.

He that dwelleth in the secret place of the most High shall abide under the shadow of the Almighty. That first verse was the one Grandfather Reece liked best, but Kate always read him the whole chapter because she liked the verses in it about the angels. *For he shall give his angels charge over thee, to keep thee in all thy ways. They shall bear thee up in their hands, lest thou dash thy foot against a stone.*

When Kate read that to her grandfather, a breath of relief went through her every time. She wasn't an angel the way Lorena kept saying. Not even close, but she liked to imagine she felt the flutter of a guardian angel's wings around her and Lorena. She asked her grandfather if that was what the verse meant—that angels were watching over them—or if the Lord sent angels just for Bible people like King David. He tried to answer her, but she couldn't quite get his meaning. Too many words still in wrong places. But he smiled and lightly caressed the Bible page, so unless his smiling and frowning were mixed up the way Daddy said, Kate thought he was telling her that yes, she could believe in guardian angels.

As she and her mother walked home that afternoon, Kate told her about the verses that promised angels would lift a believer up and not let him so much as stump his toe. She asked her mother the same question she'd asked Grandfather Reece.

"Angels." Mama stared at the gravel on the road a moment before she looked up at Kate. "The Bible does speak of them, and I believe what the Bible says."

"Right, but are the angels out there, or rather right here?" Kate held her hand up toward the blue sky over them. "Guarding over us all the time, or was that just for David? Or remember that story Grandfather used to preach about where Elisha opened his servant's eyes so he could see the horses and chariots of fire guarding the city where he lived? That would be something to see." She looked around. All she saw were houses and trees.

"It would of a truth." Mama smiled at her. "Perhaps even a bit unnerving."

"Might explain why it's so hot." Kate grinned over at her mother.

"Oh, Kate." Mama laughed. "The things you come up with. But I think the heat has more to do with the way the sun's beating down on us."

"Yeah, I know. The chariots of fire were probably just for Elisha. But having a guardian angel is different, don't you think? Something we might all have."

Her mother stopped as they came to the edge of their yard and looked off at the trees behind the house for a long moment before she answered. "Unseen angels. Perhaps they are always around us. The Bible says we can entertain angels unaware."

"But we're doing the helping then. How about them helping us? Do you think that happens?" Kate pushed her for an answer.

"It might, Kate. The Lord can use any means he wants to help us, whether that is his angels, other people, the Bible. It's all in his power." She looked back at Kate with eyes that were kind of sad. "At the same time, bad things do happen. We do dash our feet on the stones along the pathways of life. All the time."

"But is that because we're not trusting enough? If we can trust enough, will that keep the bad things away? Keep the angels guarding over us?"

"I don't know, Kate. I wish I could say yes, but I just don't know." Mama laid a hand on Kate's cheek. "What you have to remember is that bad things happened to people in the Bible too. Even David, who was a man after God's own heart. Sometimes it was because they had fallen out of the will of the Lord, and sometimes the sins of others brought hard times into their lives. Think about Joseph and how his brothers sold him into slavery. We can't control what everybody around us does."

"God made that turn out to be good."

"He did, but I doubt it felt good to Joseph when he was carried off to Egypt and later ended up in prison. He surely had to wonder if he was trusting enough."

"Do you think something bad is going to happen to us?" Kate was sorry she'd asked the question as soon as it was out of her mouth because it was too easy to see the worry in her mother's eyes.

"Some would say bad things have happened already with Father's stroke."

"He's getting better."

"He is, but he will probably never be truly well again. Perhaps never be able to preach, and preaching has always been Father's life. Plus other things could happen." Mama put her hands on Kate's shoulders and stared straight into her eyes. "I pray not, but if it does, I know the Lord will help us make it through whatever might happen the same as the good Lord is helping us and the church walk through this hard time with Father. As he's walked us through other hard times in the past."

"Like when Daddy's brother drowned?"

Mama looked surprised as she dropped her hands off Kate's shoulders. "Who told you about that?" She was frowning.

"Graham." Kate felt like she needed to backpedal and not bring up how this uncle of hers died. She should have stuck with the angel questions, even though she was definitely curious about what Graham told her.

"Graham? Are you sure? I don't think I've ever heard him speak of it. Ever." Mama's frown got deeper.

"Well, he only did because of Fern. She saw us fishing there the other day and came out and talked to us."

"Fern talked to you?"

Kate wasn't sure whether her mother looked more surprised or alarmed. "Yeah, but it was okay. She wanted to see Lorena. She said Lorena looked like her when she was little. Well, her hair did anyway." Kate hesitated a moment as she thought about how much to tell her. Definitely nothing about Fern waving her hatchet around and threatening to cut off Kate's nose. She'd already warned Tori and Lorena to keep mum about that if they wanted to go fishing over at Graham's pond ever again. But she could tell the rest. "And she said I looked like him. I didn't know who she was talking about, but Graham said Fern was talking about Daddy's brother. Press Jr. He said Fern was in love with him. Do I really look like him?"

"That's certainly a possibility since you take back after the Merritt side of the family, but I only have a vague recollection of a tall boy with brown hair. I wasn't but eight or nine when he died. I do remember how sad everybody was."

"Daddy remembers him, doesn't he?"

"Of course he does, but now is not a good time to be bothering your father about this. You know he's already having nightmares about the war. No need bringing back more sorrows for him to remember." Mama bent her head a bit and gave Kate a stern look. "Understand?"

"Yes, ma'am." Kate ducked her head. "I won't bother him about it. I promise. It's just that when Fern said I looked like him, it made me curious."

266

"My curious Kate." Mama reached out and gave her a quick hug. "But there are times to be curious and times to let things be."

Kate wanted to ask her about the other thing Fern had said. About Graham letting him die, but her mother wouldn't know about that. And Graham had already explained it. Fern had it all mixed up in her head. She had to. Graham wouldn't even kill the raccoons he and Poe treed out in the woods. He would never purposely let anyone die the way Fern made it sound.

To keep that question at bay, she said, "Do you think he was in love with Fern? She used to be pretty."

"She was. Very pretty. But I never knew her to have a suitor. Even before the influenza damaged her. She was well into her twenties by then. Poor Fern." Mama seemed to remember then her worries about Fern talking to them. "I'm sorry for her, but at the same time, you need to be careful around her. Maybe you shouldn't take Lorena back over to the pond for a while. At least not until I talk to Graham about it."

"Sure. It's too hot to fish anyway," Kate said. "I'll help her and Tori make paper dolls, or even better, we can find a shady place and I'll read them *Little Women*."

On Sunday, they went to church and listened to the young preacher from the seminary the deacons had called to fill in while they prayed for Grandfather Reece to get better. Kate kept feeling as if they were surely in the wrong church. Brother Champion was nothing like her grandfather behind the pulpit. He was young with dark wavy hair and very blue eyes. He smiled all the time except when he was preaching and sometimes even then. He actually told a funny story in the pulpit.

Kate laughed and felt disloyal for a moment, but then Brother Champion was smiling directly at her as though she were the only person in the church. Her heart did some kind of weird somersault, and her mouth went dry. It didn't matter that he looked at her for no more than a second or two before he swept his eyes to another person in the church with the same smile. Kate was sunk.

Before the first hymn was over, all the girls in the church, marrying age and younger, were watching Brother Champion's every move. That included Evie, who seemed to forget all about George even though he was sitting right beside her on the pew, holding her hand out of sight under her full skirt.

After the final prayer had been said and the new preacher walked to the door to give everybody on the way out the hand of fellowship, Evie shook off George's hand and beat everybody else to the door. Kate couldn't believe it when she heard

Evie inviting Brother Champion to dinner without even thinking about what they had to put on the table. No company fare for sure. Maybe she didn't know that, because sometimes Evie acted as if she believed things just fell out of the sky when she wanted them.

Kate grabbed her arm and pulled her to the side. "Evie, are you out of your mind?" Kate whispered in her ear. "We don't have anything ready to eat. Nothing for a preacher anyway. Bologna and cheese and leftover bean soup. We can't ask him to come eat that."

"Mama might have cooked something else," Evie said.

"Mama went to Grandfather Reece's early this morning so Carla could come to church, remember? She won't be back until suppertime."

"She made a brown sugar pie yesterday. She left it in the pie safe. I saw it this morning. That's preacher food." Evie lifted her chin and stared at Kate. "Besides, I've already asked him. Maybe we can fry some chicken."

"Are you going to catch a chicken and cut off its head?" Kate shivered at the thought. "Besides, we let the fire go out. It would take forever to get water boiling to pluck the feathers."

"You always see problems. You should learn to look for solutions." Evie pulled away from Kate. "I asked him and he said yes, so that's that. He might like bologna."

Kate looked over at the preacher, who was talking to other people on the way out the door, and her heart did another funny bounce inside her chest. Maybe Evie was right. Some people did like bologna. Tori thought it was a special treat. And it would be nice to have him sitting at the table with them, smiling at her.

One of the deacons' wives, Mrs. Spaulding, came up behind them. "Evangeline, I'm not sure it's proper you inviting the preacher home with you. Carla says your mother is sitting with your grandfather this morning."

"Our father is at home," Evie said.

"Well, of course, but . . . ," Mrs. Spaulding sputtered and seemed to run out of words.

Ella Baxter had no such problem when she joined their huddle. "While it's a well-known fact your father could use some personal time with a preacher, you can't even depend on him to be there."

"He's there." Kate tried to keep her voice civil, but it came out a bit harsh. She didn't like talking to Ella Baxter. She didn't like being in the same room with Ella Baxter. She didn't like Ella Baxter being anywhere close to Lorena. Kate tried to peer out the door into the churchyard to be sure Lorena was safe with Tori. She'd told them they could go out and play with the other kids, but now she wished she'd grabbed her hand and hurried on across the pasture field toward

270

home. She'd let herself get distracted by Brother Champion's good looks.

"Yes, but in what sort of shape?" Mrs. Baxter said with a scornful lift of her eyebrows.

"Now, Ella," Mrs. Spaulding said. "The girls have no control over that."

"Exactly," Mrs. Baxter said with a sniff that said more than words.

Red heat swept through Kate. She forgot she was in church. She forgot the new preacher was standing there behind them. She forgot that she was a kid and Ella Baxter an adult. She barely felt Evie's fingers digging into her arm. "You don't know anything about my father." She wasn't exactly yelling, but she was very close.

"Oh, my poor dear child. I certainly didn't intend to upset you." Mrs. Baxter's smile looked fake to Kate. "I pray for you and your sisters each and every day."

Evie was practically pinching a plug out of Kate now as she leaned close to whisper in her ear. "Katherine Reece Merritt, don't you dare do something to embarrass me in front of the new preacher. Remember where you are."

"Is there a problem here, ladies?" Brother Champion must have finished shaking everybody else's hands.

"No, no problem at all," Evie said quickly. She gave Kate a look as if the whole confrontation was all her fault before she smiled back at the preacher. "Miss Ella was just saying how she prayed for us. Because of our grandfather's unfortunate stroke, I'm sure. They were of the mind that I might have spoken out of turn asking you to dinner."

Then she was smiling at Ella Baxter and Mrs. Spaulding while Kate made herself unclench her fists. Evie was right. She couldn't sock Ella Baxter in church. Not because she might embarrass Evie, but because of Lorena. If Kate let her temper get the best of her, that might give them reason to claim she wasn't good for Lorena.

Kate pulled in a deep breath and blew it out slowly. Some of the heat went out with it. The Bible said she was supposed to love her enemies and pray for them. That wasn't just the Bible. It was straight from the Sermon on the Mount. Her grandfather preached on that all the time. Going the extra mile. Turning the other cheek. But Kate wasn't ready to turn any cheek or do any praying for Ella Baxter. Even if Kate was standing in church with the new preacher eyeing her as if somebody definitely needed to be praying. For Kate.

Brother Champion settled where he would be eating dinner when he turned to Evie to say, "Not out of turn at all, Miss Merritt. I'm looking forward to eating dinner with your family. I had hoped to visit Reverend Reece this afternoon, and who better to introduce me to him than his

272

own family? Don't you agree, ladies?" He showered them with one of his bright smiles. The two women looked about as near a swoon as Evie. Neither of them opened her mouth to argue.

Evie looked at Kate with a winning smile. "You go on ahead, Kate. I'll wait for Brother Champion and ride down to the house with him."

"What about George?" Kate said just for meanness. She'd already seen George go out of the church in a huff. Even if he was hanging around outside, it was a sure thing Evie wasn't riding anywhere with him today. "Don't you usually ride home with him?"

Evie shot another warning look at Kate before she casually flipped her hair back away from her face and said airily, "He said he was busy this afternoon."

Kate started to tell Evie it was probably as bad to tell a lie in church as it was to want to sock somebody in the mouth, but some things were better left unsaid. Besides, she needed to beat Ella Baxter out of the church. She needed to get Lorena away from her sight, because every time Mrs. Baxter looked at Lorena, it was like her eyes were grabbing hold of the little girl, and one of these days she wasn't going to turn her loose.

26

Kate's father looked up from his book with a bit of consternation when Kate, Tori, and Lorena came tearing home and passed him on the porch. Kate let Tori explain they were having company while she rushed on to the kitchen to shove the dirty breakfast dishes out of sight into the oven. Lorena helped her do a whirlwind pickup of books and papers in the sitting room while Tori ran out to hang a clean towel on the hook by the washpans on the back porch. By the time the preacher drove up with Evie, the house, while not up to her mother's company standards, was at least presentable.

The preacher won over Kate's father before they came in off the porch by talking about how much he liked H. G. Wells. Then he came right on out to the kitchen and sat down at the table while they were setting out the food, as if he'd known them forever.

He told them to call him Brother Mike. "Or just Mike if that suits you better. I've been praying for a chance to serve a church like yours." He seemed to think about what he'd said and rushed on, sounding a bit flustered. "Not that I think the Lord answered my prayers by causing Reverend Reece to get sick."

Kate's father helped him out. "It's an ill wind that blows no one any good."

"Yes, yes, and the Bible does say the Lord can make good come out of the worst circumstances." Brother Mike looked relieved. "We'll be praying for Reverend Reece's recovery, but until he's able to take over the church again, I'm looking forward to being here to help the church all I can. Of course with going to seminary, I'll mostly be here on the weekends unless there's a special need." He flashed them his smile.

"And your wife? Is she going to be able to come with you?" Kate's father asked.

Kate froze as she reached in the cabinet to get out the good plates. Beside her, Evie looked as if she had forgotten how to breathe as all the color drained out of her face. Surely he would have mentioned having a wife back in Louisville.

"No, no. No wife yet." Brother Mike laughed. "Right now I'm focusing all my attention on learning more about the Lord and what he wants me to do. When the right girl comes along to share in that work, I trust the Lord will point her out to me."

Evie tried to hide her sigh of relief by laughing a little. Kate made a face at her as she shoved the plates toward her. Evie was acting like she thought the good Lord had a big finger pointing at her already.

Their father smiled as he said, "I'm sure he's busy sorting through applications."

Brother Mike's cheeks colored up a bit. "Well, I don't know about that. But I do think the Lord's hand is evident in all good marriages. How about you and your wife, sir? Do you think the Lord helped you find each other?"

"We didn't have to go far to find each other since we both grew up right here in Rosey Corner, but Nadine was definitely an answer to prayer."

"How long have you been married?" Brother Mike seemed anxious to switch the attention off his love life onto something else. Anything else.

"We got married in 1917 a few months before I shipped out to France." Kate's father picked up the glass of tea Kate sat in front of him and took a sip. "But I'd been in love with her since I was a boy."

"So you were sweethearts all the way through school?" Brother Mike grinned at Kate as she dropped a piece of ice she'd chipped off the block in the icebox into his tea.

"Not at all. I said *I* was in love with *her*. For her part, she barely knew I existed until we were seniors in high school."

Evie jumped in to tell part of the story. "And then Daddy was reading a poem about a girl named Evangeline at school and Mother fell head over heels in love with him. That's where I got my name." Evie put her hands over her heart and sighed. "Isn't that just so romantic?"

"Ah, romantic love. One of the nicest gifts the Lord bestows on us." Brother Mike smiled at Evie and then turned back to their father. "And so now you have four beautiful daughters?"

"Three. We're just keeping the youngest here, Lorena, until her parents get back on their feet." Kate's father reached over to pat Lorena's head. "But I'd be proud to say she was my daughter."

"Lorena," the preacher said. "Yes, one of the ladies at church, Mrs. Baxter I think, was telling me about her." A frown flickered across his face as he looked over at Lorena. "I understood that she was caring for the little girl."

Kate stepped over behind Lorena and put her arms around her. "No. We are."

Lorena smiled up at her. "Kate's my angel. The Lord gave her to me."

"It's a long story," Kate's father said. "But right now it looks like the girls have our dinner ready, such as it is. If you'll say grace, Brother Mike, we'll eat."

Brother Mike did like bologna or at least pretended to as he ate his sandwich with a smile. After they all had a slice of the brown sugar pie, Kate's father and Brother Mike carried their tea out to the front porch while Evie and Kate cleared off the table.

"I'm going with them over to see Grandfather,"

Evie said. "You can stay home with Lorena and Tori. We can't all go."

"You haven't been to see Grandfather Reece once since he had his stroke." Kate stacked up the plates and set them beside the dishpan. She'd heat water later to wash them. Along with the breakfast dishes.

"More reason that I should go instead of you." Evie lifted her chin defiantly as she put the leftover pie back in the pie safe.

"Right, as if seeing Grandfather has anything to do with you wanting to go today. Maybe I want to go with Brother Mike." Kate looked up from wiping off the table.

"I can see you think he's cute. Who wouldn't? He's every bit dreamy." Evie sighed a little before she narrowed her eyes on Kate. "But you're too young, Kate. Way too young."

"And you're not?" Kate stood up and stared back at her.

"I'm sixteen already. And mature for my age. Besides, he likes me. I can tell by the way he smiles when he looks at me." Evie gave Kate a haughty look. "That's just something a girl can tell after she gets older. You'll understand someday."

"Oh, for heaven's sake." Sometimes Evie drove her crazy. Kate tried to swallow her irritation as she went on. "He smiled at everybody this morning. Even old Mrs. Jacobson. She must be close to a hundred."

"But not the way he smiled at me." Evie sighed again.

Kate blew some air out of her mouth. No way was Evie going to let her win this one. She might as well give in gracefully. "Okay, you go. But you'd better be nice to Grandfather Reece and not just keep making eyes at Brother Mike."

Evie frowned at her. "Whenever did you start worrying about being nice to Grandfather Reece? You're always fussing about how he keeps wanting to pray over you for this or that."

"Not since his stroke. Now all he wants me to do is read his Bible to him when I go over there. He's different. Like maybe he even understands about Lorena and the angels now."

"You're not an angel, Kate." Evie leaned closer to Kate till their noses were almost touching. "Really. You can trust me on this one. You're not an angel." She enunciated the last four words very distinctly.

"I know that, so leave me alone." Kate backed up a step. "But that doesn't change Lorena being my little sister. *Our* little sister, because that's what God wants. And I think Grandfather Reece would say the same thing if he could get the words out right."

"And I think you must be dreaming. You heard what Brother Mike said about Ella Baxter." Evie made a face. "That nasty woman. I don't know who's worse. Her or Miss Carla. But you know and I know that Grandfather Reece has always done whatever Miss Carla wanted. You can ask Mama about that. She'll say the same thing."

"It might be different now."

"Yeah, and the moon might come up and be purple tonight, but I don't think that's going to happen, do you?"

Kate didn't like losing arguments to Evie. She was usually the one demanding Evie open her eyes and stop dreaming up things that weren't going to happen. But even if she knew Evie was right, Kate couldn't completely give in on this one. "The Bible says if we have faith the size of a mustard seed, we can tell a mountain to move from one place to another and it will."

"Jesus must have been talking to Peter or James and John when he said that. Either that or nobody we've ever heard about had a mustard seed's worth of faith. And we aren't going to have a purple moon tonight either. We'll have to find another way if that's what it takes."

"Then we'll find it," Kate said. "I'll find it."

Evie's face softened. "Maybe you will, Kate. If anybody can, you will."

"Are you girls about through in there?" their father called back to the kitchen. "We need to get on over to your grandfather's."

Evie gave Kate a quick hug, yanked off her apron, and pushed her hair into place as she hurried toward the front door.

An hour later Kate was reading the fifth chapter of *Little Women* to Tori and Lorena on a blanket under the apple tree out back when they came. Grandfather Merritt led the way around the house with Ella and Joseph Baxter following him. His feet were hitting the ground hard and forceful, like he was marching.

Kate's heart jerked and then began thudding as she looked at her grandfather's face. She slowly stood up, letting the book fall closed without even checking which page they were on. Lorena looked up at Kate, scrambled to her feet, and edged behind her. Only Tori didn't seem to notice anything amiss as she called out a friendly greeting to Grandfather Merritt.

"Hello, Victoria. Kate." Their grandfather nodded curtly at them. He ignored Lorena completely. "Where are your mother and father?"

Kate felt as if somebody was grabbing the breath right out of her chest, and for a second her head spun around. Then she pulled in one slow breath and then another. She had to be ready to do battle. They were going to try to take Lorena. She licked her lips and made herself speak even as the blood began beating through her so hard that it made her voice shake. "They're at Grandfather Reece's house. You knew that already."

"I knew your mother was there," Grandfather Merritt said. "It's anybody's guess where your father might be."

"Daddy doesn't drink on Sundays." It was the very worst thing Kate could have said, but the words were out. There wasn't any way she could take them back.

"Then that's without a doubt the only day," Ella Baxter muttered.

Grandfather Merritt frowned at Mrs. Baxter and said, "I'll do the talking."

"You need to go away." Kate stared straight at her grandfather. Lorena wrapped her arms around one of Kate's legs and held on so tightly she almost pulled Kate off balance.

He glared at her. "Young lady, you are not permitted to talk to me that way."

Kate's eyes didn't waver on his as she pushed all the force she could into her voice and repeated, "Go away!" She wanted to pick Lorena up and run, but she couldn't outrun them. She had to try to face him down. She had to believe the Lord would help her face him down.

This time he pretended she hadn't spoken. "We're here to get the child." His eyes touched on Lorena, who buried her face in Kate's skirt. "Mr. and Mrs. Baxter will provide her a good home."

"Yes, little child, come see what I've brought you. A brand-new doll." Ella Baxter held a doll out toward Lorena. It had black curls painted on its china head and was dressed in a pink satin dress. Kate had never owned a doll half as pretty.

Mrs. Baxter kept talking in a sweet voice that didn't sound a bit like her usual voice. "We'll make new clothes for it. And we've fixed up a nice room for you. With pink walls and ruffled curtains."

Lorena didn't even look toward the doll. "No. Don't like pink," she said against Kate's leg. "I have to stay with my angel. With Kate." She raised her head a little to peek up toward Kate. "Mommy told me." Her eyes begged Kate to say it was so.

Tori was on her feet now too as she stared first at Kate, then Grandfather Merritt. She looked scared, but Kate couldn't worry about Tori. It was Lorena who needed her. The Lord was going to give Kate the power to win this battle. She knew he was. She had way more than a mustard seed's worth of faith about that. He wanted her to take care of Lorena. She was sure of that.

"She doesn't want to go with you," Kate said.

Grandfather Merritt mashed his mouth together and snorted as he glared at Kate for a moment before he spoke. "This is a matter for adults to decide, Katherine. It's not something you as a child can understand. Now these good people have decided to give this gypsy child a home, and she will learn to be grateful for it. And that's that. I don't want to hear one more word out of you." He glowered at her. "Not one."

Kate didn't say anything, but she tightened her

hold on Lorena. The Lord would help her. He had to. Even if he had to strike Grandfather Merritt down the same as Grandfather Reece.

"This is ridiculous," her grandfather muttered as he covered the distance between them in two steps. He grabbed Lorena and yanked her away from Kate.

Lorena screamed and Kate reached for her. They clasped hands. Tori started bawling.

"Let go of the child this instant, Katherine," Grandfather Merritt ordered.

But Kate wouldn't let go. She would never let go. She felt as if her grandfather was trying to peel her very skin away. "No!" she yelled.

"You will do as I say." He raised his hand and struck Kate across the face.

It was a hard blow that stunned Kate and knocked her off balance. She fell and hit her head on the apple tree. For a second she was dazed. She sat up slowly as something warm began running down beside her eye. She put a hand up to it and was surprised when her fingers came away red with blood.

Lorena jerked free from Grandfather Merritt and stepped between him and Kate. "Don't hurt my angel sister. Please, don't hurt Kate. I'll go with you." Tears rolled down Lorena's cheeks as she held her hand up toward Grandfather Merritt.

Kate was weeping too. She wasn't going to win this fight. The Lord wasn't going to help her, and she couldn't do it by herself. She swallowed her tears enough to say, "Let me tell her goodbye."

Grandfather Merritt pulled out his handkerchief and threw it toward Kate. "Here, use this. We'll wait on the back porch."

"Tori, go get Lorena's clothes and the doll she sleeps with." Kate picked up the handkerchief and dabbed at the cut on her head before she held her arms out to Lorena. "Come here, baby."

She held her close against her without worrying about the blood that dripped down her face to mix with her tears. Lorena nuzzled her head up against Kate. For a minute they sat like that without saying a word. Then Kate whispered in her ear, "I'll still take care of you, Lorena. They can't keep me from doing that. I'll always take care of you. I promise."

"I know," Lorena said. "You're my angel."

If only, Kate thought as she tightened her arms around Lorena and kissed her head. "I love you."

"I know." Lorena reached up and touched the hurt place on Kate's head. "I know."

Then she pushed away from Kate to stand up. She looked at Kate a long moment before she turned and slowly began walking over toward the porch where Grandfather Merritt and the Baxters were waiting with the bundle of clothes Tori had gathered up. Lorena let Ella Baxter take her hand and lead her away.

Kate sat like stone as they walked around the

house and disappeared from sight. Tori's voice came through to Kate as if it was traveling through a long tunnel. "What do you want me to do now, Kate?"

"Nothing. There's nothing to be done." Kate stood up and began walking across the field toward the woods. Her feet felt as if they each weighed three hundred pounds, but she kept walking. She was glad when Tori didn't follow her. Then she noticed the handkerchief her grandfather had given her still in her hand. She opened her hand and let it fall to the ground.

27

They were on the porch saying their goodbyes when Victoria came running across the yard. As soon as Victor saw her, his throat tightened and his muscles went stiff. Something bad had happened. Something he probably wasn't going to be able to fix, from the look on Victoria's face. There were so many things he couldn't fix. He could bend and shape iron horseshoes to keep a horse's feet in good shape. He could fashion iron pins to fix a broken gate or wagon, but the iron of life wasn't so easily shaped. Instead it was always bending and twisting him. He dreaded her news as his mouth went dry. Too dry. He needed a drink.

It was almost a relief when she leaned on the porch rail by the steps and blurted out her news between pants for breath. "They came and took Lorena."

At least everybody was still breathing. That was the way he'd always felt in France with the German shells exploding around him. It came down to whether you and the buddy next to you were still breathing when the battle was over. Sometimes the buddy wasn't. Then you were just glad to feel the breath filling your own lungs.

Not that he didn't see Victoria's sorrow and, even more, ache for Kate.

Nadine hurried off the porch to wrap her arms around Victoria. Evangeline followed her halfway down the steps before she stopped to look back at Brother Mike as if hung between her duty to her family and her desire to stay close to the young preacher.

"Who came?" Nadine asked. "Her parents?"

"No, no." Victoria had caught her breath and was able to talk now. "Mr. and Mrs. Baxter. Grandfather Merritt brought them. Kate told him to go away, but he wouldn't." Victoria looked up at her mother with big sad eyes. "He hit Kate."

"Your grandfather hit Kate?" Nadine's voice sounded disbelieving.

Victoria nodded her head. "But she didn't cry. Not then. Not until she had to tell Lorena goodbye." Then Victoria burst out in tears.

Nadine put her arms around Victoria and looked over the top of her head at Victor. In her eyes he could see the same thought he'd had earlier. He wasn't going to be able to fix this. Pain came with life, but it was doubly painful when it was your daughters hurting.

On the porch behind them, Brother Mike's smile was gone. "Is there some way I can help?" he asked.

Carla pushed her heavy frame up from her porch rocker to face the young preacher. "There's no reason to help, Brother Mike. This is the way it was supposed to be. The way Orrin said before he was felled by the stroke. My sister will give that child a fine home. Finer than she could have ever had with those vagabond parents of hers who just pushed her out of their car and drove off without her. That's for certain."

"Or with me?" Nadine straightened her shoulders a little and looked directly at Carla. "Is that what you're saying?"

"Well no, I don't think I said that exactly." Carla fanned herself with her handkerchief as beads of sweat popped out on her upper lip and forehead. Then she patted her upper lip with her handkerchief and pulled herself together. "But now that you say so, it's the truth. You have your hands more than full already with your three girls. Ella doesn't have any children. So it's only fair and reasonable."

"How about for Lorena? What's fair and reasonable for her? Or for Kate?" Nadine asked. She looked ready to burst into tears like Victoria, who was sobbing beside her.

Victor stepped down off the porch past Evangeline to stand beside Nadine. He wanted to hold Nadine, tell her he could make it right, but she wouldn't believe him. He put his hand on her shoulder, and she shot him a look as if she blamed him for what his father had done.

On the porch, Carla made a sound of disgust. "Kate needs to remember her place. That child . . ."

Nadine's father stirred in his chair and waved his good hand to silence Carla. "Wrong," he said. "Wrong."

"See." Carla looked pleased. "Listen to what your father's trying to tell you. You're wrong. Ella will be a wonderful mother."

"I'm sure she will." Brother Mike tried to his smile back on his face. "Perhaps we pray for her and for the little girl. For al' His voice held a hint of panic as b Brother Orrin grew more agitated.

Nadine looked at her father an Victoria to Victor. She rushed ba steps to lean over her father. "F the doctor told you not to g want to have another st voice level and calm a hand to calm him. She gl

"Run get some cool water and a cloth."

He jerked his hand loose from Nadine even as Evangeline ran into the house for the cold water. The screen door slammed behind her.

"No," he said as he gripped the arm of the chair he was sitting in and breathed in and out two or three times.

"Now look what you've done," Carla was saying. "Gotten him all in a stir."

"No," Nadine's father repeated. "Wrong. I was wrong." He said the words very distinctly. "Kate right."

"Why, Orrin, what in the world are you saying?" Carla asked. She looked over at Brother Mike. "Poor man. That stroke has addled his thinking. That can happen, you know, with a stroke. The doctor told me that right up front so I'd be prepared."

Brother Orrin raised his head and glared at her efore he picked up his cane and poked it against er. He looked like he wanted to preach her an ire sermon, but all he came out with was ush, woman."

rla's eyes flew open wide as she gasped, l, I never." She gave her husband a look as owly lowered herself back down in her The chair groaned under her weight. She ack and began fanning herself furiously of the wooden handled cardboard fans have carried home from the church. She

kept muttering under her breath, but Victor didn't try to hear what she was saying. The woman was always talking. She seemed to need the sound of her voice in her ears.

The new preacher shifted back and forth on his feet as if he wasn't sure what to do first. He was still young enough to think he could fix things.

Brother Orrin ignored him and Carla as he looked at Nadine and said, "Tell . . . Kate. Sorry." His chin drooped down on his chest, and for one awful moment Victor thought he might have suffered another stroke, but then he realized the old preacher was coming face-to-face with the same thing Victor was. He couldn't fix it and he knew it.

At least Victor hadn't been part of the reason for the problem. He wasn't, but his father was. His father who thought he could control everything that happened in Rosey Corner. But he hadn't always been able to fix everything either. Victor closed his mind to old, long-dead memories. Weren't there enough problems dancing around him already? He didn't want to think about Press Jr. and how his father hadn't been able to fix that. All he'd been able to do was get a boat with grappling hooks and drag the bottom of the river until they found Press Jr.

His father had made him go out in the boat with him along with Graham, who had pointed out the place where he'd seen Press Jr. go under. But

Press hadn't been there. He'd been downriver. When the men working the hooks had snagged the body and pulled it up out of the water, Victor had been sure it couldn't be his brother. It didn't matter that he recognized the blue college sweater with his fraternity symbol on the sleeve. The face was all wrong—misshapen and gray. Not a thing like Press Jr. It wasn't until his father cried out, fell across the body, and began weeping that Victor knew it had to be his brother.

Victor had never seen his father cry. It frightened him. The sight of his brother's dead body frightened him. He was ten years old and only hours before had nearly drowned himself. Would have drowned if Graham hadn't pulled him out of the river. He began sobbing uncontrollably. His father rose up off Press Jr.'s body and backhanded Victor across the face. Victor had to clutch the hard metal seat to keep from falling out into the river. His father drew back his hand to strike him again.

The owner of the boat, a man Victor had never seen before, grabbed his father's arm. "What's the matter with you, man? You've just lost one son. Are you trying to kill the only one you have left?"

Victor's father shook off the man's hand. For a moment he kept his arm raised as he glared at Victor. Beside Victor, Graham spoke up. "If you have to hit somebody, hit me. Not the kid."

Graham's voice was flat, nothing at all like he usually sounded. It was as if all the dives into the river to try to save Press Jr. had drained the life out of him too.

Graham didn't duck away from the blow or raise his hands to ward it off. Victor's father's fist smashed into Graham's face with a sickening thud. The force of the blow knocked Graham against the side of the boat, which began rocking back and forth violently. The man in the front of the boat was yelling again, but Victor didn't hear what he was saying. He was staring at his father, who was trying to keep his balance, and then at the body of Press Jr. behind him. The legs jerked and one of the hands with its fingers curled into claws reached up into the air. The whole body rolled toward Victor and one of the eyelids popped open.

Victor stared at what was left of Press Jr. and wondered if he was glad he was moving or sorry. Then he leaned his head over the side of the boat and began heaving. Nothing came out but hot water. It seemed like days had passed since he'd last eaten, and he didn't care if he ever ate again. He almost hoped his father would knock him back into the river. If he did, Victor was going to sink down below the velvety water and not make a ripple. But then he thought about those grappling hooks digging into his body and he heaved again.

A hand grabbed his shoulder and held him steady as he heaved. For one crazy moment Victor thought his father was holding him, but when his heaving stopped and he turned to look, it was Graham, not his father. His father stood in the middle of the boat, staring at him with disgust. Then he turned away from Victor to sit back down beside Press Jr., who once more was still as stone. Victor's father kept his fists clenched like he thought there might yet be someone he could hit to change who had lived and who had died.

And now he had hit Kate. Victor's own hands curled into fists. He squeezed them so tight that pain shot up past his elbows to his shoulders. Somewhere behind him in a voice that seemed far away, the young preacher was trying to pray over the sound of Victoria's sobbing and Carla's muttering and Brother Orrin's labored breathing. Victor wondered if Nadine was listening to the man's prayer. She had always been more devout than Victor. More sure of her faith. Sure the Lord would help her through whatever troubles came. Maybe she'd be sure he'd help her through this one too, but would he help Kate?

Kate. He had to go find her. Victor blew air out of his lungs and made his hands relax before he took hold of Victoria's shoulders. "Hush, baby. You're going to make yourself sick," he said softly and pulled her close against him. Behind them the preacher stopped praying. Victor didn't know if he said amen or not. Evangeline might know. She'd come back outside with the water. She stood there staring at Victor with a face almost as pale as the white rag Nadine wrung out to dab off her father's face.

After a moment, Victor leaned down to look right into Victoria's face. She was still crying. He took out his handkerchief and gently wiped away the tears on her cheeks. "Shh. It will be all right."

She looked at him as if she wanted to believe him, as she hiccupped and swallowed her tears. He handed her the handkerchief so she could blow her nose. Once she was through mopping up, he asked, "Where's Kate now?"

"I don't know. She went into the woods. I yelled at her, but she just kept walking. She didn't even look back." New tears slid out of the corners of her eyes and made tracks down her cheeks.

He hugged her again as he looked over the top of his head toward where Nadine was ministering to her father. She didn't look up. "You stay with your mother and Evangeline. I'll go find her."

"But what about Lorena?" Victoria asked.

"One daughter at a time," he said. He turned her loose and walked across the yard and through the gate. He didn't look back at Nadine. He wanted to, but he was afraid of what he might see on her face.

28

He found Kate on the bank of Graham's pond, staring out at the water. She didn't turn her head to look at him even after he sat down beside her.

"I'm sorry, baby." Blood was seeping out of an ugly scrape on her forehead. Victoria hadn't told them Kate was bleeding. He felt the hurt of it all the way down in his gut. "Did he do this to you?"

His fingers trembled as he dabbed at the wound with his handkerchief. Inside he was raging. He wanted to hit somebody in return. No, not just somebody. He wanted to smash his father into the ground and stomp on him.

"I told him to go away." Kate's voice wasn't much above a whisper. "I thought God would help me. That he'd make him go away. I thought I had enough faith. That I could be Lorena's angel like she kept saying. But I couldn't." Now her voice carried pain. "Evie told me. She said there was no way I could be an angel. She was right."

Finally she turned to look at him, and the bruise in her eyes was far worse than the cut on her head. The scrape would heal quickly. Not so the bruises to her soul. He knew, for he carried like bruises inside himself. "You're still Lorena's angel," he said.

"Lorena didn't want to go with them. She cried." She looked back out at the water. "An angel who can't protect you is not much good."

"You can go see her."

"I told her that." She kept her eyes on the water. "But Grandfather Merritt may not let me make it true."

"We'll make him." Victor put his arm around her shoulder, but she stayed stiff under his touch.

"Nobody makes Grandfather Merritt do anything."

He didn't see any need in pushing useless words at her. Words she wouldn't believe. Words even he couldn't believe. He couldn't make his father do anything. Even if he was able to smash him to the ground. He could only sit there beside his wounded daughter and share her pain. And try not to think about how much he could use a drink.

It was hot there on the pond bank. Not a breath of air came off the water to cool them. Now and again a ripple disturbed the surface of the water when a fish came up to check out a bug. Behind them the bushes rustled, but when Victor turned his head to look, he could see nothing there. Perhaps Fern on her way past them to her cedar palace. He was just as glad she didn't show herself.

The minutes passed, didn't get any easier. The sun began to head toward the western horizon. The pond bank got harder, but still they didn't move, as if waiting for some miracle to spring out of the water and change everything.

At last Kate spoke. "Do you believe in God?" She kept her eyes on the pond.

Nobody had asked him that since he'd come home from France. Over there it was a question often voiced but not always answered. No sense risking a wrong answer when at any moment a man might be sent straight out into eternity to discover the true answer once and for all.

Victor stared out at the pond too and wished Nadine was there to answer her. Or Aunt Hattie. Neither of them had ever once doubted that the Lord walked beside them even through the worst of times. That's when the good Lord carried you, Aunt Hattie always told him. They would know the words to say to keep the joy from leaking out of Kate's heart.

At last he said, "I believe there is a God." What kind of man would tell his young daughter any different? And it wasn't a lie. He did believe there was a God. He just had never been sure he'd done anything to deserve his favor. But Kate surely did. Kate had always been a mirror of joy.

"I don't." Her voice was flat and devoid of feeling. "If there was a God, he wouldn't have let them take Lorena when she didn't want to go. He wouldn't have let that happen."

Her words stabbed through him. *If there was a God.* How could a loving God let bad things happen? But bad things did happen. Over and over. The war was proof enough of that.

The pond in front of him faded away, and he was back in the shattered forests of France, moving into the face of German fire, fearing each step could be his last, but going forward nevertheless. What other choice did he have? What other choice did any of them have? It was war. Shells blew men apart whether they carried belief of the Lord in their hearts or not.

Half the men in his company were dead, their bodies scattered through the woods before they advanced a half-mile. But their orders were plain. Overrun the German guns or die trying. They'd gathered to pray before they'd gone over the top of the trenches to begin their assault on the Germans. Perhaps the Germans were praying too. When darkness fell and the only light was the artillery shells exploding over their heads, they crouched down in holes dug out in the mud and tried to keep the cold rain off their heads with their blankets, too miserable to sleep. Victor's teeth chattered so violently that he feared the Germans would hear and aim their artillery straight toward his muddy hole. A hole that would become his grave. He shut his eyes and tried to make his body believe he was back home in Maudie McElroy's feather bed with Nadine cuddled close against him.

The next morning those still breathing ate their meager rations, climbed out of their holes, and forced their legs to carry them forward. The artillery had turned the trees into giant rooted toothpicks. Fragments of the branches rolled under their feet in the mud and made for hard going. Sometimes they stepped on something soft and dared not look too closely for fear of seeing whatever was left of one of the men they'd exchanged greetings with just the day before. And finally they took out the German guns.

Victor stumbled over the top of the earthen barrier and fell right on top of a dead German soldier. He stared up at Victor with lifeless eyes. He wore a German uniform, but he could have been Victor. He looked that much like him. He'd come halfway across the world to kill a man who looked just like him.

He scrambled away from the body. Then he slowly crept back for another look, sure he'd been imagining things. But the man had his eyes and nose and mouth. He stared at the dead German, mesmerized even as he heard his captain yelling at him. There was something unnerving staring down at what you would look like if you were dead. Victor's captain yelled again. Victor reached down and yanked one of the buttons off the man's uniform. He didn't know why.

That afternoon he took shrapnel in his shoulder, and the war ended for him just as it had ended for his German twin earlier in the day. He'd made his slow way back through the lines to the medical tents and then sat half out of his head with pain and watched other men waiting for treatment die. The artillery went on booming. He wasn't sure he could really hear it or if it was an echo in his head that would never go away. He thought he should say a prayer thanking the Lord for letting him live when so many others had died, but that seemed wrong. What about him was any worthier of continuing to breathe than any of the others? Than the German boy who had looked like him? Victor had put his hand in his pocket and felt the button. And he'd been glad for the pain in his shoulder.

He kept the button. It was in a cigar box under the Purple Heart he'd received for being wounded, under the letter from Nadine that said his mother had died of influenza, under the scrap of yellowed newsprint that reported the death of one Negro soldier from Rosey Corner, Bo Johnson. On the bottom rattling around with the button was an Indian-head penny Press Jr. had pitched to him the week before he died.

A box filled with death. It was stuck back in the corner of the wardrobe in the bedroom. He hadn't pulled the button out of the box to look at it since he'd put it there. There was no need. He knew exactly what it looked like. He didn't know why he'd kept it. There was so much he didn't know. And now he didn't know what to say to his daughter who was hurting.

"Come on, baby. Let's go home. Your mama will be worried about you." He stood up and held his hand down to her. She let him pull her to her feet. "Besides, it's going on night. Old Ruby will be waiting at the barn door to be milked, and somebody has to feed the chickens before they go to roost."

Too late Victor remembered that gathering the eggs had been Lorena's job, as Kate got a stricken look on her face. "She won't get to see the baby chicks hatch out," Kate said. "The old red hen went to setting last week, and Mama put extra eggs under her. Mrs. Baxter doesn't have hens."

He didn't try to tell her that Lorena could come see the little chicks. Kate was right about that. Who knew what the Baxters would let her do? And could be it might be for the best to make a clean break, if indeed the break had to be made.

Kate followed him obediently through the woods back to the house. It was the quietest he could ever remember her being. Usually she was pointing out the birds that flew up in front of them or badgering him for a story about the crow family in the back pasture. Or laughing when he ran his face into a spiderweb across the path. Quiet didn't suit Kate.

Nadine was on the front porch watching for them when they came across the yard. Victoria and Evangeline stood a step behind her, frozen in the late afternoon light. His beautiful girls, blessings he didn't deserve. Blessings he couldn't protect from the hard knocks of life.

He thought of the cut on Kate's forehead again and wanted to walk on past the house straight to his father's house and knock him out of the chair he'd be sitting in on his back porch. Sitting there no doubt full of the righteous assurance that he'd done what needed to be done. For the good of them all.

Victor didn't notice Aunt Hattie on the porch until she stood up from the swing and set it to shaking on its chains. She and the girls followed Nadine down off the porch but stood back as Nadine wrapped her arms around Kate.

"It'll be all right, sweetheart. I don't know how, but it will," Nadine whispered into Kate's hair.

"Of course it'll be all right," Aunt Hattie said behind them. "You're still breathing. That little girl child is still breathing over at Ella Baxter's house. Ain't nobody died."

Kate pulled away from her mother to look at Aunt Hattie. "It feels like somebody did."

Aunt Hattie mashed her mouth together and

shook her head. "That's just because you ain't never felt what it really feels like when somebody you love ain't never comin' home no more. And that's good. I'm glad you ain't had to feel that way yet in your young life." The old woman stepped over closer to Kate and peered at the scrape on her head. "Appears you's bleedin', child."

"Grandfather Merritt," Kate started and then stopped. She stared down at the ground for a long moment before she went on. "I shouldn't have talked back to Grandfather Merritt. He slapped me."

Nadine pulled in a sharp breath and reached out to wrap her arms around Kate again, but Aunt Hattie put a hand out to stop her.

"Give the child time to tell us all of it." Aunt Hattie peered into Kate's face. "And that's what made your head bleed?"

"It made me fall down, and my head hit the apple tree."

Across from Victor, Nadine mashed her fist against her tightly closed lips. He could tell she was having to fight to hold back the words she wanted to say and that she was hurting just as much as Kate. Maybe more. He wanted to go to her, but he stayed rooted to his spot, afraid she'd push him away.

"All right then, now that we've heard what happened, we'd best flush it out good and bandage it up proper so's you won't have to live with the sight of an ugly scar each and every time you look in the mirror to comb out your hair."

Aunt Hattie ordered Evangeline and Victoria to fetch the things she needed. Soap and water. A chair off the porch before the light faded too much to see what she was doing. Bandages and tape. Watkins' brown salve.

Once everything was gathered, Nadine held Kate's hair back while Aunt Hattie wrung out a cloth and began to bathe the cut. Evangeline shivered and looked away, but Victoria leaned in close to be sure to see it all. Her nose was still red from her earlier tears. Kate stared straight ahead without flinching, while Aunt Hattie probed the cut to be sure it was clean.

Victor watched a moment before he asked, "What are you doing here so late, Aunt Hattie? Did my father tell you to come?"

"No, I ain't seen Mr. Preston for a spell now. The man must be washin' his own shirts. I just got the feelin' in my bones that my doctorin' might be needed. Like as how the Lord maybe was tapping me on the shoulder, tellin' me there was something to do. 'Course I didn't know about this scrape." Aunt Hattie concentrated on dabbing her rag on the cut a few times before she went on. "I was thinkin' more on soul sickness." She raised her eyes to peer across at Victor.

He met the little black woman's eyes. She'd

always known him too well. He said, "Kate is feeling low in the spirit."

"Uh-huh, 'pears the soul sickness is goin' round." Aunt Hattie laid her rag down and picked up the salve.

"I prayed, Aunt Hattie," Kate said softly. "And nobody listened."

Aunt Hattie clucked her tongue and shook her head. "Now, you just wrong about that, child. Wrong as can be. The good Lord always listens. Always." When Kate didn't say anything more, she went on. "Your mama here can tell you that. Even in the worst times. Even when it seems like there ain't no answers to be had. Ain't that right, Nadine?"

"It is," Nadine answered without a hint of doubt in her voice. "But there are times when you have to trust the Lord's answer to come in his own perfect time."

"Or the answer ain't what you's wantin' to hear but you know the Lord is gonna get you through it anyhows. Like when my Bo died. When you feel like there ain't nothin' out there to trust, that's when you's got to trust the most. That's how a body's faith grows." Aunt Hattie put her hand on Kate's shoulder as if she could transfer some of her mighty faith straight to the hurting girl. "If ever'thing was honey and sweet berries all the time, there wouldn't be no need for faith."

"But what can I do, Aunt Hattie? I know Lorena's crying. I can hear her in my heart."

At Kate's words, Victoria began sniffling, and Evangeline reached over to put her arm around her little sister. Nadine's lips were mashed together in a fierce line that Victor knew meant she was fighting tears too.

"Hush that crying now." Aunt Hattie frowned over at Victoria before she turned back to Kate and squeezed her shoulder.

"It ain't over yet, children. It ain't over. We got to keep trusting, and when the time comes, the Lord will let us know what to do."

"How?" Kate asked.

"I can't tell you that, but we'll know. We'll surely know. So long as we don't turn our backs on him." She didn't look over at Victor, but he knew the next words were for him. "There is some who do that. Who give up on the Lord helping 'em. I ain't knowing how they stand the pain. Don't let that be us, children. The good Lord won't never turn his back on us. He's a lovin' us right on through this."

She made it sound so easy. Like all he had to do was turn around and face the other direction. Look up and say, *Here am I, Lord. Take away my pain.* Take away the way his mouth wanted a drink. Out behind the house, he heard old Ruby bawling. He was glad for the reason to walk away from Aunt Hattie's sermon.

"I've got to go milk the cow," he said.

He hated himself every step out to the barn, but even before he fastened Ruby in the stanchion, he climbed up into the loft and found the bottle he'd hid in behind one of the posts. He twisted off the top and breathed in the smell. He stared at the bottle in his hand for a long moment while below him Ruby bawled for her feed before he tipped it up and let the fiery liquid roll down his throat.

29

Aunt Hattie shook her head as Kate's father disappeared around the house. Then she lifted her hands to the sky and started talking to the Lord as though he was perched up on the first star of evening, leaning his ear down toward her to hear her better.

"Lord Almighty, we's hurtin' down here, but you knows that already. You hears ever' beat of our hearts, sees ever' tear that trickles down off our cheeks. You even keep count of the very hairs on our head. So's we knows you can take care of this little child. And that you can help our hurtin'. And Lord, we's gonna do our best to be ready if'n you give us something to do back. Let your powerful love fall down on us, Lord. Amen and amen."

Aunt Hattie stared up at the sky as her prayer

shot straight up to heaven. Kate looked up too and waited to feel something, certain some answer would spring up in her heart, but she just felt empty. Useless and empty. She couldn't feel even a speck of that mustard seed of faith left in her soul. No mountains were going to get up and walk anywhere for her. That thought scared her. She'd heard Grandfather Reece preach about how it was empty hearts the devil had no problem moving into. She didn't want to be wicked.

Aunt Hattie must have read her mind, because before the sound of her amen faded into the gloaming, she stepped right in front of Kate, grabbed hold of Kate's chin, and gave it a little shake as she stared her straight in the eye. "Don't you push yo'self down in no hole of your own making, Katherine Reece. Not even the thickest blanket of suffering can smother out our Lord. I knows that for a fact. I been covered with some mighty thick blankets now and again myself, but the good Lord was always right there beside me holdin' my hand. He's got hold of your hand too and he ain't goin' nowheres. You'll see. And you be ready in case he speaks somethin' for you to do."

Aunt Hattie turned loose of Kate's chin and took another look toward the barn out back of the house, then she shook her head again and headed off through the gathering twilight toward home. They watched her till she was out of sight. Then

Evie picked up the washpan and salve. Mama carried the chair back up on the porch, and they went inside to go through the motions of putting supper on the table.

After a while, Kate's father carried the milk in from the barn. The smell of whiskey rode on him into the kitchen. Kate's mother turned her face to the wall away from him. He reached a hand out toward her, but he didn't touch her before he turned around and went back to the barn.

Kate picked up the bucket of milk to pour it through the cloth strainer into the brown crock jar. Her mother rubbed off her face with her apron and helped hold the cloth in place as the milk seeped through.

"We'll have to make butter tomorrow," she said. "And the beans will need picking again. This might be the last picking if it doesn't rain soon."

Talk of the garden helped them be able to sit down and eat their crackers and cheese, but nobody wanted the last of the brown sugar pie. Kate thought about offering to carry it out to her father, but then she didn't. As they got ready for bed, Evie chattered some about the new preacher, but it seemed like weeks instead of hours had passed since Kate's heart had done a flip-flop when he smiled across the table at her over their bologna and cheese dinner.

Tori looked at her cot and then climbed into the

bed with Evie and Kate. It was hot with all three of them in the same bed, but none of them complained. Tori kissed Kate's cheek, and Evie squeezed Kate's hand and whispered, "She'll always be our sister no matter where she is."

"Three sisters plus one," Kate said into the darkness of the room.

Tori scrambled back out of bed to stand and say, "Her name is Lorena Birdsong."

Kate and Evie got back up to hold hands in a circle with Tori and repeat it again. "Her name is Lorena Birdsong." And somewhere out of the depths of Kate's heart, there was an echo.

Once back in the bed, Evie and Tori settled down and went right to sleep. Kate told herself to do the same. It didn't do Lorena a bit of good for Kate to stare out at the grainy darkness with wide-open eyes. Even so, she didn't go to sleep. The clock had already struck twelve when her father came into the house, but she didn't get up to see if he needed help even after he bumped into the table. She couldn't get up. She had to lie quiet as a mouse to keep from disturbing Evie and Tori, but then after her father landed on the couch and started snoring, Kate's arms and legs kept twitching as though ants were crawling around inside her skin. She had to move.

Slowly she scooted down to the end of the bed and out from in between Evie and Tori. She stood there a moment to see if she'd woken them, but neither of them stirred. The silence of the house pushed in on her until she could barely breathe. She grabbed the pillow off Tori's bed and tiptoed out of the bedroom, past her father on the couch. In the moonlight coming in the windows she could see he had on his shoes, and she felt guilty. She should have helped him take them off. She stopped and carefully loosed the laces, but she didn't try to pull the shoes off for fear of waking him. Better to let him sleep it off.

It would be better if she could sleep it off. Not drinking. She was never going to touch that stuff. Ever. But the grief of how she had failed Lorena. That's what she wished she could sleep off.

She stuffed the pillow behind her in the swing and stared out at the trees bathed in moonlight. The sound of tree frogs, katydids, and crickets filled the night air. The swing swayed back and forth and then stopped when she kept her feet up on the swing seat. Kate felt very alone. She wished one of the barn cats would come find her on the porch and settle in her lap, but they would all be sleeping on the hay or hunting midnight mice.

The screen door eased open and her mother stepped out onto the porch. "Too hot to sleep?" she asked softly.

"I guess," Kate said.

Her mother came over to stand in front of Kate. "You want to talk about it?"

"I don't know." Kate moved her feet to make room for her mother to sit down on the swing beside her.

"We could pray about it," Mama suggested.

"Aunt Hattie already did," Kate said.

"So she did."

Her mother pulled Kate's feet over into her lap and began massaging them without saying anything more. They sat there and let the night noises fill their ears. It should have felt peaceful, but it didn't. After a while, Kate asked her mother the same question she'd asked her father earlier over at the pond. "Do you believe in God?" She kept her eyes on the few stars the moonlight wasn't blotting out.

Mama's hands stilled on Kate's feet for a moment before her fingers began kneading Kate's toes again. "Yes," she said.

"Even when he doesn't answer your prayers?"

"Yes," Mama said again.

"Have you ever said a prayer that wasn't answered?"

"I have. I prayed for my mother to live with all my heart, and then after she died, I prayed even harder for my baby sister. Poor, dear little Essie. She was so pretty. She lived almost three weeks."

Kate felt ashamed when she remembered how Aunt Hattie had taken her to task by saying at least she and Lorena were still breathing. Just the thought of losing her mother was enough to make her heart hurt. Kate reached over and clutched her mother's arm. "Promise you won't die, Mama. Not for a long, long time."

"I plan to hold your babies and be an old granny." Mama put her hand over Kate's and squeezed it, but then she smiled a little sadly as she said, "You know, I asked your father to make that same promise to me before he went overseas to the war."

"Did he promise?"

"He wanted to, but he said no truthful man could make that kind of promise going to war. That no one had the promise of tomorrow. And I knew that then and I know it now. Tomorrow is in the Lord's hands, but your father promised something even better. He promised his love for me would never die. That no matter what happened in the war, his love would always be alive in my heart." Kate's mother looked toward the window into the living room. Through it, they could see Kate's father asleep on the couch.

"Did you believe him?"

"I believed him, but I wanted more. I wanted him back with me. I wanted to have babies with him. I wanted to have you." Mama poked Kate's leg with her finger. "So I prayed and prayed that the Lord would let your father come home to me."

"And he did."

"He did." Kate's mother rocked the swing back and forth with her foot. "And I was thankful. Am thankful. A lot of men didn't come home."

"Like Aunt Hattie's son."

Mama's face looked sad in the moonlight. "That's right. And nobody could have prayed more than Aunt Hattie did for her Bo."

"Then why did the Lord answer the prayers for Daddy and not for him?" Kate was trying hard to understand.

"He answered both our prayers. Aunt Hattie would be the first to tell you that. Just in different ways. We can't escape the sad parts of living no matter how much we pray. In wars, people die. Mothers die having babies. Bad things happen. But that doesn't mean we should stop believing. Or praying. The Lord helps in good times and bad. And he'll answer your prayers too, Kate. However he sees best."

"It can't be best for Lorena to be there with the Baxters instead of with us. It just can't."

Mama sighed. "I know. I feel the same way, but maybe we're wrong. Why don't we pray for Ella Baxter? That she will be a loving mother to Lorena."

"I don't want to pray that. I want Lorena to be here," Kate said.

"Come here, sweetheart." Her mother held out her arms and waited while Kate shifted in the swing to lean back against her. She wrapped her arms around her and kissed the top of her head. "It'll work out. I don't know how, but it will."

"Do you think Mrs. Baxter let Lorena say her name before she went to bed?"

"I don't see why not. It's very important to Lorena."

They sat there in silence then for a while as Kate's mother kept the swing swaying gently. Inside Kate's father cried out in his sleep and her mother and Kate both jumped a little and held their breath until they heard him snoring again.

Kate said, "Daddy must be having a bad dream."

"Sounds like it."

"About the war, you think?" Kate asked.

"Probably."

"The war must have been really bad."

"Worse than anything we can imagine."

"Is that why he drinks?" The question was out before Kate thought about it. She and her mother never talked about her father drinking in plain, out-in-the-open words, as though as long as they didn't mention it, it might not be happening.

Mama's voice sounded a little stiff as she said, "That's a question your father will have to answer for you."

"I hate it when he drinks."

Her mother tightened her arms around Kate. She kissed her hair again. "So do I, sweetheart. So do I."

The swing chains creaked a little as they

swayed back and forth. After a minute, Kate said, "Daddy hates it too."

"Then he could quit." The stiffness was back in Mama's voice.

"Do you think he could?" Kate twisted her head around to look at her mother.

"A person can do whatever he sets his mind to," Mama said firmly, but then she relented a little. "It might not be easy, but with the Lord's help he could do it. He doesn't seem to want to ask for that help."

"Maybe he's afraid to ask."

"Why would anyone be afraid to ask the Lord anything? The Lord wants us to ask him for help." Her mother sounded almost angry.

"Maybe he thinks the Lord doesn't love him enough to help him." That was the way Kate was feeling. If there was a God and he was love the way the Bible said, then the problem had to be that she, Kate, wasn't lovable enough.

Again her mother's arms were tight around her. "The Lord's love never changes. It's always there, has always been there for us, and will always be there. All he wants is for us to step into that love. He won't make us do that. He won't make us pray and ask for help, but he's there ready. Always there ready to help."

"But we're supposed to love one another too, aren't we?"

"Yes. Love thy neighbor as thyself."

"I can't love Ella Baxter." Kate hesitated a moment before she blurted out, "Or Grandfather Merritt."

"Sometimes it's hard to love those around you." Mama didn't sound shocked by what Kate said. "Even those we love the most."

Kate didn't know what to say to that. Her mother's words didn't make any sense.

After a few more minutes of gently swaying in the swing, her mother rubbed the hair back from Kate's face and kissed her forehead before she said, "It's been a long day. We'd better go to bed and try to sleep now." She moved to stand up.

"Can I just stay out here and sleep on the swing tonight? It's too hot inside." Kate stayed on the swing.

"I suppose, but you need to shut your eyes and go to sleep."

"I will. I promise."

Her mother leaned down and kissed her before she went back inside. Through the window, Kate saw her stop beside the couch. Gently she eased Kate's father's shoes off his feet. She set the shoes down beside the couch and began to move away when he cried out again in his sleep. Her mother stopped and stood there for a moment before she turned around to reach over the back of the couch to stroke his head.

Out on the porch, Kate's heart didn't feel quite as empty.

30

Nadine softly rubbed Victor's hair. It was wet with sweat from the heat of the night, the same as it had been that night so long ago when she'd sat propped up in the bed in Maudie McElroy's attic room and watched him sleep before he had to board the train to go away from her to the war.

She was so frightened that night. And angry. The anger had surprised her. He'd courted her, made her fall desperately in love with him, and then he was leaving her. He hadn't had to volunteer for the army. He wasn't draft age. Her anger that night had been childish, selfish, but easier to feel than the heart-rending fear that she might never look on his face again.

Now all these years later she was angry with him again. A different kind of anger. A slow-burning, sorrowful anger. How could he have gone out and found a bottle on this night when Kate needed him? When she needed him. She pulled her hand away from his head and went on into her lonesome bedroom.

She sat by her open window and tried to imagine a breeze coming in as she wondered what better things she might have said to comfort Kate. Dear Kate who couldn't bear standing in front of a door that she couldn't open. Even Victor's drinking wasn't that big an obstacle for her. She was used to it. Not happy about it, but used to it. It was different having a father who drank than a husband who did. There was no reason for a daughter to think she shared any of the blame for a father who chose booze over her. But what else could a wife think? Something wasn't quite right between a man and his wife when that man had to get comfort from a bottle.

Nadine loved Victor every bit as much—even more, much more—than she had loved him the day she held his hand in front of that preacher in Edgeville and promised to stand by him through sickness and in health till death parted them. Then she hadn't really known much about love except what she read in the Bible and in her poetry books. Two people becoming one, cleaving together. Jacob working fourteen years for Rachel. David's desire for Bathsheba leading him into sin. Evangeline searching for her love only to find him too late. Romeo and Juliet.

It seemed in literature the greatest loves always ended in tragedy. And sometimes tragedy struck in real life. She was a firsthand witness to that when her mother had reached for her father's hand and pulled it to her cheek before she breathed her last. So it was no wonder that she imagined all the worst possible things when it was time for Victor to board that train to go over there to fight the war. People you loved too much died. Tragically.

And what could be more tragic than a war? She'd read reports in the newspapers of American soldiers dying in France. Regular doughboys just like Victor.

So she clung to him that last night and begged him to promise her he would come back. "I can't live without you."

He held her and stroked her cheek as he tried to allay her worries. "You won't have to. I'll be back."

"Promise me. Swear to it on my mother's Bible." She twisted away from him to reach for the Bible on the table beside the bed, but he stopped her.

"Look at me, Nadine."

She turned back to him. He put both hands on her cheeks and held her face very close to his. His breath was warm against her lips. Her heart began beating faster. She loved him so much.

"Please promise me," she whispered.

His eyes were intent on hers as he said, "You and I both know that some things can't be promised. We can want to promise. We can even make promises in our hearts, but tomorrow isn't promised to any of us. We trust that tomorrow will come. We pray that tomorrow will come. We have hope for tomorrow, and tomorrow does come for most of us." He paused for just a second as if to be sure she understood how important his next words were. "So while I can't swear to it on your mother's Bible, I do believe we will have a tomorrow. And I want you to believe that too."

"I do believe it," she whispered.

He dropped his lips down to cover hers. She wrapped her arms around him and gave every inch of herself to him. She thought he was through talking, but then he lifted his lips away from hers. Again he was looking into her eyes as though he could see into her soul.

"This promise I can make. Be assured, Nadine Reece Merritt, and know without any doubt in your heart that I love you more than life itself, but if that life is taken from me before I see you again, then you can still be sure that my love for you will live beyond the beating of my heart and on in eternity."

She didn't have to wait for eternity. He came home to her and brought his love back to her. Armistice was declared in November, but it took time to get the paperwork for his release through and the released soldiers transported back across the ocean. Each day seemed a week long as she waited to feel his arms around her again.

Finally the day came late in January 1919 when Father Merritt went with her to Louisville to meet Victor's train. He said he needed to buy stock for the store, but she thought he needed to lay his eyes on Victor to be sure he was all right the same as she did, even though he would never admit to it. They caught the train in Edgeville. Nadine stared out at snow-covered fields and didn't try to force idle chatter between them. Instead she thought about the last time she'd seen Victor almost a year and a half ago. She knew that man. The man who had ridden the train away from her. She loved that man. Would the man riding the train back to her be the same? Was she the same? She could feel her heart pounding in her chest, and she couldn't be sure whether it was from excitement or fear. Perhaps they would both be too changed.

Victor's father's thoughts mirrored her own. "He'll be different," he said abruptly as they bounced across the countryside toward Louisville. "War changes men."

Nadine pulled her eyes away from the window to look at the ramrod-straight man in the seat beside her. He wasn't looking at her, but instead was staring toward the front of the train as if he could already see Victor and knew how changed he'd be.

She said softly, "We're all changed."

"Not so much," he said.

She didn't say anything to that. She'd learned it was an exercise in futility to disagree with Father Merritt. The man did not entertain the possibility of being wrong. And perhaps he wasn't wrong. Perhaps he hadn't changed. But she knew the changes in herself. She wasn't the same girl Victor had left behind and promised to love forever. She'd mourned a baby. She'd watched the influenza take Victor's mother and many friends. She'd separated herself from her father. She'd learned to work beside the hard man who sat beside her without caring if he ever offered her a kind word.

She looked away from Father Merritt's face down at her hands clutching her purse. Through the soft velvet cloth she felt the edges of the last letter she'd gotten from Victor. She took courage from the memory of the words crowded on the thin paper.

I can't wait to see your beautiful face and hold you in my arms once more. I want to kiss you until our lips are numb. The other guys talk about going home to their wives and sweethearts, but I pity them because they aren't coming home to you. I am the luckiest man in the world to have you for my wife. Sometimes I think my heart will explode—it's so full of love for you. So I try to count the ways I love you but I never get through counting. If I did, the ways would number more than the stars in the sky.

He hadn't forgotten his love for her, and she hadn't forgotten her love for him. It would be all right. Love would conquer any problems or changes the months they had been apart might cause.

Until he spoke, she had almost forgotten Father Merritt there beside her while she shut her eyes and mentally read Victor's words of love. His voice was not only an intrusion into her thoughts, it was almost as if Father Merritt had read her mind. "Young people think love will solve everything. It doesn't. It doesn't even come close."

"Were you never in love?" Nadine asked.

"Once, long ago." He stared straight ahead, and his voice was matter-of-fact, with no more feeling than if he were talking about how much sugar was left in the sugar barrel at the store.

His words surprised Nadine. She hadn't expected an answer. She'd never known the man to share any personal feelings with anyone, and yet he seemed to be waiting for her to ask more. The throb of the train wheels carried them forward toward Louisville, but there were miles to go before the outskirts of the town. "With Miss Juanita?" she asked.

"No. Juanita and I were ill matched. I should have let her go back to Virginia, but she was already carrying Preston Jr. I couldn't give up my son."

"Then who?" Nadine was curious not only about his past, but why he was telling her.

"Her name was Estelle Glynn."

Nadine's mouth dropped open. She couldn't believe what he was saying, but why would he lie about such a thing? Her throat felt tight as she pushed out her next words. "My mother?"

He didn't seem to notice the shock in her voice or even that she had spoken. Instead he almost seemed to be talking to himself. "She was a beautiful woman. Much like you." He glanced over at Nadine and then turned his head back to the front.

Nadine stared at his chiseled profile and could not think of one word to say.

After a moment he started talking again. "I didn't think she'd turn me down, but she said she'd made a promise to a man of God. That no matter how she felt in her heart, she was honor bound to live up to that promise and the calling she felt from the Lord."

Nadine's world rumbled and shook just as the train did when they went over some rough track. She couldn't quite take in what the man was telling her. Surely he wasn't saying that her mother had once been in love with him. Her mother and father had been devoted to one another. That had been plain enough to see. While her father might have always been stern with Nadine, he'd been gentle and loving with her mother. Their house had been filled with peace and contentment until her mother died.

"My mother loved my father," Nadine said, with no doubt at all in her voice.

"Perhaps she did. I couldn't say for sure about

that, but I know she loved me. As sure as I'm sitting here beside her daughter, she loved me, but she had a calling. A man can fight another man. A man can't fight against the Lord." He stared down at his hands resting on his knees. Slowly he curled them into fists and then opened them back up and stared at his empty hands. "I turned my back on her, wished her dead. Love can turn to hate, you know." He looked over at Nadine.

"Not true love," Nadine said.

"True love." His voice was scornful as he shook his head at her. "You're not that young, are you? That you still believe in fairy tales and happily ever after?"

"I'll be twenty soon." Nadine refused to let him beat her down. She was not a child, and no matter what he might say, she did believe. If not in fairy tales, then in love.

"Then perhaps you are that young." He looked back down at his hands. "Time will teach you many lessons as it has me."

Nadine looked out the window and saw they had gotten to Louisville and the station was just ahead. She started to stay quiet, allow their conversation to die, but her curiosity got the best of her. "What lessons?" she asked.

"That with discipline a man can overcome anything. Anything. Love. Loss. Even hate."

"I don't want to overcome love. I want to feel love."

He turned to pin her against her seat with his hard gray eyes. "There may come a day when you change your mind. When love hurts too much."

The train screeched to a halt and he stood up. He pushed his way through the other passengers toward the door. He didn't look back to be sure Nadine was behind him. He expected her to follow him.

They stood together on the platform and waited for Victor's train. She was glad for the silence between them. She tried to push what he'd told her on the train into a far corner of her mind, but it kept sneaking out to worry her. She'd never known him to lie, even for kindness' sake, but he must have been deluded when he thought her mother loved him. It simply could not be true.

A train whistle sounded in the distance. The train bringing Victor home to her. Nadine let loose the past. What difference did anything Father Merritt said make? Even if it were true. The past was gone. This very moment in time was all she had for sure, and she intended to rejoice in the moment. She was going to grab happiness with both hands and let it pull her into the future with the man she loved.

Father Merritt stood back and watched with a disapproving eye as Nadine threw herself into Victor's arms as soon as he stepped off his train.

Victor lifted her off her feet and hugged her as though he'd never turn her loose. Her worries dissolved like mist on a hot summer day. He was changed. She saw that as soon as she looked at him. Lines creased his face that hadn't been there when he left. His eyes looked older, sadder. But at the same time his love for her had not changed. He paid no attention to his father there beside them as he laughed and then kissed her until she had to push him away to get her breath. He laughed again. It was a good sound. A sound she needed to hear.

Finally she said, "Aren't you going to say hello to your father?"

He kept his eyes on her face. "First things first." Then he kissed her again.

At last he pulled her close against his side and turned to look at his father. Neither man smiled or made the first move to embrace or even shake hands. "Hello, Father. It was good of you to come meet me."

"I had to buy stock for the store anyway, so it worked out."

"Yes, of course. Have you gone to see about that already?"

"No. We just got here a few minutes ago. I have time before the train back to Edgeville. We have three tickets for the five o'clock train."

"That's kind of you, but Nadine and I are going to stay in Louisville and see the sights tonight.

I'll see if they will exchange our tickets for tomorrow's train."

Father Merritt's eyes narrowed. "It's a little cold for taking in any sights."

Victor's arm tightened around Nadine. "Not for the sights we're going to be seeing." He smiled down at her.

Nadine's face flushed hot as she stared down at the platform. Victor laughed, and Father Merritt pushed a snort of air out his nose. "You always did lack self-control."

Victor's eyes on his father were icy cold. "I spent months in the trenches practicing self-control. I ran into the face of enemy fire when I wanted to run the other way. Don't tell me I lack self-control." His voice softened. "But I lived and today I'm home with my beautiful wife here beside me. It's time to celebrate being alive."

"Very well. Do what you will." His father reached into his coat pocket and pulled out two of the tickets. He handed them to Victor. "If they won't trade them for tomorrow's train, you'll have to find your own way home."

"We can do it," Victor said.

"We can only hope so. For the Merritt name to live on." Father Merritt turned away and then stopped and looked back at them. "Hattie says the baby Nadine lost was a boy. So that means the next one could be as well."

"That's good to know," Victor said, but he

didn't sound as if he was thinking anything good.

"Yes. Yes, it is," his father said before he turned and walked away without even once smiling at his son home from the war.

Victor felt stiff against her as they watched him walk across the platform without giving an inch to anyone he met. "I'm sorry," Nadine said. "I should have come alone."

"No, no. I'm glad he came with you." Victor shook himself a little and laughed again. "But now I'm even gladder he's gone." He picked her up and swung her around. "You are the most beautiful thing I have ever seen. Let's go see if Maudie has saved us a room so we can get started on making that Merritt heir Father wants so much."

But they hadn't ever made another boy after that first dear baby who had not lived in Nadine's womb. Three beautiful girls. Enough for her and enough for Victor—he'd never shown the first hint of disappointment that she hadn't had a boy child. But not enough for Father Merritt.

She had nearly died with childbirth fever after Victoria was born, and the doctor said she'd never have another baby. There would be no sons born to her and Victor. But oh, the beautiful daughters they had. Evangeline Estelle, Katherine Reece, and Victoria Gale. Nadine stared out the window and whispered another name. "And her name is Lorena Birdsong." Her little angel daughter.

Surely Kate was right in that the Lord had sent

the little girl to them. That was the only way they could have planted her in their hearts so quickly and so deeply. Without closing her eyes, Nadine sent up a fervent prayer for Lorena. But like Kate, she heard Lorena crying in her heart. If only she could hold the child in her lap and comfort her. If only she had someone to hold and comfort her.

31

The dreams tormented Victor. He'd given up years ago thinking they'd fade away. He'd always had bad dreams. Even before the war. His mother used to tell him to quit reading the far-fetched stories he loved, that reading all those fantastic and impossible imaginings planted strange seeds in his brain that took root and gave flower to scary monsters that jumped out at him when he went to sleep.

But he didn't dream about men from Mars or three-headed monsters or one-eyed Cyclops. He dreamed about water swallowing him up. About dead eyes staring at him. About gray hands reaching for him to pull him into the world of the dead. And then came the war with hundreds more reasons for nightmares. The mud and the water mixed, pulled him down into a soupy muck he couldn't escape.

His father told him he could—with self-control. Aunt Hattie told him he could—with prayer. Nadine told him he could—with love. And the love had worked for a while. He'd had the dreams, but he'd also had Nadine. Now he felt as if he were losing her. As if he wasn't man enough to keep her. He couldn't even be man enough to help a little child in need. Or his own daughter. He'd let the siren call of the alcohol lure him away from the ones who needed him to be strong for them.

His weakness disgusted him. Out in the barn, he'd stared at the bottle in his hand and hated it while at the same time wishing it held more whiskey. Enough to make him numb to the pain of his failings. He thought about using his belt to hang himself from one of the barn rafters. Had gone so far as to pull his belt off. He sat in the hayloft and stared at the leather belt a long time. The leather was worn white where the buckle hit.

Kate will find you. The words whispered through his head. In his mind's eye he could see Kate coming to the barn after the sun came up in the morning to tell him breakfast was ready. She would try to rescue him even though it would be hours too late. He'd pass the nightmares on to her. He couldn't do that to Kate.

He stood up and put the belt back on. He needed to get it out of his hands. Away from his neck. He didn't really want to die. He wanted to live. He just needed to figure out how.

He spotted the bottle there in the chaff of the hay beside him. It wasn't completely empty. He could tip it all the way up and get that one last swallow his tongue could taste just looking at it. He picked the bottle up and threw it against the far wall. It shattered and fell into the hay. He'd have to pick up the pieces of glass tomorrow to keep the girls from getting cut. Victoria and Lorena liked to play with the kittens in the loft.

The thought made Victor sad. Lorena wouldn't be there tomorrow to play. His father had decreed they couldn't invite the child into their hearts. His father said she couldn't be a Merritt. But then wasn't that what his father had always said about him too? And wasn't he a Merritt in spite of it?

His father was wrong about Lorena too. She was already snuggled down in their hearts. Nothing Preston Merritt did was going to change that now.

Victor stumbled to the house. Where else could he go? His home. His family. The door hadn't been bolted against him as yet. The bedroom door perhaps, but not the door to the house.

He was relieved when Kate didn't come out to help him. He sat down on the couch and thought about taking off his shoes, but what difference did it really make? He was tired. Bone weary.

And tomorrow he had to shape more iron. Tomorrow he had to find a way to be strong.

The dream had come to mock him. To show him he wasn't strong. That the mud and water were going to pull him down and under and he'd never be free of it. When he cried out, he half woke. At first he thought he was imagining the touch of Nadine's hand on his head. As if he'd gone back in time to when things were easier between the two of them, to when she thought she could carry him past the dreams. When they both thought their love would be enough. Before hard times made him swallow his pride and ask his father for credit at the store. His girls had to eat.

He kept pushing his breath in and out slow and steady, as though he were still asleep, but every nerve in his body was awake to her touch. He wasn't dreaming. She was there behind him. Her fragrance settled around him, and it was all he could do to keep from reaching up and taking her hand in his. He wanted to hold her, to feel her body against his, to know without a doubt that she loved him.

She lifted her hand away from his hair, and he heard the whisper of her bare feet against the floor as she went back into her bedroom. Their bedroom.

He opened his eyes and stared out at the dark air in front of him. He wanted to follow her. More than he wanted to breathe, he wanted to follow her, but he stayed on the couch. He was afraid. What if she slammed the door in his face and locked it for all time? Yet she had laid her hand on his hair. She had caressed his head. She didn't want a drunken husband, but she did still want him. He saw that in her eyes, heard it in her voice. She wanted them to have the closeness they'd shared when the girls were young, before the years had worn away at him. Before he'd surrendered to the drink.

You can quit. The words were there in his head. *For her, you can do anything. You smashed the bottle in the barn. You can smash the other bottles. Not just for her. For the girls. For yourself.*

He had planned to quit every week for months. But then the bottle would be before him, and his resolve would weaken. He couldn't bear the pain without the booze. It would be too hard to live without the drink. He didn't know how to quit. He was afraid.

Be strong and of good courage. The voice was speaking in his head again. That was Scripture. He didn't know the Bible the way Nadine did, but he did know that. Perhaps a psalm penned by King David as he remembered how the Lord had given him courage and strength against Goliath. Victor didn't know where in the Bible the words were, but he knew they were words he needed.

He could be strong and have courage. He'd proved that during the war. He'd been afraid but he'd beaten down the fear and fought the enemy.

He could do the same with this enemy that threatened to destroy him now. But he couldn't do it alone. He needed help. He sat up on the couch and tried to pray. Every word that he pushed up toward the Lord felt weak and wrong. It was as if the ceiling above his head was a barrier bouncing his puny attempts at praying back at him.

Nadine knew how to pray. Hadn't he depended on her prayers while he was in France? Didn't he know she prayed for him still, even though he defied those prayers? Suddenly he knew it wasn't the barrier over his head making his prayers weak. The barrier he needed to knock down was between him and Nadine.

Be strong and of good courage. He stood up. For a minute he was frozen there in the grainy dark of the night. Maybe he should go wash the smell of liquor off him before he went to Nadine. But he was afraid that if he went out the back door, he wouldn't find the courage to come back inside no matter how much the Scripture words echoed in his head.

He didn't knock on the bedroom door. It wasn't closed, so he just stepped through into the room. He stood inside the door and breathed in her fragrance. His heart was doing a funny skip inside his chest, and his hands felt sweaty. He thought about trying to pray again, but he had no words. Perhaps the Scripture running through his head would be prayer enough.

She wasn't in the bed. Instead she sat by the window, her head in her arms on the windowsill. Her white nightgown and the scarf she used to tie back her hair while she slept showed up plainly in the dim light drifting through the window. For a moment he thought she might be asleep, but then she sat up. She didn't turn to look at him, but she knew he was there.

He made himself move across the floor even though he sensed no welcome in the air. He went right over to stand behind her and put his hands gently on her shoulders. Her body felt stiff under his touch. "Nadine," he said. "I need your help."

"Oh?" Her voice was only a whisper in the dark. "You mean to get Kate to bed? I told her she could sleep on the porch."

"No, not Kate. Me. I need you to help me." It was hard for him to say the words. To admit he was weak, even though he knew he was. A man was supposed to be strong for his wife.

Her shoulders stayed stiff as she stared out the window. Her silence beat against his eardrums. His hands turned to rock on her shoulders. He shouldn't have come in here. He'd made a mistake. He had in fact surely been dreaming when he'd felt her hand stroking his head. And now they would no longer be able to pretend that things might someday get better. The barrier that had built up between them was too thick to penetrate.

He moistened his lips and pushed out the words. "I'm sorry. I had no right to ask for your help. I don't deserve your help or prayers after the way I've let you down. Let everybody down." Sorrow mashed down on him and made it hard to breathe as he lifted his hands off her shoulders and turned away.

"Wait," she said.

He stopped. His heart started pounding as if he'd just had to back a fractious horse into the corner of the fence to nail his shoes on. It took all his strength to stand there and wait for her next words.

"Do you love me?" She turned half around in her chair to look toward him.

Her face was only a shadow in the dark, but he heard her heart's longing in her words. And her fear. He knelt beside her and found her hands in her lap. He grasped them and peered at her face. "I told you once that I loved you more than life itself and that if I lost my life, my love would live on in your heart forever. Nothing has changed. Nothing could ever change that. I do love you, Nadine Reece Merritt. With my whole heart, with every fiber in my being."

"Then why do you drink?" Her voice was stiff,

but she didn't try to pull her hands away from him.

"Because the demons chase me and I am weak." He hesitated for a moment but made himself go on and say it all. "Because I fear you no longer love me."

"Oh, Victor, I could never stop loving you. You are my life. You and our girls." She did pull a hand free then, to lay against his cheek. "And you aren't weak. You are the strength of my heart. Even when you're drinking."

"No one could love me then. Not even the Lord."

"That's not true." Her voice was gentle, yet sure of what she was saying. "The Lord always loves us no matter what we do. He'll help you. You just have to ask."

"I tried to pray, but I couldn't come up with the right words. I thought if you prayed for me—"

She jumped in front of his words. "I do pray for you, Victor."

"Your prayers haven't kept me from drinking."

"No, but they always brought you home."

"I'm home now," Victor said. "I want to stay here. Pray that I won't fail you again, Nadine."

"All right. If you will pray the same for me, for I have surely failed you as often as you have me."

"No," he started to protest, but she put her finger over his lips.

Then she put both hands on his head. "Here we

are, Lord, two sinners standing in the need of prayer. Help us. Amen."

So simple, but he felt the prayer rise up out of her heart and his. "Amen," he echoed.

For a few minutes they stayed motionless in the dark of the night. She in her chair, with him still on his knees beside her. No lightning bolts flashed in the dark. No trumpets sounded, but somehow Victor felt different. It took him a minute to understand why. He felt loved. By Nadine. By the Lord.

Nadine stood up and took his hand to pull him up beside her. "The night has cooled. Let's go to bed."

Victor felt all atremble, the way he had years ago when he'd been a young man following Nadine up the stairs to Maudie McElroy's attic room.

32

The pink fingers of dawn nudged Kate awake. For a few seconds she didn't know why she was in the swing on the porch. The swing chains bounced against their hooks as she sat up and leaned her head to one side and then the other to get the crick out of her neck. She was stiff all over and her left arm was asleep from where it had been mashed up against the back of the swing. She shook it to start it tingling awake.

Her brain came awake too as everything that had happened the day before slammed back into her head. Grandfather Merritt taking Lorena and giving her to the Baxters as if she were no more than a stray kitten. Kate touched the scrape on her forehead. She didn't really care about that. She'd had lots of bumps and bruises. It was the empty ache inside her that made her want to walk down the porch steps and off into the woods to get lost in the trees.

Not that that would solve anything.

And she couldn't really go off walking in the woods in her nightdress. People would be talking about her the way they did Fern. It was bad enough Kate was standing on the porch in broad daylight in her old gown worn so thin a person could see right through it. Who knew when a car might go by out on the road or a neighbor might take a shortcut through the yard on his way to the store?

She picked up the pillow off the swing and held it in front of her as she backed toward the door. Lorena would be laughing her head off at Kate if she were there. Lorena liked to laugh. Kate wished she could believe Lorena would have a reason to laugh this morning at Ella Baxter's house, but she couldn't.

Kate paused before she went in the front door to look up the road in the direction of the

Baxters' house. She couldn't see even a bit of its roof, but she knew it was there. She knew Lorena was there. "Your name is Lorena Birdsong," Kate said very softly.

The sun was pushing more rosy light into the sky in the east, but it wasn't up. The tree frogs and katydids hadn't hushed their night songs. Behind her in the house, there was absolutely no noise of anyone stirring. She could go see Lorena before breakfast.

Her father wasn't on the couch, so maybe she was wrong about nobody being up. She peeked toward her mother's bedroom. The door wasn't quite closed, and through the crack Kate could see her mother curled against her father. They were both sound asleep.

They looked right lying there together, so right that a thankful prayer almost took wing in Kate's heart before she remembered that she didn't believe praying did any good anymore. If it did, Lorena would be in the other bedroom waking up beside Tori.

Kate tried to dress as quietly as possible, but Tori opened her eyes before Kate finished buttoning up the back of her dress.

"Go back to sleep," Kate whispered. "It's too early to get up. Mama and Daddy aren't up yet."

"You're up." Tori raised up on her elbow to look at Kate. She was still in Evie and Kate's bed instead of her own.

"Yeah, well, that doesn't mean you have to be."

"We could go fishing. They might bite this early."

"Not today." Kate ran her fingers through her hair.

"I guess it would be too sad. Without Lorena." Tori's mouth turned down. "Do you think Mrs. Baxter will let her go fishing with us sometime?"

"I doubt it. She probably doesn't think little girls should go fishing."

Evie groaned beside Tori. "Good gosh. Will you two hush up?" She squinted open one of her eyes and peeked toward the window. "The sun's not even up yet."

"Sorry," Kate said. "I was trying to be quiet."

Evie groaned again and pulled her pillow up around her head to cover her ears. "Then go be quiet somewhere else, for Pete's sake."

"Right," Kate whispered. She picked up her shoes and then put them back down. She was used to going barefoot. She didn't need shoes.

"Where are you going, Kate?" Tori asked.

"For a walk."

"Can I go too? I can get dressed fast." She swung her feet over the side of the bed.

"Not this morning." Kate kissed the top of Tori's head and pushed her back down on the pillow. "Tell Mama not to save any breakfast for me, but that I'll be back in time to wash the dishes."

Kate was almost to the bedroom door when Evie dropped her pillow away from her ears and whispered, "Give her a hug for us too."

The sun was just beginning to pop up over the horizon when Kate got to the Baxter house. She didn't go up to the front door. It was way too early for visiting, and she didn't want to visit the Baxters. She just wanted to see Lorena.

Kate settled down cross-legged behind the big forsythia bush in Ella Baxter's backyard. From where she sat, she had a good view of the outhouse but nobody could see her. She was beginning to feel more and more like Fern, out sneaking around in the early morning before anybody else was awake. Kate touched her hair. She hadn't even taken time to properly comb her hair. Fern didn't worry much with combs either. All Kate needed was a little axe.

Shivers tickled Kate's back. She looked over her shoulder, almost expecting to see Fern behind her, but no one was there. Kate was alone. With each minute that ticked by, she felt even more alone until she thought she might not mind Fern showing up to sit beside her.

Mr. Baxter came out the back door and made his way to the outhouse. Kate held her breath and sat perfectly still. He didn't look right or left, but kept his eyes on the ground as he walked the worn path. The hinges on the door creaked as he opened it and disappeared inside. Kate let out her breath and scooted around to the other side of the bush where she was sure he wouldn't spot her when he came out of the outhouse. While Joseph Baxter never seemed to have much to say, Kate was afraid he might say plenty if he caught her hiding in his yard spying on his outhouse.

Kate breathed easier when she heard the outhouse door creak open and shut again and then a few minutes later the house door slam. On the air she caught the smell of bacon frying. That was good. Lorena liked bacon.

Ella Baxter was the next one out the back door, but she didn't come up the path toward the outhouse. She was carrying a chamber pot that she emptied at the back fence. Again Kate eased around the bush to stay out of sight. Spying on someone from behind a bush wasn't as easy as Kate had thought it would be. She should have paid more attention to how Fern did it. Except that Fern was so good at it that most of the time Kate never knew she was there. Or maybe she wasn't. Who could be sure?

Kate didn't feel sure of anything right now. Where was Lorena? She always had to go to the outhouse first thing when she got up at Kate's house, but perhaps she'd used the chamber pot. Or she was sleeping late. Or Mr. and Mrs. Baxter had decided they didn't want the little girl and had given her away to someone else.

That thought, as far-fetched as it was, made

Kate's heart bound up into her throat. She was getting up to go to the door when the back door opened again and Lorena came out. She kept her head down as she walked slowly to the outhouse. She would never go to the outhouse alone at Kate's house. She was terrified that rats would come out of the corners to chew on her toes while she did her business. Even though Kate kept telling Lorena she'd never once seen a rat in the outhouse, she or Mama always went with Lorena to stand in the door to be sure no stray rats sneaked in to scare her.

Lorena hesitated halfway up the path and looked back over her shoulder toward the house. The back door stayed closed, and Kate couldn't see anybody peeking out the windows watching Lorena. In fact, in front of the house Mr. Baxter was starting his car to head off to work at his shoe store in Edgeville. Aunt Gertie said he was a different person when he was trying to sell a person a pair of shoes. All smiles and full of talk about this or that leather. Kate didn't know. She'd never been in his store there. They bought all their shoes at Grandfather Merritt's store.

But she was pretty sure that Mrs. Baxter would be at the front door waving goodbye to him, so she edged around the bush and peeked out. "Lorena," she said softly. "Over here."

Lorena jumped and then her eyes flew open,

and the next second she was throwing herself at Kate behind the bush. "Oh, Kate. I knew you'd come. I knew it."

"I told you I would." Kate kissed Lorena's forehead and then smoothed her curly hair back from her face. "How are things going? They're being good to you, aren't they? I mean, it must be nice having your own room with pink walls and everything."

"I like your house better." Lorena looked down at her hands and then back up at Kate. "Can I come home with you now? Please. I'll be very good. I promise."

Kate pulled her close and hugged her for a long moment before she pushed her back to say, "I want you to. You know I want you to, but you'll have to stay here for a little while. Till I figure out what to do."

"Did you ask Jesus to help you?"

"Not today," Kate said.

"Why not? Mommy told me Jesus would always help me. That's how come you're here, because I was afraid to go to the toilet by myself. Miss Ella said I couldn't use the pot inside during the daytime and that I'd better not mess my new underwear. It's real white." Lorena lifted the edge of her skirt to show Kate her bloomers with lace around the legs.

"They're pretty," Kate said.

"I don't like them. They're scratchy. I wanted

to take them off last night, but Miss Ella said only bomians did things like that."

"Bohemians?"

"I don't know. Some kind of bad people. I told her I wanted to be a bo- whatever you said." Lorena's lips trembled as she looked down at the ground. "She got all mad and hit me with her flyswatter."

"Oh, sweetie." Kate pulled her close in a hug again.

"It's okay. It didn't hurt much. But Miss Ella gets mad real easy. She got mad awhile ago when I told her rats might live in outhouses. She said if she had to go with me, she'd take the flyswatter too. So I shut my eyes and told Jesus I was scared, and then you were here." Lorena pulled away from Kate. She grabbed between her legs and hopped up and down as she said, "Now come on. I really got to go."

Kate peeked around the bush at the house. She didn't see any sign of Ella Baxter, so she ran to the outhouse and slipped inside with Lorena. Light sifted in through the cracks between the boards of the outhouse. There were spiderwebs up in the corners and it was stinky, but then all outhouses had spiders and were a little stinky. The seat with the two holes in it was too high for Lorena to get up on by herself.

"You need a stool," Kate said as she lifted Lorena up to sit on the hole.

Lorena kept a tight hold on Kate's arms. "Don't let go of me. I might fall in."

"No, sweetie. The hole's not that big."

Lorena clung even tighter to Kate. "It feels big to me."

"Just do what you have to do so we can get out of here."

"You're scared there are rats too." Lorena stared up at her with big eyes.

"No. No rats. I promise."

The little girl didn't look convinced. "Cross your heart?"

"Cross my heart." Kate didn't blame Lorena for looking doubtful. Too many promises to her had been broken already. But Kate was pretty sure no rats would pop out of the corners of the Baxters' outhouse, so a no-rats promise was probably safe to make.

"I don't like rats."

"I know. Tell you what. Before I leave, I'll sprinkle some rat-proof powder all around the door so if you have to go to the toilet when I'm not here, you'll be fine." Kate looked around as she helped Lorena down. "And look, there's an old bucket you can turn upside down and stand on to get up on the toilet. You'll be able to do it by yourself, Lorena."

"I'll still be scared." She reached down to pull up her underwear.

"I know, sweetie. I know, but even scared, you can do it."

"And you're sure about the rats?"

"I'm sure. No rats." Kate touched Lorena's cheek. "Remember rat-proof powder."

"And Jesus," Lorena added. "He can help me be brave."

A door slammed. Kate peeked out the cracks. Ella Baxter was on the back step looking toward the outhouse. "Polly! Where are you, Polly?" she called.

"Polly? Does Miss Ella have a cat named Polly?"

"No." Lorena sniffed a little and leaned against Kate. "She says I have to be Polly. I told her my name, but she said that wasn't a good name, that Polly was better and from now on I'd be Polly, but I won't. I don't care how much she hits me with her flyswatter. My name is Lorena Birdsong."

"Yes. Yes, it is. But maybe right now, you should yell back at her that you're coming."

Ella Baxter had started up the path to the outhouse. Kate had no idea what she might do if she caught Kate there with Lorena, but she had a feeling it wouldn't be anything Kate or Lorena wanted to happen.

"Coming!" Lorena yelled as loud as she could.

"What in the world are you doing in there?" Ella stopped on the path and stared at the outhouse.

Kate whispered, "Go on out. I'll come back

after breakfast. I'll knock on the front door." She gave Lorena a quick kiss and then scooted back as far as she could into the corner when Lorena opened the door and hurried out. She slammed the door closed behind her.

"Well, it's about time. And make sure you fasten that door good and tight. We don't want any possums taking up residence in there, do we?"

"No, ma'am." Lorena turned the wooden button to hold the door shut. She peeked through the cracks toward Kate.

"What are you doing?"

"Looking for possums. Are they like rats?"

"Bigger and meaner. Now quit poking along. I've got work to do." Mrs. Baxter grabbed hold of Lorena's arm and yanked her along the path toward the house.

"Can't I stay outside and play?"

"Not now. I told you. Chores first, then playtime. You've got to straighten your room."

"I haven't messed it up yet," Lorena said.

"Don't back talk me, young lady. You've been around that Kate Merritt too long. You need to learn how to behave, and I'm the one that can teach you." She kept fussing as she pulled Lorena through the back door and shut it behind them.

Kate waited a few minutes longer before she pushed against the outhouse door. The wooden button held tight. She softly bounced the door back and forth against the wood fastener in hopes that it might make the button slide around on its nail. No such luck. She was stuck inside there until somebody came up the path, and then what?

Her heart started beating a little faster. She wasn't exactly scared. She didn't think rats were going to start crawling out of the corners toward her. Spiders maybe, but not rats. She peered up toward the spiderwebs above her head and wished she hadn't thought about the spiders. She felt all crawly as she brushed through her hair with her hands and shook her arms and legs. She didn't see a spider anywhere, but that didn't mean they weren't there. The light was dim in the outhouse and some spiders were really small.

She squeezed her eyes shut and breathed in and out slowly to keep from screaming. The spiders would stay in their webs. They wouldn't hurt her. But who knew what might happen if Mrs. Baxter caught her there? She'd tell Grandfather Merritt and he'd say she couldn't come see Lorena ever. It had to be just a matter of time until Mrs. Baxter needed to use the toilet and then Kate would be caught for sure.

You could ask Jesus to help you. Lorena's words echoed in Kate's head, but the Lord hadn't helped her the day before. Even if she said the words, *Please, Jesus, help me,* out loud there wasn't anybody to hear them. Nobody. But the words seemed to rise inside her in spite of herself. It was as if she couldn't stop the prayer even though she knew nobody was listening.

All of a sudden the button on the outside of the door turned. Kate hadn't heard anybody come up the path. She hadn't heard anything at all. Her heart jumped up in her throat as her eyes flew open. She peeked out of the cracks between the planks on the door. No one was there. Gingerly she pushed open the door and peered out. No sign of anybody there. Not Mrs. Baxter. No one.

Kate stepped out of the outhouse, pushed the door shut, and locked it. She looked toward the house before she slipped around behind the outhouse where she could walk away without being seen.

And there was her rescuer, already climbing the fence behind the house to head toward the trees in the distance. Kate called out to her, but Fern didn't look back. She just kept walking.

33

You can't go bothering people before breakfast, Kate," her mother said while Kate poured water out of the teakettle into the dishpan. She was trying to sound stern, but Kate thought she really wanted to skip the lecture and just ask about Lorena.

They were alone in the kitchen. Tori had tagged

along with Kate's father to the shop, and Evie had gone to the store to get some salt.

"Mrs. Baxter didn't see me." Kate set the teakettle back on the stove.

"Yes, but you still should have waited." Mama paused a moment before she asked, "Was Lorena all right?"

"I guess, but she'd been crying." Kate didn't look at her mother as she concentrated on washing her father's coffee cup just so. A couple of tears slid out of the corners of her eyes when she thought about leaving Lorena there with Mrs. Baxter, but her mother didn't notice. The tears rolled down to join the beads of sweat on Kate's face. The kitchen was hot.

"Well, that might be expected. Poor child's had some upheavals." Her mother dropped a handful of the lima beans she was shelling into a pan.

"She said Mrs. Baxter wanted to change her name to Polly, and when Lorena said she wouldn't, she hit her with a flyswatter."

"Polly." Mama mashed her mouth together and shook her head. "I don't know what Ella's thinking." She sounded almost like she was talking to herself, before she blew out a breath and looked up at Kate. "But I suppose there's nothing wrong with the name Polly."

"I'm not calling her Polly," Kate said as she attacked the dried egg and ketchup on Tori's plate.

"No. Not unless Lorena decides she likes the name."

"She won't." Kate propped the clean plate in the draining pan and started scrubbing on the skillet.

Her mother sighed and picked up a new bean to shell. "You're no doubt right about that. Her name is important to her. It's her last connection with her mother."

"Do you think her parents will ever come back to get her?"

"I don't know. Who knows what might have happened to them after they drove away from Rosey Corner? It's awful to be so poor."

Kate wiped the skillet dry with a tea towel and looked around for any dishes she might have missed as she said, "But we're poor too, aren't we? We don't have money."

"We may not have a lot of money, but we get by. We don't go hungry." Mama's voice sounded stiff.

Kate wrung out the dishrag and draped it over the edge of the cabinet. "But what if Grandfather Merritt quits letting us run a tab at his store?"

"He won't."

Kate carried the dishpan out the back door and threw the water out in the yard. Some hens came running to frantically peck at the bits of food in the dishwater. Kate went back in the kitchen and sat down at the table beside her mother. She picked up a handful of the lima beans and began hulling them. "Is that why Grandfather Merritt can tell people what to do in Rosey Corner? Because people owe him money for the stuff they buy?"

Mama was quiet for so long that Kate didn't think she was going to answer her, but at last she said, "No, I don't think that's it. I think it has more to do with your grandfather's strength of character and how he feels about Rosey Corner. While he may seem harsh at times, I believe he really does want what's best for the community. The same as Father always wanted what was best for the church."

"He doesn't want what's best for Lorena." Kate stared at the beans in her hand. "Neither did Grandfather Reece. He wanted Mrs. Baxter to have her."

"Not now. With all that happened, I forgot to tell you what Father said yesterday. He told me to tell you he was wrong and you were right." Mama put her hand on Kate's arm and looked straight into her face. "I don't think I've ever heard him say he was wrong before."

Kate stared at her. "Can't we just go get Lorena back? She wants to come, and we want her to be here. Mrs. Baxter doesn't even act like she likes her."

Kate's mother reached across the beans in her lap to give Kate a hug. "I wish I could make all this better, but I can't. All I can do is pray that an answer will come. An answer that will be best for Lorena. And for you."

Kate shifted uneasily in her chair. She couldn't tell her mother she didn't believe in prayer anymore. Mama thought prayer could solve everything, but Kate knew that wasn't true. So what if Fern had let her out of the outhouse right after a prayer had sort of sprung up inside of Kate's head all on its own. That didn't mean a thing.

Evie came in the back door and set the salt down on the table. She looked at Kate. "Grandfather Merritt told me to tell you not to go see Lorena. He didn't know you'd already been over there and I didn't tell him, but he said you had to stay away from Lorena so she could get used to being with the Baxters."

"But I promised Lorena I'd come back after breakfast. I can go, can't I?" Kate begged her mother. "I have to. I promised."

Mama studied the lima bean in her hand for a long moment before she finally looked up and said, "You can go, but you have to be respectful of Mrs. Baxter."

"But she's been hitting Lorena with a flyswatter."

"I've waved a flyswatter your way a few times myself when you needed it."

"That's different," Kate said.

"How so?" Mama looked at her with raised eyebrows.

"You love us. Mrs. Baxter doesn't love Lorena."

"Now, Kate, you can't be sure of that."

"Mama, she can't love her. Not and try to change her name to Polly. She just wouldn't do that if she loved her."

Before Kate could go back to see Lorena, she had to help finish up the lima beans and then carry some food and a raisin pie to Grandfather Reece's house. When she got there, Grandfather Reece had his Bible marked at Luke 11 for her to read to him. That was the chapter with the Lord's Prayer in it.

Grandfather Reece had to know those verses by heart, but he shut his eyes and seemed to absorb the words as Kate read them. Then when she got to the ninth and tenth verses about asking and receiving, seeking and finding, knocking and it opening up, he reached over and poked the Bible with his finger, then poked her. She knew he was preaching at her even though she was the one reading the Scripture and he wasn't saying a word. What she didn't know was how he knew she felt all prayed out and empty.

So it was already the middle of the afternoon before Kate finally walked up to the Baxters' front door and knocked on the screen door. She wanted to just yell for Lorena, but she'd promised her mother to be respectful of Mrs. Baxter. Kate peered through the screen door in hopes of seeing Lorena running to the door. The living room looked like something out of a magazine, with a cream-colored couch and books perfectly arranged on a coffee table in front of it.

The room was not a thing like her sister's house. The only time Miss Carla's house got any kind of cleaning was when Kate's mother took pity on Grandfather Reece and straightened up the mess. Mama said cleaning wasn't Miss Carla's talent. Kate didn't think cleaning took talent, but if it did, then from the looks of Mrs. Baxter's living room, she had loads of that talent.

And it was quiet. Too quiet. Like nobody was home. Kate knocked again. She was about to turn away and go see if Lorena was out in the backyard when Mrs. Baxter came out of a side room into the living room. From the way she fluffed her hair as she came toward the door, Kate guessed she must have been lying down.

"Kate." Mrs. Baxter made no move to open the screen door. She looked surprised and not at all happy to see Kate. "Didn't your grandfather talk to you?"

"I haven't seen him today." It wasn't a lie. Kate hadn't seen him. "I came to see Lorena. Can she come outside?"

"No Lorena here." Mrs. Baxter had a smug look on her face.

"Not here? Then where is she?" Kate asked.

"Oh, you must mean Polly." Mrs. Baxter emphasized the name Polly.

"Polly? No, I mean Lorena. Lorena Birdsong."

Mrs. Baxter got a pained look on her face and covered her ears with her fingertips. "Please. That name is not to be spoken in this house."

"Why not? That's Lorena's name."

"Not anymore. She's my responsibility now and she'll be called what I say and not some gypsy Indian–sounding name. Polly Baxter is a good, respectable name." Mrs. Baxter put her hands on her hips and glared at Kate through the screen. "Now it's time for you to go home."

"But I have to see Lo—" Kate stopped when she saw the frown on Mrs. Baxter's face deepen. She had to get past this woman to see Lorena. Kate licked her lips and said, "I mean Polly."

"That's more like it." Mrs. Baxter smiled as if she'd beaten Kate in some kind of contest. Then her smile was gone as she narrowed her eyes on Kate. "But I'm afraid Polly can't have visitors right now. She needs to spend some time alone while she readjusts her attitude. And I'm sure it will be much better for her if you stay away from her. You're not a good influence, Kate Merritt. And you can tell your mother I said so. Goodbye." She stepped back and shut the wooden door in Kate's face.

Right before the door slammed shut, Kate called out, "Lorena!"

From somewhere back in the house, Kate heard a muffled cry and then her name yelled over and over. "Kate! Kate!"

Kate pulled on the screen door, but it was locked. She yanked on it, but it wouldn't open. She stood there and stared at the closed door and didn't know what to do.

From inside she heard Mrs. Baxter's voice. "Stop all that caterwauling or you'll have to stay in there an hour longer."

Lorena quit yelling, and things got very quiet again.

Kate's heart was pounding up in her throat, but she couldn't tear down the door no matter how much she wanted to. She turned around and went down the porch steps and out of the yard. Maybe her mother would know what to do.

Kate nearly jumped out of her skin when somebody put a hand on her shoulder. She whirled around to come face-to-face with Fern. "You scared me," Kate said when she caught her breath.

"Sorry." Fern's lips turned up a bare bit. She had on a faded red flowered dress and rubber boots. She had to be walking in puddles of sweat inside those boots. Her gray hair was tied down with a rolled-up kerchief around her head like an Indian headdress. Her face was clean. She didn't have the hatchet, and her eyes looked almost sane. Her mouth straightened out as all hint of a smile vanished from her face. "You help her. That woman put her in a closet. Little girl's scared."

"How do you know?"

"I looked through the window."

"But what can I do? Mrs. Baxter won't let me in."

Fern's eyes bored into Kate. "The back door's open." She grabbed Kate's shoulder and gave it a shake. "You help her."

Kate turned back toward the Baxters' house. Fern was right. She couldn't just walk away when Lorena needed her. Her parents would understand. Grandfather Merritt wouldn't, but her parents surely would. But even if they didn't, she had to do it. She looked around behind her, but Fern was gone. Kate took a deep breath and began creeping toward Mrs. Baxter's back door.

The back screen door was unlocked just the way Fern said. Kate slowly pulled it open, hoping against hope that it wouldn't squeak on its hinges. She hesitated just inside the door and looked around. The kitchen was empty. Kate's heart was beating so loud inside her chest that she was sure Mrs. Baxter would be able to hear it from wherever she was in the house. She should have asked Fern which closet in which room.

She held her breath and listened. When she heard steps in the next room, she looked around

363

frantically for someplace to hide if the steps started toward the kitchen. But they didn't. The front door opened and Mrs. Baxter went out on the porch. Kate pulled in a shaky breath. From behind a closed door on the other side of the kitchen, she heard a sniffle.

Kate moved silently across the floor on her bare feet and opened the door. Lorena was huddled back in the corner of the pantry with her feet pulled up under her and her hands over her toes. Her eyes flew wide open when she saw Kate, and she scrambled up toward her. Kate shushed her by putting a finger against her lips and pulled the door of the pantry shut behind her just as the front door opened and closed again.

"You better not be trying to open that door, missy," Mrs. Baxter called back toward the kitchen. "Not if you don't want to stay in there till bedtime."

Kate hugged Lorena close to her as her eyes adjusted to the dim light. The pantry was big enough to walk between two rows of shelves filled with canned food, cracker boxes, and sacks of flour and sugar. Kate had never seen so many groceries in one place except at her grandfather's store. The shelves stopped a couple of feet from the door where brooms and mops leaned against the wall behind a lard can on one side. On the other side, aprons and old flour sacks hung from hooks on the end of the shelves.

From somewhere in the house, music started playing and then a voice was talking. A radio. While the electric lines weren't to Kate's house yet, parts of Rosey Corner had gotten on the line last fall. Kate breathed easier. Perhaps Mrs. Baxter would be so tuned in to her program, she wouldn't be listening for any noises coming from the pantry.

Kate sat down on the floor beside Lorena and used her skirt tail to rub the tears off her cheeks. She whispered into Lorena's ear, "We have to be real quiet."

"I knew Jesus would tell you to come. I prayed." She threw her arms around Kate's neck and kissed her cheek a half dozen times.

"Then he must have told Fern."

"Fern?" Lorena leaned back to look at Kate. Her forehead wrinkled as she asked, "The woman who tried to chop off your nose?"

"She was just trying to scare me. She wouldn't really chop off my nose."

"Did she scare you?"

"A little," Kate admitted.

"Oh." Lorena grabbed Kate around the neck again and hugged tight. Her whisper was muffled against Kate's shoulder. "I was scared. Before you got here. The rats were coming to chew off my toes. I heard them sneaking up under the shelves."

"Shh, sweetie. It's all right. I won't let the rats

get anywhere close to your toes. I promise." Kate rubbed her hand up and down Lorena's back.

"I know." Lorena sniffed a little and raised up her head to look at Kate. "Can you sprinkle your special rat-proof angel powder in here? Like you did around the toilet this morning?"

"Sure. I've got some in my pocket." Kate put her hand in her pocket and pretended to pull out some powder to scatter around. "Now listen." She stopped talking and held her breath. "Do you hear anything?"

"No," Lorena whispered.

"Good. That means it worked." Kate kissed Lorena's nose and then pulled her close again. She stroked Lorena's hair and whispered nursery rhymes in her ear. In the middle of Little Bo Peep losing her sheep, Lorena's head relaxed against Kate's shoulder as she fell asleep.

Kate kept stroking Lorena's hair. How could she leave her here? She had to get her mother and father to do something. They had to. Even if they had to get the sheriff in Edgeville to come and sort it all out. Of course, the sheriff might just haul Kate away for sneaking into Mrs. Baxter's house without permission.

The radio stopped playing. Kate kissed Lorena and shook her a little. Lorena blinked open her eyes and looked at Kate.

Kate whispered in her ear. "Just do whatever she tells you to do, Lorena."

"But she gets mad when I say my name, and I have to say my name."

"Whisper it after you go to bed. And we'll be saying it real loud at our house. Your mommy will know."

Lorena sounded sad, but she said, "Okay."

Footsteps came toward the kitchen. Kate slid Lorena out of her lap down to the floor and quietly edged back in the corner behind the flour sacks. She held her breath as Mrs. Baxter jerked open the door.

Mrs. Baxter stared at Lorena. "You can come out now if you think you can behave, Polly."

"Yes, ma'am." Lorena sounded even sadder as she slowly stood up and went out into the kitchen. After Mrs. Baxter pushed the door shut, Lorena said, "Can I go play with my doll out on the porch?"

"I suppose. If you stay on the porch and don't get your feet dirty."

Kate heard Lorena go out of the kitchen, but she didn't hear Mrs. Baxter following her. Kate's heart began pounding again. Her breathing sounded loud in her ears. What if Mrs. Baxter heard her? Or opened the door again to get her apron?

"I can't get the door unhooked," Lorena called.

"Oh, my heavenly days. I've never seen such a helpless child." Mrs. Baxter sounded cross, but she walked across the kitchen into the next room.

"I think we may have made a big mistake taking you in."

Kate slipped out of the pantry and ran on tiptoes across the kitchen. She was out the door and behind the forsythia bush in ten seconds flat. Just in time too. Mrs. Baxter stuck her head out the back door to look around as if she'd heard something. After Mrs. Baxter closed the door, Kate counted to a hundred twice before she ran for the woods. If Fern was watching, she didn't see her.

34

It was hard being sober. Forever sober. Victor had gone without drinking for days at a stretch before, but he'd always known where a bottle was hidden away to give the promise of relief if things got bad. Things always got bad. He didn't have any bottles hidden away now. He'd broken them all. And he wasn't going to buy any more. He wasn't. No matter how much his hands shook. No matter how much it felt like the cooties were crawling around under his skin. No matter how the dreams tormented him. He wasn't. He'd promised Nadine.

She'd prayed for him. For them. She believed he could quit. All he had to do was find a way to believe it too. And he did. Most of the time. He could quit because he loved Nadine more than life itself. He loved her more than booze. He loved his girls more than booze. And he was trying to love himself more than booze.

He was appealing to the Lord on that one. He whispered Nadine's simple prayer a dozen times a day. "Lord, here am I. Help me." So far he had. So far the prayers had kept Victor from turning up the familiar path to the place in Rosey Corner where the bottles beckoned. But the prayers hadn't kept him from wanting to.

What he needed was for the Lord to take the wanting of it away from him. To erase it from his mind. That's what he told Aunt Hattie on the third day when she brought a jug of lemonade by the shop. Because it was so hot, she claimed, but Victor figured Nadine had enlisted Aunt Hattie to help pray him through.

"Has you told the Lord that?" Aunt Hattie peered over at him as he chugged down the lemonade.

"What do you mean?" Victor frowned a little as he lowered the jar of lemonade and wiped the sweat off his face with a blue bandana. "Doesn't he already know what I need? Better than me."

"Ain't no doubtin' that. But that don't mean he don't want to hear us ask it."

"I'm not too good at prayer words." Victor stared down at the lemon slices floating in what was left of the lemonade. He wondered how many shirts she'd had to wash and iron to buy the lemon and sugar.

"You think the Lord don't understand common talk? Just speak it out straight."

Victor could feel her eyes boring into him. He looked up at her. "Now?"

"What better time than when you needs to? Ain't nobody here but me and you and the Lord. So go ahead. He's got his ear bent down towards us."

"All right." Victor stared up at the ceiling in his shop. It was black from the forge fire. He shifted uneasily on his feet and tried to think up what to say with both the Lord and Aunt Hattie listening. At last he pushed out, "Lord, help me stay sober."

Aunt Hattie gave his arm a little shake. "That ain't what you's wantin' to pray."

Victor looked at her and then back up at the ceiling. Why was it so hard to lay himself open to the Lord? The Lord already knew him, every inch. Inside and out. Even better than Aunt Hattie, who had caught him when he was born. "Take this desire to hide in a bottle away from me."

"Amen," Aunt Hattie said. "That's more like it."

Victor looked down at his hands. His fingers were still trembling. "I don't feel any different."

"And you might never. That old thorn might always be prickin' you."

Victor frowned at Aunt Hattie. "Then what good did it do to pray the words?"

"'My grace is sufficient for thee; for my strength is made perfect in weakness.' That's what the good Lord told Paul about his thorn in the flesh. That's what the good Lord told me when I told him I couldn't make it without my Bo livin' and breathin'. Whether he takes the want to away from you or not, his grace will turn your weakness into strength."

"But what if I'm too weak?" He rubbed his finger down through the moisture on the outside of the lemonade jar. "What if it's too hard?"

"Ain't nothin' too hard for the Lord. You hear me now." She poked his chest with a bony finger. "We ain't promised no easy ride through this life. Life ain't easy. Ain't never been since Adam and Eve was thrown out of the garden. Ain't never gonna be. Leastways not for the most of us. Hard times come."

They both fell silent as they considered the hard times they'd seen and might yet see. After a minute, Aunt Hattie shook her head and said sadly, "I guess our Kate's done findin' that out right now, what with having that li'l child ripped away from her."

"She's struggling with it." Victor felt the familiar sorrow rising in him that he always felt when one of his girls was hurting.

"I hear Mr. Preston done told Kate not to go see the girl. She listenin'?"

"No. She's been over there every morning

before breakfast and maybe other times too. We haven't told her not to."

"Mr. Preston must not be knowin' about that yet, but best you keep in mind, don't much stay secret long from Mr. Preston in Rosey Corner. And he ain't gonna be happy with our Kate. Or with you," Aunt Hattie warned as she picked up her bag and headed for the door. "He done wrong about all this, but we both knows your daddy ain't one for ever admittin' that. The more wrong he is, the more he's out to prove he's right."

That afternoon Victor was banking the coals in the forge to leave for home when his father appeared in the doorway. The light was behind him so Victor couldn't see his face in the shadow, but he wouldn't be there for any good reason. In the seventeen years Victor had done blacksmithing in Rosey Corner, his father had rarely darkened the door of his shop. Even when he had owned a horse that needed shoeing, Victor had always gone and fetched the horse and then taken it home.

Victor squared his shoulders as if readying himself for a punch and faced his father. He didn't bother with a greeting. "What do you want, Father?"

"I want a son who doesn't defy his father's orders." It was easy to hear the anger in his father's voice.

Victor kept his voice calm as he picked his

words carefully. "I'm not a child, Father. It's been years since I had to do as you said, but out of respect, I've never intentionally defied you."

"If you believe that, you surely must have a faulty memory." He stepped into the shop. His mouth was hard and set, and his eyes were shooting sparks at Victor.

"How so?" Victor stared straight at his father, not shying away from his anger.

"I told you not to take over this place. I told you there wasn't any money in smithing, but you wouldn't listen."

"I've gotten by." Victor turned away from his father and pulled his leather apron off. He hated the way his hand trembled as he hung the apron up on its hook.

"Hmph." His father made a sound of disgust. "If you can call it that."

Victor took an extra moment to straighten the handles of his hammers on the shelf before he turned back to his father. "This is old stuff. Why don't you say what you've come to say and get it over with?"

"Can't take looking at the truth, can you? Especially not sober. You've always been too weak to face the truth."

Blood rose in Victor's face as he clenched his fists. "I faced the truth a long time ago, Father. The truth that I'd never be able to be the son you wanted. I'd never be able to be Press Jr."

"You aren't even good enough to say his name." His father was yelling now. "If it wasn't for you, he'd still be alive."

"I don't know what you're talking about." Victor's heart began pounding in his chest. It always came down to this. Him being alive and Press Jr. being dead. "I don't even remember what happened."

"You don't want to remember."

"Then why don't you tell me?" Victor stepped over right in front of his father and stared him in the face. "What did happen?"

"He died saving you." He wasn't yelling now, but his eyes were full of contempt.

Victor didn't back down from him. He kept his eyes locked on his father's face. "Graham pulled me out of the river. Not Press."

"I thought you couldn't remember."

"I don't remember how I got in the river, but I do know Graham pulled me out."

"You don't know anything."

Victor stared at his father. This man who had never accepted him as a man or even as a son. He wasn't going to change now. Victor made himself step away from him. He stopped beside his anvil and ran his hand over its familiar shape.

He knew the anvil as well as he knew his own hands. When he was working the iron, it became part of him. He knew where to lay the shoes on its hard surface to shape them. When he brought his hammer down with care, the iron bent to his will. That's what his father had never done. He'd tried to hammer Victor into the shape he thought he should be, but he'd never done it with any kind of caring. He'd just hammered him down. Victor should have long ago stopped worrying about what the man thought of him.

Victor blew out his breath slowly. What good did it do to keep pounding on cold iron? "That's all long past, Father. Done and over. What do you want today? Now."

His father kept glaring at him. "I want your daughter to stop defying my orders."

"If you're talking about Kate going to see Lorena, that's not harming anybody." Victor felt tired. He just wanted his father to go away.

"I told her not to." His father's face stayed as hard as the anvil Victor was leaning against.

"But I haven't told her not to. What you did with Lorena was wrong." Victor kept his eyes on his father's face. "You can't just take a child and give her to this or that person like she's no more than a stray dog."

"Oh, can't I? I did, didn't I?"

"But it was a wrong thing to do." Victor's eyes didn't waver on his father's face.

His father's eyes narrowed a little as he said, "I told you I wasn't going to let you make that gypsy child into a Merritt. And I'm not. Mark my words on that. You tell Katherine to stay away from the Baxters."

"Or what?"

"I'll disown you." He shot the words at Victor. "I'll write you out of my will."

"You think I care about that?" Victor almost smiled. "About your money? Go ahead. Cut us out of your life. You'll be the one losing there. I have my family. I don't need you. I learned not to need you years ago. And what will you have if you disown us? A safe full of money and nobody to give it to."

"I could marry again. Have more children."

"Then why don't you? Why didn't you?" Victor had never seen his father any angrier, but he didn't care. He kept on. "What was the matter? Were you afraid you couldn't find anybody worthy enough for you? Nobody who would give you strong Merritt children? Afraid that maybe it wasn't the Gale blood that was weak, but maybe the blood in your own veins? That you'd have more weak children like me and Gertie?"

Victor's father crossed the space between them in two steps and backhanded Victor like he was still a child instead of a man bigger and stronger than he was. Victor didn't raise his hands to defend himself. He just looked at his father and suddenly felt sorry for him. "Hit me again if it makes you feel better."

His father raised his hand up again, but then he

laughed. It wasn't a happy sound. He reached into his pocket and pulled out a bottle of whiskey. "I bought this for you. I thought you probably would need it by now." He held it out toward Victor.

Victor kept his hands on the anvil. He tried to absorb the hardness of the iron to keep his hands from shaking.

"You want it. I can tell you do." His father's voice was mocking as he stepped back and pitched the bottle toward Victor.

When Victor didn't raise his hands to catch it, the bottle hit the anvil and shattered. Whiskey splashed all over his pants and shoes. The smell of it filled the shop.

His father laughed again. "When I leave, you can lick it up off the floor." He turned on his heel and went out the door without looking back.

Victor looked down at the broken glass. He felt no regret at all over the spilled whiskey. He stooped down and picked up the pieces of the bottle and threw them in a bucket by the forge. He only hoped Nadine would believe him when he came in with the whiskey smell on his clothes. That was his only worry.

35

The alcohol smell came through the kitchen's screen door as soon as Victor stepped up on the back porch. Nadine's heart sank and the prayers she'd been circling in her head all week crashed down with it. He hadn't been able to keep his promise. She blinked back tears and turned away from the door to stir the vegetable soup on the stove even though she'd just laid down her spoon from stirring it a moment ago.

She couldn't look at him. Not and trust herself to keep her tongue still. She didn't want to lash out at him. Not with Kate right behind her setting the table for supper. The last few days had been hard enough on Kate without Nadine piling more grief on her head.

All week Kate had moped around the house, a faint shadow of her normal self. At mealtimes, she picked at her food. She didn't fuss with Evangeline. She didn't play with Victoria or go out to talk to any of the neighbor kids when they showed up in the yard. They all thought she was sick.

Jesse Granger had even brought her a mason jar filled with daisies and Queen Anne's lace. "Flowers for the sick," he'd said when he showed up at the front door.

Kate looked at the flowers and said, "I'm not sick."

"Well, something's wrong with you." He shoved the flowers at Kate and left.

And he was right. She was sick. Sick at heart. So Kate already had enough sorrow in her heart without being witness to Nadine's disappointment. No, more than disappointment. Despair. He had promised. Worse, she had believed him.

Victor opened the screen door and stepped into the kitchen. Nadine kept her eyes on the vegetable soup she was stirring as though her sanity depended on it being mixed just so. The whiskey smell was strong. She'd never known him to drink so much so early in the day.

The clank of the spoon against the pan was the only sound in the kitchen. Kate had quit rattling the plates, and Victor had to be standing stock-still just inside the door. What did he want from her? Forgiveness? She had none left to give. He had promised. They had prayed together. They'd never done that before. Not about the drinking.

Not about anything, really. She had always kept her prayers private, but wasn't that what the Bible said to do? She did pray out loud at times. She taught the girls the Lord's Prayer. She said grace. But other prayers were between her and the Lord. In the prayer closet of her heart.

She prayed Victor through the war. She prayed for her babies as she carried them and still lost that first precious child. She prayed to live through giving birth to each of them. She prayed her girls would be healthy. She prayed for rain. She prayed Victor would stop drinking. But until he came to her in the night and asked her to, she'd never prayed with Victor. Now he had betrayed that prayer.

"Nadine. Look at me." He didn't sound drunk. His words weren't slurred. When she didn't move, he added, "Please." His voice trembled a bit.

She couldn't refuse him. Not with Kate standing there between them. She scooted the pot of soup to the back of the stove where the fire wasn't as hot and carefully laid the spoon across the top of the kettle. As she turned around, she wiped her face with her apron to hide her despair from Kate. "All right, Victor." She managed to keep the sound of tears out of her voice.

His eyes grabbed hers. "You have to trust me," he said.

She felt like she was drowning in his eyes. Beautiful eyes. Loving eyes. "I want to," she said. But the whiskey smell was there, sickening her and giving lie to all his promises.

"Have I ever lied to you?" When she hesitated, he went on. "I haven't always done what I should. I don't deny that. I've let you down many times, but I've never lied to you. I've never spoken a promise to you I didn't keep. Never."

His eyes burned into her as he waited for her to speak. She wanted to say yes, he was right. He had kept his spoken promises to her, but there were other promises as well. Promises of the heart. She didn't know what to say. She believed his eyes, but her nose couldn't deny the stench of the whiskey.

Again he spoke before she could find words to say. "You have to trust me. Without trust, we have nothing."

Nadine could feel Kate's eyes on her as she stood frozen at the end of the table watching them. Nadine had to say the right words, but when she finally spoke, her words were not because of Kate. They were true words from her heart. "I do trust you, Victor."

"Thank you." Relief flooded his face, but he still didn't step across the floor to her. "I haven't been drinking. I know you smell it on me, but I haven't swallowed a drop. Someone broke a bottle on the anvil, and the drink splashed all over me."

"Why in the world did they do that?" Nadine frowned.

"I guess I made him mad." Victor attempted a smile as he shrugged his shoulders, but Nadine saw the pain in his eyes.

"Who?"

Victor's eyes slid sideways to touch on Kate and then came back to Nadine's face. "Nobody important." Then he was looking at Kate again. "Why don't you go fetch me a clean pair of britches, Kate, and I'll change out back? We wouldn't want you girls to think you were eating in a saloon tonight."

Kate giggled, more from nerves than because anything was funny. Then instead of going straight to find his britches, she stepped around the table to the door and wrapped her arms around Victor. "I love you, Daddy," she said. Then she turned loose of him and came back around the table to grab Nadine in a hug. "And you, Mama."

"That's more than she's said all week," Victor said after Kate ran out of the room. "Do you think the worst is over?"

"For us maybe, but not for her." Nadine stepped around the table to put her arms around him.

He put out his hands and tried to step back. "I'll get you dirty, Nadine."

"Then I'll be dirty," she said and stepped into his embrace. "Thank you, Victor."

"For what? Not drinking?"

"For making me fall in love with you. For coming home to me once again. For being the good man you are."

"My father doesn't share your opinion on that last, I fear." Victor's voice sounded strained. "Or so he just got through telling me."

"He was the one?" Nadine leaned back away

from him to look at his face. "He had the whiskey? But he doesn't drink."

"He bought it for me."

"Why would he do that?"

"I don't know, Nadine. Aunt Hattie must have told him I'd quit drinking."

"But that doesn't make sense."

"Not much does when it comes to me and my father." Victor sounded resigned. Then he tightened his arms around her. "But you have always made sense to me. You are the most wonderful woman in the world, and I'm the one who needs to be thanking you. My beautiful Nadine. If only I could write a poem to do you justice. My Nadine. She keeps me clean. My love for my Nadine would fill a ravine."

"Keeps you clean? Fill a ravine? Surely you can come up with something more romantic than that." Nadine laughed.

"All right. How about this? No eye has ever seen a prettier girl than my Nadine."

"Better, but I don't need poetry. I just need you." She lifted her mouth to meet his lips and didn't push him away even when she heard Kate come back into the kitchen.

After a minute, Kate cleared her throat. "Should I go away?"

Nadine pushed back from Victor. She looked around at Kate. "No, no. It's time for supper." Nadine's face was warm and not just from the heat in the kitchen. She normally didn't behave so wantonly in front of her children, but she'd felt like a new bride. It wasn't a bad feeling.

Victor kept his arms around her and leaned down to whisper in her ear. "Later." Then he grinned over at Kate. "It's okay, Kate. We're married."

"Oh, Daddy!" Kate rolled her eyes at him as she handed him the clean britches. She looked at Nadine. "You want me to tell Tori and Evie supper's ready?"

"Give your father a few minutes to change," Nadine said. "You can put water in the glasses."

Victor was still on the back porch washing up when somebody started pounding on the front door. "Who could that be?" Nadine muttered as Victoria came running into the kitchen. Her face was white and her eyes wide open.

"It's Grandfather Merritt and Mr. and Mrs. Baxter," she said.

"Do they have Lorena with them?" Kate asked with a look of hope on her face. "Maybe they're bringing her home." She set down the glass she was filling and ran toward the front room.

"Wait, Kate!" Nadine tried to stop her.

Nobody pounding on the door like that was there for any good purpose, but Kate was already out of the kitchen. Nadine wiped her hands on her apron as she hurried after her. She wouldn't let Father Merritt hurt Kate again. He'd already tried to do enough harm on this day.

Evangeline was at the door, doing her best to greet her grandfather as if he'd just come to visit. "Grandfather, come in. And Mr. and Mrs. Baxter. How nice to . . ."

Her grandfather pushed past her without a word to her. His eyes locked on Kate as he demanded, "Where is she?"

Kate stopped in her tracks at the look on his face. "Who?" The blood drained out of her face.

He crossed the space between them in two steps and was in front of Kate before Nadine could step between them. He shouted in her face. "You know who. That gypsy child."

"Lorena's missing?" Kate edged back a step, but he stayed in her face.

"You know she is. Where are you hiding her?"

Kate stood her ground this time. "What are you talking about?" She looked over her grandfather's shoulder at Ella Baxter. "What did you do to her?"

"Don't play Miss Innocent with me," Father Merritt said. "I'll make you tell the truth." He reached toward Kate, but Nadine pushed Kate aside and stepped in front of him.

"Don't you ever touch my daughter again. Ever." Nadine kept her voice low, but she put every bit of force she could in it.

Then Victor was there beside her, strong and unbending. "I don't know what's going on here, but I think it might be best if you all leave."

"We'll leave when we find the girl," Father Merritt said.

"Are you talking about Lorena?" Victor said.

"Polly," Mrs. Baxter corrected. "Polly's gone. She was in the . . ." She hesitated and then quickly went on. "The kitchen. When I went to check on her, she was gone."

"She stuck her in the closet again." Kate's voice was matter-of-fact.

Nadine looked at Ella with disgust. "You surely didn't lock her in a closet? The poor child is terrified of dark places. No wonder she ran away."

"It was for her own good." Ella raised her chin and sniffed as she stared at Nadine. "She's a willful child who needs correction. Isn't that right, Joseph?"

She looked around at her husband, standing just inside the front door with his hat in his hands. He twisted his hatband and sounded worried as he said, "I don't know, Ella. I'd say she's been more unhappy than willful." He touched his eyes on Nadine's face and then looked back at Ella. "Could be you shouldn't have locked her in the closet if she was scared."

Ella whipped her head around to glare at Joseph, who stared down at his feet as if he hoped a hole might open up in the floor to let him fall through.

Father Merritt spoke before Ella could explode. "The point is, the child is gone."

"That's right." Ella recovered and wagged her finger at Nadine. "Your daughter must have come into my house without permission and helped her run away. Talk about a willful child."

"Enough!" Victor's voice had the force of his biggest hammer slamming down on his anvil.

Everyone in the room fell silent and stared at him. Even his father was quiet as he stared at Victor with narrowed eyes and his mouth screwed up in a tight circle.

Victor pulled in a breath and waited a brief moment before he went on. "If Kate knows where Lorena is, she'll tell us."

They all turned toward where Kate had been standing behind Nadine. She was gone.

36

As soon as Kate realized her grandfather had come hunting for Lorena instead of bringing the little girl home, she started easing toward the kitchen. Her bare feet didn't make even a whisper of noise on the wood floor. In the kitchen she stepped around the spot in front of the icebox where the floorboards always squeaked before she carefully pushed open the screen door and eased out on the back porch. The screen door slipped out of her hand and rattled shut. Kate pulled in her breath and froze in place as she peered back through the screen to see if anybody was coming after her. Nobody was. They were still in the front room arguing about why Lorena had run away.

That was no mystery. Lorena would do anything to get out of that closet when she heard the rats coming after her toes. After all, who could expect her to keep believing in rat-proof angel powder when the angel had deserted her? Kate hadn't wanted to desert her. She just didn't know what to do to help Lorena.

She hadn't helped her today. She'd stolen a few minutes with her early that morning, but she'd had to help her mother clean Grandfather Reece's house that afternoon. She'd been planning to go see Lorena after supper. So she hadn't let Lorena out of the closet, but she knew who had.

Kate slipped on the shoes she'd left on the back porch before she jumped off the end of the porch and took off across the yard. Two old hens pecking in the dirt squawked and flapped out of the way. Kate didn't look back. She just ran faster across the open field toward the woods. She didn't hear any doors slamming. She didn't hear anybody yell her name. She wouldn't have stopped even if she had. She had to find Lorena and make sure she was all right.

Once out of sight in the trees, she slowed to a walk and caught her breath. She went by Graham's little cabin first, but he wasn't there. It was no telling where he and Poe might be. Fishing in the pond. Hunting raccoons. At the Lindell house dusting his mother's hats. Kate looked in the direction of the big house, but she had no way of knowing for sure whether he was there or not. He could be anywhere and she didn't have a lot of time to waste. The sun was already sinking behind the trees to the west. She didn't want to be hunting Fern after dark.

Of course that was who had opened the closet and taken Lorena. Fern. Just the same as she'd let Kate out of the Baxters' outhouse on Monday morning. Kate looked around and listened. She fervently wished Graham would appear out of the trees, but there was no sign of him. She didn't hear Poe baying in the woods. She didn't hear Graham whistling. She didn't hear anything except some crows fussing over her head and the crickets and tree frogs beginning to tune up their night songs.

She made herself walk away from Graham's house. She could find Fern by herself. She wasn't afraid of Fern. Not really afraid. That wasn't why her heart was pounding in her chest. She'd been running. She was scared for Lorena. She was worried about what her mother and father might do to her when she had to go home. She would have to go home. She and Lorena couldn't live in the woods the way Fern did.

She breathed in and out slowly as she hurried

through the trees. Each time she heard the brush rustle near her, her heart bounded up in her throat as she imagined tramps stepping out on the path in front of her or rabid foxes or Fern with her hatchet. But she wanted to find Fern, and the only way to do that was to keep moving deeper into the woods. And stay calm so she could think. If she didn't pay attention to where she was in the woods, she might start walking in circles and never find anybody.

She didn't know where Fern's newest cedar palace was, but she did know where the cedars grew. If she walked back and forth through the cedar thicket, she'd surely find it eventually. She bent down and pushed her way into the cedars and entered a different world where the thick canopy of evergreens blocked out the dying rays of sunlight. It was going to be very dark under there soon.

Kate moved as fast as she could on the thick layer of fallen cedar needles as she ducked and twisted to get through the low-growing trees. When she ran smack into a spiderweb, she yelped and slapped frantically at her hair to knock away the spider. She pulled in one deep breath and then another before she managed to calm down enough to pick the sticky web off her face.

She couldn't let a little spider stop her. She had to find Lorena. After grabbing up a stick to do battle with any new spiderwebs, she pushed on through the trees. The sound of a screech owl sent chills down her back.

She wanted to pray. The "want to" scratched at the inside of her heart, but she mashed her mouth together and didn't allow the words to whisper up inside her. It would do no good to pray. The Lord didn't answer prayers. Not for people like her who went around pretending to be angels. Besides, she didn't believe there was a God anymore. Wasn't that what she'd told her father? That if there was a God, he wouldn't have let Grandfather Merritt take Lorena away?

You don't believe that. You know there's a God and you want him to help you. So pray, for heaven's sake. Kate didn't know where the voice came from, but it was there in her mind. Maybe her mother. Maybe Aunt Hattie.

A dog started howling off in the distance. It could be Poe. She wasn't sure. It sounded so far away. She felt separated from the rest of the world here in this cedar thicket. Lost and alone.

Stop it, she ordered. *You're not lost. You know exactly where you are.* But the lost feeling didn't go away as she made her feet keep moving. Somehow even while waving the stick back and forth in front of her face, she ran into another spiderweb. She hit at her dress and hair again as she felt spiders crawling all over her. She wanted to sit down and cry, and she never did that. Not boohoo crying like Tori or Evie. Never. And she

391

still wanted to pray. So much that she could hardly breathe.

She dropped down on the cedar needles under the trees, pulled her legs up against her chest, and laid her forehead down on her knees. "Dear Lord," she whispered. "I don't know if you're really there or not, but if you are, I could use some help. I don't know what to do. I thought you wanted me to help Lorena, but then you didn't stop them from coming and taking her away. I thought you'd help me. And now I don't know where she is. If you're there, if you're listening, please help me find her. Please help me know what to do. And don't let the spiders get me. You know how much I don't like spiders."

No answer came falling down out of the cedars over her head, but she felt better. She stood up and started walking again. She still felt a little lost but not nearly so alone. She could almost see the words in her Grandfather Reece's Bible. *And lo, I am with you always, even unto the end of the world.*

She wasn't to the end of the world. She was right in the middle of Lindell Woods, and it wasn't dark yet. She had time to find Fern. And Lorena. She didn't know what she would do then, but there wasn't any use letting her worries race on ahead of her.

She smelled the pungent odor of newly cut red cedar before she stumbled across a freshly chopped stump. She touched the sticky sap oozing up from the bark on the stump and looked around. In the dimming light, she spotted other stumps here and there among the cedars. She had to be close.

Fern hadn't exactly cleared out a path through the cedars. The cut cedars were more like stepping-stones through a creek. Then there were dozens of cut stumps, and rising up in front of Kate a wall of green cedars piled on top of one another higher than her head. She'd seen Fern's cedar palaces before, but never one this big or this green. Usually Fern had already deserted the place by the time Kate came across it, and the dead cedars shed their needles at the slightest touch.

Kate reached out and felt the cedar walls. The trees on the bottom felt dry and brittle, but the top trees were soft and green as if they'd only been cut that day. Fern had to be close by, and she didn't like people messing around her palaces. Kate thought about all the stories she'd heard on the school playground about kids being swallowed up in Fern's cedars never to be seen again.

She never believed the stories. When she asked what kid, nobody could come up with one single missing kid, but that didn't make the idea of it any less scary. Or keep them from believing it might happen, and now maybe it had. To Lorena.

Kate held her breath and listened. She heard the screech owl again and another dog barking in the distance. This one definitely not Poe. It wasn't a hound. Bugs were chirping from among the cut cedars and a whippoorwill sang its name not far away. Kate could almost feel night falling around her as she stood there.

"Lorena." Her voice was barely above a whisper. There was no way Lorena would hear that even if she was right on the other side of the cedar wall. Kate opened her mouth to say Lorena's name louder, but then she shut it again as she stared at the barrier of cedars. She had the uneasy feeling they might all fall on top of her if she made too much noise.

She started walking along the wall. There had to be a way inside. A faded pink flour sack hung over an opening at one of the corners. Kate reached to pull it back and then hesitated. Fern might be waiting on the other side of the cedar wall for Kate to stick her head through the opening. She'd have her hatchet.

The back of Kate's neck suddenly felt very bare, but she swallowed hard and got down on her knees to push back the flour sack and crawl through the low opening. Fern had never actually killed anybody. At least not that Kate knew about. But that didn't mean it hadn't happened. Hadn't she been finding out about other things she'd never known about before now? Fern chopping somebody's head off could be one of those things nobody in Rosey Corner talked about.

"Lorena? Are you in here?" Kate kept her voice low as she gingerly crawled through the opening. Her heart was pounding so hard she thought it might jump out of her chest.

"Kate!" Lorena piled into Kate and started hugging her before she got all the way through the opening. "I told Fern you'd come."

"Wait, sweetie. Let me get in here. We don't want all these trees to fall on our heads."

"Don't worry." Lorena giggled as she backed up to let Kate scramble the rest of the way through the opening. "Fern says none of her palaces have ever fell down while they're green. Just after they turn brown."

Kate looked around as she sat down and let Lorena crawl into her lap. It was lighter inside the cedar room than outside under the cedars because the space was open to the sky where the first stars of evening were appearing. A wooden table sat in the center of the cedar room. Its legs had been sawn off to make it low enough so the blocks of wood around it could serve as chairs. A couple of quart mason jars sat on the table. One was filled with daisies and black-eyed Susans. The other one had water in it. To Kate's left against the cedar wall a gray-looking sheet covered a mound of more cedars. Fern was nowhere in sight.

"It's pretty, isn't it? Me and Mommy and Daddy and Kenton could have lived here."

"But there's no roof." Kate was breathing easier without Fern and her hatchet to worry about. She kissed Lorena's head. The little girl's hair smelled like cedar, but then everything smelled like cedar in here.

"Fern likes stars." Lorena looked up at the sky. "I do too."

"What does she do when it rains?"

"She takes a bath," Lorena said as if Fern had figured out the perfect way to live.

Kate had to laugh and then Lorena was laughing too. It was all just too crazy. Sitting out in the middle of the woods in a batty woman's cedar palace as night fell. Yet she didn't want to go home where people might be waiting to grab Lorena away from her.

She tightened her arms around the little girl. "Whatever are we going to do, sweetie?"

"I don't know, but I told Fern you'd think of something." Lorena didn't sound a bit worried.

"Where is Fern?"

"She went to get something for us to eat," Lorena said. Then she looked over Kate's shoulder. "She's back now."

Kate jerked around and couldn't keep from jumping. She hadn't heard even a whisper of noise as the woman came through the cedars, but there she was standing a few paces behind Kate, holding a sack and the hatchet. Kate tore her eyes away from the hatchet and tried to think of the right thing to say, but Fern spoke first.

"They're coming." Her voice was flat without feeling. But then a look of sadness settled on her face as if she knew her cedar palace couldn't keep them away.

37

The fervor of the hunt quickly overtook the men in spite of Victor's plea for calm heads. After they had discovered Kate missing, everybody trailed Victor out of the house to wait while he yelled for her. His voice had rung out over the yard and the fields, but there'd been no answer.

At least not from Kate. His cow had bawled for her nightly milking. Victoria sat down on the edge of the porch and began sobbing. Haskell Cox's dog down the road started barking and kept it up when his barks echoed back to him off the barn behind Alvin Holt's house. Other dogs in the neighborhood joined in. Haskell and a couple of other neighbors came over to see what was going on.

"Two girls are missing," Victor's father told them, not bothering to explain that Kate had only been "missing" a bare ten minutes.

"Nobody's missing," Victor said. "At least not Kate."

"What about Polly?" Ella Baxter said. "She's run away. No matter what else we think, we're obligated to try to find her before something out in the woods gets her."

Victor tried to be the voice of reason. "Nothing is going to hurt them out in the woods. All we need to do is give them time to come home. Kate's a sensible girl. She'll bring Lorena home."

"Then you're admitting that your daughter stole her out of my house," Ella said.

Nadine got right in Ella's face. "Kate didn't set foot in your house and do anything of the sort. She's been with me all afternoon."

Ella backed up a few steps, but she didn't let Nadine silence her. "Then why did she run away? She had to know where Polly was or she wouldn't have done that."

"The child's name is not Polly." Nadine was almost shouting. Victor put his hand on her shoulder, and she took a deep breath before she went on in a calmer voice. "Her name is Lorena. Lorena Birdsong."

"That's not a decent name. And not one a child of mine will ever have."

"She's not your child," Nadine said.

"She's not yours either," Ella shot back.

"She is now." Nadine looked from Ella to

Victor's father as though defying him to say the first thing against that.

He twisted his mouth with disgust, turned away from her, and spat on the ground.

When he didn't say anything, Ella started in again. "If you ever find her. She could be gone for good. You and your Kate with her. The gypsies may have stolen them both or who knows what tramps are out in the woods. Not to mention that crazy Lindell woman. We know she's out there somewhere. By now she may have chopped them to pieces and be burying their parts out in the woods where you'll never find them."

"Ella!" Joseph Baxter said, his face pale. "We don't want nothing bad to happen to the little girl. Or Kate either."

"Speak for yourself, Joseph Baxter. I'm sick of the whole bunch and I'm going home." She started for the road. When Joseph didn't follow her, she looked over her shoulder at him and said, "Come on."

"I think I ought to stay and help with the search, Ella." He winced a little as he spoke in anticipation of her displeasure, but he stood his ground.

She turned and threw a challenge at him. "You'd better come with me if you want breakfast in the morning."

The man stayed put as he almost twisted his hat

in two. "I guess it won't hurt me to miss breakfast."

Ella stared at him as her face turned as red as his was pale. "Well, I do declare." She spun on her heel away from him and stomped off.

The men standing around in the yard sneaked looks at Joseph, who straightened out his hat as best he could and jammed it on his head. Then Haskell spoke up. "She could be right. About the tramps and all. We can't just stand here and not go looking for them."

"There's nothing in that woods to hurt them," Victor said.

"What about Fern Lindell?" It was Victor's father talking again. He seemed to want to stir up the men. "Ella's right. Who knows what that woman might do?"

"Fern has never hurt anybody. She just chops down cedars," Victor said, but nobody paid any attention.

"It's going to be dark soon," one of the men said. "We'd better get some torches."

"I ain't going in there without a gun," another man shouted.

"No guns. We don't need guns." Again Victor's words fell on deaf ears. He stepped over to his father. "Stop them, Father."

"I can't stop them," his father said as the men ran back to their houses to get what they thought they needed for the search.

Victor stared at him. His father was almost

smiling. "What is the matter with you? Have you lost your mind?"

"You should have listened to me. You should have done what I said."

Victor frowned. His father wasn't making any sense. "I don't know what you're talking about. All my life I've done what you said."

"No." The look on his father's face changed. "I told you to follow Press Jr. To make sure he didn't get into trouble with that girl."

"What's Press Jr. got to do with any of this? He's been dead for years."

"Because of you."

Victor shut his eyes and pulled in a long breath. His father had gone around the bend. He wasn't making sense. Victor wasn't going to be able to reason with him. He let his breath out slowly. "All right, Father. Punish me if you must. But don't put my daughter—your granddaughter—in danger by inciting some kind of wild search."

"She should have listened to me."

Victor turned his back on his father then. He touched Nadine's cheek. "Stay with Evangeline and Victoria. I'll find Kate and bring her home."

Nadine looked frightened. "Be careful."

"Don't worry. I'll get Graham to help me. If Kate and Lorena are in the woods, he'll know where."

"What about your father?"

"I don't have a father." The words set something free inside Victor. Too long he'd tried to be what he could not be. Too long he'd tried to please a man who could not be pleased. But at the same time he knew it wasn't that easy to shake off years of guilt.

"I'll tell him to go home," Nadine said.

"Tell them all to go home. I can find the girls without help." He could only hope they would listen to her better than they had him as he saw Haskell coming across his yard with a torch, and another man running down the road with a gun. He turned his back on them and walked swiftly toward the woods.

He didn't know why they were all so sure Kate had run to the woods. None of them had seen where she'd gone. She might be hiding out in the barn with Lorena. Or be at the Baxters' house. She could be at Aunt Hattie's. Yet he kept walking into the woods. She'd gone this way. He sensed it.

The light was already fading under the trees, and an eerie stillness filled the air as night crept closer. His feet crunched down the carpet of leaf litter, and a crow flew up out of the tree beside him and cawed out a warning to the woods creatures.

He'd walked through the woods the night Press Jr. had died. Not these woods, but the woods on the other side of Rosey Corner that went down to the river. The memory came out of nowhere. Perhaps his father was right. Maybe he hadn't forgotten it all. Maybe he'd just pushed it away for so long that he thought he'd forgotten it.

He wasn't going to think about it now. He could do nothing for Press Jr. or for his father. He could find Kate. He didn't think she had anything to fear in the woods, but he'd feel better when she was safe back at the house. Both her and Lorena.

He hadn't walked far into the woods when Graham stepped up beside him. "What's going on, Victor? I heard you hollering for Kate. Is she all right?" His dog was right behind him as always.

"I don't know, Graham. I was hoping you could tell me. Lorena ran away from the Baxters' house, and my father came looking for her, thinking Kate had something to do with it. Then while everybody was yelling at everybody else, Kate took off."

"Are you sure she's here in the woods?" Graham frowned a little.

"So you haven't seen her."

"Nope, but then I was over at the big house for a spell. I can't hear what's going on so good when I'm over there. And fact is, when we went back to the cabin a bit ago, Poe was doing a powerful lot of sniffing around. Could be she came by and we missed her." He touched the hound's head, and Poe flapped his tail back and forth. "I should've paid more attention, but the girl don't ever come this close to dark so I figured it was a coon or a possum that had his ears perking up."

"Do you think he could track her down?" Victor looked at the coonhound.

"Hard to say. He might run down a coon instead if one crossed his trail. But we could give it a try if you're a mind to."

"It's a big woods. She could have gone in any direction. We need some help." Victor looked back over his shoulder toward his house. He couldn't see anything through the trees, but he could hear the men in the distance. No words. Just excited babble. "And not that help back there."

"I saw them gathering. Looked like a couple of them were carrying torches." Graham shook his head. "It's not a good time to be carrying torches around in here. Everything's awful dry. Hot like it's been and with no rain."

"I told Nadine to tell them to go on home. If they'll listen. Somebody said something about tramps in the woods and got them all in a stir."

"No tramps around here. They mostly stay to the road."

"I know that and you know that, but they're not thinking straight. And my father's not helping. It's like he wants to stir them up, but heaven only knows why. He's talking strange today. Even talked about Fern maybe hurting the girls. I don't know why."

"Your daddy hasn't ever found a way to forgive himself. You keep poison like that inside you long enough, it eventually comes out and does damage to your thinking."

"What do you mean? What does he have to forgive himself for?"

"For it all," Graham said sadly. "For it all. But we don't have time to worry about that right now. We've got to find Kate. And you say the little girl is missing too?"

"According to Ella Baxter, somebody came in her house and let Lorena out of the closet she'd locked her in. She was punishing the poor child for something."

"Somebody ought to lock Ella Baxter in a closet." Graham's voice was close to a growl. He walked on without saying anything for a minute before he asked, "And was it Kate that let the girl out?"

"No. She was with Nadine all afternoon. It couldn't have been her."

"Then I don't guess we need to depend on Poe's nose. We just need to find Fern. She's been practically obsessed with the little thing ever since she saw her fishing over at the pond. Said Lorena looks like her when she was little. She's been watching her some, but I didn't think there'd be any harm in that."

"If she let her out of the closet, she wasn't hurting her. She was helping her."

"But will anybody believe that?" Graham looked worried in the dying light of the day. "Your daddy hasn't ever liked Fern."

"What difference does that make?"

"Sometimes in Rosey Corner, all the difference." Graham turned and cut through the woods away from his cabin. "We better hurry. It's going to be dark as spades soon."

38

Victor pulled in a long breath to steady himself as he tried to quell the nervous worry ballooning up inside him. He didn't know why he was so worried. Kate was a sensible girl, and she knew the woods. Hairs on the back of his neck had no reason to stand on end, but it was happening, as every inch of his body braced for danger.

Dusk was stealing the daylight, but there was nothing fearful in Lindell Woods. Day or night. No wolves. No mountain lions. A skunk or fox might cross their path, but that was all. Victor liked the woods. As a boy he spent many happy days with Graham and Bo in among these very trees.

Then after he got home from the war, a walk under the huge first-growth trees in the heart of

Lindell Woods helped him get a peaceful silence back in the center of his thoughts instead of the unending echo of exploding shells and the screams of dying men. He never should have let his busy life pull him away from the spiritual refreshing he found in the woods that he couldn't find sitting in a church pew. But the girls had come along, and every minute not spent at the forge shaping horseshoes was needed to tend the garden and his bees, or cut wood for the stove and keep the roof from leaking. Besides, he thought he had found his peace with his beautiful daughters and loving wife.

But somehow he'd lost sight of that peace. Money got scarce. The pain in his shoulder got worse with every swing of his striking hammer, and the hard memories had come edging back in his dreams to haunt him. Instead of looking to his family or to the Lord for help, he'd tried to drown it all out in a bottle of whiskey.

It hadn't mattered how many times Nadine said she loved him, how many times Aunt Hattie assured him the Lord loved him, he could never quite believe it could be true. Not when he knew how weak he was. Not when he knew how scared he was. Not when he knew how often he'd failed. It was better to keep his head low and hope the Lord might not notice that the wrong men had died. The stronger men—Bo and Press Jr.

So Victor hadn't prayed. He hadn't laid his

burdens down at the Lord's feet. He'd kept trying to shoulder them all alone, and always failing. At least until a few nights before when he'd asked Nadine to pray for him.

Nadine would be praying for him now. And for Kate. She had that kind of trust in the Lord. She would be reaching for his mighty help, and knowing that made Victor feel better as he followed Graham. Then he wondered if it was wrong for him to always lean on her prayers. So he let the words whisper through his mind as they hurried through the trees. *Please, Lord. Protect my Kate.*

They found Fern's cedar palace, but even before they crawled through the opening, Graham was muttering under his breath. When they stood up inside the walls of cedar, he shook his head and said, "This isn't it. I guess it's been longer than I thought since I'd been over this way. She must have a new one."

"Maybe she's just not here." Victor looked around and then up at the sky. Stars were coming out. But no evening dew was falling and the cedars smelled dry.

"No, Fern always has flowers or what passes for flowers even if it's nothing but the fuzzy ends of grass. She used to help Mother keep flowers on the table. Big bouquets. In the winter they brought in cedar branches to keep the house smelling good."

"I remember." Victor had liked going in Graham's house where there was laughter and flowers and teacakes, but even then Fern hadn't shared in the laughter. Her father had treated her for melancholia, but she'd always seemed withdrawn and sad even before the influenza fever burned through her and destroyed whatever part of a person it was that reached out for the companionship of other people. Or maybe it wasn't completely destroyed. She must have felt some kind of connection with Lorena.

They crawled back out of the piles of cedars. Victor brushed against the side of the opening, and cedar needles showered down in his hair and on his neck. The things made him itch. Always had. He tried to brush them off his sweaty skin as he asked Graham, "Which way from here?"

"Give me a second to think where I last saw her chopping cedars." Graham rubbed his forehead as if that would help him remember. He was still thinking when his dog pointed his nose back the way they'd come and started baying.

Victor turned and caught the flicker of light through the trees. "I guess Nadine couldn't talk them into going on home."

Graham reached down and put his hand on Poe's head. The dog fell silent at once. "No need barking, boy. They aren't going to run from us." He straightened up and listened a minute before he went on. "Sounds like a herd of buffaloes."

Back through the trees a man let out a yell. A second later a gunshot echoed through the woods. "Worse than buffalo," Victor said. "I don't like the feel of this."

"Me neither, Victor. Me neither. And this might scare Fern silly. She doesn't like strangers in our woods."

"They're not strangers. Just some of the neighbors. And Father."

"They're acting strange enough." Graham sounded worried. "We need to find the girls and get them out of here."

"You think you can find them?" Victor could barely make out the features of Graham's face as night began falling over them like a curtain.

"I've an idea where they might be." Graham pointed west where some fingers of pink still colored the sky. "Fern was over that way a piece a couple of days ago."

"Then you go get them. I'll head off the men."

"You're liable to get yourself shot for your trouble," Graham warned. "Might be best you just come on with me."

Victor hesitated a second but then said, "No, I need to stop them before they do something foolish. You go. Take the girls back to my house. Fern too."

"If she'll go. Fern hasn't done much she didn't want to do for a long time now, but could be she might listen to me." Graham touched his dog's head again and turned away from Victor. "Fern, Poe. Go find Fern, boy."

The dog stuck his head up in the air for a moment before he put his nose to the ground and took off through the trees. Graham trotted after the dog as they headed away from the sound of the men crashing through the trees. The searchers were coming straight toward Victor, obviously homing in on the sound of Poe's barking. The dog was running silently now. Victor didn't think it was possible to teach a hound to run without baying, but then the bond between Poe and Graham wasn't normal.

Nothing seemed normal this night. Victor caught a whiff of the whiskey that had spilt on his shoes, and all at once his hands felt shaky. He squeezed them into fists and shut the thought of booze from his mind. He was through with the bottle forever. He didn't care how many demons he had to fight. The Lord would help him. Had already helped him. He'd wipe that lingering desire for the bottle right out of Victor's head.

What was it Nadine used to tell him all the time? Her God was able. That he'd saved Shadrach, Meshach, and Abednego from the fiery furnace. That he'd parted the Red Sea. That he'd brought Victor home from the war. Her God was his God.

The men were closer. Victor shouted out to them. As he made his way through the undergrowth, he was again pushed back to that night so long ago when Press Jr. had died. There'd been men with torches that night. They'd gathered in clusters on the riverbank before the man with the boat had come. Victor had wanted the men to go away, for all the torches to go black. He'd wanted the river edge to be the way it had been before he came out of the trees and found his brother on the wooden dock.

There'd been a girl there with long black hair. Press was kissing her. That was why Victor was there. His father had sent him to spy on Press Jr. The girl turned away and started crying when they heard him in the shadows. He had a cold and couldn't keep from coughing. Press was so angry. Victor had never seen him so mad. Not at him. Not at anyone.

Not even at their father. Press had always laughed whenever Victor complained about their father. "You just have to know how to get along with him, kid. That's all. It's not so hard as long as you remember a few rules."

"Yeah. Be biggest and strongest and best. At everything." They'd been walking down the road toward the house after a baseball game in the schoolyard. Victor had hung out behind the plate to chase down foul balls. Press had hit two home runs and would have had a third if Bo hadn't made a great catch to steal it away from him. Victor kept his eyes on the ground as he said, "But me, I'm scrawniest and worst at everything."

"You're going to get bigger. Why, look at those feet!" Press pointed at Victor's bare feet on the dusty path. "You grow to those feet, you'll be bigger than me or Dad, either one."

"I don't think so. Nobody could be bigger and stronger than you, Press."

Press laughed and mussed Victor's hair. "Don't forget handsome. The girls like handsome."

"You got a girlfriend, Press?" Victor peered up at him.

His brother's smile flickered a little as if he was having trouble holding on to it, but then he was laughing even more. "I got dozens of them, kid. Dozens." He put his finger over his lips and added, "But don't tell Dad. He says girls just mess a man up. Hold him back. Dad doesn't have to know everything, even if he thinks he does. Last time I read my history book, every governor we've had in our great state had a wife. Of course our father would say they had to have the right wife." And this time Press didn't hold onto the smile.

Two weeks later his father had ordered Victor to follow Press. It was a Saturday night. Press left the store early, said he was meeting some friends down by the river. He told Victor to tell their mother not to worry if he didn't come home till morning. His friend had a camp down there, and they'd probably fish all night. Victor made the mistake of telling their father first.

Press hadn't been gone from the store long when Jack Price came in the store talking about fishing. Victor liked Mr. Price because he always had a kind word for him. It seemed a natural enough thing to say Press Jr. had gone fishing too. Victor's father grabbed him by the collar and propelled him to the back storeroom.

Once away from Mr. Price's eyes and ears, he got right down in Victor's face and demanded to know exactly what Press had told him. Victor was so afraid he couldn't keep from stammering a little as he said, "He went fishing. Said he might fish all night."

"Fishing." Victor's father snorted in disbelief. His breath was hot on Victor's face. "You're lying to me. Press doesn't like to fish."

"That's what he told me. Honest." Victor wanted to jerk free of his father and run, but instead he stood still and braced himself for whatever his father was going to do to him. Later he wished his father had given him a licking and sent him home the way he usually did when Victor did something to upset him. That would have been better than having to chase after Press through the trees as night was falling. Victor didn't like being alone in the dark, but he had to do what his father said. All his life he'd had to do whatever his father told him to do.

Victor couldn't find Press in the woods, so he just went to the only camp on the river he knew about. Graham's grandfather owned it. Victor had been fishing there with Bo and Graham. He never planned to spy on Press and go running to their father with tales. He'd rather take a beating than do that, but if he could find Graham and Graham could help him find Press, then Press could tell him what to do. Press would know.

But it wasn't Graham at the camp. It was Press and the girl in an embrace. Victor stepped back into the shadows. And then he coughed. The girl started crying, and Press started yelling.

"What are you doing here?" Press reached for Victor, but Victor edged away from him across the dock. He'd never been afraid of Press, but he'd never seen Press like this. "Have you been down here spying on me every night?"

"No, no," Victor said. "I'm looking for Graham."

"You're lying. Father sent you, didn't he?"

Victor hung his head as tears pushed at his eyes. He didn't want Press to hate him. "He said you weren't fishing, and that I had to find out what you were really doing."

The girl turned toward them. "It's no use, Press. Your father will never let us marry. Never." Her face in the shadows was beautiful and tragic.

Press looked at the girl. "Once I'm out of school, it won't matter what he says."

"You could tell him now. If you loved me enough."

"It's not so long until I'm out of school. Just a few years. We can wait that long." Press put his hands on her arms.

"I can wait, but will it matter?" She stared at Press for a moment before she said sadly, "You won't ever go against him. I don't think you can." She jerked away from him and ran toward the wooden steps that led up to the small house on the bank above the river.

"Wait, Maia," Press called, but the girl kept running up the steps. "I do love you. You have to believe me."

Victor should have run for home, but instead he stood frozen in his spot on the dock. They'd had storms the week before and the river was up. In the dying light of the day, the brown water bounced against the underpinnings of the dock and splashed up on the wooden planks and over his shoes, but he still didn't move. He'd ruined things for his brother, and he had no idea how to fix it.

Press turned back toward him, his face almost unrecognizable with the anger flooding it. "You rotten little sneak. This is all your fault." He ran toward Victor and slammed him down on the dock. Victor scrambled to his feet to get away from him, but Press caught him and shook him so hard Victor's teeth rattled.

Victor didn't fight. He couldn't fight Press. He loved Press. Then there were more footsteps, running down the steps and across the dock. Graham was yelling at Press. "It's not the boy you want to kill."

Press whirled to face Graham, and Victor fell backward off the dock. The water swallowed him up and carried him away.

39

Another gunshot jerked Victor back to the present. He gasped as if he really had been swallowing the river water and drowning. But that was years ago. This was now. He shouted again and waited for the men to come to him.

There were five of them. All good men, but they'd let their imaginings push them down panic's path until now they seemed to have lost all common sense. Victor blamed his father for that. His father could have stopped them. He knew Fern wasn't dangerous. He knew Kate was sensible and would come home eventually. And yet he was egging the men on, encouraging their foolishness for some purpose of his own.

Again in his mind's eye, Victor saw Fern running up the steps away from Press. His father would know it was Fern whom Press had been going to meet. It could be he blamed her just as much as he blamed Victor for what happened that night. Perhaps even more.

Whatever his father was trying to do, Victor had to stop him. He stepped out in front of the men with torches. "It's all right, men. Graham found the girls and is taking them home." It wasn't a lie so much as a prediction. Graham would find Kate and Lorena and take them home. Given time. That's what Victor planned to give him. Time.

"That's good to hear." Victor's father spoke up, but he wasn't ready to give up the hunt. "If it's true. We want to see for ourselves. We want to be sure they're safe."

"Fine." Victor kept his voice level and calm. "Go on back to the house and there they'll be. But nobody's here." Victor pointed at the piled cedars behind him.

"How do you know? Did you go inside?" Alvin Holt held his torch up higher and peered past Victor.

"I did. No one's here," Victor repeated.

"You know Fern can move quiet as a cat and disappear behind a bush until you couldn't spot her even in broad daylight. A couple of you men need to make sure she's not in there," Victor's father said.

"Go ahead." Victor shrugged. "Just leave the torches out here. You can't crawl in there with them."

"I'm not going in there without some light." Alvin backed up a few steps, and all the other men stopped in their tracks alongside him.

"Surely you're not afraid of a woman," Victor's father said as he turned to glare at his posse. "If she's in there, we need to know. We need to know what she's done."

Victor grabbed his father's arm and spun him around to face him. "What are you doing? Fern hasn't hurt anyone."

"That's what you think. She's the cause of it all."

Victor stared at his father. The man's eyes shone with a strange fervor in the light of the torches. "She wasn't the reason Press ended up in the river any more than I was."

"So you do remember."

"I do now. You were the reason Press ended up in the river. Not Fern. Not me. Not Graham. You." Anger boiled up inside Victor, but then just as quickly it was gone. He simply felt tired. Most of his life he'd carried that heavy sack of guilt on his back. His father had made sure it stayed loaded and in place, but maybe it was time Victor shrugged it off and laid it down. His voice was sad as he went on. "All these years you've tried to blame other people, but it was always you. You killed the son you loved."

"You don't know what you're talking about. I wasn't even there!" His father was shouting.

The other men lowered their torches a bit and stepped back. They wanted no part of this argument between father and son.

"But you were the reason I was. You were the reason Press was. The reason he had to sneak around to see Fern. What was wrong with her? Why wasn't she good enough for you?"

"It wasn't me she wasn't good enough for. It was Press. He needed someone special. Not someone from Rosey Corner with nothing on her mind but tying him down with babies too soon."

"Her grandfather was a senator." Victor was trying to understand. He needed to understand.

"Fulton Barclay was a buffoon. A Populist. The man had to buy votes to get elected." His father's voice was scornful. "Any connection with that man would have been a disaster. I wasn't about to let Press ruin his future because of a girl."

"So you sent me to spy on him?"

"I had to know what was happening so I could stop it. He would have thanked me in time. When he was governor. He was going to be governor. Everybody knew that. Everybody. You know it's true." Victor's father looked at the men around them as if expecting a shout of support. When none of them said anything, he went on in a louder voice. "You all know it's true."

The men ducked their heads and stared down at the ground. The silence full of unsaid things pounded against their ears. Finally Alvin spoke up. "Maybe Victor's right. We should just go on home. Graham won't let no harm come to the girls."

Victor felt a subtle shifting of the way things had always been in Rosey Corner as the rest of the men murmured in agreement and began turning toward home. They were listening to him and not his father.

Victor's father must have felt the same shift as he glared at Victor in the shadowy light of the torches. He wasn't about to surrender his power over the men without a fight. "You aren't going to listen to a drunk, are you?" he shouted at the men. "A useless, worthless drunk."

Victor didn't attempt to defend himself against his father. It didn't matter anymore what he said, but one of the other men looked back and said, "Come on, Preston. Ain't no call to be talking about your own son that way."

Alvin turned around and reached toward Victor's father. "Yeah, we know you don't mean it. Victor might take a nip or two now and again, but we all know he's a good boy. A good man. Let's just go on home and get some supper. Victor's done told us Kate and that little girl are safe, and that's all we were worrying about, wasn't it?"

"Don't you talk to me like I don't know what I'm doing. I know. Give me that torch and I'll go do what has to be done if the rest of you are too afraid." Victor's father tried to grab the torch out of Alvin's hand.

Alvin lifted it high over his head out of reach. "We're going home, Preston, and that's—"

Before he could finish, Victor's father punched Alvin in the stomach. The torch went flying as the man doubled over. It landed in the pile of dry cedars behind them. Victor scrambled after it. He jerked it out of the cedars, but it was too late. Already the fire was whooshing up through the dry needles. Victor and the other men tried to pull some of the cedars away from the flames, but the fire leapt up through the stacked cedars and took on a life of its own. There was no stopping it.

The other men and Victor stepped back and shielded their faces from the heat. The flames were leaping into the air and spreading sparks across the dry woods.

Victor stared at the fire and said, "What have you done, Father?"

His father showed no remorse. "This cedar thicket needs clearing out."

Victor stared at the wall of flames as fear gripped his heart. "Kate may still be in there."

"I thought you said Graham was taking her home."

"He may not have had time to get them out of the woods yet."

"So you were lying." His father made a little snorting laugh. "Could be you're going to find out the same as I did how it feels to lose a child."

Victor looked over at his father and felt sick all the way down to his toes. "Kate's your grandchild."

"She is." His father didn't look at him but kept his eyes on the flames. "But the fire is the same as the water was. Things happen. That's what everybody told me. Things happen."

"Sometimes because people cause them to happen."

"They still happen. And there's nothing you can do to change that."

"Kate will be all right." Victor pushed all the certainty he could into his words. "She'll have time to get out of the woods."

"The fire will spread fast." His father turned to look at him then. In the reflection of the fire there was a look of sorrow on his face, but Victor wasn't sure who he was grieving. "As dry as it is, it could take all of Rosey Corner if we don't stop it."

Alvin was yelling at them then. "We gotta get back away from here."

"They need someone to tell them what to do," Victor's father said. "To make a firebreak. And you'd better pray the wind doesn't start blowing our way."

"You tell them," Victor said. "I've got to go find Kate."

"You can't find her. You know that. And they won't listen to me. Not now. It's up to you. You decide. Kate or the rest of your family and Rosey Corner." His father's voice was flat and his face now emotionless. He turned away from Victor and started walking away.

"Where are you going?"

"Home."

"Come on, Victor," Alvin yelled again.

For a few seconds longer Victor didn't move. The heat was getting intense, and the flames began making their own wind as the smoke rose up to the sky, blotting out the stars overhead. His father was right. He couldn't find Kate. There were too many acres to cover.

"Dear Lord," Victor spoke aloud, but he could barely hear his own words above the roar of the flames. "Have mercy on us. Oh dear Lord, I beg you."

Then he turned away from the fire and ran with the other men through the trees back toward Rosey Corner. Already somebody had seen the flames and was ringing the church bell.

40

K ate perched uneasily on one of the stumps around the table in the middle of Fern's cedar palace and nibbled on a peanut butter sandwich while she tried to think of what to do next. It wasn't going to work for them to just sit there and try to hide. She had realized that as soon as Fern came back with the food and said Kate's grandfather and some other men were in the woods hunting for them.

"Where's Daddy?" Kate had asked.

"Don't know. Didn't see him. Or Brother. Could be hunting too." Fern had pulled out a loaf of bread and a jar of peanut butter. She looked at Kate as if guessing her thoughts. "I didn't steal it. Brother bought it at that man's store."

"Does Graham know where you are?" Kate looked around. "Where this is?"

"No." Fern shoved her hand deep into her overall pocket and pulled out a knife. She handed it and the peanut butter to Kate. "Here. You fix her food."

Lorena was staring at the peanut butter jar as though she was worried it might disappear. "Can I have a spoonful?"

"Sorry, sweetie. I don't have a spoon." Kate twisted the top off the peanut butter.

"Fingers came before spoons," Fern said.

"But," Kate started to protest. Her mother would never let anybody dip peanut butter out of a jar with a fingertip even if the person's hands were squeaky clean.

"She's hungry." Fern yanked the jar away from Kate and held it out to Lorena, who gave Kate a guilty look before she stuck her finger down into the peanut butter.

"Are you that hungry?" Kate asked.

Lorena nodded her head as she licked the peanut butter off her finger. "She told me I couldn't have anything to eat until I said my name was Polly. But I wouldn't. I told her my name was Lorena Birdsong. I said it real loud. She got mad and hit me and put me in the closet with the rats." Lorena's voice trembled a little as she went on. "I saw their eyes under the shelves, and I prayed for you to come. But Fern came first."

Kate swallowed hard to keep from crying at the thought of Lorena alone in the closet all day with nothing to eat while she was terrified the rats were going to eat her toes. "It's okay, Lorena. I'll fix you a sandwich and we'll have a picnic here while we decide what to do next."

"I'm not going back there." Lorena planted her feet and crossed her arms. "I'll live here with Fern before I go back. Fern will let me, won't you, Fern?" She looked at Fern, who didn't say anything.

"You can't live with Fern," Kate said gently. "They won't let you."

"But they wouldn't let me live with you either." Lorena crumpled to the ground and started crying.

"You made her cry." Fern hit Kate's shoulder so hard Kate staggered back a few steps. "Make her stop."

Kate rubbed her shoulder, then knelt down to pick Lorena up off the ground. She held her very close. "Shh, sweetie. They'll let you live with me now. We'll make them."

"We can't. We're too little." Lorena sounded ready to start sobbing again.

"God's big." Fern was standing over them. She reached a hand out to awkwardly pat Lorena's head. Then she pointed at Kate. "Pray!"

Kate looked at Fern. Her face was hard and tight, and her eyes were burning into Kate. "What if he doesn't answer?" Kate said softly.

"Bible says he'll answer. He answered when you prayed in the cedars."

"You saw me?"

Fern didn't answer her. Instead she said, " 'God is our refuge and strength, a very present help in trouble.' "

"That's out of the Bible," Kate said. Fern was the last person on earth Kate expected to quote Bible to her.

Fern's eyes narrowed on Kate. "You think I'm a heathen."

Kate cringed as she tightened her arms around Lorena and braced for Fern to hit her again. Lorena pushed her hands against Kate's chest and wiggled free. She put her small face close to Kate's. "Fern won't hurt you. She just wants you to pray. Please. So God will help us."

"He didn't help us before. What makes you

think he will now?" Kate immediately regretted her words when she saw Lorena's bottom lip start trembling again. Besides, it was surely sinful to doubt the Lord's help. Especially when he'd answered her plea for help just moments before and guided her to Lorena.

"He will. I know he will," Lorena said. "He has to."

Kate looked right into Lorena's eyes. "I'm sorry I said that. I was wrong. The Lord will help us."

Lorena smiled a little. "So you'll pray like she says? We can all pray together." She grabbed Kate's hand and then Fern's. She looked impatiently at Fern and Kate. "You two have to hold hands too."

Kate held out her hand toward Fern. Fern hesitated a moment before she grabbed hold.

"All right," Fern said. "Pray. Like Preacher Reece."

"I can't pray like him."

"Pray like you. Like an angel." Lorena squeezed her hand.

"I'm not an angel, but I can pray. At least I think I can." Kate held the two hands, one soft and small, the other hard and rough, and looked up at the stars. Her heart was pounding inside her. She'd never prayed out loud in front of anyone except for saying grace at the table. If anything needed praying about out loud, somebody else, somebody older and better at praying, had always been there to take the lead, and she'd just followed along in her head. Now she had to come up with the words and not just for Fern and Lorena to hear, but for the Lord to hear.

Kate licked her lips and began. "Dear Lord." She stopped and stared up at the stars. She didn't know what to say. Then she thought about how Aunt Hattie prayed. Like the Lord might be standing right beside her, listening.

She tried again. "Dear Lord. I know you're there. That you're listening and watching over us. I was wrong when I kept saying you weren't up there paying attention last week. I know you're always there. A present help in trouble just like Fern said. Like the Bible says. And we're in trouble now. So if there's any way you can, please help us tonight. We don't know what to do, but Lorena loves you. Fern loves you." Kate paused and let the silence pound against her ears before she added in a quavering whisper. "I love you."

She let the words hang in the air a minute before she swallowed down the lump in her throat and finished her prayer. "And thank you for Fern. For the way she helped Lorena." She squeezed both Lorena's hand and Fern's hand as she said, "Amen."

"Amen," Lorena echoed her.

But Fern shook Kate's hand a little and said, "You didn't thank him for the food so we can eat."

"Oh." Kate bowed her head this time. "Thank you for the food we have to eat. Amen."

So now they were eating the peanut butter sandwiches Kate had made and drinking water out of the mason jar, but Kate still didn't know what to do. Except go home. She looked over toward Lorena. She couldn't see her face. Night had fallen and the quarter moon didn't push much light down into the trees. Fern was sitting on the other side of Lorena, silent as a stone. Kate slid her eyes over to her and then back to Lorena as she said, "We can't stay here. We have to go back to the house."

Lorena sighed heavily and stood up to come lean against Kate. "If we have to."

"Go then," Fern said. "They've got guns, but they won't shoot you."

"They won't shoot you either," Kate said.

"They aim to shoot something."

"Not us. Not you." Kate stared at Fern, but shadows hid her face. "I can't find the way home in the dark."

Lorena went over to her. "We'll get lost without you, Fern."

"Then wait till daylight," Fern said.

"We can't," Kate said. "Mama and Daddy will be worried."

"He worried about his mother and father worrying too. Too much."

"Who? Graham?" Kate asked.

"No, him. The one you look like." Fern stood up. "I'll take you partway."

They crawled out of the cedar house. As soon as Fern stood up she stopped and raised her head as if listening for something. "Smoke," she said. "Cedar smoke."

Kate smelled it too. "Is the woods on fire?"

Fern didn't answer. She just pointed behind them where the glow of flames was lighting up the sky.

"Are we going to burn up?" Lorena asked in a small scared voice.

"No, of course not," Kate said. "The fire's not here. We've got time."

"Coming fast." Fern licked her finger and held it up. "Wind's picking up. Blowing this way. The fire will jump ahead."

"I'm scared, Kate." Lorena grabbed hold of Kate's leg. "Maybe we should pray again."

"No time." Fern turned and started walking fast through the cedars.

Kate took Lorena's hand and hurried after her. She couldn't let Fern get out of sight. They hadn't gone far when they heard something crashing through the woods toward them. Kate picked up Lorena and tried to run, but it was no use. It was coming too fast. She couldn't outrun it. She pushed Lorena behind her and picked up a stick.

An animal bounded out of the trees and jumped straight at Kate. She screamed and fell backward. Then paws were on her chest and a big tongue was licking her face.

"Poe!" Kate sat up and pushed him away from her face. "You crazy dog. You nearly scared me to death."

"Sorry about that, Kate," Graham said as he followed the dog out of the trees. "I should've told Poe to bark before we got here." He snapped his fingers once, and the dog backed away from Kate. "He was glad to see you. Truth is, so am I. You find the girl?"

"She's here."

"Hi." Lorena peeked out from behind Kate. She laughed when Poe ran toward her to wash her face with his big tongue too.

"No time." Fern came back down the trace of a path they were on. "Fire's bigger."

The smell of smoke was getting stronger, and they could hear the fire crackling and popping now. It didn't sound all that far away.

"Fern was showing us the way home," Kate said. "But then when we got out of her cedar house we smelled the smoke. Is it bad?"

"Bad." Graham's voice sounded sad. "The whole place may go up in flames."

"The house too?" Fern asked.

"A possibility." Graham and Fern stared at one another.

"What about Mama's picture?" Fern said. "And the money?"

"You and the girls matter more than a picture," Graham said, but he sounded even sadder. "More than money. And the men may stop the fire before it gets to the house."

Fern raised her head and listened a moment. "No stopping this. Too dry."

"We better get moving." Graham picked up Lorena. "You lead the way, Fern."

"You take them, Brother. I'll get the picture."

"No, Fern. It might not be safe." Graham grabbed her arm as she turned away.

She pulled away from him. "I thought the woods was safe, but nothing's safe. Nothing." With that she was gone.

"Fern, come back," Lorena yelled after her. When Fern didn't answer her, she started crying.

Graham patted Lorena's back. "Now, now. Don't take on so. Fern's tough. She'll keep out of the way of the fire. You just trust old Graham and Poe on this one. We're all going to be fine."

"But what about Fern's trees?" Lorena whimpered.

"Trees grow back," Graham said. "Tell her, Kate."

"Right. Trees grow back." Kate kept her voice steady and calm, but she felt anything but. The fire seemed to be on all sides, closing in on them. "We'd better go, hadn't we?"

They took off through the trees. Graham carried Lorena and held her head down close to his shoulder as he ducked under the branches. Kate followed on his heels. Behind her the fire was roaring, and she imagined she could feel the heat of the flames. She had no idea where they were in the woods with the smoke swirling around them. She could only hope that Graham knew where he was going.

Then the fire jumped the way Fern warned it would, and instead of running away from the flames, they were running toward them. The fire was coming toward them from every direction. Kate could barely get her breath. She didn't know if it was from the smoke or the running or the fear. She tried to pray, but she was too scared. Fern's words from earlier popped into her head. God's big. He could save them.

Graham leaned over and spoke right into her ear. "We can make the pond. Grab hold of my shirttail. Poe will show us the way."

Up ahead she heard Poe bay like he was on the trail of a coon. They ran after him, not paying any mind to the bushes grabbing at their legs and arms. When they came out on the pond bank, the water looked red in the light of the fire chasing after them and coming in from the other side. Poe stopped on the bank, but Graham didn't slow down. He plunged right into the water and kept walking until the water was waist deep. Kate was right behind him. Her shoes got stuck in the mud. She pulled her feet out of them and kept going. The mud squishing up between her toes was the most wonderful thing she had ever felt. Poe swam in after them.

41

Nadine stood at the fence and waited. She'd done as Victor asked and told the men to go home, but Father Merritt had pushed past her and led the men on across the pasture field and into the trees. She hadn't stopped praying since.

When she saw the first flames rising up out of the trees, she sent Evangeline and Victoria to Gertie's house to sound the alarm. The church bells were still pealing. Over and over. The evening air vibrated with the sound. With danger.

Behind Nadine, doors were slamming and people were yelling, but she stayed by the fence, staring at the edge of the woods, straining to see Victor and Kate and Lorena come out of the trees and run across the field to her. Night was falling, but there was enough light to see.

Father Merritt came out first. He walked across the field to the road in front of the house without glancing once toward the fence where

Nadine stood. Nor did he look behind him. She called to him, but he didn't raise his eyes from the ground in front of his feet as he kept walking. He didn't seem to be aware of the church bells ringing or the fire blooming up out of the trees behind him or the men yelling at him as he passed.

A few minutes later the other men broke free from the trees and hurried across the field toward their houses. Victor was with them, but Kate and Lorena were not. His eyes were fastened on her as he came straight toward her.

When he was near enough, he asked, "Has Graham brought the girls out?"

"No." Her heart leapt up in her throat so that she could barely push out the next words as he stopped on the other side of the fence in front of her. "So you saw them? They're all right?"

"I did not." He put his hands on the top rail of the fence and lifted himself over. He put his arms around her for a moment. "But Graham went for them. He'll find them. He thinks they're with Fern. That she must have been the one who rescued Lorena from Ella's closet."

"We never should have let your father take her from us and give her to Ella."

"My father." Victor's voice was flat. "He's the reason for this." He waved behind him at the fire.

"What do you mean?"

"No time to explain now. I've got to get my

axe. We need to cut a fire break to slow down the fire."

Nadine looked over Victor's shoulder. The fire had tripled in size already. "Will you be able to save Graham's house?"

"The big house maybe. I don't know. As dry as it is and the way the wind's blowing, the cedar thickets will go up like tinder. There may be no stopping it." Victor tightened his arms around her and then turned loose. "I've got to get my axe."

She followed him around the house. "I can go with you. Help somehow."

"No, you stay here and wait for Kate." The door creaked when he opened the shed to pull out his axe. The cow heard it and began bawling again. "You'd better milk her or else her bag will go bad and we won't have milk. Just don't leave her in the barn." He started back toward the woods.

Nadine grabbed his arm and made him turn back toward her. "Surely we don't have to worry about the fire getting the barn. Do we?"

"No, I don't think so. We'll stop it. But if we don't, no sense losing the cow." His voice softened as he touched her cheek. "Kate will be all right, Nadine. I know she will." Then he was gone, running across the field back toward the fire.

Nadine didn't bother putting the cow in the barn. She just poured some corn out on the ground and milked her where she stood. The old cow had always been extra gentle, and even with the smell of smoke in the air, she only lifted her feet a couple of times to show her uneasiness. Each time Nadine took hold of the cow's leg and gently pushed her hoof back down on the ground. The barn would be dark. She didn't want to light a lantern and take the chance it might get knocked over and start a new fire.

It was bad enough the fire was growing by leaps and bounds in the woods right across from her. Bad enough that she had to worry about Kate and Lorena somewhere in the middle of that. She leaned her head against the old cow's side and patiently stripped the milk out of her teats into the bucket. Some things had to be done no matter if the world was burning up around you.

And hadn't she always done what had to be done? So had Kate. She was the one child of Nadine's who was most like her in that way. Kate knew what had to be done and did it. That's why she'd run away to the woods to get Lorena. She knew Lorena would need her. That was why now she'd be running away from the fire and finding somewhere safe. Besides, Nadine didn't just have to depend on Kate's own good sense. Graham would have found her. He knew every tree in Lindell Woods. He'd find a way out. He'd see that the girls were safe even while his whole world was burning down.

Poor Graham. He'd already been through one life tragedy back when the influenza had taken his parents and the same as taken Fern. He'd had to give up his dream of being a doctor to care for Fern. Such a gentle man with such a kind spirit. Nadine had never seen him be hateful to anyone. Even when they made fun of him or Fern and the way they lived, keeping the big house as a shrine to his mother. Now it looked like that might all go up in smoke.

She patted the old cow's rump to let her know she was through milking her and carried the bucket of milk into the house. She left it sitting on the kitchen table. She didn't bother lighting a lamp, but she did light a lantern now. She'd told the girls to stay at Gertie's, so she was alone in the house. She couldn't go search for Kate and Lorena. She couldn't be all that much help on the fire line. She thought about her father and how the church bells ringing and the sight of the fire moving closer to his house and the church might upset him. She'd go there second.

First she walked across the field and straight toward the Lindell house. The fire wasn't there yet, but the smoke was. She had time. She could hear the men shouting back and forth as they felled trees and worked frantically to clear a firebreak. The noise of the flames consuming the trees was terrifying, and Nadine prayed out loud and walked faster.

The house was still standing, but it would take a miracle for the men to save it. The woods had edged too close on all sides since the house had held a family. She looked over her shoulder at the flames lighting the sky as she pushed open the door and stepped through it into the front hall. Here Mrs. Lindell had once greeted people and held lavish parties for her father, the senator. She had been a beautiful woman with a heart as kind as Graham's. The air in the house felt too still, as if the house itself was holding its breath as it awaited its fate.

Nadine had the eerie feeling she wasn't alone, but she shook it away. The spirits of Mr. and Mrs. Lindell had long been gone from this place. Long removed from the worries of this world. She had come for one thing and one thing only. It was the least she could do for Graham while he was saving Kate and Lorena. She had to believe he was saving Kate and Lorena.

The painting of his mother hung in the parlor over the mantel. Nadine had never been in the house with Graham when he didn't show her the painting and talk about how beautiful his mother was. Sometimes he talked to the painting as if the woman gazing out at him might even yet hear his voice. He'd be heartbroken if it was lost. Nadine set her lantern down on the hearth and pushed a chair over to the mantel.

She ignored the feeling that she was being

watched and resisted the urge to talk to the woman's face in front of her the way Graham did as she lifted the painting off the wall. It was heavier than she had expected and awkward to hold. The chair that had seemed steady enough when she'd first stepped up on it now felt wobbly as she tried to shift the painting in her hands to set it down on the floor.

"What are you doing?" The voice spoke right behind her.

Nadine jumped and would have fallen if rough hands hadn't grabbed her and lifted her off the chair and set her on the floor. She kept hold of the painting and looked around at Fern. "You scared me, Fern."

"I scare a lot of people," she said. "What are you doing with Mother's portrait?"

"I wanted to save it in case the men couldn't stop the fire. I know how much it means to Graham." Nadine looked at Fern in the dim light of the lantern. "And you."

"Brother says paintings don't matter. People matter."

"Where is Graham?"

"That's why you're here. You think if you save his painting he'll save her. Like a trade." Fern stared at Nadine for a moment before she shook her head sadly. "But it doesn't work that way. People die no matter what you try to trade."

Nadine moistened her lips and tried to mash

down the panic growing in her. Kate and Lorena had to be with Graham. They had to be safe. "They aren't going to die."

"Maybe not," Fern said. "Probably not. Brother had them. He'll get them out but not because of this." She pointed at the painting.

Relief washed through Nadine and made her legs weak. She set the painting down against the wall and held onto the back of the chair.

Fern grabbed Nadine's arm again to keep her from falling. "I used to swoon. Stopped that."

"I never swoon." Nadine straightened up.

"Could be the smoke, but looked more like a swoon." Fern let go of Nadine and went to push open a window and lean out it. "Fire's not here yet, but it will be." She pulled her head back in and went to the middle of the room. Her shadow in the light of the lantern stretched across the room and up the wall. "Laughter here. Once."

"Did you come back to say goodbye to the house?" Nadine asked softly.

Fern turned to Nadine. "Houses don't have ears."

"Maybe not, but their walls ring with memories." Nadine looked around at the faded rose wallpaper and sheet-covered furniture. There was something so lonesome about an empty house.

"Bad memories too." Fern went over and leaned the painting out from the wall to pat the back of its canvas. She stood up and stared toward Nadine. "Brother keeps money there. If you bother it, I'll know. Got to get my box." Without hurrying she went to the hall where the stairs climbed up to the second floor.

Nadine picked up her lantern and the painting to follow her. The smoke was getting thicker, and she couldn't keep from coughing a little as she said, "Hurry."

Fern stopped halfway up the stairs and looked down at Nadine. "Go home before you swoon again."

"I won't leave you," Nadine said.

"That's what he said. I didn't believe him. The boy came and I ran away. I shouldn't have run away. I could have stopped it. Kept him from knocking the boy into the water. Kept Brother from hitting him. Stopped it all." She stared over top of Nadine's head, seeing something that Nadine knew nothing of. "Boy came up and Brother saved him, but the water took my love away. Stole him from me, but it wasn't the water's fault. It was mine. I want to blame that man, but it was my fault. All mine."

So many words seemed to empty Fern out, and she had to grasp hold of the banister for a moment before she gained the strength to keep climbing. Nadine stood at the bottom of the staircase and tried not to think about the thickening smoke as she waited for Fern. She could hear the woman walking around in the room above her, and Nadine wanted to run up the stairs and grab Fern and pull her out of the house. But the fire hadn't reached the house. There was surely time for Fern to get whatever dear possession she wanted to save. Nadine wouldn't deny her that when the poor woman had been denied so much already.

She blew out a breath in relief when Fern started back down the steps. Fern almost smiled when she got to the bottom of the stairs and looked at Nadine. "Faithful like Brother." She thrust a small wooden box at Nadine. "Here. Take that and Mother. I can chop trees. Stop the fire."

Nadine took the box, but before she picked up the painting, she surprised both Fern and herself by grabbing Fern in a hug. "I'm sorry."

Fern pulled loose. "For what?"

"I don't know, but you do."

Fern looked at her for another minute before she went out the front door, picked up her hatchet, and started toward where the men were working against the fire that was leaping out of the trees toward the sky now. The men looked small in front of the flames.

It was awkward carrying the painting, the box, and the lantern. Halfway across the field back toward Rosey Corner, Nadine blew out the lantern and set it down on the ground. The fire was throwing enough light her way that she didn't need it anymore. She didn't stop at her house but carried the painting and Fern's box to Gertie's house in the middle of Rosey Corner. If Gertie's house burned, all of Rosey Corner would be lost.

Gertie and the girls ran down off the porch to meet her. They were full of questions Nadine couldn't answer, but she told them Kate and Lorena were safe with Graham. She needed to believe it was true as much as they did. Then she left them with Gertie and walked to her father's house. Here the fire was much closer, only a short open field away.

Carla and her father were on the porch in their rocking chairs. Carla was rocking furiously and talking nonstop. Nadine could hear her before she went through the yard gate. Nadine's father wasn't rocking at all as he stared out toward the fire.

"Nadine!" Carla jumped up out of her chair when she saw Nadine. She ran down the steps to grab Nadine's arms. "Tell your father we have to leave. He won't listen to me. For a while he kept praying the Lord would keep the church building safe, but then he sat down and now he won't say anything. Just sits there."

"Calm down, Carla," Nadine said.

"Calm down!? How could anybody be calm with that right on their doorstep?" Carla gestured wildly toward the fire.

Nadine pushed Carla's hands away and stepped past her to the porch. She knew why her father was so silent even before she went up the steps. The fire had claimed its first victim.

42

The men worked feverishly to get a firebreak cleared to save the Lindell house, but the fire was too big to stop. Fern was working beside Victor when the house caught.

When she'd shown up earlier with an axe and her hatchet and started to chop down the nearest bushes without a word, he'd shouted to her over the noise of the fire and the axes. "Where are the girls?"

She stood up and looked straight at him. "With Brother."

He could barely hear her. "Safe?"

She just kept looking at him, her face not showing any feeling in the reflection of the fire. She didn't look a thing like the girl he'd remembered weeping and running up the steps away from Press Jr. that night so long ago. Finally, without making any kind of answer, she turned back to the brush and began chopping again. He'd done the same. There was nothing else to do. Nothing but pray. Pray and keep fighting the fire.

The fire was a ravenous monster riding on the wind. The more it ate, the hungrier it got. They would fight it back in one place only to see a new bush farther along flash into flames as though gasoline had been poured on it.

The wind was the reason they lost the Lindell house. It was blowing hard against them almost as if a storm was brewing. Victor even thought he heard a clap of thunder, but when he looked up to check for clouds, all he could see was the glow of the flames dancing against the black sky.

And then they were dancing across the roof of the Lindell house. At first it was just a spark or two, but minutes later flames were chasing each other across the old shingles and sliding down the walls.

Beside him, Fern straightened up and stared at the house. Victor moved over beside her. He touched her shoulder, but she shrugged off his hand. "Just a house," she said.

Victor dropped his hand to his side, but didn't move away from her. "But your house," he said.

"Brother's house. Trees mine." She looked from the house to the trees flaming around them. "All gone. No place left."

"We'll find you a place. Don't worry."

Fern looked at him. "That's what he would always say. Don't worry. And then he would smile. Do you remember? That smile."

He knew whose smile she was talking about. "Press was my hero."

"He said don't worry, but I did. Worry, worry. Weep, weep. Hurt, hurt." She put her hand over her heart as she turned her eyes back toward the house. Her voice didn't change as she went on. "Then I stopped. Like swooning. Didn't help."

"I'm sorry," Victor said.

"Sorry don't help any more than swooning."

The roof of the house fell in, and flames exploded out the windows. They watched it silently for a moment before Fern said, "Brother will cry." Then she picked up her axe and moved to where the other men had started clearing a new line.

Victor followed her, as the prayer rose inside him that Graham would have the chance to cry over his lost house. That would mean he was still alive along with the girls. They had to be alive.

A half hour later he again heard a rumbling boom. This time there was no denying it was thunder. Several of the men stopped working to look up at the sky. Victor knew they were praying, and he lifted his own prayer up to join theirs.

"Rain. Dear Lord, send rain down on the fire."

The first big drops hit his head before all the words were out of his mouth.

Kate had no idea how long they'd been standing in the water. It seemed like an eternity as the fire flashed through the trees and surrounded them while the reflection of the flames shimmered on top the water. The fire was terrible to see, yet at the same time so awesome Kate couldn't turn her eyes away from it.

Graham stared at the fire and whispered, "We shall behold the great and mighty works of the Lord."

Lorena kept her face hidden against Graham's shoulder. "I'm scared."

"I know, they can be fearsome acts," Graham said as he stroked Lorena's back. "But don't you worry. The Lord, he's taking care of us. Helped us find the pond. And appears like we're not the only ones. Look over there." He pointed. "That looks like old Carson Coon. Me and Poe have been chasing that old rascal all summer, and here he is coming out to swim with us. And here comes a possum. The good Lord sure didn't waste no pretty parts on him, now did he?"

Lorena lifted her feet out of the water. "He won't eat my toes, will he?"

"No, your toenails would be way too crunchy for him," Graham said.

Lorena giggled and let her feet dip down in the water again. More animals came out of the woods to ease into the water as they kept a wary eye on the humans and dog in the pond. Kate was beginning to feel like she was in a soup pot in the middle of a campfire. No more had that thought run through her mind than she imagined the water was getting warmer.

Kate leaned over to whisper to Graham. "The water won't get too hot, will it?"

She could see his smile in the light of the fire. "You don't have to worry none about that. We won't be onions in fish soup here. It's a big pond, and the fire's moving past us fast. Just burning the cedars and underbrush. It may not get the old trees."

Kate stared back at the fire and couldn't imagine it leaving anything standing. It seemed to be devouring everything in its path the way the fire Elijah had called down from heaven had consumed his sacrifice, the wood, the rocks, and even licked up the water in the trough around the altar. Kate shook her head a little. She didn't want to think about fire licking up water. She dipped down until her chin was level with the pond surface.

A few minutes later, Kate almost laughed out loud when the first raindrop hit the pond water beside her. "It's raining!" she shouted to Graham.

"It's raining," Lorena echoed.

Even Poe got into the spirit with a howl, and then Graham did laugh out loud.

The raindrops began making circles in the water around them, and then the rain came down in a swoosh that swept across the pond surface. The water dashed against their faces and felt cool and refreshing. Kate opened her mouth and stuck out her tongue to catch some of the raindrops. In the woods around the pond, the rain beat down the flames as steamy fog mixed with smoke rose from the ground.

Above their heads thunder rumbled and lightning lit up the sky. The rain kept falling. "Will it put the fire out?" Kate asked Graham.

"Enough of it. See, look. Some of the critters are heading out already." When the lightning lit up the pond, Graham pointed toward the raccoon swimming toward the bank.

"Can we go home now?" Kate asked. She wanted to go home more than anything in the world. She wanted to see her mother and father. She wanted them to know she and Lorena were safe. "Please."

"Home. I don't see why not." Graham leaned over close to her ear. "A person can always go home."

Lorena pushed her head in between Graham and Kate. "I want to go too. Home with Kate."

They stomped around in the mud close to the pond bank to try to find Kate's shoes, but the mud must have swallowed the shoes whole.

"Oh well," Kate said as she climbed on out of the pond. "I can go barefoot. My feet are tough."

"Tough enough till you step on a hot coal." Graham followed her out on the bank and set Lorena down. He pulled off his shirt and began tearing it into strips. "We'll have to make you some shoes of a sort."

Kate tore a few strips off her dress tail to add to what Graham was wrapping around her feet. The first heavy dash of rain gave way to a gentle, steady shower that was slowly quenching the flames. But the fire smoldered in the old logs and put out thick, choking smoke. After Graham wrapped the rags around her feet, he soaked strips of what was left of his shirt to tie over their noses and mouths before they left the pond.

It was very dark with the rain falling around them and the clouds blotting out any sign of the moon or stars. Kate had walked between her house and Graham's pond a hundred times, but now nothing was the same. She had no idea if they were going the right direction as they made their way between snags of burned tree trunks and fallen trees. The lingering smoke burned her nose even with the wet rag to filter out the worst of the ash. Kate couldn't imagine what the place would look like in the morning light. She didn't want to imagine it. Sunrise would bring the truth soon enough.

And then they stepped into a different world. A world where the trees were still standing and the rain was filtering through a canopy of leaves over their heads to wash away the smoke that lingered in the air.

Graham pulled the rag down off his nose and

then off Lorena's face too, as he sat her down on her feet. He looked back at Kate.

"See, I told you the old girls would make it through." He stepped up beside one of the oak trees and laughed as he laid his hand on its trunk.

Kate freed her face from the wet rag and looked up. The night was very dark, but she could sense the trees towering over her. Trees that had been there since long before Rosey Corner had been settled. The fire had gone through, but it hadn't taken any of the trees down. When the song rose up inside her, she let it out. "Praise God from whom all blessings flow." Kate always wanted to sing when she was under the great trees, and never more than now.

Graham joined in with her. He didn't have much of a singing voice, but he sounded joyful. "Praise him all creatures here below."

Lorena sang the amen with them.

"The strong find a way to keep standing. No matter what happens." Graham patted the tree trunk closest to him. Then he put his hand on Lorena's head and Kate's shoulder. "That's us. Strong. We're still standing."

"Because you knew where the pond was." Kate wasn't feeling very strong, just blessed. Mightily blessed.

"It's the Lord who gives us strength," Graham said. "To face all the fires of life."

"You sound like Grandfather Reece," Kate said.

"If a fellow can't preach a little after what we've seen tonight, there's something wrong inside his heart."

"Can we go on home now?" Lorena asked in a small voice. "Or are we lost?"

Kate picked up Lorena. "No, sweetie. We aren't lost. We know where we are and who we are. Why don't you say your name now?"

"Okay, but put me down so I can say it right." Lorena stood down on the ground and lifted up her head to shout at the tops of the trees. "My name is Lorena Birdsong."

Kate laughed and shouted after her. "My name is Katherine Reece Merritt."

Graham echoed his name right behind them. "My name is Graham Barclay Lindell."

Then Kate shouted. "And we are alive."

The word *alive* bounced off the trees around them. She pulled in a deep breath and wanted to sing again. And dance. And laugh. She'd never before thought about how good it felt to breathe.

43

Nadine had to leave her father in his chair on the porch. She couldn't move his body by herself, and Carla was next to useless. It didn't seem right at first, but then she stood up and looked across the field toward the church. While the fire was devouring the woods behind her and a blanket of smoke was settling across the land, the church stayed a calm and serene picture of peace. Her father had always liked reading his Bible out on the porch in the evening where he could look up and see the church. His church. He'd given his whole life to that church, so now perhaps it was good that he could be where he could see it. Of course he wasn't seeing anything. Not here on this earth anyway. He'd gone home.

The rain started hitting the roof as Nadine went inside to fetch a cover off her father's bed. When Nadine draped the quilt over her father's body, Carla set up a keening wail. Nadine did her best to be kind as she led Carla into the house out of the rain blowing up under the porch roof.

"We can't leave him out there," Carla cried. "Not alone."

"He's not alone. He's with the angels now." Nadine kept her voice soft. "With Mama and my little sister. He's happy again."

"Again? What's that supposed to mean? That he wasn't happy with me?" Carla glared at her as Nadine lit one of the oil lamps.

"I meant before he got sick," Nadine said quickly. She gently urged Carla down on the couch. The rain was peppering against the tin roof. "The rain will put the fire out. You'll be safe here now."

Carla grabbed Nadine's arm. "You can't leave.

You have to stay here with him until help comes."

"Father is beyond our help now. You have to be strong, Carla." Nadine tried to pull away from Carla, but the woman gripped harder until Nadine thought her arm would be bruised. "You have to turn me loose."

"I can't be here alone with him. Not and him dead." Carla's eyes got big. "His spirit might still be in the house."

"No," Nadine said firmly as she pried Carla's fingers off her arm. "If you don't want to stay here, you can walk to Ella's, but I have to go see about my family."

"Your father's your family. Where's your respect for the dead?"

Nadine backed away from Carla. "I'll send someone for the undertaker as soon as the men come back from fighting the fire. You'll need to get his suit ready."

"I can't," Carla moaned.

Nadine relented. "All right, don't worry about that. I'll come see to it when the undertaker comes."

Carla half rose off the couch to grab at Nadine again, but Nadine stepped away toward the door. So Carla tried to stop her with words instead. "Your father always said you were an ungrateful daughter."

Nadine didn't stop. She went on through the

door, past her father's body on the porch, and down the steps into the rain. She welcomed the feel of the rain on her face and arms, washing her clean. At the yard gate she turned around and looked back at the porch. It was so dark now she could barely see the shape of her father's body under the quilt. She stared at it a moment and then whispered into the rain. "I was a good daughter." Then she looked up at the dark sky. "Wasn't I, Lord?"

She stood still as the night seemed to push in on her soul. Her father was dead, gone from her forever in this life. Perhaps she had failed him. Perhaps Carla was right and she'd never been the daughter he had wanted her to be. It could be she'd failed all those she loved. That she was the reason Victor had turned to alcohol for comfort. Because she wasn't the wife she should be. Perhaps she wasn't the mother she should be either, and that was why Kate was in danger. She'd certainly failed to protect Lorena, who might not be her daughter in the natural manner but was every bit the daughter of her heart.

Tears mixed with the rain on her face, and for a moment she felt too much despair to move her feet on down the path toward her own house. What if bad news awaited her there as it had at her father's house? Wouldn't it be better to just stay in the darkness not knowing?

A Bible verse slipped into her mind. She hadn't

prayed, but the answer was there in her mind anyway. *Be of good courage, and he shall strengthen your heart, all ye that hope in the Lord.*

She did hope in the Lord. She had always leaned on the Lord. He knew she wasn't perfect, but he loved her anyway. She carried that love, that hope in her heart, and now she felt a renewed strength as she began walking again. She hadn't always done everything right, but she had always tried to do her best. The Lord would honor that.

It didn't matter what Carla said. It didn't even matter what Nadine's father might have said before he died. Nadine had been a dutiful daughter. Perhaps too dutiful. She and Victor had both let their fathers' expectations of them color too much of their life together. Expectations that neither of them had ever been able to live up to.

Nadine didn't go back to Gertie's. She went straight to her house from her father's. She was glad she didn't meet anyone on the road. Glad she didn't yet have to speak of her father's death. There would be time for that.

It began to rain harder, and beyond her in the trees, the flames began to die down. Smoke that carried more than the smell of wood ash settled around her. The Lindell house must have burned, and she was glad she and Fern had saved the painting for Graham, even if she knew Fern was right. That didn't promise his safety. Or that of the girls.

She refused to let panic grab hold of her heart again and kept putting one foot in front of the other until she was climbing her front porch steps. The house was dark. And very empty. She moved through the familiar rooms to the kitchen where she lit a taper from the coals in the cookstove to light a lamp. For a moment she wished she'd brought Evangeline and Victoria home with her so she wouldn't feel so alone. She thought of Carla and wondered if she still sat cowering on her couch. It could be Carla was right and the church people would look down on Nadine for leaving her there alone with the body.

She shook away that worry. Her place was where she was standing, waiting for her husband, waiting for Kate and Lorena. They would come. She had to believe that. Her hand shook a little as she lit a second lamp and then blew out the taper. Cream was beginning to rise in the milk on the table. She looked at it a long moment before she set down the lamp and fixed the straining rag over the crock on the cabinet. Carefully she poured the milk through the rag into the crock and then rinsed out the bucket so it would be ready for the morning milking.

She drank a dipper full of water and felt guilty as she swallowed, thinking of how thirsty Victor or Kate and Lorena might be. She pulled three glasses out of the cabinet and filled them with water to have them ready. Then she added a fourth glass for Graham. They would come. They would all come.

She carried the lamp to the table in front of the window in the sitting room. She paid no mind to her wet dress and hair as she went out to wait on the porch. Some things had to be done. Others could wait.

Victor came first. With Fern in tow. Both their faces were streaked with smoke and ash as their hair and clothes dripped from the rain. "Kate?" Victor asked as he came up on the porch.

"Not yet." Nadine swallowed hard to keep the worry out of her voice, but Victor heard it anyway and put his arms around her.

"They'll come." Victor kissed the top of her head and held her tightly for a moment before he stepped back and motioned toward Fern, who didn't seem to pay any mind to the rain as she waited on the steps. "Fern's house burned. She needs some dry clothes and a place to sleep."

"Clothes will dry," Fern said without moving out of the rain.

Nadine reached and took her hand to pull her up on the porch beside them. "Come, Fern. Let us help you."

"Don't need help." But she followed Nadine into the house. The woman looked oddly diminished with her gray hair plastered down around her face and the wet shirt under the overalls showing how very slim she was.

Nadine went into the kitchen to get a towel, and Fern followed her. She counted the glasses of water on the table. "One, two, three, four. Hope. Good to have hope. When you lose that, you lose everything." She picked up one of the glasses and drank it dry before she held out the empty glass to Nadine. "Fill it up again for Brother."

While Nadine was filling the glass, Fern stepped out the back door. Nadine set the glass down and hurried after her. "Wait, Fern."

Fern was standing at the edge of the back porch. "Listen," she told Nadine.

Nadine stopped half out the screen door and listened. All she could hear was the rain hitting the roof and dripping down into the rain barrels. After a moment she asked, "For what?"

"They're coming," Fern said.

"Who?" Nadine said as hope began bouncing around wildly inside her chest.

"Brother. Your girl who looks like him and the little one who looks like me." Fern pointed into the darkness.

Nadine strained to see, but she couldn't. "Are you sure?"

Fern made a sound that might have been a laugh and put her fingers in her mouth to give a shrill whistle. In a moment, the same whistle echoed back to them. "Brother taught me the whistle."

Nadine was off the porch and running past Fern

toward the sound before Fern had all the words out. "Kate!" she shouted.

"Mama!" Kate's beautiful voice came back to her.

Lorena's voice echoed hers. "Mama Angel."

Then they were hugging and laughing, and she had Lorena in one arm and the other arm around Kate and they were alive. Gloriously alive. Victor was there too with his arms around them all. Rejoicing in hope. *Let thy mercy, O Lord, be upon us, according as we hope in thee.* The Bible verse bubbled up inside Nadine's head. The merciful Lord had brought her children out of the fire. And Graham.

Nadine reached toward where Graham stood just out of their circle and grabbed his hand. "Thank you, Graham."

"Don't give me all the credit. Poe here helped, didn't he, girls?"

Poe lifted his head and let out a long howl.

"That's about as happy as he gets," Graham said.

Lorena giggled and reached down to touch Poe's head. Victor took Lorena and carried her back to the house, but Nadine kept one hand touching her and one touching Kate.

When they went up on the back porch, Fern stepped out of the shadows. "Hope came," she said.

"Oh yes, Fern," Nadine said. "They're home."

Lorena jumped down from Victor's arms as she shouted, "Fern." She ran right to her and wrapped her arms around her waist. "I prayed that the fire wouldn't get you."

Fern stayed stiff for a moment, but then she lifted her hand and softly laid it on Lorena's wet tangle of curls.

44

The church was packed for the funeral. Everybody in Rosey Corner had to be there along with people from Edgeville and beyond who had grown up in the church thinking Preacher Reece was Rosey Corner's Moses. The two sons had come in from Indiana. It had been years since they'd been back to Rosey Corner, and the oldest, Orrin Jr., caused a stir when he came in the church because of how much he looked like his father. The younger brother, James Robert, still had the gentle look that, according to Nadine, was so like his mother. When he first got out of the car at Rosey Corner, he and Nadine held each other and wept—not so much for their father, Victor thought, but for the years they'd been apart.

There was one notable absence. Victor's father. He hadn't been seen since the fire. Hadn't opened his store Friday or Saturday. Nobody in Rosey

Corner could remember Merritt's Dry Goods Store ever being closed two days in a row, not even during the influenza epidemic when Victor's mother had died.

Aunt Hattie checked on him on Saturday and came back shaking her head. "I ain't seen him like this since Press Jr. drowned." She had called Victor out in the yard away from the family and friends gathered to comfort Nadine. They stood under the big oak with the rope swing hanging down from one of its branches.

Victor watched the swing move slightly in the breeze before he looked at Aunt Hattie. "You think I should care, but I don't. He caused this." He swept his hand out toward the blackened woods where logs were still smoldering. He looked back at Aunt Hattie. "He wanted me to lose Kate, to know what it was like to lose a child."

"No, no," Aunt Hattie protested. "He couldn't have wanted that. He loves that girl. Most of any of your girls."

"He said it."

Aunt Hattie peered up at Victor. "And you've never said an'thing you didn't mean in a moment of anger? A moment of grief?"

"A moment? It's been nearly thirty years since Press died."

Aunt Hattie's eyes bored into Victor. "How long do you think you would have grieved our

Kate if she hadn't made it out of the fire?" She didn't wait for him to answer. "I'll tell you 'cause I know. A heart never stops achin' over a lost child." She hit her chest with a balled up fist and kept it over her heart. "My Bo, he's right here with me ever' day."

Victor's eyes softened on Aunt Hattie's wrinkled face. "I know, Aunt Hattie. I'm sorry. But you didn't turn bitter. You kept loving the rest of us."

"True enough. Ain't much left if you stop lovin' folks around you. And the good Lord, he helped me forgive."

"Forgive who?"

"The government that sent him to war. The army that pushed him out there on the front lines with those French soldiers. The Germans that shot him. Whoever the Lord laid on my heart to forgive so's I could keep on breathing. Your daddy, he couldn't never forgive." She put her hand up on Victor's cheek. "Don't you be like him. You forgive. You got your family. You's laid down the bottle." She eyed him a minute until he nodded before she went on. "You got the Lord. You can forgive."

"So could he. It wasn't Fern's fault. It wasn't my fault."

Aunt Hattie smiled sadly. "Oh, but child, don't you see? That's how come it was so hard for him to forgive. The one he had to forgive the most was his own self and he couldn't do that. He had to lay the blame somewhere's else."

Victor stared at her without saying anything. He couldn't forgive his father. Not yet. When he thought of Kate and how near he'd come to losing her, he didn't think he ever would.

Aunt Hattie didn't look disappointed in him. "You pray about it some and your heart might soften. You'll see it weren't all his fault. Things were set in motion. Things happened. We all stand in need of forgiveness."

She'd gone inside then and gotten Fern to take home with her. Fern was sitting by her now on the back pew in the church. She had on a dress, and Aunt Hattie must have cut her hair. Fern's eyes kept darting to the door like a trapped animal looking for a way out, but she stayed beside Aunt Hattie.

Brother Mike, the young preacher, looked nervous too as he stared out at the people assembled to pay their last respects to their preacher. Many of them had never known any other preacher at Rosey Corner Baptist Church, and they'd made sure the young preacher knew that. He swallowed hard and stared down at his Bible, but then as he began reading the Twenty-third Psalm, his voice got stronger. People sat up and listened and were comforted by the familiar words.

Victor took Nadine's hand. Lorena was in

Kate's lap next to Nadine. She'd hardly let any of the girls out of her sight since the fire. Victoria was scooted up close to Kate on the other side.

Only Evangeline didn't seem especially bothered by Kate's near escape. The night of the fire, she'd just looked at Kate and said, "I knew you'd be all right. You always are. No matter what crazy thing you do." Now Evangeline wasn't bothered about anything except Brother Mike. She was trying to be serious and proper, but there was a shine to her eyes that had nothing to do with tears for her grandfather.

After the funeral sermon, the Rosey Corner Baptist Church deacons carried their preacher out to his final resting place in the cemetery beside the church. Carla began moaning as Orrin Jr. and Joseph Baxter helped her out to the graveyard. Nadine didn't even glance in her direction. Many of the women were weeping, but Nadine watched dry-eyed as the young preacher read again from the Bible.

"'All are of the dust, and all turn to dust again.'" He flipped a few pages and read again. "'Let us hear the conclusion of the whole matter: Fear God, and keep his commandments: for this is the whole duty of man.'" He looked up at the people gathered around the grave. "A duty this good man kept faithfully for many years as a pastor, a husband, a father, a grandfather, and friend. Let us who loved him do no less." The men slowly lowered the casket into the grave.

Each of the deacons took a handful of the dirt beside the grave and dropped it in on top of the casket. Everybody began to walk back toward the church where the ladies had set up a meal on a wagon pulled up into the front churchyard, but Nadine stayed. Victor waited with her.

After a long minute, she picked up a handful of dirt herself and dropped it into the grave. "I forgive you," she whispered. Then she looked up at the sky. "Pray God you forgive me in return."

Then she turned to Victor. "I should have told him that while he was alive."

"Do you think he would have listened?" Victor looked at the grave.

"I don't know. He wouldn't have thought there was any reason for me to forgive him or so he would have pretended, but perhaps deep in his heart he would have listened and accepted my words. But no matter how he felt, I needed to say them. To turn loose of the past and pay more attention to the blessings of this day, this time." She looked intently at Victor. "You. The girls. Our home."

"Are you trying to tell me I need to turn loose of the past too?" Victor asked.

"And forgive your father."

"He doesn't want my forgiveness."

"Perhaps not. But you need to give it. Inasmuch as we forgive, so we are forgiven."

"Are you going to step into the pulpit behind your father?" Victor asked.

Nadine smiled and took his hand. "No. I'm happy being your wife and the mother of your children. Our children."

She was so beautiful that Victor could hardly breathe for a moment. Then he said, "Have you been happy, Nadine? With me?"

"Not every minute, Victor. But more minutes than not."

"It's you I should beg forgiveness. I haven't—"

"Shh." She put her fingers over his lips to stop him talking. "There's nothing to forgive. I love you, Victor Merritt."

He wanted to grab her and kiss her, to hold her until the sun sank in the west, but the men were waiting respectfully to the side to fill in the grave, and Kate and Victoria were calling to them from the front of the church. "And I love you, Nadine Reece Merritt."

"Then you'll forgive Father Merritt?"

Victor hesitated before he gave in. "All right. For you, Nadine, but he doesn't deserve forgiveness."

The next morning, Victor went by the store on his way to the blacksmith shop. The store was still closed. Something white was nailed to the door. Stan Groggin, a man who sometimes worked part-time for his father, was sitting on the steps. When he saw Victor, he stood up and came to meet him.

"Are you closing the store?" he asked without any other greeting. He was a wiry little man who was usually ready with a story and a smile, but he wasn't smiling today.

Victor wasn't sure he'd heard him right. "You mean the blacksmith shop?"

"No, the store."

"I guess you'd better ask my father that."

"I did." Stan looked a little uncomfortable as he took off his cap, stared at it a few seconds, and then jammed it back on his head. He looked past Victor toward the store's door. "He was by here early. Stuck that up on the door and said you were the man with the answers now. Then he filled up his car at the pumps and drove off."

Victor looked around. "Where?"

"Didn't say. Didn't seem to be in a talkative mood. Headed west toward Louisville." Stan nodded toward the envelope on the door. "It's got your name on it. I didn't bother it. If you hadn't a showed up, I was gonna come find you."

Victor stared at his name on the envelope before he took it off the door. He pulled out the nail and stuck it in his pocket. He couldn't remember his father ever writing him a letter. Not even when he was in the war. For a minute he thought about just tearing it up without reading it, but then he remembered promising Nadine to forgive his father. He opened the envelope and pulled out the sheet of paper.

I've gone. Heading to Oregon. Always wanted to see the West. Tell Nadine she can run the store. Tell her to make them pay their bills. Most of them can. You know which ones. You're the man with the answers now. Let Hattie live in the house.

It looked like he had started to put his name, but then scratched it out and wrote: *Tell Kate I'm sorry.*

And that was all. He didn't sign his name. Victor looked up and stared down the road that went west. He needed more. More words. Then he looked back down and read again. *Tell Kate I'm sorry.* Maybe that was enough. The past couldn't be changed.

"What's he say?" Stan asked, peering toward the paper in Victor's hand.

"He's going to Oregon," Victor said.

"But what about the store?" Stan sounded worried. "You can't just close up the store. Bill Baxter's store don't have half what your daddy carries."

"He wants Nadine to run it while he's gone."

"You think she'll do it?" Stan asked.

"I don't know. She'll have to decide on that."

"Say what you want about Preston, but he always did know the answer." Stan smiled and shook his head a little. "Nadine worked in the

471

store while you were over there fighting the war, you know."

"I know."

"They tell me you quit drinking." Stan's smile got bigger. "Wouldn't it be something if she took over the store and you went to preaching?"

Victor laughed. "I haven't ever felt the call to preach, Stan."

"Not yet, but I've hear'd of it happening. A man getting the call from the Lord later on in life. Especially a man standing in some need of forgiveness." Stan looked flustered as he rushed on. "Not to say that you do or anything. At least no more than a lot of the rest of us."

"It's all right, Stan. I guess we all stand in need of forgiveness, and I'm not denying I might more than most." Victor clapped Stan on the shoulder and smiled. "But if the good Lord wants me to preach, he's going to have to call loud and clear before I believe it."

He left Stan chuckling as he headed home to show Nadine the note. Halfway there, Victor met Kate coming up the road. She didn't look happy when she stopped in front of him. "Mama needs some things from the store. I told her I didn't want to go. I don't want to talk to Grandfather Merritt, but she says I have to."

"I guess she told you to forgive him."

Kate looked up at Victor a little surprised. "How did you know?"

472

"She told me the same thing. That I had to tell him I forgive him."

"Why?" Kate looked puzzled. "Because of Lorena?"

"That and other things. Your grandfather and I have had our differences."

"Oh, so did you have to ask him to forgive you too? Mama says I have to. Even if I don't think I've done anything he needed to forgive me for." Kate ducked her head and stared down at the gravel on the road. She dug out a little hole with her toes. "But I guess I was sort of disrespectful. Even if I was right." She looked up at Victor. "Do you think he will? Forgive me if I ask him, I mean."

"I think he already has." Victor held out the note to her to read.

Her eyes swept over the few words and then flew back up to Victor's face. "Oregon?"

"That's what it says. One of his brothers went out there and settled years ago. Before I was born. Maybe he's going to visit him."

She looked down at the note again. "You think he'll ever come back?"

"I don't know."

"But I didn't get to say I was sorry."

"Me either," Victor said.

"I feel bad now." Kate's face drooped. "What if Grandfather Merritt thinks I don't love him? I was mad at him, but I didn't really stop loving him. He's my grandfather."

"And my father." Victor wasn't sure he had that automatic love in his heart the way Kate did, but the man was his father. That surely meant something. He looked at Kate. "Tell you what. We can still tell him. Just say it out loud and maybe the words will follow him down the road."

"You mean the way Lorena's mother told her to say her name so Lorena won't forget who she really is?"

"Why not? It seems to work for Lorena." He put his arm around Kate's shoulders, and they turned to stare down the road. They were quiet for a moment as if neither of them knew exactly what to say.

Kate spoke first. "I'm sorry, Grandfather. Please forgive me. And I forgive you." She put her hand over her heart. "For true."

Victor took a deep breath and echoed her words. "I'm sorry, Father. Forgive me. And I forgive you." Silently he added *I forgive you for not loving me.* A weight seemed to drop off his shoulders as those words passed through his mind. A weight he'd carried way too long. He'd been wrong to harbor so much resentment for his father's lack of love. Hadn't the Lord blessed him with abundant love from Nadine and his girls even when he didn't always deserve such love?

"The Bible says there are angels watching over us, Daddy." Kate's eyes were still on the road. "Do you believe that?"

"If the Bible says it, it must be true."

"Then maybe they can catch our words in their hands and carry them to Grandfather Merritt's ears."

"Maybe they can," Victor said.

Kate turned to wrap her arms around him in a tight hug. "Thank you, Daddy."

"For what?"

She leaned back and looked up at him. "For being my daddy. For loving me. For coming home at suppertime." Her cheeks warmed a little as she said that last.

"You can count on me, baby. I made your mama a promise. No more drinking, and I always keep my promises to your mama. And you."

Kate laughed and turned loose of him. "You think Mama will want to run the store?"

"I think she might."

Kate laughed again. "You know what I think?"

"No, tell me."

"I think Merritt's Dry Goods Store is going to see some changes."

She twirled out in front of him. She looked so happy she was almost sparkling. No wonder Lorena called her angel sister. Victor wouldn't have been a bit surprised to see angels dancing right along beside her as they walked down the road toward home.

AUTHOR'S NOTES
AND ACKNOWLEDGMENTS

Angel Sister is a story from the heart. My heart and my mother's heart. The events and characters in the book all rose up out of that mysterious deep well that is a writer's imagination and are completely fictitious, but that well was fed by the many stories I heard from my mother and her sisters about growing up in the small community of Alton during the Depression years. My Rosey Corner is the Alton of their memories. My Merritt family is very, very loosely based on their family. My grandmother and grandfather did love to read. My grandfather was a blacksmith and did at one time have a drinking problem. He did serve in France during World War I. That much of the story is based on fact. But he was a cook and didn't have to go "over the top" and up out of the trenches into combat. My Fern and Graham are the fleshed-out characters brought to mind by the stories my aunts and mother used to tell about some of the odder characters in their community. The place seemed to have more than its share of odd characters, including, as my aunt Bill used to say, "them"—the four Hawkins sisters. And then she would laugh.

I took the feeling of the wonderful memories

they shared and from those seeds created my Rosey Corner and my family of four sisters. So to the first four sisters—Evelyn, Olga, Margaret, and Bill—I am completely indebted for the atmosphere and background of this book. The rest I made up by imagining how it might have been and what would have happened if. That is a fiction writer's privilege and joy. My aunts and mother loved to laugh and talk about the days back when. My mother is the only sister left now, but if my aunts were still living, I know they would have enjoyed going back to Rosey Corner with me.

Once a story makes it out of a writer's heart and onto paper, many people have to help it along its journey toward becoming a book. I'm grateful to my wonderful editor, Lonnie Hull DuPont, who is always ready to share an encouraging word. I'm especially thankful for her enthusiasm for this story that had her digging through trash cans to find out the "rest of the story" after accidently throwing away part of the original manuscript. I appreciate all the people at Revell Books and Baker Publishing Group who do so much to help make my books better with careful editing, make them look good with great cover art, and then get them out there in front of readers. I also thank Lettie Lee for believing in my stories through the years. And I can't forget to mention the friendship and support of Wendy

Lawton, who stands ready to help me in so many ways.

Always I thank the Lord for giving me the desire to write and for gifting me with this story. Last of all, I appreciate each of you who picked up this book and let my story come to life in your imagination. Thank you for inviting the Merritt family into your heart.

Ann H. Gabhart and her husband live on a farm just over the hill from where she grew up in central Kentucky. She's active in her country church, and her husband sings bass in a Southern Gospel quartet. Ann is the author of over twenty novels for adults and young adults. Her first inspirational novel, *The Scent of Lilacs*, was one of Booklist's top ten inspirational novels of 2006. Her novel *The Outsider* was a finalist for the 2009 Christian Book Awards in the fiction category.

Visit Ann's website at www.annhgabhart.com.

Center Point Publishing
600 Brooks Road ● PO Box 1
Thorndike ME 04986-0001 USA

(207) 568-3717

US & Canada:
1 800 929-9108
www.centerpointlargeprint.com